Bound

by

Loyalty

Book One of the
Victoria Chronicles

J. Robert Whittle

Publisher's note: This book is a work of fiction set in the City of Victoria, Municipality of Saanich, and other areas of British Columbia, as well as Washington State. To enhance the story, real places and people's names have sometimes been used, although the characters are fictional and are in no way intended to represent any person living or dead.

Contact the author or purchase copies of any
of his books through the publisher :

Whitlands Publishing Ltd.
4444 Tremblay Drive
Victoria, BC Canada V8N 4W5
250-477-0192
www.whitlands.com
info@whitlands.com

Original cover artwork by Barbara Porter
Cover design by Jim Bisakowski, Desktop Publishing
Back cover photo by Terry Seney

National Library of Canada Cataloguing in Publication Data

Whittle, J. Robert (John Robert), 1933-
Bound by loyalty

(Victoria chronicles ; 1)

I. Title. II. Series: Whittle, J. Robert (John Robert), 1933- Victoria chronicles ; 1.

PS8595.H4985B68 2001 C813'.54 C2001-911456-7

PR9199.3.W458B68 2001

ISBN: 09685061-4-3

Printed in Canada by Friesens, Altona, MB

To Dorothy,
a lady of indomitable spirit, bubbling humour,
and enthusiastic encouragement.
You're more than a mother-in-law;
you're a very special lady, and my pal.

Acknowledgements

Over the past three years, many hundreds of supportive people have taken the time to communicate their encouraging words of praise and demands that I 'keep writing'. Be it through snail or email, fax, telephone, or at the hundreds of market/craftshow days Joyce and I have now attended over the past 2 ½ years, each of your comments is gratefully received and we are so very pleased that so many gain so much enjoyment from our 3 books.

Early on realizing the disadvantages of self-publishing and the uphill battle we would encounter by taking on such a project, we soon happily discovered the benefits of marketing our own titles to the general public. Then, in spite of our awareness of the gruelling schedule to come, Joyce and I found ourselves jumping in with both feet in the summer of 2001. Thanks to the BC Ferries Market Place at the Swartz Bay Terminal, Victoria's Bastion Square Festival of Fine Arts, Sidney Summer Market, Chemainus Market Days, and several weekly local markets which we amazingly found time to fit in. It has been a most memorable, successful, and exceedingly enjoyable 'summer' season which we will undoubtably repeat.

Fortunately, we live in a popular tourist destination, and because of this our Lizzie Books are now in at least 26 countries, every US state, and many corners of our Canadian provinces, all because of the loyal support of people like you. It continues to be a most humbling experience to meet our public.

With the addition of *Bound by Loyalty* to our list of proud achievements, we now eagerly await the 2001Christmas season (and beyond). We have already received some measure of the excitement this book is generating when we found people willingly pre-buying copies or demanding we let them know when our 'Victoria Book' was available.

Our thanks to the archive staff at the City of Victoria, BC Archives, local municipalities, libraries, the Hallmark Society, and other private archives, and those families who shared verbal memoirs or let me have a peek into their fascinating collections. A special thanks to Carey Pallister, archivist and historical researcher at the City of Victoria Archives who so willingly shared her knowledge and whose enthusiasm and friendship is deeply appreciated. Her crucial critique and always helpful wisdom throughout the writing and editing process, have been invaluable.

Thanks also to Barbara Porter, a local-born artist residing in California, for her perfect interpretation of *Cunningham Manor* for our cover; Jim Bisakowski, our cover designer, for his patience; Micheline Keating, for her

vii

enthusiasm and marketing assistance; our many understanding and supportive friends; and our children, Robert Jr., Carol, James (for keeping our computers running), Christine, and your families, for your love and support across the miles and now thankfully, the internet.

A very special thanks to my Victoria-born wife, long-suffering editor, publisher, and children's book co-author, Joyce Sandilands, whose favourite comeback of late has become, 'I have other more important top priorities, honey!' Without her 14-hour plus days, her critique, support, and love, none of our books would have been possible. It was she who suggested a story set in Victoria and as she had researched her family history some years before, our library was already bursting with local research materials. Whether at her computer or at markets, she continually assures me she doesn't mind the pace because she enjoys 'her job' and her boss usually appreciates her! A singer since a teen, herself, her knowledge of music and performing was most helpful in setting up the musical scenes.

And finally, to Dorothy Carlson (nee Joyce), Joyce's forever-supportive Victoria-born mother. Eighty-two years young, her parents came from the Maritimes in the late 1800s—her mother, Harriet Strickland, as a 5-year-old orphan separated from her siblings, travelling the long train journey to Victoria in 1892, where she found a home with relatives on Davie Street. Over the past two years, I often found myself asking her to turn back the pages of her memory to give me a feel of the 'Olde Victoria'. She remembered swimming in the Gorge, biking to Elk Lake, streetcars, and living on a farm near the Willows Fairground. The fictitious Joyce brothers' were added as a tribute to Dorothy's father, grandfathers, and other family members who were whalers and fishermen in Newfoundland and Nova Scotia in the 1800s, and particularly her maternal grandfather, Joshu Strickland, who was lost at sea off the Grand Banks in 1892.

The success of my violence-free novels indicates to me that it *is* possible to change people's thinking about the entertainment they seek. And so, I continue my journey to entertain. We hope you enjoy our momentary digression from Lizzie, however, we anticipate her return in 2002.

On behalf of Joyce and myself, a most sincere 'thank you' to all.

J. Robert "Bob" Whittle
November 2001
jrw@whitlands.com

Main Characters (in order of appearance)

Nancy Wilson – young English girl
Tom Wilson – Nancy's father
Rev. Charles & Emilia Garvey – couple on ship
Captain Welch – Captain of emmigrant ship
Dan Brown – boy at orphanage
Billy and Rose – Indian children
Louise – cook at Temperance Hotel
Ned and Tim Joyce – owners of whaling company
Jack and Nellie Duggan – bricklayer and wife
Jack Cunningham - English Jack, a goldminer
Meg MacDonald – Scottish secretary to Joyce brothers
Waldo Skillings – owner of Victoria Baggage Company
Charlotte Townend – political organizer
John Mount Langley – Police Chief
Jebediah Judd – Pinkerton detective from USA
Sergeant Walker – City policeman
George and Mrs. Dunn – proprietors of Occidental Hotel
Tom Ben – salesman for E.A. Morris, tobacco merchant
Jane Newcolm – Vancouver artist
Richard McBride – Premier of BC
Harry Tabour – Balmoral Hotel Dining Room Manager
Jack Dumpford (Dumpy) – helmsman on *Belfast*
Mary – cook at Balmoral Hotel
Elizabeth (Eliza) Marshall – owner of Gorge Hotel
Gus and Beth Jorgensen – Seattle businessman and wife
Dick – newspaper vendor

(cont'd)

Main Characters (continued)

William Wilson – co-owner of W & J Wilson, drapers
Bob Leighton - manager of Willows racetrack
Terry O'Reilly – Seattle gangster
John Bryant – stunt flyer
Harry Maynard - owner of Crystal Springs Brewer
Millie Maynard - pianist, wife of Harry Maynard
Tom Irvine – local farmer
Mr. Davis – owner of Spencer's Store
Joseph Wilson – co-owner of W & J Wilson, drapers
Bill Foster – Jorgensen lawyer
Fred Barrett – manager of local Coast Guard station
Emerson Turpel – William Turpel drydock
Sister Mary – friend of Charlotte Townend
Nellie Cashman – goldminer and businesswomen
Capt. Percy Neville – British Army Captain
Brian Harper – owner of Harper and Well's, automobile dealer
Sam Smith and Flash – hermit and his dog
Katherine (Kate) – waitress at Balmoral Hotel
Al O'Malley – owner of Finnegan's Restaurant, Seattle

Bound
by
Loyalty

Prologue

Panic-stricken and with tears streaming down her young face, Nancy peered through the ship's rails to catch a last heartbreaking glimpse of the only mother she had ever known. As the great vessel pulled slowly away from the Liverpool dock, she tightly clasped her father's hand and waved until her tired fingers would move no more.

Whimpering softly, the 3-year-old cautiously looked up at the man who was almost a stranger to her. Suddenly, she began to realize something of her father's own pain as she watched his tears roll silently from distraught eyes, splashing onto his beard.

In the past weeks, Nancy's young mind had been trying desperately to grasp the reality of the situation she was facing. She looked out again at the diminishing figure of her handkerchief-waving aunt and couldn't bear to believe that she would never see her again … and then the great ship turned, and both the crowd and her aunt disappeared from view.

One of her father's tears fell onto her hand bringing her back to the present and again she looked up at him. Seeing his young daughter's forlorn expression and her red, tear-stained cheeks, he whispered helplessly, "God help us lass, it's the best ah could do."

Then, for the first time she could remember, he scooped her up in his arms and hugged her. Holding her tightly to his chest, he began to sob … and the land slipped slowly away.

Chapter 1

Life, for Nancy, began on June 10th, 1896, in the small, Northern England village of Grange Moor … the daughter of Tom Wilson, a young coal miner. Her mother died soon after childbirth, leaving Nancy's heartbroken father an embittered and broken man, who never really forgave her. He took to drink to drown his sorrows, leaving his baby's care in the hands of an aunt who lived a day's journey away.

Nancy was a happy child and her aunt and uncle loved her dearly. Her young life was uncomplicated until one day early in the year 1900 when her father made an infrequent and fateful visit. He had decided to emigrate to Canada he said with a trace of disinterest in his voice. They were advertising for miners and he was taking Nancy with him.

The long and treacherous sea voyage to Victoria on Canada's rugged westcoast, began as a nightmare of discomfort. For the first two weeks the ship wallowed in mountainous seas and fog banks just off the English coast—common for April. Freezing winds whistled around corners and through every opening. Sickness was rife among the one hundred and ten frightened and unhappy passengers crammed together in the dark bowels of the four-masted ship.

Among the passengers were a Presbyterian minister, Charles Garvey and his wife, Emilia. A middle-aged, childless couple, they had sought a calling in the New World and been rewarded with the opportunity to save souls in a new town called New Westminster. They became aware of Nancy's plight early on in the voyage. Making friends with Wilson and his daughter, they soon found themselves the little girl's protectors when sickness overcame her father rendering him totally helpless.

The Garveys were kind, but didn't understand the fears of a child, and Nancy became more and more lost in a world of her own. In her troubled moments she tried to find solace in the sounds and rhythm of the sea. Sally, a ragdoll her aunt had given her, became her constant companion never complaining when Nancy clutched her fiercely giving her a bath of tears.

During those horrid days of calm, which happened far too often, she stood on deck with the Garveys and watched as sailcloth-wrapped bodies were dropped over the side of the ship into the dark, foreboding sea.

Hopelessness and fear often consumed the little girl and she would run sobbing to her father's bedside. But Tom Wilson was no longer aware of his daughter's presence as his will to survive lessened. With nowhere to run and no loving arms to hold her, the child slipped into a world of make believe, as the vessel plied relentlessly across the Atlantic.

Captain Welch, a leather-skinned man of ageing years and a vicious temper, soon found himself drawn to the wide-eyed, motherless child. Having been at sea nearly all his life, he had still found time to marry and father two children. He had received word recently that he was a grandfather and he wondered when, if ever, he would see them again. Gaining permission for Nancy to accompany him when weather and time allowed, she was often seen on deck and in the wheelhouse with him where he found her an easy subject to amuse.

Very soon both crew and passengers began to notice that the gnarled seaman was softening under Nancy's spell. The child grew happier, looking forward to their visits—his sailing implements and incessant chatter amusing her for hours. Nancy began to accept the noises made by the pounding sea as she listened to the ravings of this strange man. They had interesting conversations and her vocabulary improved as did her confidence. She grew more able to deal with the monotony and boredom of shipboard living. When forced to remain below deck, she often lay for long periods on her blankets listening to the once horrifying sounds that now sent her imagination racing.

4

Past the windswept islands of the Azores and Cape Verde they sailed. Then, the weather changed and they began to feel the oppressive heat as they neared the equator. At Salvador, Nancy stood by the rail with the other passengers. They looked out longingly at the tropical, green hills and wide sandy beaches and watched the loading of precious barrels of life-giving water into their hold.

On deck, constant winds tore at her clothes when they dared venture out. About thirty days from Salvador, a hurricane-force wind battered them ruthlessly blowing up mountainous sheets of water. Thankfully, Captain Welch found shelter in the naturally protected harbour of Santa Cruz, a large Argentinian city.

Remarkably, Nancy's resilient young mind seemed to take it all in stride, although like the others, she quietly wondered when the nightmare would end.

On the twelfth of July, they rounded the tip of South America—Cape Horn, Captain Welch called it—when no one was allowed on deck and capsizing became a very real danger. Later, Nancy lay sobbing in Emilia's arms as she watched her poor father succumb once again to the dreadful sea sickness.

One very humid afternoon, she and Emilia remained on deck after the others had gone below following an enjoyable time in the sun. Sitting on a blanket happily studying the pictures in the clouds, they were totally unaware of the impending danger. Suddenly, a warning sounded as sails were buffeted by the wind causing them to crack like the sound of lightning. The ship lurched violently as the wind-whipped waves tossed them about like a toy. Emilia frantically gathered their precious belongings but the strong winds threatened everything on deck.

"AAAHHH!!" screamed Nancy, as the wind picked her up and tossed her toward the railing.

"HELP ... OH HELP US, PLEASE ... SOMEONE!" Emilia cried, dropping the precious blanket and making a desperate attempt to catch her before she moved out of reach. With every ounce of her diminishing strength, Emilia pulled herself toward the child's tiny outstretched arm. Finally being close enough to grasp her, she pulled her close, shouting, "PUT YOUR ARMS AROUND MY NECK, NANCY … HOLD ON TIGHTLY!" Wrapping one arm tightly around the little girl's waist, she heaved them slowly along the railing toward the hatch.

But the few steps felt like a mile and panic now clutched at her throat as tears stung her face. *Where is everyone?* she thought desperately. *Haven't they noticed our absence? Why doesn't someone come to help us?* She knew she shouldn't waste her precious energy, so she pushed fearful thoughts aside concentrating only on saving Nancy … and herself. Finally, they reached the hatch and safety … but the relentless wind sent them tumbling back across the deck wrenching the girl from her arms.

"AAAHHHHH!!" she screamed. *Oh God, please help us!"* her inner voice cried as she desperately summoned her strength to reach the screaming child.

"MRS. GARVEY!" shouted the familiar voice of Captain Welch, but Emilia could see neither he nor Nancy.

"I HAVE HER, I HAVE THE CHILD. GET TO THE HATCH NOW!!" the Captain roared above the deafening noise.

Suddenly, there were sailors running about in all directions. One of them grabbed her roughly, pushing her toward the hatch before he joined the others in the rigging. The Captain caught her and handing the limp child into her arms, grabbed her waist and literally heaved them both through the opening, banging the hatch shut behind them.

As the shock of darkness enveloped her, Emilia tried to catch her breath. Heart pounding in her throat, she found it difficult to catch her breath and Nancy's weight didn't help. Thankfully, she could feel the child's laboured breathing. They were alive and safe but needed to get below and she couldn't see a thing. She called out to Charles and above the din, someone called her name and willing hands soon took Nancy from her and led her down the dark, steep stairs. She could hear Nancy crying and tried to call out to her but the noise of crashing seas made it hopeless.

Suddenly, just as she reached for the bottom step, a terrible crash sounded above and the ship lurched violently. She fell into a sea of bodies as people screamed and flailed about in fear. Then there was calm as the ship stopped pitching and someone lit a candle.

"Emilia ... Emilia, I was so worried," cried a familiar voice at her side. It was Charles, and she fell thankfully into his arms as sobs wracked her body.

Captain Welch had mere seconds after closing the hatch to heed the warning crack as one of the masts, hit by lightening, shattered, then thundered to the deck. Leaping out of the way, he saw the bodies of his men fall with the rigging ... writhing ... desperately reaching for anything to break their fall.

The winds abated soon after doing their damage, but relentless rain pounded them for two days before they were able to limp into the harbour at Manta, Ecuador. In unbearable heat, the hungry and frightened passengers began to grumble loudly. They were allowed to disembark during the next two days as a new mast was put into place. The crew tended to their injured and began the job of refitting new sails. While ashore the passengers managed to buy fresh fruit substantially improving their disposition.

However, on the third day, the captain announced they would be leaving on the next tide. Obviously counting on fair weather, he told them the crew would be completing repairs as they travelled. He also refused to purchase further stores, except a small supply of fresh water. The rumble of disapproval became anger, moving quickly from crew to passenger ... and the unbearable heat continued.

Captain Welch began spending even more time with Nancy. As they sailed westward from Ecuador his ramblings told the child they were looking for a large group of islands. Two days later, he found them, calling them Galapagos. He said they would now take a bearing north-west which would bring them, at last, into the waters of North America—they were nearing their destination.

With new sails in place, they were blessed with fair winds and soon regained their former speed. The steaming heat dissipated as the

Pacific Ocean and favourable winds took them northwards. The Captain soon found himself facing open revolt from both crew and passengers who could no longer abide the lack of quality food. He was often seen pacing the deck until finally upon reaching San Francisco, he purchased hard biscuits, potatoes, and oranges, to augment their rations. Nancy's young teeth became adept at nibbling raw potato to settle the hunger pains, although often receiving extra rations when visiting the Captain.

Rev. Garvey had learned that Nancy would need someone to care for her in Victoria as her father was travelling north to the Nanaimo coalfields to seek work. Feeling compassion for Tom Wilson's situation, the Garveys offered to escort the child to the local orphanage upon their arrival. Nancy's father accepted the offer knowing he had no choice and little energy for long goodbyes. He would return for Nancy once he had settled into his job and found a home ... a few months at most.

Pleasant weather permitted more time on deck and even Wilson and his fellow sufferers began to feel like moving about again. Finally, he was able to spend time with his little girl and they were often seen on deck together. Nancy, now four, stayed protectively close to her father and they were not often seen apart during the final weeks of the voyage.

Finally, one sunny morning in early October, Captain Welch pointed out the rolling green hills in the distance, explaining they were trees ... thousands of acres of larger and taller trees than they had ever seen before. This was their destination ... Vancouver Island, he called it.

A great cheer arose but later in the day strong winds and a relentless rain restricted their time on deck as they entered the Straits of Juan de Fuca. It eased during the night and early the next morning they caught their first glimpse of Victoria ... before black rain clouds enveloped them once again.

Lining the railing, the passengers watched expectantly as they sailed into a crowded and noisy Victoria Harbour ... 'whaling ships and gold seekers,' someone said knowingly, but many were travellers and emigrants just like themselves. They had developed a preconceived idea of Victoria, and the lack of modern buildings, homes, and visible inhabitants, coupled with the distressing weather, now greatly dismayed them.

A depressing overcast sky matched Tom Wilson's countenance as he clutched his daughter in his arms. He was still very tired from his long ordeal but he knew he must put on a brave front for the child. Tears were difficult to contain and several escaped, running down his haggardly pale face. Nancy clung tightly to his neck, kissing his cheek and brushing away each tear as it escaped. Tom found it difficult to look at her. He had tried to explain that he must find work and would return soon, but he had no way of knowing if a child so young could really understand and would ever forgive him.

The familiar *bump* was felt and the passengers began to line up at the disembarking area. It was still raining and the gangway was treacherously slippery as they helped each other down to the safety of the wharf. Underfoot, the solid nature of Victoria's dock seemed strangely foreign as they disembarked and searched for their baggage and belongings, brought up by crew members. They found the sun comfortably warm when it came out momentarily, but it was not to last as ominous grey clouds brought rain once again and they were soon wet through.

And then it was time for Tom to leave. Tearfully, Nancy said goodbye to her father, holding so tightly to his neck Charles had to pry her hands away. Taking her into his own arms, her little body began to shake and her face contorted with pain as the realization of their final parting set in. As she watched the last of her family walk away, a heart-wrenching cry escaped her lips.

"DAAADDYYY!!"

Her father turned for one last pitiful glance wanting desperately to stay but knowing it was impossible. With shoulders stooped and heart breaking, he turned and quickly disappeared into the rain and the jostling crowd.

Sobbing quietly now, Nancy held tightly to Charles' hand as they left the dock area and walked up the hill to the main street, they called

Government. It was a hazardous journey along the now muddy, pothole-strewn road. As they walked up the uneven boardwalk, greasy from the rain which had now stopped, a dreadful mixture of noises filled the air. All manner of transportation lumbered by often splashing pedestrians in their eagerness to get to their destination. Rough voices shouted and whips cracked coaxing on heavily-loaded drays that creaked and groaned from the strain, terrifying the little girl as she held more tightly to Charles' hand.

Just as they reached Courtney Street, a stagecoach with the words *Victoria Transfer Co. Tally-Ho* emblazoned on the side, lumbered by causing them to hastily seek safety.

A stern-faced churchman dressed in a long, black cloak awaited their arrival at the corner. He offered the Reverend a lifeless handshake and grumbled at the sight of the child.

"The orphanage is full," he said coldly, upon hearing Rev. Garvey's explanation for the girl's presence. "And you, sir, force us to take in another one of these homeless waifs!"

In a show of temper, the sinister-looking churchman turned on his heel and slipping slightly on the slick surface, marched across the street his long cloak dragging in the mire. Wondering if he should follow, Charles hesitated but Emilia carefully hoisted her skirts in a vain attempt to keep them out of the mud, and stepped from the safety of the boardwalk.

"Come, Charles," she ordered over her shoulder, picking her way between the potholes. Then, noticing Nancy's appearance, she adding more gently, "Pick her up, Charles, the child can barely stay awake."

He picked up the weary little girl and hurried across the road. Reaching the opposite side, he stopped to look about him and noticed for the first time the rows of shacks that purported to be businesses—many of them desperately in need of repair. For a fleeting moment, he was glad they were not staying.

With his temper wearing thin at the poor welcome being afforded them, Charles Garvey called harshly after the churchman who was hurrying ahead. "Good gracious man, could you at least tell us where you're taking us!"

An arm appeared from under the churchman's cloak, though he never turned his head nor spoke a word. He pointed through the mist to a brick church spire at the end of the block. Seeing their destination at last, they hurried on and soon found themselves standing at the entrance of a somewhat familiar-looking place of worship. The sign read, SAINT ANDREWS PRESBYTERIAN CHURCH. Although it was much smaller than most English churches, they were nonetheless grateful.

Emilia's clothes were now quite wet and streaked with mud. She was barely able to contain her anger as they arrived at the side door. Her husband tightly gripped the distressed child who now whimpered in fitful sleep on his shoulder. Their guide rang a bell and they waited. By the time the Chinese houseboy opened the door, Emilia was fuming. The thoughts in her head were anything except charitable. Charles, who was normally a patient man, was making a feeble attempt to calm his wife without waking Nancy.

Stepping inside the dark hallway, it was quite noticeable that their guide had been left outside in the rain. Emilia sighed, biting her lip as they slipped wet coats from tired shoulders, finally waking Nancy when they removed her cape. Frightened by the dark room, she clung even more tightly to Charles.

The houseboy showed them into a comfortably furnished parlour, and disappeared. Polished maple floors were scattered with oriental rugs arranged in an orderly fashion about the room. Dark leather upholstered chairs with enough embroidered cushions to suggest a women's hand, and heavy vases, stood on miniature tables. A large, unhealthy-looking plant spread its branches from a dark corner. Pictures of horses and hounds adorned the walls in true English tradition. Several long, narrow windows were draped with dark velvet curtains, allowing little light to penetrate the room.

The houseboy returned quickly leading them down a short hall and into another, cheerier looking room. Teacups of fine china were laid out neatly on a low centre table. The short, kindly-looking, but portly, resident clergy, stood with his back to the fire peering over his spectacles, hands clasped behind him. His wife sat stern-faced in an overlarge chair, giving the impression she was casually reading the Bible, which lay open on her lap.

"Come in, come in," Rev. Gosworth's powerful voice boomed. "Now what have we here?" he asked, moving closer to study the now wide-awake child in Charles' arms.

Nancy recoiled and the clergyman stopped, noting her distress. Instead, he inquired of their voyage as he rang a bell and a young maid quickly entered.

"Take the child to the kitchen, Jane, and feed her," he ordered. "She is no doubt hungry and Rector Swift from St. John's will soon be here to collect her." When the maid had left the room, he turned to Charles and growled, "Your promises are most inconvenient, sir!"

The last they heard of Nancy was a pitiful cry as the maid carried her down the long hallway toward the kitchen. "You'll feel better with something in your stomach, little miss," she said, charitably.

Shocked alert by the recurring thread of impoliteness, Emilia took a deep breath. "Our luggage should be arriving in a fine state after sitting on the dock in all this rain. I daresay you have a most unwelcome manner of treating guests!" she said, forcing a cold smile.

The biting comment was not lost on the clergyman's wife. Frowning, she slammed her Bible shut with a thud. Seeing the danger, her husband quickly interceded by assuring Emilia, their trunks would be arriving shortly … they had been well taken care of. Noting the fire in the eyes of this gentle-looking English lady, he decided it would be better not to raise the ire of this women for the steamship to the mainland would be leaving in a couple of days.

"I think the tea is steeped, Gertrude dear. I've no doubt our guests have not had a decent cup of tea in months," said the Reverend, prodding his wife into action.

In the kitchen, Nancy picked at the food on her tin plate. Finally, unable to hold her head up any longer, she fell into merciful sleep—her lovely, but frightfully matted, red hair almost covered her tear-stained face as it rested on the table. Jimmy, the houseboy, looked sympathetically at the child, gently patting her shoulder.

Suddenly, the bell for the front door bounced frantically on the end of its spring, ringing just once before Jimmy leapt into action.

At the door stood the tall figure of Rector Swift. Framed in the light and with water dripping liberally from his wide-brimmed hat, he made no effort to enter. "There's a waif, I believe, a girl from a ship."

Jimmy nodded and closed the door. Soon it swung open again.

Looking disdainfully at the dripping man, Rev. Gosworth snapped, "Back door, man, you're wet!"

Grinning to himself as the door banged shut, the old rector of the Iron Church, more formally known as St. John's Anglican, slowly made his way to the servant's entrance. It would have come as a tremendous shock if the minister of St. Andrews had invited him in—they were colleagues, in a manner of speaking, yet decidedly different, and obviously so. Rev. Gosworth was a social climber, entertainer of the rich and powerful men of the city, and intent on being ordained a Bishop as a just reward.

But the rector of the Iron Church had no such illusions. He was getting old and happy to serve the Lord and his congregation as the hard life of the working class would allow. The flock to whom he administered in the rattling, old corrugated building he called a House of Worship at the corner of Douglas and Herald, was set amid the sprawling shacks of the poor. They came from different countries, most seeking their fortune or already losing it, in the goldfields of British Columbia and farther north. His habit of befriending the Indians often raised the ire of his parishioners. The Iron Church had served its purpose, but like him, it was getting old and soon would be cast aside in the name of progress.

Arriving at the back door, he tapped lightly. The door opened and the sleeping child was thrust into his arms along with a small suitcase. He heard the door bang shut behind him and he shuddered at the thought of this innocent waif all alone. He looked into the face of the beautiful little girl and turned his solemn face toward the sky. "Lord," he whispered, "please help this poor, lonely child."

Chapter 2

Waking to the unexpected sounds of soft children's voices, Nancy sat up slowly and wondered where she was. Letting her eyes roam fearfully around the room, she realized the Garveys were nowhere in sight. Instead, there were many children about, quietly getting out of beds and dressing themselves.

A young girl moved cautiously toward her, buttoning her frock. "Better get up before *she* gets here, or you'll be in trouble!" she whispered, urgently.

But Nancy couldn't move and in her confusion, began to cry. An older, sandy-haired lad hurried over to help her. He urged her out of bed, helped her to dress, and stood beside her holding her hand.

Suddenly, the dormitory door banged open. A stern-faced women, dressed in black, entered and stood scowling at the children. She marched down the row of beds, stopping to glower at Nancy and the boy still holding her hand.

This must be 'she'! Nancy thought, shuddering.

"That your bed, lad?" matron hissed disdainfully, flicking the boy's bare arm with the wet cloth in her hand.

Nancy flinched and heard the boy's sudden intake of breath. She looked up at him fearfully, but no tears came to his eyes. He slowly shook his head.

"Then get to your own bed, Dan Brown! You know the rules." She flicked him again with the cloth as he moved past her.

Nancy stood rock still, watching her ally run back across the room and stand silently beside his bed.

An ominous silence now descended on that room—except for the heavy tread of matron's feet on the bare wooden floor. She marched slowly down the row, casting her haughty gaze over each of the sullen-faced children. Then marching back toward the door, she

14

turned back to face them. "We have a new mouth to feed," she announced, with a growl. Casting a withering look at Nancy, she sneered, "You lot had better explain my two golden rules to her, silence and obedience, in case you've forgotten!" She moved toward the door, her long black dress rustling behind her. "You know the drill … toilet first, then wash for breakfast or there will be none!"

Following matron in single file, the children left the security of the dormitory. They hurried to keep up, going along a dimly lit passage that led past two other large rooms, and then down a wide dark stairway. Matron turned off at one of the rooms telling them to 'hurry up' one last time.

Passing her, Dan reached out and grasped Nancy's hand giving her a cautious smile of encouragement. Leading the confused little girl behind him, he showed her the outside toilet and helped her to wash before lining up with the others.

After a long wait, matron's voice finally called them to breakfast. The room they entered had only one picture on the wall and beside it a stark white cross. The only furniture was a long, bare wooden table which took up the entire centre of the room. Chairs were lined up on both sides of the table and the children moved quickly to their places. Dan pulled Nancy along with him. Standing to attention behind their chairs, she timidly followed his example.

"We will say grace," Matron's voice droned from the head of the table, "and thank the Lord for his blessing."

The children stood stiffly to attention with heads bowed and the lady in black began her monotonous recitation. Nancy, not being familiar with this ritual, lifted her head and looked around the room. Making unexpected eye contact with the dark glaring eyes of the matron, she shuddered, her lips quivering fearfully, and she quickly dropped her head.

Finally finished, she barked, "AMEN … NOW SIT, AND NO NOISE!" Remaining standing, with her hands on the table, she leaned across the table and glared at them as chairs scraped on the rough wooden floor.

Small dishes were passed along the table and Dan made sure Nancy got one. A cup of water and a spoon came next, each child unsmiling and silently passing them along the row ... the stern eye of matron watching their every move. A scoop of oatmeal was sloshed haphazardly into each dish by a uniformed kitchen maid as she passed behind each chair.

Forgetting to watch Dan, Nancy reached for her spoon but stopped abruptly when she heard matron's voice. "NOT YET, GIRL!"

Scuttling away to the kitchen, the maid returned with matron's plate. Nancy couldn't believe her eyes. She had never seen so much food on one plate in her entire life. As the smell of eggs and ham floated slowly down the table, she looked around at the expressionless faces about her and realized this was a normal sight for them.

"Eat and be grateful!" matron growled, smiling a little at the sight of her own meal. As she shoveled in the first mouthful, she glanced down the row of faces with their now pleading eyes. BANG! went the handle of her knife, striking the table. Her mouth full of food, she snarled, "I SAID ... EAT!"

In five minutes it was all over. On a sign from matron, they formed a single file and carried their dirty dishes into the kitchen, each washing their own. Then they lined up again and waited. Dan kept Nancy beside him, often smiling at her reassuringly although he never spoke.

Finally matron finished her breakfast, and after mopping her plate with a thick slice of dark bread, she rose. Pointing her long finger at Dan, making Nancy tremble, she announced loudly, "You, Dan Brown, will go to the bakery again today. Sweeping floors should keep you out of trouble for awhile. Next, she turned her attention to the older girls. "You two will go to the seamstress and continue your sewing lessons," she said, her finger rising again. "The rest of you upstairs ... AND NO NOISE!"

Filing off in orderly fashion and closing the door quietly behind themselves, they retraced their steps back through the hallways and up the dark stairs. When they could go no farther, they made their way to the large room next to the bedroom. This room, Nancy would learn, was both play area and schoolroom for the younger children.

The two older girls quickly and silently gathered together what they needed and went back downstairs. Leaving the building, they hurried down the path together, neither daring to speak until they were well out of sight.

Dan took Nancy's hand and knelt down beside her, whispering urgent instructions to his little charge. "Follow the others and do what they do and you'll be fine. I'll be back at six with some treats," he said gently, taking her over to one of the other girls.

"Look after her, Barbara. I have to leave now," he said, to the little girl who had spoken to her earlier that morning.

Nancy cast her eyes to the floor but Barbara took her hand and led her over to a corner where some of the others were playing with wooden toys on the bare floor.

At precisely twelve noon, a bell rang and the children ran for the doorway … it was lunchtime, Barbara said. Afterwards, they were allowed one hour of playtime out in the yard with only the old kitchen maid watching them.

Off to one side, peeking through the tall iron fence, Nancy noticed two chubby brown faces looking at them. Slowly, she walked closer to the fence and stood staring back at the two native children. She was curious, but not frightened, as she had often seen brown-skinned people when the ship stopped in various ports.

"Hello!" said the taller one, a boy of about six, grinning at her.

Nancy stepped back in surprise.

"You're new! Can we be friends? My name is Billy," the boy whispered, pushing his head against the fence.

Nancy nodded. It seemed strange to hear another child talking when the lady in black insisted that they should always be quiet. Inch by inch she crept closer until finally their fingers touched.

"My daddy's gone away," she informed them.

The younger one was about her age, and no doubt Billy's sister. She was holding out a strange-looking black stick to her.

"You hungry? Here," she said, putting it into her hand.

17

Despite having just eaten, the thought of more food was awfully tempting and her tummy still felt empty. Cautiously, Nancy reached for the stick and put it to her lips. She took a small bite. A puzzled look came over her face at the surprisingly pleasant taste.

"It's salmon fish! You eat it," said Billy. As Nancy finished, the maid appeared and the children stepped quickly away from the fence. "We'll come tomorrow," he whispered, and they ran away.

The rest of the afternoon was spent in the big room upstairs. The younger children quietly amused themselves but Nancy, suddenly feeling very tired, crouched sleepily in a corner. The older children sat at wooden-topped, iron desks doing school lessons under the watchful eye of their teacher, Miss Simpson. She was not at all like matron—she was friendly and really nice. Nancy wished she was old enough to go to school so Miss Simpson could be her teacher, too.

At six o'clock, Dan and the two girls returned home just in time for supper. Nancy was very relieved to see Dan's smiling face again. As they stood behind their chairs in the dining room, he winked at her and she smiled ... for the first time since she had arrived in this frightening place. Surreptitiously, he took her hand under the table, and she felt warm all over. *Maybe I will like it here, if I can be with Dan,* she thought.

After cleaning their plates and sweeping the floor, the children were allowed outside again. It had been a wet week and they welcomed the opportunity to run around outside where they could make noise out of earshot of matron. Dan organized a game of leapfrog on the grass and they watched matron leave for home. Then, Dan took Nancy to one side and emptied his pockets. He had bits of crusty bread, broken buns, and cake wrapped in brown paper and soon all the children were gathered around enjoying pieces of his treasure.

"You can talk now," announced Dan, "but not too loudly."

Dan Brown was almost twelve years old. An orphan since the age of six, when he had arrived at this place. He was the oldest and as their chosen leader cared for the others as best he was able. He had learnt early that he was no match for matron.

A month later, he was put out as an apprentice baker at the shop in Douglas Street where he'd been sweeping the floors for the past four months. Although he was glad of his partial freedom, he hated having to leave Nancy. It was little ones like her that bothered him the most. His nature being gentle and kind, he fostered a deep-seated hatred for matron and a system that treated children so harshly.

Nancy settled into the bitter existence of an orphan's life waiting for the day her father would return. In Dan's absence, she looked forward to seeing the Indian children who came to visit her often.

Billy and his younger sister, Rose, explained to her one day that one of their ancestors was the Chief of the Stamiss tribe, the original peoples of this place the white man calls Victoria. "White men called him Freezy," Billy giggled, "but I don't know why."

Before long, the weather grew colder and the children were no longer allowed outside. The days seemed longer and Nancy wished for warmth and sunshine again so Dan and the native children would return.

At the end of February, matron called her to the office one day. Standing over her with a solemn face she gave her news that chilled her to the bone. "You can stop thinking about your father now, girl. He is never going to come. He is dead and that is all there is to it. The mining company in Cumberland send us a letter about an accident in which many men were killed. Your father was one of them."

Nancy only heard the first part of the matron's dissertation. She didn't understand it all. She just knew he was never coming back. She was just like the others now … an orphan that no one cared about. For two days she sat in a corner and cried. Barbara asked her what was wrong and Miss Simpson came over to talk to her. After that she tried very hard not to cry anymore and with their help she began to feel better.

Over the next four years, despite her many hardships, Nancy grew into a pretty little girl with a quick aptitude for learning. Dan visited often, bringing a bagful of treats to the fence whenever he was able.

Then, one day early in April 1904, Dan announced he had turned 16 ... gaining his freedom from the orphanage and the bakery. He wanted to be a goldminer but the goldfields were now too far away in Alaska, so he had decided to join on as a crew member of a whaling boat. Nancy was heartbroken but she tried not to show it. Dan had taught her much about coping on her own and she had to prove to him she had learned well and would be brave. She would miss him so much. He had always been like a brother to her, the brother she had never had.

Before he said goodbye, he took her aside and told her that one day he would find her again. He hugged her quickly, and then he was gone. Feeling more alone than she could ever remember, she walked slowly over to the far corner of the yard and sat down, just as she had on that very first day. Shaking inside, she pulled her legs up against her chest. For the first time since matron had told her that her daddy was dead, she wept uncontrollably.

When she was 11, matron announced to Nancy that she had completed her schooling and would now be required to earn her own keep. She and the new rector had arranged a job as dishwasher at the Temperance Hotel—a non-alcoholic establishment on Langley Street approved by the Church. Janet, one of the older girls, was going for an interview downtown and would deliver Nancy on her first day. However, matron warned in no uncertain terms that she would have to remember her way back.

Nancy had not been into downtown Victoria since the day she and her father arrived at the harbour so many years before. This was her first trip outside the orphanage walls unaccompanied by the eagle-eyed matron who occasionally took them for walks up Douglas or through Chinatown. Nancy was so very excited, she barely even considered the ramifications of her first job.

As they neared the city she watched in wonder as streetcars rumbled by, filled with people. Queens Market, at the corner of Johnson and Douglas, held a grizzly fascination with carcasses of meat hanging in full view. But it was the patrons of the cigar shops that really kept her amused—important-looking men strutting about in top hats puffing on their curiously-shaped pipes, as vile smelling clouds of smoke followed them.

Nancy peered curiously in the windows of the haberdashery emporiums, marvelling at the wonderful array of goods made especially for women, forgetting all about her appointment. But Janet was kind and reminded her to hurry, warning her that matron would hear of their tardiness.

The first few days at her new job were exhausting and Nancy could barely find the energy to walk home. However, she was soon impressing her sour-faced employers and although the work was exhausting, she learned to do it well and quickly. In no time, even the walk home became a measure of her freedom and she savoured it each day, learning to keep a smile on her face attracting many admirers.

For two and a half long years she washed dishes and did other menial tasks about the hotel, always in the background away from the patrons. As the months passed, the tasks grew less tiring as both her mind and body developed and her willingness to learn became obvious to those around her.

Early in 1910, Louise joined the staff as cook. Before long, this kindly lady became her friend taking an extreme liking to the wispy young girl. Relief from the drudgery of dirty crockery arrived just prior to her 14th birthday when Louise made a request that Nancy be allowed to assist her in preparing the vegetables. For six months under her watchful eye, they worked together as a closely knit team.

Then one day, the friendly, oversized woman took the girl to one side and whispered confidentially, "I'm leaving at the end of the month. I have a new job at the Occidental."

Nancy's eyes opened wide in amazement. "Oh no!" she gasped in utter desperation, her hand clasping her mouth as her throat tightened and she turned to escape.

"Wait … wait," Louise urged, grasping the girl's arm and turning her around to face her. "You are going with me, Nancy!"

Nancy shook her head, tears welling up in her eyes. "They'll never let me go."

"Yes, they will, it's already arranged," Louise insisted. She smiled and took Nancy's hand. "I've already talked to matron and rector, and if you agree to an apprenticeship of eighteen months, they'll allow it." She paused, looking serious again. "Do you understand what that means, Nancy?" Not waiting for the speechless girl to answer, she pulled her tiny body toward her ample bosom and hugged her. "It means they will take half your wages for a year and a half," she whispered into her ear, sarcastically adding, "for all the love and caring they've given you!"

Nancy pulled away, wiping her damp eyes with the back of her hand. "You mean, I get to live away from that place?" she asked, as she began to realize what Louise was trying to tell her.

Louise nodded, and smiled encouragingly.

"You mean, I'm free ... I'm free?" she cried, hugging Louise fiercely.

Near the end of October, matron watched through the window as the redheaded girl marched confidently down the path for the last time. Nancy never looked back ... she'd finally finished with this horrible place forever. She tightly grasped the handle of the old suitcase, held her chin high, letting the wind blow through her hair, and walked out of the gate ... her thoughts on nothing but freedom.

Chapter 3

On October 26th, 1910, she entered the Occidental Hotel at the foot of Johnson Street and began the next phase of her young life. But this day was to hold unexpected and horrifying excitement. By noon, news was being shouted by passersby that a fire was raging mere blocks away, threatening the city's oldest businesses on Fort Street. Hurrying outside, she and Louise watched the angry red and orange flames leaping over the rooftops, sending great clouds of black smoke skyward from the wooden buildings mere blocks away. Firebells rang their message of doom as firemen and their horse-drawn engines, aided by many civilians, showed their eagerness to pit their strength against the quickly spreading blaze.

Word passed quickly through the Occidental. Built of solid bricks and mortar and several blocks away from the inferno, the staff didn't even consider the risk. However, frightened patrons packed their belongings quickly and vacated their rooms, some without paying. Concern soon escalated as word came that Broad Street was also in flames.

Pandemonium raged in the streets as men, women, and horses screamed in fear, running in every direction to escape the heat and flames. Streetcars rattled to a halt at Government and Yates quickly backing away from the danger as nearby shop owners desperately threw buckets of water on storefronts.

Rumors spread like wildfire through the city as the crackle of burning buildings could be heard blocks away. Smoke hung heavy over the city and people began to struggle with the enormity of the disaster. City businessmen wept openly when hard-won fortunes were swept away in a sea of flames. Fighting valiantly, the firemen found themselves often in a position of retreat from the blazing inferno, looking desperately for a place to hold the spread as fireballs leapt from rooftop to rooftop.

Adding to the tragedy, a fear-crazed horse galloped headlong into the path of a moving railway engine on Johnson Street leaving its Chinese owner wailing hysterically over the battered body.

Hundreds of sandwiches and buckets of tea and coffee were sent to the firefighters, keeping Louise, Nancy, and other hotel kitchens very busy. Updates poured into both the Victoria Times and Daily Colonist offices as word circulated around the city—even as the latter was itself threatened with fire raging about them. Bars were full to bursting as both injured and frightened sought a place of shelter.

Finally, word came that the devastation had been stopped at Trounce Alley and as the coolness of the October evening settled over the city, the last flames were extinguished and fireman were left with the job of ensuring the safety of the remaining buildings. Acrid fumes and smothering ruins that lasted for days were the only sad reminder of the horror the city had experienced that fateful day. Mayor Beckwith and several city councillors roamed the smoky streets lamenting the loss, praising the firemen, and telling anyone who'd listen that the electric power should be back on in a week.

Throughout that winter, an extensive cleanup campaign consumed the city. Streetcar schedules were withdrawn or changed and Government Street was closed to all but workmen and carts as they began the slow process of clearing away debris.

Finally, the spring of 1911 saw workmen commence the rebuilding with renewed and urgent vigour. Streetcar schedules resumed but the rattling monsters were often disrupted for hours. People learned to be tolerant and either walked or spent their time curiously watching the new buildings take shape. The topic of conversation naturally centred on the rebuilding, everyone seeming to have a conflicting view of how to proceed with the huge task.

The Occidental Hotel was several blocks north of the Temperance where Nancy had previously worked, and far enough away from the fire not to be harmed. It had a bar with entertainment and a dining room and lounge. Large rooms were fitted with all the modern amenities and being at the corner of Johnson and Wharf Streets, little seaview balconies overlooked the harbour, although Nancy hardly ever had the luxury of enjoying the view.

Being the lowest of a flock of kitchen maids, her job was to help prepare the mountain of vegetables consumed daily. This now came easily to her and with her bright eyes and sweet smile she was a diligent and well-liked worker. Expectations of freedom ran high in Nancy's mind and she soon noticed that time passed more quickly when she applied herself.

Her wages were paid weekly, half to her and half to the church for the orphanage fund. After that first year and a half, it would all be hers—a day she looked forward to with great anticipation.

The hotel staff were happy, kindly people. They gave her meals and a space to sleep under the stairs, and she made many new friends. Aprons were provided and the staff were permitted to share any clothes left in the rooms. After that first year, she graduated to helping the serving staff in the dining room. Her now lithesome, well-rounded young body, and winsome smile, quickly drew her a sizable amount in tips from the many male patrons that travelled in and out of the city. Eighteen months was passing very quickly.

Freedom! she thought, waking early to the noises of a hotel getting ready for a new day. It was the 30th day of April 1912 … a day to celebrate. It was the last day of her contract. She was almost 16-years-old and the thought of finally being able to do what she wanted with her own life exhilarated her.

Later that day, her money bulging in the top of her stocking—stretching her suspender to almost breaking point—she affectionately patted the lump before hiding it away in her shoe and getting ready for bed. After today, her savings account would grow much faster and she had already begun making plans for spending some of it on desperately needed new clothes.

Several days later, the staff was shocked and saddened when Louise was badly scalded in the kitchen and had to leave her job.

Doctors were scarce, expensive, and their services way out of reach of the working class. People often resorted to herbal remedies acquired at the Chinese druggists on lower Fisgard Street.

Keeping in touch with Louise became extremely difficult for Nancy, having to rely on hearsay and messages passed from one worker to another. Several weeks later, she was told that Louise had moved out to Saanich where her relatives could more easily look after her. Sadly, the bond was broken. She had just celebrated her 16th birthday and she was on her own once more.

Being advanced to a waitress soon after Louise's departure, Nancy quickly learned that this position had many advantages for her. Apart from the tips, she was continually meeting new people—many of them locals who soon became her friends. When working the evening shift she enjoyed watching the patrons come in dressed in all their finery, nothing like the upper class she saw on the streets when she occasionally went for a walk, but the ladies looked awfully nice in their fancy dresses, large hats and accessories. She wondered if she would ever be able to dress up like that. Some of the men carried walking sticks and looked so funny as they walked out onto the street, it was all she could do not to laugh.

She was fascinated and amused with the snatches of confidential conversations she overheard as she moved between tables. Later, in her lonely room, she often passed the time by making up stories, imagining the missing portions of what she had heard. Most patrons treated her exceptionally well, finding her pleasant and efficient and the days passed quickly.

The unbearably hot summer was just a memory when early in October, she heard a city councilman talking to a businessman about the hotel. Rushing back to the kitchen to get her next order, she served it slowly at the next table, listening intently. The councillor was telling his guest that the hotel had gained a bad reputation and was being discussed in Victoria's City Council meetings.

Nancy pondered on this all afternoon. Her mind in a whirl as she wondered what he was referring to. The owners were kind to the staff and it was a happy place to work, but curiosity gnawed at her brain.

Finally, a few days later while serving a group of regulars, she was about to ask them when a group of noisy sailors walked in calling loudly for service.

In an effort to quiet them down, she moved to their table giving them menus and waiting to take their order. She scratched notes on her pad as each one made his choice. The fourth member of the group took more time to decide and as their eyes met across the table Nancy gasped, dropping her pencil.

"Danny ... Dan Brown ... is that really you?" she asked, staring at him incredulously.

"Aye lass, it is," the sailor answered, studying her face with more interest. Then his puzzled look changed to one of disbelief and a smile lit up his face. "Nancy?" he whispered.

One of his companions broke the spell. "Later, Danny m'lad! I'm hungry," he insisted, in an agitated manner.

In a daze, Nancy took his order and quickly returned to the kitchen, her mind spinning. Cook noticed her confusion.

"What's wrong lass, yer seen a ghost?"

Too bewildered to speak, she merely shook her head as she filled her tray and quickly returned to the dining room. Serving the first three men she avoided eye contact with Dan. Returning with the second tray, she purposely left him until last.

She had just emptied the tray when Dan lightly touched her hand. Pushing his chair away from the table and rising, he took the tray from her and placed it on his seat. He reached for her hand and raised it slowly to his lips. He kissed it gently, causing a tear to slip silently down Nancy's cheek.

Dan's shipmates were remarkably silent, although watching their friend intently. "Who is she, Danny?" the older man asked, almost reverently, laying his knife and fork back down on the table.

"This is Nancy, the little girl I left in the orphanage ... so long ago," he said in a near whisper, not taking his eyes off the girl's face. "I want you to meet me later, Nancy. Can you be at the front door of The Empress at eight?"

A voice at a nearby table called for service interrupting them, but Nancy quickly nodded her reply, smiling shyly as she pulled her hand free of his grasp. Then hurriedly picking up her tray, she moved on, leaving Dan's companions in stunned silence behind her.

Later, she returned to clear their table and present the bill. Dan winked at her and stood up, dropping a ten dollar bill in the centre of the table. The others followed Dan's example until four, ten dollar bills lay in a heap.

"That's for you, lass," said the oldest sailor.

Nancy was flabbergasted and busied herself with clearing the table as the men paid the cashier and left. Only then did her faltering hands scoop up the money which represented more than three months wages.

"Do you know those sailors?" one of the waitresses asked later.

"No," Nancy murmured, turning to face the older girl.

"Whalers, love," she grinned. "They are the Irish crew, the Highliners, they're called ... the best on the coast. Got lots of money, they have. Bet you got a good tip the way that young one was watching you!" she added, with a giggle.

Nancy merely smiled, happy that Dan was doing well for himself. For a moment her mind went back to the days at the orphanage and those special moments when he had brought treats for her and the others. Finding it difficult to get the sandy-haired young man off her mind, she kept watching the clock in the bar wishing she could will it to strike six.

After a long day at work, Nancy was normally too tired to wander very far from the hotel. Once in awhile, she did enjoy a walk down to the causeway which was becoming the centre of activity for tourists. From this vantage point, CPN steamships and other ocean-going vessels could often be seen quietly riding the tide of the inner harbour. She remembered the way the old coal-oil lamps had twinkled dimly along the harbour but they were now being replaced by modern electric lamps. Tall masts stretched to the sky and seemed to conjure up vague memories from her own past. But tonight, all traces of exhaustion were forgotten as she eagerly awaited her appointment and the short walk down to The Empress. She was going to see Danny and a strange excitement gripped her.

Taking her supper back to her tiny room under the stairs, she ate slowly, her thoughts turning over and over. This would be the first time she'd ever gone inside The Empress, and she had never met a man by appointment before.

She changed into her heavy cotton petticoat, and her best warm hose. Happily, she pulled on her new high-topped shiny black boots which had been left by a moneyed patron the week before. *What a bit of luck that I had the smallest feet!* she thought smugly. She looked at her long-sleeved, high-necked, white cotton blouse trimmed with layers of lace on the cuffs and held it to her chest. She had been saving this for just such a special occasion. Lastly, came a dark blue full-skirted dress with broad shoulder straps. The hem came just below her boot-tops and she thought she looked rather smart. Finally, she pinned her green tam carefully in place. She was ready, but if it wasn't for the new clothes purchased with her now larger salary, she would have been embarrassed to meet Dan tonight.

At 7:35 pm, she stepped out into the alley lighted only by a single lightbulb, pulled her warm woollen shawl even tighter about her slim body and hurried up to Johnson Street. Turning east, she went one block and turned south. Most of the stores on Government were absolutely dark but at least the street was now paved and sported lights and sidewalks, new additions that were appreciated by all. The roads had previously been so poor with many hidden obstructions and holes few people had dared venture out in the dark.

As she went past the Rogers' grocery and chocolate shop, she looked down toward The Empress having a clear view of the newly paved road and seawall. The Empress had been built on reclaimed land once known as James Bay, a very smelly slough used for a garbage dump, she had been told. Now, a causeway stood on the site of the old James Bay Bridge and it was a wonderful area for walking.

Tonight, the lights on the causeway did twinkle in the crisp October air, bringing a smile to her lips. A chill was definitely in the air and she was glad she had worn warm clothes.

In the background, the illuminated Parliament Buildings shone brightly as darkness enfolded the harbour, but tonight her attention was on the magnificent hotel which someone told her had over 200 guest rooms. Waiting for a break in the slowly lumbering traffic, she hurried across the road and made her way toward the steps, looking around to see if she could find Dan in the crowd.

Suddenly, a voice at her elbow, startled her. "Glad you came, Nancy," Dan said softly, stepping out from behind a group of people. "Let's take a little walk before we go inside," he suggested, reaching for her hand and tucking it under his arm.

Without speaking they walked down to the end of the block and across the front of the Parliament Buildings ... both deep in their own thoughts. Nancy's mind was in a whirl, and completely out of character for this usually outspoken girl, she found herself unable to speak. She had been 8-years-old when she had last seen Danny and her memories were very vague. It had been amazing that she had recognized him. So much had happened since that day. She tried to remember ... *he said he was going far away on a boat ... he said they would meet again one day ... he had been right!* Her vision blurred as tears began. *I don't want to cry the first time I see him. He taught me to be brave ... keep calm, oh please be calm,* she thought desperately.

Slowing his stride, Dan looked down at her but not being able to see her face, he could not imagine what was going through her mind. He turned into the breeze and looked out across the harbour. He realized this was going to be difficult for her. *She was so young when I left. I need to give her time. What a beautiful girl she has become.*

"That's my ship over there, the *Belfast*," he said, pointing to the dim shape of a ship with several twinkling red lights. "I once told you I was going whaling. Well, this is the ship I found and the Joyce brothers that I work for became family to me, and I stayed. We live on the boat and that building on the dock ...," pointing to a faint outline to the right, "is the company office." Taking her hand, he applied gentle pressure to emphasize his next statement. "The Joyce Bros. office, that's where you can contact me. I spend a lot of time at sea but go see Meg McDonald, she lives there. She's a really nice lady and will be very glad to see you."

30

Nancy returned his squeeze, looking up at him and moving a bit closer as she felt his reassurance. The wind picked up and Dan hurried her back across the street toward The Empress. They moved up the roadway, darting between cars and carriages lined up at the side entrance. Joining a group of elegantly dressed guests, he led her into the foyer where more guests milled about talking loudly.

To Nancy, it was like they had entered another world. The room was huge with fancy chairs and heavy velvet curtains. Women in wonderful dresses and furs were everywhere but no one seemed to be in a hurry. They heard music playing and Dan pulled her toward the Crystal Ballroom where a dance was just beginning. A few couples were dancing a waltz covering the floor in long gliding strides as an orchestra played in a corner. It was a breathtaking sight and Nancy stood with her mouth open as she looked at the huge chandeliers and wonderful flower arrangements. Ladies in beautiful gowns trimmed in pearls and lace swished by on the arms of grand-looking men in long-jacketed black suits and smartly-creased trousers.

Dan gently pulled her away and they made their way to a small dining room down a wide hallway. A man sat playing a piano in the corner, the soft music almost lost amongst the noises of conversation and cutlery. He gave his name to a uniformed man, he later told her was called a maitre'd. Taking her shawl, Dan handed it to a lady in a little room nearby. The maitre'd showed them to their table and held Nancy's chair as she sat down.

Her eyes nervously swept the room. "But Danny ...," was all she managed before he interrupted.

"Listen, Nancy, you need to see this. We've experienced the other side, you and me. Well, this is how the rich live, and I can afford to treat you, so don't worry."

"I feel so out of place," she whispered, as a waitress in a black dress with a white, highly starched apron, approached.

"Two teas and cake for me and my sister," Dan said with authority, not looking at Nancy. The waitress bobbed a quick curtsy before turning away. "From now on, you're my sister. I have no family and neither have you, so let's invent one!" He watched her

31

closely for her reaction. When she nodded shyly, he chuckled. "Right then, that's settled!"

The waitress returned with a tray of little cakes and poured their tea. "Will that be all, sir?" she inquired, curtsying again.

Nancy finally began to relax and soon she and Dan were catching up on their missing years—getting to know each other all over again. Later, as Dan walked her to the back door of the Occidental, he announced that he was sailing again at the end of the week. However, he promised to see her tomorrow because they had things to look after before he went away.

Exchanging uncomfortable goodnights on the doorstep, he gently kissed her cheek and then grabbed her in a fierce embrace. Nancy still wasn't sure how to react to Dan but when he took her into his arms she melted, returning his embrace willingly.

Sleep didn't come easy to Nancy as she lay in her tiny cot under the service stairs. She wondered what Dan meant when he said they had things to do first. She didn't really care, she was just so glad they had found each other again. She suddenly realized how lonely she had been, especially since Louise's accident. She tossed and turned for a long time before sleep overtook her that night.

Waking tiredly at seven o'clock, her heart was full of joy as she ate a quick breakfast and went to work as if in a dream. Dan was alone when he came into the dining room at lunchtime. She watched him curiously as she served tables nearby. He had some papers which he spread out in front of him and seemed to be studying. When finished, he stacked them neatly together.

"Nancy," he whispered as she passed his table. "I want you to sign these papers for me." Puzzled, but after several attempts between customers, she had finally signed them all. Her eyes asked questions of Dan but she had no time to listen to his answers.

Dan ordered lunch as two of the sailors he had been with the day before, walked in and joined him. He handed one of them a pen and he also signed the papers. When Nancy came to get their orders, Dan introduced them.

"Meet Ned Joyce and his brother Tim, Nancy." The two men smiled, rose from their chairs, and reached over to shake the girl's hand. "They're from Newfoundland and Irish as hell, but good men and true. I've worked for them ever since I left the orphanage. They're my family, too!"

Going into the kitchen, she waited for the lunch plates to be filled.

"What's going on out there, lass? Are them sailors bothering you?" Alice asked, as she scooped food onto the plates.

"No, no, it's my brother!" she giggled, causing the cook's head to jerk up.

"But you don't have one!" Alice gasped, handing her the order.

"Didn't ... but do now!" she said happily, picking up the hot plates and exiting quickly through the door leaving cook and another waitress open-mouthed behind her.

As the dining room grew busier, Nancy had no time to speak with the men. Later, she noticed they'd gone. On the table was a neat stack of coins and a note from Dan that she was to pay the bill and keep the rest. It also said, MEET YOU AT SEVEN AT THE BACK DOOR. Slipping the note into her pocket, she paid the cashier, discovering they had left a nice tip.

She found she couldn't stop watching the clock all afternoon. Re-reading the note during a hurried break, her spirits soared. At six o'clock, she grabbed a quick meal, changed her clothes and fussed with her hair. By 6:55, she let herself out the back door, and looked for Dan in the alley. Heavy-booted footsteps alerted her that he was on his way. Beaming, he opened his arms and embraced her.

"Come on, sis, we've some people to meet," he said, taking her arm.

Nancy allowed herself to be led over to Yates Street and the streetcar stop. Soon the rattling, clanging transport could be heard coming along Government. She had never ridden the streetcar before, though she had often watched them in fascination.

"Spring Ridge," Dan told the conductor, paying the fare and accepting their tickets.

"That's the terminus, lad," the ruddy-faced conductor chuckled, "up by the quarry."

Nancy enjoyed the closeness as she sat next to Dan and watched as the new lights of the city brightened the sky.

It's so beautiful," murmured Nancy, squeezing even closer.

"You're so right, love," he agreed, casting his eyes on her lovely auburn hair as they jerked and bounced along.

Rattling and grinding to its last stop, the conductor yelled, "Terminus ... everybody off!"

They were the only passengers by now and Dan leapt down offering her a hand. Nancy pulled her hat down over her ears and buttoned up her coat against the cold wind that rustled the last of the leaves from the trees.

Where are we going?" she asked, looking through the darkness as Dan pointed to a large brick house a few doors away.

Irish Jack Duggan's," he announced. "He's a master bricklayer and housebuilder, and works for the Parfitt Brothers." He paused to open the gate. "Built this house himself. He's another eastcoaster."

"Eastcoaster?"

"Yep, Irish decent like my bosses, the Joyces. They all come from Newfoundland," Dan explained as he picked up the large brass knocker and rapped confidently on the door. He slipped his arm around Nancy's shoulder as the door opened exposing a tall grey-bearded man with a grin that reached from ear to ear.

"Come in, lad," the big man quietly invited, his voice soft with affection. "And bring that beautiful young lady with yer."

As the door closed the two men shook hands warmly. Jack hung their coats up in a nearby closet before leading them through to the parlor. Mrs. Nellie Duggan rose from her chair to welcome the guests with such a friendly, enthusiastic greeting it set Nancy instantly at ease. There were two other men in the room and Nancy recognized them as the two men who had been in the hotel dining room with Dan ... his bosses, the Joyces.

"My, you're a pretty one!" Mrs. Duggan declared. Grasping her hand, she whispered, "Come, sit next to me, dear."

34

Irish Jack served tea to the ladies, his big hands having difficulty with his wife's fine china. The cups rattled as he presented the tray and the men helped themselves to the bottle of Irish whisky set on the low table in front of them. Nellie Duggan chattered quietly to Nancy, enjoying the company of a younger woman. The Duggan's had never had children, a sad quirk of fate for such a kind and devoted couple.

"Come into the dining room, friends," Jack called, sliding back the highly polished dark mahogany doors and leading the way. "There are name cards on the table," he announced. Then with a mischievous chuckle, he added, "That's if you two can read!" winking at his old friends the Joyces.

"Stop that right now, Jack," his wife giggled. "You know they understand pictures."

"Well, I guess we've got a problem then," Ned admitted. "I don't see any pictures on these cards!"

Everyone laughed as they found their names and sat down. Dan and Nancy not surprisingly found themselves sitting next to each other. When the laughter settled and everyone was sitting except Jack, he cleared his throat to get their attention.

"As most of you know, Dan asked that we get together tonight for a specific purpose. Nancy, Dan wants us to witness a document that makes you the sole beneficiary of his estate should he become demised."

Nancy's face went quite pale and Dan reached over and took her hand.

"You silly old Irishman!" Nellie chortled. "Nobody becomes demised. You should say ... upon his demise, shouldn't he?"

When the room quieted down, Jack tried again. "It means ...," he continued, trying to keep a straight face, "that you get all his money if he wakes up dead one morning!"

Again the house erupted in laughter, causing Nellie to pull out her handkerchief to dab her eyes. "Now you be quiet. I think you've said quite enough, dear," she scolded. "You're frightening the poor girl half to death." Then turning to Nancy, who was looking quite confused, she explained. "It's simple, love. Dan has no family, so he's making you his heir in case of an accident. We're all going to witness the papers."

"B - b - but," Nancy stammered. "Why me?"

"Because you are my sister," Dan muttered, lowering his eyes to the table, his voice cracking with emotion. "You were the bravest little thing I had ever seen and I never forgot."

The room was so quiet you could hear a pin drop as they watched the heart-wrenching interplay between the two orphans. Nancy's eyes filled with tears as memories of those early days flooded back. Dan moved closer and slipped his arm reassuringly around her shoulder as she wiped her tears and desperately tried to keep her composure. Jack produced a paper and as it went around the table each signed their names in silence.

"Come on, you two," Nellie whispered, patting the girl's arm affectionately, "this is a happy day. Now you both have a family. Let's get on with our meal ... I'm famished!"

It was almost ten o'clock when the party broke up. Ned offered Dan and Nancy a ride back to the city but Nancy had her own ideas.

"We'll walk," she said, with a wink at Nellie. "He's got some explaining to do!"

Facing the cold wind blowing up the hill from the sea, they pulled their hats down, their collars up, linked arms and hurried up the street. A dog barked a warning as they passed a darkened house and up ahead the glow of Victoria's streetlights and noise from the taverns told them the city was far from asleep.

When the moon found a space in the clouds, it cast a shadow-filled light over buildings and trees, illuminating their breath as they talked. Reaching the much better lit Douglas Street, Nancy shuddered and a chill moved up her spine. Grasping Dan's hand even tighter her gaze strayed up the street past the City Hall to the empty lot where the orphanage and Iron Church once stood. Word around was that this would soon be a construction site for the new Hudson's Bay store.

They hurried past the outskirts of Chinatown, with its squalor and stacked up homes of the hardworking, but desperately poor. These streets had suffered terribly in the 1907 fire that had taken out this whole area right up to Quadra Street, but now it was abuzz with activity as the much maligned Chinese immigrants moved about the area. Their traditions and culture were different which brought them into regular conflict with the stuffy self-serving upperclass white folk.

"Looks like there's a good trade going on in opium smoking tonight!" Dan commented, noting the large number of men heading into the area near Fan Tan Alley.

"Smoking ... what?" Nancy asked.

Dan laughed as he tried to explain, urging her never to try it. He quickly added that he only knew from what other men had told him, never having tried it himself. Then a bit self-consciously he mentioned the brothels that were frequented by sailors, miners and local residents. Nancy lapsed into an unusual silence.

"What ya thinking, love?"

"I know what brothels are," she whispered, "but do married men go there, too?"

"Aye, lass," he growled, uncomfortably. "An some mighty prominent names too, I'm told."

Nancy was intrigued and wanted to question Dan further. However, as they turned into the alley behind the Occidental they saw two men fighting. Dan released his grip on her hand and told her to stand still and wait as he moved boldly towards them. Her vision impaired by the darkness and Dan's body, she couldn't see what was happening. Then she heard a dull crack, followed by a groan and a thud, and Dan was quickly back at her side.

"What happened?"

"Nothing much, the drunken fools banged their heads together. They'll be friends when they wake up! It's safe now." Hardly glancing at the two prone figures, he hurried her past.

But Nancy did look and what she saw surprised her. "I know them, Danny, they were in the hotel today," she said, stopping to stare at the men. Dan took her arm and urged her forward. As she moved toward the door, her foot kicked something hard and she bent to pick it up, moving under the light to study it.

"It's a gold sack," she gasped, "and it looks awfully familiar. I know why, it's English Jack's. It has a unique pattern and I'd recognize it anywhere. Do you think they could have stolen it? We'd better find him, Dan!"

"Not tonight, my girl," Dan ordered, taking her arm and steering her toward the door. "He'll not be needing it until tomorrow, when he's sober. Put it in your pocket; I have something to tell you."

Reluctantly she complied although not feeling very comfortable with it. "Something to tell me?" she asked, her hand on the doorknob.

"Don't go in yet," he whispered, pulling her toward him. "We're leaving tomorrow, Nancy."

She looked up at him in disbelief then wrapped her arms around him tightly. "No, Danny, I can't bear you to leave so soon," she pleaded, her head dropping onto his chest.

"Silly goose," he chided gently, hugging her affectionately. "Six months will go by very quickly. Just wait and see! I'm never going to lose you again and that's a promise!" Lightly kissing her cheek, he opened the door and pushed her inside, then turned and strode away.

Chapter 4

In the days that followed Nancy watched carefully hoping to see English Jack. Making discreet inquires she learned he had probably gone back up north although no one had seen him leave. He seemed to have completely disappeared ... it just made no sense. *Hadn't he noticed his gold was missing?* she wondered. *Surely he wouldn't leave without it.*

As the rain continued, bringing the month to a close, she wandered down to the docks after work one evening. It was cold and windy and she was relieved when she saw a light in the window of the Joyce Bros. office. Tapping lightly on the door, she was pleased to hear a feminine voice answer.

"Come on in!" it called loudly.

Stepping into the room, she felt the welcome warmth of the pot-bellied stove as the door pulled itself shut with a bang.

"Well, what have we here?" asked a smiling, but obviously friendly, older woman, sitting behind a desk. Laying down her pen, she sat back in her chair and looked over her glasses at the visitor.

"Beg your pardon ma'am, but have you heard any news from Dan?"

"Dan?" the lady asked, somewhat blankly. "Dan who?" She pushed her chair back, laid her glasses on the desk and stood up, not taking her eyes off the stranger who now appeared quite confused.

Although still a child when she left Scotland, Meg MacDonald was a true Scot from the Isle of Skye. Her family emigrated to Nova Scotia in 1873 where her father and three brothers continued the family tradition as men of the sea. They were the last of an old Scottish seafaring family. She had never forgotten that terrible day the deadly August Gale of 1892 stole the lives of her father and elder brother when their fishing schooner, *George Foote,* disappeared off the Grand Banks with all aboard. Her mother died of a broken heart some years later and in 1906, she and her two younger brothers, came by train to Victoria. They purchased a little cottage in the country near Elk Lake where Meg had a lovely little garden and was terribly happy. However, fate once again struck the MacDonald family a heart-crushing blow. The boy's whaler capsized in a storm off the rugged coast of Vancouver Island.

When the *Belfast* returned with their bodies, they met Meg for the first time. Through all the heartbreak, a special friendship was forged between them. The next year she moved back into town and became their housekeeper, office-worker, tormentor and friend ... fiercely protective and loyal. She had been with them for three years now and for all intents and purpose, they were family.

"Dan ... Dan Brown," Nancy repeated, stepping back toward the door, bringing Meg back to reality.

"Come in, lassie, am noo goin ta bite you!" she chuckled, breaking into her Scottish brogue. "We don't make it a habit to give out information to strangers ... even pretty ones!" She paused, tipping her head to one side. "Just let me see the colour of your hair now, lassie."

Nancy felt a little uncomfortable, but she stepped forward into the light. Turning down her coat collar, she removed her hat. Her beautiful auburn hair fell about her shoulders, sparkling in the light.

"Nancy!" Meg gasped, moving toward her. "Glory be, Danny was right. You are a beauty!"

"You do know him!" Nancy reddened, sighing with relief.

"Yes, of course I know him. We all know you, too!"

Taking the girl's arm, she took her coat and led her to a chair near the stove. Her hair, knotted tightly in a bun, now bounced around like a ball on a string as she bubbled with enthusiasm

"He talks of nothing but you, lass," she cooed. "How old are you, dear?"

"Sixteen and a half," she answered, warming to the woman's friendly nature.

"Well, my name is Meg MacDonald. I'm the Joyce's housekeeper, clerk and just about everything else!" she exclaimed, smiling at the girl. "Their ship is named the *Belfast*. It's a one hundred and ten foot whaler with a steam engine and an eleven-man-crew … although they often run it with less." Pausing to pour them each a cup of tea and put out a plate of cookies, she continued. "Many years ago, they sailed her all the way from Newfoundland on the eastern seaboard. Good seamen are those Joyces, your Danny, too." The pride in Meg's voice made Nancy smile.

Ever so slowly, the woman coaxed more information out of the girl and was impressed with her resolve and good nature.

"But where have they gone?" Nancy asked.

"Oh, they've gone up the coast to the Queen Charlottes and Rose Harbour. They have an arrangement with the whaling station there." Checking the teapot on top of the stove, without asking Meg poured another cup of tea for each of them. "The staff at Rose Harbour renders down their catch. They keep one-quarter of the oil and the boys bring home the rest and sell it. That's why I'm in the office … I take their orders and keep their books straight."

Nancy drank the last of her tea and stood up. "I thought whaling ended in October?"

"Yer right, lass, it does around here, but the boys often run right through the winter 'cause they hunt seal up north, too."

The girl pulled on her coat and adjusted her scarf about her neck. "Thank you for the tea and letting me visit with you, Miss MacDonald," she said, reaching for the door.

Meg smiled and held out her arms. "Come give me a hug, child, and please call me Meg! You've been real good company tonight. Do come again." Holding the door against the wind, she called after her, "Ach, hurry home, lassie. It's a miserable one out there tonight."

Nancy picked her way cautiously up the slippery boardwalk, dimly lit by two small lights on a pole. Once onto Wharf Street, she could see a bit better but she kept to the side of buildings as the strong wind buffeted her slim body.

Connie, one of the kitchen's evening staff, grimaced as the cold air whistled through the open door as Nancy hurried inside. "Brrr, feels like a touch of frost tonight, Nancy."

Nancy nodded, her teeth chattering and so chilled she offered no reply, merely waving, and hurried to her warm room. When she climbed into bed her thoughts returned to her newfound friend. She had a good feeling about Meg MacDonald—at last she would have a place to go when loneliness overtook her on dark winter evenings.

During the next few days she tried again to find news of English Jack by catching snatches of the patron's conversations. Then, on the third day a stranger came into the dining room. He found a seat in the corner and ordered a huge meal, drinking cup after cup of steaming hot tea. He was a kindly-looking old soul, tall and slim, but slightly hunched. He had the look of an outdoorsman, having at least a week's growth of grey beard and an odour suggesting he was sorely in need of a bath. She thought it strange when she found his chatter friendly and educated.

He finished his meal, ordered a beer, and after the table was cleared, he produced a newspaper and spread it out in front of him. Nancy noticed the banner which read NEW YORK TIMES. Her curiosity aroused, she read the headline over his shoulder. TITANIC SUNK BY ICEBERG, 1000 LIVES LOST. Stunned at first, then thinking she had heard about this sometime before, her eyes moved to the date of the issue, April 16th, 1912.

"Why that newspaper is eight-months-old!" she gasped.

"New to me, young lady!" the old man growled. "Got it from an American some while back." When he had read the newspaper thoroughly he folded it carefully, stood up, and slipped it into his coat pocket. As he slowly moved toward the exit, his eyes darted about the room. They came to rest on a middle-aged, well-dressed man sitting at a nearby table.

"I need a bath," he muttered, loudly enough for the man to hear.

"You sure do!" Bill Wallace replied, nose twitching as his senses became aware of the foul odour.

Nancy recognized Bill Wallace as a frequent customer. She had been told he was a sharp one making his money from any means he

42

could—totally without scruples or morals. He was not at all popular with the hotel staff.

Bill rose to his feet and began to move in the direction of the door which took him past the old man. As they passed, he spoke quietly out of the side of his mouth, "Bath, two dollars fifty—bath and a woman, ten!"

"Pimp!" the scruffy old man threw back loudly enough for all to hear.

Wallace stopped in mid-stride. Slowly and deliberately, he turned to face his accuser as the other patrons watched in silent anticipation. "You say what?" he thundered, his eyes shooting daggers.

"Hard of hearing are you, sonny?" the answer cracked across the quiet room.

Tension rose as Wallace took a step toward the old man. Crash! went Nancy's tray of dirty dishes as she dropped them onto a table and quickly moved in front of the advancing man.

"Oh no, you don't!" she cried, wagging her fist under Bill Wallace's nose.

An evil grin spread over his face. He raised his hand to strike her but it stopped in mid-air as a new voice interceded.

"Don't you even think about it, Wallace, or you'll be dealing with me!"

Half turning, Bill Wallace's haughty gaze came to rest on Waldo Skillings, the Victoria Baggage Company owner. Immediately, his mood changed and totally subdued, he lowered his hand and backed toward the door. Nancy sighed with relief.

"Come here, Nancy," said Mr. Skillings in a gentler voice. "I'd like you to meet Charlotte Townend. Charlotte is the wife of one of our local politicians and a busy organizer for our party.

"Would you really have defended that old man?" Charlotte asked.

"Hush, Charlotte," Waldo interrupted. "You're a brave girl, Nancy, your Danny was right."

"You know my Dan, Mr. Skillings?"

"Yes, I do. I buy my oil from the Joyces." He patted her hand and looked up at her. "When I saw him recently, he talked of nothing else but you. Now off you go. We don't want you getting into trouble on our account."

Nancy smiled and began to walk away, but Charlotte rose and gently caught her arm. "Wait Nancy, we need more women with your courage. I hope we can be friends ...."

A call from a customer drew Nancy's attention and she escaped without having to answer. When she returned with a tray of food a few minutes later, she noticed the old man had sat down again and was watching her closely. She delivered her order and went over to him. "Can I get you something more, sir?"

"Aye lass, that you can," he chuckled. "A bath, a barber, a tailor, and a talk with you ... and in that order!"

"Just a minute while I serve these customers, then I'll write the information down for you," she offered. Ten minutes later she reappeared with his bill and a note. She put them on the table, a frown creasing her brow as she asked, "Do you have any money?"

The old man nodded almost imperceptibly as he read the note. When he finished, he raised his head and looked up at her. His soft, twinkling eyes were now full of mischief.

"Your name is Nancy, isn't it?" he asked, but not waiting for her answer, he continued, "will you do me a favour?"

She nodded, looking at him curiously.

"Then show me what you have in your hand," he said, pointing to the hand she was holding behind her back.

A pink tinge began to creep up her neck as she slowly brought out her hand, opening it to reveal three silver dollars. From under the table the old man also raised his hand turning it over to reveal four silver dollars.

"You were going to pay my bill weren't you, little lady? Well, now this is for you!" Smiling broadly, he dropped the four coins into Nancy's still-outstretched hand, jingling as they landed amongst the other three coins. Then he stood up and walked rather quickly to the cashier's desk. Nancy watched, unable to move, as he paid his bill and left the dining room without looking back.

The next evening, as Nancy lay reading a book on her bed, a knock came at the door. Opening it revealed Jessica, one of the restaurant's evening staff.

"There are two men in the dining room asking for you, shall I tell them you'll come?"

"Who are they?" Nancy asked, slipping her shoes back on and smoothing the wrinkles from her skirts.

"One of them is the police chief," replied the girl, a note of fear in her voice. "Don't know the other one."

"Right, tell them I'll be there in a moment."

Jessica nodded. Nancy closed the door and found her warm shawl. Throwing it over her shoulders, she headed for the dining room. Passing through the kitchen, she noticed the bar manager watching her as he ate supper. His eyebrows creased into a deep scowl.

"What you been up to, lass?" he growled.

"Nothing, sir," Nancy purred, squeezing past him to the door.

Entering the dining room, she looked around. Over in the far corner sat the stern-looking police chief with a well-dressed stranger.

"Go on, get over there, girl!" the bar manager snapped from behind her, giving her a shove.

John Langley saw what was happening and leapt up from his seat, striding across the room.

"Keep your damned hands to yourself!" the police chief snapped, towering over Nancy as he faced the bar manager. "Nobody touches this girl or they answer to me!" He reached for Nancy's elbow and led her over to his table. "Sit down, Nancy," he said gently. "Somebody here wants to talk with you.

As staff watched curiously, she sat down. She had the strangest feeling that she knew the other man, but didn't know how. Across the table the stranger smiled, their eyes locking for a moment.

"Told you I was coming back to talk to you," he said, with a slight American accent, keeping his eyes down.

Nancy frowned, trying to recall who had said that to her.

The stranger sat back in his chair until it was rocking on its back legs. He looked up at her with a mischievous glint in his eyes. He

45

reached into his coat pocket watching her closely. He withdrew his hand from the pocket and slowly set his chair back down. His actions were methodical and by now had the girl's curious attention. He leaned forward, laying his hand palm down on the table in front of her. He turned it over and slowly opened it to reveal two silver dollars. Then, he winked at her.

Her hand flew to her mouth. "You're the smelly old man!"

"And now he's going to tell you who he really is," Chief Langley interrupted gravely.

"Nancy, my name is Jebediah Judd. I'm a Pinkerton man from across the line."

"What's a Pinkerton man?" she asked.

Jebediah began to answer but Langley stopped him by holding up his hand. "Don't get him started, lass," the chief chuckled. "He's too long-winded for me. All it means is he's a detective, working for the American government."

"Under cover," growled Jebediah.

"But what do you want with me?" Nancy asked, nervously.

The eyes of the two lawmen locked across the table.

"First of all, my friends call me Jeb or JJ, take your pick!" he announced, smiling at the girl.

"Get on with it, man," the chief's agitated voice snapped.

Jebediah's eyebrows shot up in annoyance and his fingers began drumming on the table, then just as quickly the smile reappeared.

"What you did yesterday, Nancy," he said quietly, "showed me you have unusual courage, grit, and compassion. You're a woman who uses her brain." He paused to take a sip of his drink. "To put it in a nutshell, we want you to work with us."

"Shortest speech I've ever heard you make," the chief muttered. "Can you read and write, lass?"

"Of course she can," Jebediah answered, impatiently. "Wrote me a note didn't she?"

A smile touched Nancy's lips as she watched the police chief absent-mindedly scratch his mustache.

"Right, I'll leave you to set it up with her, Jeb," he said, pushing his chair away from the table. "She knows we're both behind her now and you can tell me about it tomorrow."

"Wait a minute!" Jeb snapped. "She ain't agreed to nothin yet."

"Then it's up to you to convince her," Langley grunted. "It was your idea!"

Rising from his chair, the impeccably dressed lawman picked up his hat, tucked his baton under his arm, and marched toward the door, striking an imposing figure as he glowered at the drinking patrons.

"He's a good man," Jeb commented, "but bad tempered as hell."

During the next hour, the lawman convinced Nancy that what they had in mind would not be dangerous. Being somewhat adventurous in nature, she agreed to give it a try.

"All you need to do is listen for bits of information while you are serving customers." He gave her three things to listen for and then they worked out a method of communication.

"How will you know who my men are?" Jeb whispered, watching her face intently.

She thought for a moment. "Because you will tell them about my code. If they work for you, they'll place a silver dollar on the floor by the leg of their chair. I'll hand him the menu, upside down, if I need to talk to him."

Jeb's fingers tapped the table; he had not misjudged this girl.

"I'll pick up the coin and put it on the table," Nancy continued, still speaking softly, noticing the colour in Jeb's face rise. "If I need to see him immediately at the back door, it will be heads up, but if it can wait until after work it will be heads down." She paused once more, smiling craftily. "If they understand, they have to say, it's not mine, you keep it. Of course, if I have no information, I will merely leave the money on the floor."

"Where you could pick it up later ... you little devil," he muttered, his eyes twinkling at her ingenuity. "You're making us pay a dollar for information."

Chapter 5

Throughout early December, Jebediah was a regular patron at the Occidental. He usually came in the late afternoon and was hardly ever alone. Then he went missing, turning up on the 20th looking tired and dishevelled. As he sat in his favourite corner picking at his food, Nancy went to talk to him.

"Been out of town?" she asked, casually.

"Vancouver," he muttered. "Fella I've been chasing for six months. Thought they had him locked up over there," he sighed, stabbing at his steak.

Nancy returned a few minutes later with a steaming pot of fresh tea. "Like some more, Jeb?"

He looked up sharply as a thought struck him, making his eyes dance with fire. "Listen lass," he whispered, "this fellow I'm looking for killed a man in Seattle a year ago." He rubbed his stubbly chin. "When he's short of money he picks pockets and he must be getting short by now. It's close to Christmas so he might be right here in town, no doubt somewhere there is a crowd. He wears a brown top hat."

"Tall? short? fat? thin? Does he always wear his top hat?"

Jeb studied the girl's face. *This girl certainly knows the right questions*, he thought. "Medium everything, just looks ordinary like everybody else." He closed his eyes in deep thought. "But does he always wear his top hat? Now there's a good question. I'm damned if I know!"

On the Saturday before Christmas, Nancy walked down Wharf Street to the Joyce Bros. office. She and Meg MacDonald had now become firm friends over the course of many visits and Meg had invited her for Christmas dinner. Determined that the girl was going to experience a proper Christmas and a special dinner with all the trimmings, Meg decided to celebrate a few days early to fit into Nancy's working schedule.

As she stepped into the room, the mixed aromas of pork and chicken assailed her senses immediately. Meg had prepared a wonderful spiced stuffing for the chicken and fresh applesauce from fruit carefully stored out in the shed. A special treat for Meg was a glass of good scotch whisky and she offered one to Nancy, although she knew it would be declined. The table was set and they were almost ready to sit down when a timid knock came at the door. Meg had her hands full, so Nancy went to open it.

Holding the door against the fierce pull of the wind, she could see the outline of two figures framed against the low light. Their faces were almost covered by blankets wrapped around their bodies and held tightly up to their noses.

"Tell them to come in," Meg called. "Quickly, close the door!"

The Indians stepped inside and removed their blankets, staring at Nancy. Meg looked over her shoulder, recognizing them. "Come over here by the stove and get warm, you must be frozen."

They did as they were told, eyes never wavering from Nancy.

"What's the matter?" Meg asked. "Have you two seen a ghost?"

Nancy's hand suddenly went to her mouth. "Oh my goodness! You're Billy! Rose!" she spluttered, as memories flooded her head. Rushing forward, her eyes welling with tears, she opened her arms and hugged the two natives.

Meg watched in fascination.

"Meg, these are the two children who visited me at the orphanage when I was young. I haven't seen them in years, you've grown so much! What are you doing here?" she asked, standing back and wiping her eyes.

"Why, lass, they've come to sell their whale oil," Meg interceded. "How many barrels have you ready, Billy?"

Billy and his sister looked very much alike, both being of medium height and stocky build, although the boy was slightly taller. "Ten, missus, they come tomorrow," he said, a grin stretching across his face.

Meg set two mugs of tea on the table. That's for you and Rose. Would you like a piece of apple pie?"

They nodded vigorously, then Billy reached out and touched Nancy's arm. "You happy now?"

Nancy smiled. "Yes, I'm very happy now," she answered, searching the faces of these two young people who had shown her such kindness so long ago.

They told Nancy that their family had recently moved to the new Songhees Reserve in Esquimalt, then picking up their blankets they suddenly moved to the door saying it was time to go. "Can we get paid today, missus?" Billy asked.

"Tomorrow, lad, when you bring the oil in," said Meg. "Just like always."

Nancy suddenly thought of something. "I would like to give you a Christmas gift, as a thank you. I owe you both so much."

Billy and his sister looked puzzled, not fully understanding the white man's traditions. They talked briefly in their native tongue then Billy turned to Nancy. "I like tall, brown hat ... like man in village?"

The smile slipped from Nancy's face.

"There's a man in your village with a brown top hat?" she asked. "A white man?"

"Billy like his hat," he said, nodding excitedly.

"Tell you what," Nancy said calmly, "you bring me that man all tied up like a chicken tomorrow night at 8:30, and I'll give you his hat!"

Meg kept quiet as the grin on the boy's face got bigger, but she couldn't help but wonder what Nancy was doing.

"Big trouble with law, eh?" Billy mused, his hand on the latch. "We'll do it. We'll bring him with oil tomorrow night." Then pulling the door open, they quickly went out into the wind and shut the door.

Nancy turned to see Meg staring at her in disbelief, hands clasped together nervously. "Good gracious, child, what have you done?" she gasped. "They'll bring that poor man in just like you asked them to.

50

She quickly moved to the table and sat down as if all her energy had suddenly dissipated.

Nancy ignored her and filled their plates. Putting an arm affectionately around the older woman's shoulders she said, "Come on, stop worrying and let's enjoy our meal. I'll tell you all about it."

Meg brightened as Nancy explained her actions. She told Meg of her talk with Jebediah Judd and Police Chief Langley and her encounter with Bill Wallace, plus Jeb's request to watch out for a man in a brown top hat.

Feeling much better, Meg clinked her glass of whisky with Nancy's cup of tea. They giggled as Meg offered a toast to absent friends ... one of the oldest of Scottish traditions, she explained.

Sundays were usually quiet days in the dining room but this was the last Sunday before Christmas and many more churchgoers than usual seemed to be eating out. It was hectic from the moment Nancy's shift began.

A light dusting of snow had fallen during the night, making sidewalks very treacherous, although the swampers tried their best to keep the front of the hotel clear. A wickedly cold wind whistled up Johnson Street as if it were coming right across the railway bridge. Regular patrons and travellers alike eagerly sought shelter inside the doors.

In the middle of the afternoon, Jebediah came in, found a table in a corner, and called for service. Nancy attended to him immediately, putting a cup of steaming coffee in front of him and a menu in his hand ... upside down. Jeb's reaction was instant, his eye flashing onto the girl's face and sitting up stiffly in his chair.

"Bring me some liver and onions, and two fingers of rum," he muttered, handing her back the menu.

Smiling to herself she made her way into the kitchen wondering if Jeb would remember the code. With her tray loaded, she called at the bar hatch and collected the two fingers of rum. Returning to his table, she noticed the silver dollar on the floor by his chair leg. Depositing the food in front of him, she bent and scooped up the silver dollar, placing it heads up on the table. Jeb's eyes fastened on it for a moment, then his head jerked up and with a frown, he whispered, "It's not mine, love."

The clock in the bar was just striking three as Jebediah left the hotel without waiting for his bill. When Nancy went to clear the table, neatly stacked beside his empty plate were three silver dollars. She paid the cashier who winked as he handed her back fifty cents.

"You had a break yet, lass?" he asked, peering over his thick spectacles as he glanced at the clock. "Go have ten minutes, you've never stopped and there's two more girls on at three."

Thanking him profusely, Nancy poured herself a cup of tea. She quickly went to her room and slipped a shawl around her shoulders. At the back door, she stepped out into the cold just as Jeb arrived, his shoulders hunched against the cold wind.

"Damn it, that were quick," he muttered. After hearing her story about the man with the top hat, he agreed to meet her at 8:15.

"You will recognize him won't you, Jeb?"

"I'll know if it's him," he chuckled, pulling his collar up and walking away.

When Nancy finished her shift she sought out the cook. "Make me a sandwich will you please, Alice. I've got to go out."

"Go out!" Alice called, across the kitchen. "It's late and it's snowing out there. You should be in bed, lass, you've worked like a dog all day." Then turning, she grinned at the girl. "Want a turkey leg? Sure, I'll put something together for you, yer only young once!"

Nancy sighed and tiredly walked the few steps to her room. Changing quickly, she buttoned her heavy coat up to the neck, added her scarf and hat and went out to the kitchen. She found her package of food and left by the back door, pulling it shut behind her. She found Jeb waiting around the corner leaning against the building smoking a cigar.

"Which way?" he asked.

Nancy pointed up Wharf Street and Jeb took her arm and they hurried through the snow, heads bent forward against the biting wind. Meg must have been waiting, for the door flew open even before they knocked. They stamped their feet to remove the snow and hurried inside. Jeb swept his hat off and reached for Nancy's coat.

"Who have we here?" Meg asked, indicating the hat stand to Jeb.

"This as Jebediah Judd, Meg. He's an American policeman."

Jeb made a face, obviously not agreeing with her description. "I'm not really an official policeman, lass," he chuckled. "I'm a detective, a Pinkerton man."

Meg indicated chairs near the fire and they were soon warm again. Nancy ate the food Alice had prepared and Meg poured tea into three cups, adding a little whisky into each. "This will warm your bones!" she said quietly.

Jeb commented on Meg's accent and soon she was happily reminiscing about Scotland. She must have heard footsteps because a minute later she jumped to her feet, calling over her shoulder as she made for the door. "They're here!"

An icy blast of air swept into the room as four snow-covered natives stepped inside, two of them struggling with a large human-size bundle. They dumped it unceremoniously onto the bare wooden floor just inside the door.

Billy came to stand in front of Nancy, indicating the older man beside him. "My father," he said.

The old man turned to his son and began talking in their native language, waving his arms to the accompaniment of nods and grunts from his companions. Billy turned back to Nancy and extracted the brown top hat from inside his coat.

"That belongs to you now, Billy. Thank you for your help," she said, trying to hide her smile as she envisioned the hat on her friend.

"My father," he said, fondling the hat, "says that you are worthy friend and he will accept you into our lodge." Pausing, he shifted a penetrating stare on Meg. "You will pay for oil now, missus?" It was more a statement than a question, as he held out his hand.

Meg produced an inkpad and a piece of paper, along with a small bag of coins, and placed them all on the table. Billy's father pressed his thumb on the inkpad, leaving a perfect imprint. Then without a sound, he scooped up the bag of coins and made for the door.

53

"Wait!" Nancy called. "What do you mean ... I'm accepted into your father's lodge?"

The older natives took no notice, as they opened the door and left, but Billy turned back. "It means, you are always welcome at our lodge, and my father will protect you at all times. You are now like family ... big honour for white face!"

Nancy's expression gave way to shock, but the door had closed behind Billy before she could say anything. Jeb wasted no time pulling the wrappings from the groaning man's head revealing his prisoner both blindfolded and gagged. Meg clucked softly.

"It's him," said Jeb. "No doubt about it, it's him."

More footsteps sounded outside.

"Now what?" said Meg.

A knock sounded and without waiting two Victoria policemen walked in, closing the door quickly behind them.

"Evening folks, you Mr. Judd?" asked the Sergeant.

"Yep, that's me," Jeb said, with a frown. "Forgive me, boys, but let's see yer warrant cards." Each man produced identification and watched as Jeb inspected them carefully before handing them back. "Just being cautious," he muttered.

"Good way to be, sir," Sergeant Walker growled. He bodily picked up the fugitive, swinging him onto the younger man's shoulder. "Good night, folks."

As the heavy footsteps faded away, Meg breathed a sigh of relief and sat down with a thump on her chair. "Pour me a cup of tea, love," she whispered. "I'm fair worn out with excitement ... and put a dram in it!"

Nancy smiled and quickly complied with her wishes. Then she noticed Jebediah was getting fidgety.

"You can go, Jeb. I'll stay awhile with Meg."

"I think I had better see you home, Nancy. Wouldn't want to lose you in a snowdrift, would we!"

Meg brightened. "You're right, Mr. Judd. You go on, lassie. I'll be just fine. It's far too late and with this terrible weather, I'd feel much better if Mr. Judd saw you home."

A look of relief swept over his face. Wasting no time, he quickly found their coats. Saying their goodnights, they were soon heading back toward the Occidental. At the back door, he reached into his pocket and drew out an envelope.

"Here's a little something for you, just to show my appreciation," he said, putting the envelope into her hand and turning to leave. "I'm leaving tomorrow, but the next time I'm back this way I'll drop in to see you." And then he disappeared behind the cloak of falling snow.

Back in her room, she removed her wet clothes and picked up the envelope. Her finger deftly broke the seal and she pulled out the contents, gasping in surprise when she found she was holding five, ten dollar bills. There was also a handwritten note which she read quickly. DEAR NANCY, WITH YOUR BRAINS AND CONNECTIONS YOU SHOULD BE A DETECTIVE, PERHAPS EVEN MY CANADIAN PARTNER! JEBEDIAH

A thoughtful smile crept across her face as she fondled the money. *A detective ... hmm, I wonder. I think Jeb would approve of my search for English Jack.* And with that comforting thought she safely put her money away in her shoe and went to bed.

Christmas added a hectic frenzy to the city with late shoppers and revelers battling their way through the streets, made worse by the blowing snow and bitterly cold wind. One situation brought on by the bad weather was the ineptitude of the new-fangled automobiles that were often seen being pulled through the snow by horses. This became quite a humorous situation, particularly appreciated by the old folks who were still not convinced they were the transport of the future.

After Boxing Day, it rained for three days washing away all trace of the snow, bringing the city almost back to normal. Nancy decided to go see Meg on the morning of New Year's Eve not having to report for work until afternoon. She hadn't seen Meg for over a week and was eager to tell her about Jeb's present. Meg was thrilled to see her having been shut in without company for days. She fussed around the little kitchen getting her a cup of tea.

"Have you had breakfast, lassie? Can I make you some eggs and toast?"

"No, no! I was up early and cook made me breakfast. Sit down and relax, Meg. I have something exciting to tell you."

Nancy must have used the right word for the older woman immediately sat down across the table and leaned forward expectantly. "Something to tell me? What's happened, love?"

Nancy told her how Jebediah had given her an envelope that night after walking her home, and then finding the money with his note.

"Fifty dollars!" she gasped. "That's a lot of money, love. Private detectives must be paid very well for him to give you that kind of money."

"I wonder how you become a detective?" Nancy mused.

"I don't know, but a detective finds things out. If you think you might like to be one, there must be something we could practice on."

"Yes, *we* could," Nancy laughed, "and there is something we could practice on. English Jack disappeared suddenly last month and I've already been trying to find him. I could use your help."

"Don't think I know him, love. Could he be dead?" she said with a worried look.

"No, not here at any rate, I'd have heard."

"Why do we want to find him?"

"Practice, and I'd like to know what happened to him." Nancy watched the smile creep back onto Meg's face, but decided not to tell her that she had Jack's gold.

Laughter rang through the wooden building as the two women exchanged ideas planning their strategy. Meg, being the organizer, produced a piece of paper and methodically began taking notes ...

1. GOLD PROSPECTOR AND A DRUNK

2. NAME INDICATES HE MIGHT BE FROM ENGLAND.

"Not much to go on," Meg muttered, frowning so hard it deepened the wrinkles on her forehead.

"And ... my dear," Nancy wagged her finger, "we haven't to let anybody know what we're doing. It must be a secret."

Warming to the adventure, the older lady glowed with anticipation. This was the most interesting thing she had ever done. Nancy explained how she could be contacted at the Occidental. She also made arrangements to come see Meg every evening after work once the dining room was back on it's normal routine after January 2nd.

"Don't you go filling up on that awful hotel food either! I'd love the company and it's always easier to cook for two," she announced, happily. "We can discuss the progress on our detective work, too!"

Nancy hugged the older woman gratefully and reached for her coat. Meg helped her on with it and gave her a hug.

"Off you go, love, and don't forget I want you to remember what everyone wears to the party tonight!"

Two days into 1913, George Dunn, the owner of the hotel and his wife, came in for a late lunch. As Nancy cleared away the last of their dirty dishes, Mrs. Dunn stopped her.

"Come here and sit down for a moment. We've something to talk to you about," she whispered, secretively.

"Can't ma'am. I've got too much to do!" Nancy replied boldly, indicating her tray full of dirty crockery.

Mrs. Dunn, not used to her orders being disobeyed, impatiently tapped the table with the tips of her well-manicured fingers. Her temper was rising to a dangerous level.

"Stop woman!" her husband ordered quietly, used to his wife's rough manner. "It shows the girl has a sense of responsibility."

The tapping fingers stopped immediately, their eyes meeting across the table, her frown changing to a sweet smile. "Yes dear, I think you're right. She'll do the job just fine."

Watching Nancy work for the next fifteen minutes, the owners sat patiently admiring her speed and efficiency. At last she made her way over to their table.

"You wish to talk to me, ma'am?"

"Sit down, deary," Mrs. Dunn said, trying to be gentle, but obviously not her usual nature.

57

"Beg pardon, ma'am, but I need to watch the room. Stella is on her break," Nancy explained, in a respectful tone, her eyes flashing around the busy dining room.

Mr. Dunn smiled at her candid answer, watching his wife's eyes twitching as she fought to keep her temper under control. "We want to offer you the job of running the dining room, Nancy. We believe you are ready for the added responsibility." His wife nodded in agreement.

"Waitress!" a customer called from a table on the other side of the room.

Nancy jumped into action, but Mrs. Dunn's hand shot out to grab a tight hold on her wrist. "Leave it!" she snapped, her eyes flashing again.

"Please let me go, ma'am," the girl begged. "They're your customers and mine. They come here for service, that's my job."

"Unhand her woman!" George hissed at his wife pushing his chair away from the table and preparing to leave. "You think about it, lass," he said calmly, as Mrs. Dunn dropped Nancy's arm allowing her to escape.

That evening, Nancy told Meg about their offer.

"Be a step up, love, although …," she said with concern on her face. "It would be a lot of responsibility for someone so young."

"There are other considerations we have to look at, too, Meg. My tips would be less and it would be harder to get information if I wasn't on the floor." She paused, biting her lip and thinking hard. "No, I think I'm better off as a waitress right now."

Meg's eyebrows shot up, impressed by the girl's common-sense logic. She wasn't going to let the lure of higher pay fog her better judgment.

In mid-February, four haggard, rough-looking men checked into the Occidental—paying in advance for separate rooms, the staff said, from a pouch of gold dust. They arrived in the dining room later that afternoon looking much more respectable.

Nancy served them, catching bits of their chatter and shuddering at some of their stories about the cold, hard life their friends were enduring by staying the winter in Alaska.

Mr. Dunn stopped her as she went by. "Know who they are, lass?"

"No sir," she quipped innocently, smiling to herself as she went into the kitchen knowing full well he intended to find out.

Mr. Dunn invited himself to their table and sat with them for some time. He was always interested in strangers with gold. It was whispered in the kitchen that he was one of the prominent businessmen who owned the bordello on lower Herald Street above the livery stables and carriage shop. There wasn't much that he missed in this town. Leaving their table, his expression told Nancy he'd learned nothing.

"That the owner?" one of the men asked Nancy, scowling.

"Yes, sir," she replied. "He's a bit nosy but a really nice man."

The men laughed at her candidness and ordered more liquor. As she hurried to the bar, one of the men called loudly after her. "Bring the bottle, girl!"

With a full bottle balanced on her tray, she quickly returned and found the men talking in very low voices. They ceased talking when she came near and one of them smiled through his whiskers watching her closely as she set the bottle down.

"Just give me a call if you need anything," she said, turning away.

"Come back when you've time, lass," one of the men growled. "Bring four big cigars and a plug of chewing tobacco."

The girl nodded and moved away. A few minutes later, she noticed Tom Ben sitting alone at a table in the far corner. He was one of the outside salesmen with E.A. Morris, the tobacconists in Government Street. She went to his table inquiring if he needed anything.

"Yes ... sales would be nice, Nancy love," he said, grinning.

Tom Ben had worked at E.A. Morris' for years and knew everyone. His happy, obliging nature made him welcome wherever he went. His five-foot, four-inch height, and an enormous girth of similar proportions helped to make him easily recognizable. Cleaning

59

his glasses, he returned them to his face and peered at the girl through extra thick lens.

"Those men over by the wall ... ," Nancy whispered, watching his eyes stray in that direction, "are smoking cigars and if you could supply them cheaper by the box, they'd probably buy some."

Tom screwed up his eyes as if that made thinking easier, and he began to push his chair back from the table.

"Not yet!" Nancy snapped, softly. "Give me an answer first."

"Yes, yes, of course I can," he laughed, a prospective sale always exciting him. "Especially if they're friends of yours!"

"Then sit still, let me ask them," she said, moving away.

Passing the bar, the girl picked up a thick plug of chewing tobacco, grimacing at the sight of the foul-smelling stuff. The men looked up as she came toward then and one man reached for the plug of tobacco before it dropped on the table.

"Cigars lass ... you've forgot 'em!" one of the others grouched.

"No, I haven't," she replied, "but if you're going to smoke cigars, you should be buying them by the box. They're much cheaper that way."

The four men laughed.

"I told you she was smart," said the big man in the stylish black suit. He spoke with an unusual slow drawl that Nancy hadn't heard before.

"You want them, yes or no? He's sat right over there."

"Yes, we want them," said the man closest to her. "Call him over. Then tell us who's a good gunsmith. We've firearms that need repairing."

Nancy waved Tom over, then she told them of the gunsmith in Yates Street.

"Gentlemen, this is Tom Ben from the tobacconist shop," said Nancy as he arrived with his samples. "This man knows almost everything about Victoria and he should be able to help you with anything you want to know." She paused as the rotund tobacco salesman beamed at her recommendation, pulled up a chair and sat

60

down. "I just need your room number or a name for the bill, to finish our business!"

The big man in the suit smiled. "Put it down to Texas Jack, in Room 26," he said brashly, then noticing his friends had gone quiet, he glanced around the room and realized others were listening. "And we all sleep with a gun in one hand!" he added in a slightly louder tone, winking at Nancy. Rising, he bathed the room with an ominous icy stare.

Nancy quaked a little at the man's words, quickly writing his name and room number on her pad.

"Here, lass," said Texas Jack, stopping her retreat as he dropped something that rolled onto the table. "That's for you ... you're honest and tried to save us money. I like that."

The odd-shaped object, about the size of a small pebble, glistened as it lay on the table catching the light. Reaching over to pick it up she rolled it in her fingers, examining it carefully.

"It's gold!" Tom gasped.

Nancy was taken aback but managed to thank Texas Jack, her eyes sparkling as her thoughts turned mischievous. "You sure your name isn't English Jack?"

The others roared with laughter, banging their fists on the table, making the now nervous salesman jump.

"English Jack, you say girl?" the big man chuckled. "Why he's drunk and in jail. We saw the police cart him off two weeks ago, up in the interior."

Surprised at this information, Nancy breathed a sigh of relief. At least the old man was alive ... drunk as usual, but not short of money it appeared.

The Texan turned serious. "Sorry lass ... kin of yours?"

"No, no," Nancy smiled. "A customer that's all."

Just before she finished her shift, the men departed for their rooms, leaving Tom still sitting at the table. He had a strange smile on his face, but she knew he had been very nervous.

"You all right, Mr. Ben?" she asked.

"Th - th - they bought eight boxes!" he stammered.

"And you don't like that!" she gasped.

"B - but I do, I do. I've never had such a day before!"

Later that evening, she told Meg about her encounter of the afternoon and how they'd solve the mystery of English Jack's whereabouts. She was showing her the gold nugget when a knock sounded on the door. Answering it, Meg found a young ship's officer standing there and asked him to come in. He said he was from a British survey vessel lying in the harbour. He acted most proper, standing inside the door with his hat tucked under his arm.

"I have a message from the *Belfast*, ma'am," he declared, in an accent that made both the women smile, "from Mr. Joyce. They'll be home on April Fool's Day." Grinning, the officer reached into his pocket producing a small package wrapped in brown paper and tied with string. "This, ma'am, is for you," he said, offering the package to Nancy. "He said I would know you by the colour of your hair, beautiful auburn … his words not mine, ma'am." The officer blushed a little, looking at the floor as he continued. "Though I tend to agree."

Holding the package carefully, Nancy's hands trembled a little, feeling a thrill run through her body. She'd never received a real present before.

Meg slipped her arm around the girl's waist. "You mean Ned Joyce said that?"

"No, ma'am," the officer chuckled, "twas Mr. Brown, her brother."

"I thought for a minute Ned had lost his senses!" Meg laughed.

Setting his cap firmly in place, he saluted them smartly. "Goodnight ladies, it's been a pleasure."

"They're coming home, lass!" Meg declared excitedly, as the door closed. "Let's see what Danny's sent you."

Meg cleared a space on the table. Picking at the string until it finally came loose, Nancy carefully unfolded the brown paper wrapping and found a lovely little wooden box inside. Easing the lid off with great anticipation, revealed two small objects with tiny drawings on them. Nancy picked one up and held it to the light.

"They're beautiful and such tiny pictures. What are they made of, Meg?"

"Oh yes, they are beautiful," said Meg, reverently. "It's known as scrimshaw. Sailors need to have something to do on their long lonely voyages and many of them use bits of whalebone and teeth to make presents for loved ones or to sell to traders. These are sperm whale teeth." She sighed as she carefully studied the beautifully crafted pieces of artwork, turning them over in her hand. "I don't think Dan did them himself, but someone is very talented."

"Can I leave them here?" Nancy asked, delicately laying her treasures back in their box.

"Of course you can, lassie. You do whatever you like, yer family now!" said Meg with a twinkle in her eyes. Then changing the subject abruptly, she continued, "It'll soon be spring and then we can walk out to the cottage and tend the garden."

"The cottage?" Nancy asked, vaguely remembering Dan had mentioned the MacDonald cottage once before.

"Yes, our cottage in Saanich behind Elk Lake," she replied, her mood turning pensive. "I haven't been out there for over a year."

"Hold it, young lady," Nancy chuckled, trying to keep the conversation light. "We can't walk all that way, work in the garden then walk back again. I know I would be dead beat just walking out there let alone coming home!"

They laughed, knowing it was true.

"Tell you what," Meg said as Nancy prepared to leave, "we'll rent a buggy and drive out. I'm used to horses, although its been a while."

"Now you're talking," said Nancy, her face lighting up as she put on her shawl. "That's a great idea, we'll practice by driving through Beacon Hill Park one Sunday when it gets a bit warmer."

She hugged Meg and shut the door behind her. Walking quickly along Wharf Street, she felt the sting of the freezing sea air on her face and fervently wished spring would hurry.

Chapter 6

The next day, the sun came out bathing the city with warmth and it wasn't long before crocuses and snowdrops were springing up all over the area. People came out of their homes seeking the sunshine and Victoria slowly began coming back to life.

In the first few weeks of March the weather turned ugly again for a few days with gale-force winds and freezing rain. Hotels were suddenly full of travellers, trapped when their ships ran for Victoria Harbour seeking shelter. For two days, Nancy worked long hours falling dead beat into bed each evening. Then just as quickly as it began, the storm went away, leaving behind a gentle breeze and brighter skies. The promise of spring once again warmed their hearts and lifted their spirits.

It had been almost a week since she had last seen Meg. So, on Saturday evening she hurriedly changed her clothes intending to pay her friend a visit. An unexpected knock sounded at her door and Sarah, one of the waitresses, informed her that a lady was waiting for her in the dining room. Puzzled over who it could be, she let her hair down, brushed it quickly, and slipped on her coat so she wouldn't have to return.

She was most surprised to find Meg sitting at a table sipping tea, looking quite edgy and glancing furtively about the room.

Another waitress stopped beside Nancy as she came through the door, asking with a giggle, "Who is she?"

Without flinching, Nancy replied, "She's a dear friend and there'll be no bill!" She moved quickly to join Meg, slipping silently into the chair opposite.

"Came looking for me did you?" she whispered, reaching out and locking hands across the table.

"Oh lassie," the older lady sighed. "I missed you so badly, I just had to come."

"Don't worry, love. I was just getting dressed to come visit you. Finish your tea and we'll go for a walk," Nancy suggested. "I know David Spencer's will still be open."

Meg calmed down, enjoying her young companion's conversation as she identified some of the more prominent patrons. It amused her to watch the men's reactions when they noticed the good-looking girl who was usually their waitress.

Nancy, used to keeping track of the goings on in the room, noticed the arrival of Charlotte Townend with another woman, obviously looking for someone as her eyes raced over the patrons. She gave a half-hearted wave and they came over to Nancy's table.

"Have you seen Mr. Skillings, Nancy?"

"Not tonight, but I've only been here half an hour."

"Oh dear!" she replied. "Can we join you?"

"Certainly, but we're not staying long. Charlotte, I'd like you to meet my friend, Meg MacDonald from the Joyce Bros. office. Meg, this is Charlotte Townend."

The women greeted the Scottish lady and Charlotte introduced her friend, Jane Newcolm, as an artist from Vancouver.

As they talked, Charlotte's eyes were constantly watching the door. Nancy ordered tea for everyone, stressing again that there would be no bill.

"Yer on edge, lass, what's the matter?" Meg asked, addressing Charlotte. "Maybe we can help."

A sinister chuckle escaped the younger woman's lips. "Wish others thought that way love, life would be so much easier!" Charlotte paused, pursing her lips before she continued. "I was supposed to meet Waldo here at seven." She glanced over at the clock. "We are having a meeting with Dick McBride."

"The Premier, Mr. McBride ... oh dear!" Meg sympathized. "And its already twenty minutes after."

"Are you sure about the time?" Nancy asked.

Charlotte screwed her face up in deep thought, then nodded.

"I'll be back in a minute," said Nancy, quickly leaving her chair and moving toward the lobby.

"Where's she going?" Jane asked.

"Don't know, lassie," Meg chuckled. "We'll have to wait and see. She's got a plan though, you can be sure of that!"

Nancy marched boldly up to the hotel's front desk. Old Joe watched her coming and smiled as he peered over his glasses. He had taken a particular interest in this girl and she had become one of his favourites. He'd watched her grow up from a hard-working 14-year-old, always eager to get him a meal or drink, to a confident and beautiful young woman.

"Any private rooms rented out tonight, Joe?" she asked.

"I'm not supposed to disclose that information," he reminded her.

"But yer going to tell me, lad!" Nancy laughed, opening the counter door and stepping inside, her finger teasing as they reached out toward him.

"No, no, don't start tickling," he laughed, turning the register around to face her. "I can't show you," he said, lowering his voice. "You'll just have to look for yourself!"

Nancy's finger ran down the dates, stopping on the 8th of March and moving across the page, *Richard McBride, Room 326.* With a wink, she turned the book back around.

"Is Waldo Skillings up there too, Joe?" she whispered.

"Three of 'em," he replied, going red in the face as she leaned over the counter and planted a kiss on his cheek.

Nancy returned to the dining room and slipped into her seat.

"He's here!" she whispered, leaning toward Charlotte.

"Where?" asked Charlotte, in a frustrated tone.

"Calm down. I know their room number but were you expecting three men?"

Charlotte shook her head, frowning.

"They're in Room 326. Follow me! You too, Meg."

"Nancy, this seems very improper. I think I'll wait down here, if you don't mind," said Meg.

"No, you won't. These are Charlotte's friends and you'll see it is all very proper. Don't worry, Meg," Nancy assured her.

Fussing with their belongings, the four women trouped out of the dining room. Nancy kept the reluctant Meg right beside her as she led them up the stairs to the private rooms. Conveniently isolated at the end of the third floor hallway, they located Room 326 and tapped lightly on the door. Muffled footsteps sounded and the door opened, revealing Waldo holding a glass in his hand.

"Come in, Charlotte! Where the devil have you been?"

The four women moved quickly into the room, grinning foolishly as they passed the startled man.

"It's alright, gents," said Waldo. "I know these women. Ladies, I'd like you to meet our esteemed Premier, Sir Richard McBride, and John Bryant, a flyer from the United States."

Charlotte completed the introductions and Waldo offered them each a drink, Nancy being the only one to decline.

"Are you really a flyer, Mr. Bryant?" Meg asked the youngest man.

"He certainly is," McBride thundered in a voice like a foghorn. "You wait until August when he'll be here doing one of his aerial displays."

Mcg was thrilled with meeting all these famous people. What a tale she'd have to tell the boys when they came home.

"So you forgot what I said," Waldo said turning to Charlottc. "How did you find us?" he asked, his brow wrinkling into a deep frown.

"Nancy found you," she admitted.

Waldo turned to face his favourite waitress. "You're becoming quite a little detective, young lady. What else have you done?"

"She found English Jack, too!" offered Meg.

"My gawd, lass, I think I should talk to you about a little problem I have!" boomed Waldo, jovially.

"Discreet are you, girl?" the Premier asked.

"I vouch for her integrity," Waldo growled.

"Me, too," said Charlotte.

"My, my," said Richard McBride. "You have a lot of friends, my dear. I'm damned glad you're not running for Premier, but seriously, I may find a use for your talent myself sometime."

Soon after, Nancy and Meg excused themselves, saying it was time for them to get home. Charlotte shouted her gratitude and they stepped out into the carpeted corridor. Nancy linked the older woman's arm and they went down the stairs and out onto Johnson Street. Nancy expressed her regret that the evening had been stolen by the troubles of others.

"Don't you be sorry, lass, that was one of the most interesting evenings I've had in my entire life!" Squeezing the girl's arm, she said excitedly, "Fancy me meeting the Premier ... and him offering you a job."

"Well, he didn't actually offer me a job," Nancy giggled. "But we sure left a mark on their minds."

Walking Meg to the office door and watching her unlock it, she said goodnight and gave her a hug. "See you tomorrow," she called over her shoulder.

"I'll be expecting you for supper," Meg called back, feeling much happier than she had in days.

The next week there was talk of the flowers blooming early in Beacon Hill Park. Meg, in her enthusiasm for an outing, had telephoned the livery stable arranging to hire a horse and buggy the following Sunday. However, cold weather returned with a vengeance and driving rain froze overnight making even walking a hazard. The new automobiles had a terrible time on the slippery streets, causing many an irate driver and pedestrian to curse their existence.

On the morning of March 16th, the weather cleared and by 11 o'clock it was comfortably warm and people filled the streets. Daffodils were now waving their heads from boxes and gardens all over the city. Meg again hired a horse and buggy and this time was pleased to find the weather co-operating. As they walked toward the livery yard, their steps seeming slightly jauntier than usual. Nancy carried a small hamper and they were going to have a picnic somewhere on the way.

"Picked you a quiet one," the old stableman announced, leading out a fine looking grey. "Which one of you is the driver?" Looking expectantly at each other, he grinned through smoke-blackened teeth.

"I am," Meg replied, tentatively. "Why do you ask?"

Shaking his head but not giving an answer, he backed the horse expertly into the shafts of a smart-looking black buggy. His knarled old hands were amazingly quick fastening chains, straps and buckles. Finally, he unfolded the reins and lay them neatly over the rack.

"There you are, ladies," he announced, with a sweep of his hand and a bow. "Be back by 3:30."

After much arranging of long skirts and coats and making sure the hamper was safely stowed, Meg shook the reins and the horse moved off at a walk.

"Oh, isn't this thrilling!" she murmured, sitting up straight and concentrating on her driving.

"We're still in the yard!" Nancy laughed. "Wait till we get out in the traffic."

Once out in Herald Street the grey broke into a gentle trot. Keeping pace with other carriages as they headed down Douglas Street, Meg cautiously watched for the hazardous tram tracks as they moved down the wide street.

"Gosh, this is easy," exclaimed Meg, clutching the reins tightly but looking very proud of herself as the horse took its own lead moving down the hill past the rear of The Empress.

Beacon Hill Park was alive with people. Families were feeding the ducks as older couples admired the wonderful show of early-blooming flowers. Daffodils and bright red alpine azaleas had been laid out in beds of random order by John Blair back in 1889. Today they were a grand credit to the Scot who had obviously been a skilled artist with gardens.

They continued on over the bridge and through the park, noticing that other vigilant drivers were being extra cautious as children darted between the horses and carriages. Shouting and laughing merrily, they dashed about the paths, followed by nannies or parents hard-pressed to keep pace.

Meg, thrilled by the adventure, paid careful attention to her driving but had no trouble guiding the grey. He knew what was expected and performed like a dream.

"Let's go down Dallas Road toward Oak Bay, Meg," Nancy suggested. "I've never been out that far from the city."

As they came in view of the sea, they saw a score of sailboats gliding across the water, making an eye-catching scene.

"They must be from the Victoria Yacht Club," Meg announced. "It looks like they are having a race." Taking Nancy's suggestion, she turned the horse along the dirt coastal road. Clucking her tongue and shaking the reins, the grey raised his head and picked up speed. Even the horse seemed happier as he covered the ground with long easy strides. A large open-topped car full of laughing young people passed them going into town at an awful speed, kicking up dust and blowing it into their faces.

"My goodness, they shouldn't be going so fast. I thought the speed limit was 20 mph?" Meg grumbled, shielding her eyes.

"Look at those waves beating on the rocks. It's so pretty here," squealed Nancy. Then a mile or so up the road, she grabbed Meg's arm. "Pull over ... pull over quickly, please Meg!"

Meg slowed the horse to a walk and pulled him off the road. "What have you seen?" she asked.

Without answering, Nancy leapt from the buggy and raced across the dusty track, disappearing into a large clump of broom. Meg could hear men shouting and laughing. Beyond the bushes she could see them swinging long sticks. Puzzling it over a moment, she had just realized they were playing the old Scottish game of golf, when Nancy returned. She had a small white ball in her hand.

"What you got there, lassie?"

"One of their golf balls from the links. Someone lost it in the bushes. My goodness, it's a frightfully hard ball!"

"Yes it is, love, could be lethal if it hit you," chuckled the older lady, clucking at the grey. Turning the buggy, they headed back towards the city.

Nancy studied the little ball, posing question after question at Meg. "They bounce like the devil," she said. "Do you know this thing bounced off two trees then smashed a small branch off a bush right next to me."

"You need to be careful when watching that game, lass. You could have been hurt and ended up over there!" Meg muttered, pointing towards some trees.

"Is it a hospital?" Nancy asked.

"No, Ross Bay Cemetery!" said Meg, trying to sound serious.

Nancy looked at Meg and they both broke into laughter. They went on in silence watching the sailboats and commenting on the many different automobiles that passed them, until they arrived back at Beacon Hill Park. They decided this was a good place for their picnic and they parked where they could watch children playing. Later, they continued up Dallas Road until they could see the large Dallas Hotel in the distance. Then Meg made a right turn onto Government Street.

"We'll go by the Parliament Buildings. They're adding some wings to it I hear," she announced.

"Oh look!" called Nancy. "There's a man who must be going golfing. He's wearing those funny trousers with their pants tied up at the knee!"

"They're called Plus Fours, lassie. We'll go into Wilson's sometime and I'll show you," Meg chuckled. "They're very popular."

They carried on up Government and in no time they were back at the livery yard. Standing in the corner leaning on a broom, one foot on a wheelbarrow half-full of dung, the old stableman puffed on his well-worn pipe as they pulled into the yard.

"Tommy!" he yelled as the buggy came to a stop.

A lad of no more than 10-years ran out of the stable door and came to their assistance, holding the horse steady as they stepped from the buggy.

71

"Had a good day, ladies?" inquired the old man.

"Yes, we did," said Meg, happily. "We shall be doing it again."

"Any time," he growled, taking their hamper out of the boot for them. "Just book a few days ahead an I'll make sure you get the grey."

As they walked up Store Street, they couldn't help but notice the large number of ramshackle buildings and warehouses. Here too, were the homes of Chinese emigrants stacked precariously one on top of another, each with its own tiny line of washing fluttering in the breeze. Meg told her they were the poorest of people but some were beginning to assert themselves by pooling their resources and building religious houses, schools and businesses.

Meg was glad when they reached the railway bridge at the bottom of Johnson Street because this meant they were almost home and she was beginning to feel quite tired.

"Did you know that a long time ago a little bridge was built here to encourage the Indians to move out of the city?" Nancy was saying. "I heard Waldo talking about it at the restaurant one day. He said it was built by someone named Roderick Finlayson."

"Strange isn't it?" added Meg. "Today it's the favoured route to their reservation in Esquimalt. This bridge is more modern, of course, so the railway can use it, too."

"That centre piece is ingenious. It's fascinating to watch the huge centre column as it pivots and opens like a huge door."

"Tim said it was necessary because now larger vessels can have access to more of the harbour. That swing bridge allows for ships with higher masts to pass," explained Meg. "My, its nice to have the streets paved. There is so much less dust," she said, changing the subject as they stepped off the sidewalk and onto the rattling boards that led to the office.

"Street lights are an improvement, too, now we have a few more of them," said Nancy, following her friend. "I don't mind going out at night anymore."

"You know," Meg said later, as she poured them each a second cup of tea. "That's the first time I've been out and about on my own."

"But you weren't on your own," Nancy laughed. "I was with you, Aunt Meg!" Realizing suddenly what she had said, she repeated it softly. "Aunt Meg, that's what I'll call you from now on ... if it's alright with you?" Pausing to reach for Meg's hand, she continued, "You have shown me so much kindness ... like my Dan, and I love you for it."

Meg MacDonald gripped the girl's hand tenderly and a tear suddenly found its way down her cheek. "Oh child, you've no idea what you mean to me. I would love you to call me aunt."

As the month came to a close, each day grew a little warmer. The women were well aware that the *Belfast* was supposed to be home by the first of April and their anticipation was building.

Nancy was aching to see Dan again, thinking of him often in his absence. She simply couldn't wait any longer to tell her self-proclaimed brother her exciting news. News she had already discussed with Meg and was probably one of the most important decisions of her young life ... whether she should accept the job offer from Mr. Tabour at the high-class Balmoral Hotel on Douglas Street.

Waldo and Charlotte had engineered the unexpected introduction just two weeks before. They had coaxed the Balmoral's Dining Room Manager, Harry Tabour, into the Occidental on the pretext of talking business during the busy lunch period. Witnessing Nancy's startling efficiency and with her lovely auburn hair flashing in the light as she moved quickly between the tables and kitchen, he was more than impressed.

"Why, that girl is a veritable wonder," Harry Tabour muttered, hardly able to take his eyes off the pretty girl. "She's a beauty as well!"

"She's more than that," Charlotte proclaimed, in a warning tone. "That girl is honest and smart ... and she's a friend of mine!"

Harry's eyebrows rose in surprise. "A friend of yours, Charlotte," he growled, "but she's only a waitress!"

Charlotte's eyes flashed a warning. She was in no mood for Harry's sarcastic comments. Leaning forward, she set her elbows solidly on the table and glared at him.

Waldo, recognizing the signs, intervened. "Don't be an idiot, Harry. You can be such a pompous ass! She's also a friend of mine!"

Harry was dumbfounded. The blood rushed into his head turning his face a bright shade of crimson and he spluttered for words.

At that very moment, Nancy passed by their table with a full tray of food. Noticing Harry's apparent difficulty, she slid the tray onto the table and rushed to his assistance. She patted his back lightly and offered him a glass of water.

"There, there sir, you'll be alright," she said gently.

Embarrassed, Harry managed a weak smile before the girl moved away. The hum of voices throughout the room resumed their normal volume and Harry fought to find his voice as his friends snickered quietly.

"My word, she's an attentive one," Harry croaked. "We could do with her at the Balmoral."

"Then offer her a job," Charlotte whispered, harshly. "And don't be cheap or I'll never let you forget it!"

Recovering quickly, he smiled as he realized he'd been hoodwinked and Charlotte meant every word. Waldo and Charlotte knew his reputation for employing only the best and he could see plainly that this girl had no equal. "You pair of conniving rogues!"

His companions merely grinned.

"Well, it's worked," he said. "Tell her to come and see me."

"Not a chance!" Charlotte snapped. "You'll do it now, so we can protect her."

"Damn it, Waldo, talk to the woman. I don't think she trusts me!" Harry snorted, feigning anger.

"NANCY," Waldo called, bringing the girl quickly to their table. "Tell her, Charlotte," he suggested impatiently.

Charlotte made the introduction, quickly adding, "He has a job in their dining room for you … as a senior waitress!" She smiled wickedly at Harry. "And he'll double the wages you get here … with all your meals free!"

"B - b - but I live here," the girl stammered, taken completely by surprise. "May I think on it for a few days, please sir?"

Receiving a silent nod from the man, she returned to her duties.

That night she told Meg, who immediately offered her a bed in the corner of her office. A few days later, with Meg's assurance she was making the right decision, she accepted the new position which would begin in early April.

Chapter 7

On the 1st of April, a gentle rain fell as Nancy rose after her second night at Meg's. Although she didn't start her new job for a week, Meg had insisted that she move immediately. So, on Sunday she had packed her meagre possessions and using a wheeled cart from the wharf, one trip was all that was needed. Now, she had two surprises for Dan.

She went to the window hoping to see the *Belfast* already tied at the dock, but even in the pre-dawn light she could tell that the empty space was still there. All day, her attention kept moving to the door of the restaurant ... with a totally new eagerness. At quitting time, she ran home and burst through the office door, red-faced and panting.

"Slow down, lassie," Meg soothed, looking up from her knitting. "They're on their way and will be here in no time."

"How do you know?" she asked brightly, her eyes sparkling as she hung her coat up and gave Meg a hug.

"Lighthouse keepers and Coast Guard keep us well informed, lass. They should be in about nine, as far as I can tell."

It was the longest three hours Nancy had ever experienced in her life, but finally, the clock said 8:30. "Will they be here soon, Aunt Meg?" she asked, somewhat impatiently, as she walked over to the window and peered through the darkness, her heart beating wildly.

"Patience, child," said Meg calmly. "Slip your coat on and take a look down the harbour. You might be able to see their lights.

"But how can I tell if it's them?"

Meg's needles stopped clicking. "Why lass, that's easy. Look for one red running-light on the bow and three green lights just above it, that's the *Belfast*. The bow is the front!"

Nancy hurried into her coat, wrapping her scarf around her neck.

"You might need mittens, too! It's cold out there," called Meg.

Nodding, the girl pulled her mittens out of her pocket and eagerly stepped out into the cold. Reaching the end of the dock, she peered out into the darkness toward the mouth of the harbour. She listened to the rhythmic slapping of waves under the dock and thought what a peaceful sound it was. Her eyes searched the darkness for the tiniest flicker of light. She was no longer apprehensive, she trusted Meg's contacts and craned her neck even harder.

She felt a gentle hand on her shoulder. "There they are!" Meg announced, excitement obvious in her voice.

Straining her eyes, Nancy picked out the single, tiny red light. Watching closely, now breathless as her heart began to beat rapidly, she forgot the cold and soon was able to make out the three green lights above the red one.

"It's them! They're home, Meg!"

"Let's light up the dock, lass, the lamps are all ready," Meg urged, as she struck a match and lit the first one. "Place them six strides apart with two together in the middle."

Nancy raced across the dock with the glowing objects, placing them according to instructions. Glancing up, as the moon streamed through a hole in the clouds making the *Belfast* clearly visible, a lump rose in her throat as she watched it come closer. Tears wetting her eyes, she felt Meg's reassuring arm around her and they stood together watching as their men came safely home.

Slowly, the large masted vessel came up alongside. A line came shooting out from the deck and Meg moved quickly, tying the line to a capstan on the dock. With a loud creaking of timber, the vessel finally stopped.

Leaping from the boat, Dan quickly tied the rest of the lines ... and then he realized Nancy was there, too. With one great whoop of joy, he ran toward her and they flew into each other's arms.

"My darling, my darling," Dan whispered, as he felt Nancy's quiet sobs. They held each other for what seemed like forever, neither wanting to let go. Dan finally released her and held her at arm's length. "Let's take a look at you. You know, sis, you're even more beautiful than I remembered!"

"Oh stop that, Danny. Can't you see you're embarrassing the poor girl," Meg admonished, as the rest of the crew joined them.

"He's just saying that, he can't even see me for the dark!" Nancy giggled.

There were hugs for Meg and much laughter as they all greeted each other; the crew finished their duties and each headed for home. They had a cup of tea together and then Dan took Nancy out for a quiet walk. He was thrilled to hear she was staying with Meg, a much better situation for both of them. An hour later, they returned.

"I'll see you in the morning, love," he whispered, kissing her tenderly on the cheek, then he pushed her through the office door and turned toward the ship.

During the next few weeks Nancy spent all of her spare time with Dan. His bonus from their last trip had been highly profitable and neither of them being used to spending money, they piled it into a savings account at the bank, and it was growing rapidly.

She started her new job at the imposing looking Balmoral Hotel on Douglas Street a week after Dan arrived home. Mr. Tabour told her he wanted to break her in gently. She was to start out as senior waitress but as he didn't have a head waitress at the present time, he was confident he could soon promote her to that position.

The Joyces decided to add a small room for Nancy adjacent to the office making Meg extremely happy she was a permanent resident. With Dan's help, it was completed within the week and the *Belfast* left again for Rose Harbour to recover the rest of the whale oil. Dan had some business to attend to so their helmsman, Jack Dumpford, affectionately known as Dumpy, went along with them. Ned said they'd be back for Nancy's birthday but no one was mentioning that fact to her.

As he watched them go, Dan's mind slipped back in time as he remembered when he and Dumpy began working together back in 1904. That was when he had said goodbye to Nancy and left the orphanage for good. Dumpy had been the Joyce's crewman and friend ever since the boat arrived from Newfoundland back in '96. Now, at age 32, he remained unmarried, living with his mother in the tiny house where he was born on Mason Street. His father had built the house from money scratched from the goldfields before Jack was born and a few years later he was killed by a runaway horse on Douglas Street. There were many hard years for the boy and his mother until he joined the Joyces. He was reliable and honest, and idolized Dan for his confidence and skills.

By the end of May, the days were much longer and regular sunshine was turning Victoria into a destination for hundreds of tourists, from high-born Germans and English nobility, to rich American industrialists. It was not uncommon to see vessels flying American and English flags in the already crowded harbour even though more docks were constructed to accommodate them.

Dan had been so proud of her when she told him of her new job. She had settled into it nicely as she knew many of the staff, some of them having worked with her at the Occidental or the Temperance. She grew especially close to Mary, the day cook, whose husband had recently been in a boating accident losing his leg. This only added to the poor woman's troubles as she was already working extra hours to support her family.

Harry Tabour turned out to be an easy man to get along with and he was not the least bit surprised when some of Nancy's regulars followed the popular girl, he had counted on it, in fact. He derived much pleasure hearing from friends that George Dunn was whining as usual. He had often accused Harry of stealing the best girls, and customers, in town!

With Nancy's surprise birthday party coming in a couple of weeks, Charlotte, having already coaxed George Dunn into giving her the day off, now found herself having to deal with Harry Tabour. After explaining how Nancy had never been given a party before and giving him a short rundown on his new waitress's life, he acquiesced and gave his permission willingly.

On Sunday, June 8th, Meg and Nancy arose bright and early expecting Dan who had arranged to take them out to Meg's cottage at Elk lake. The sun was already throwing its early morning brilliance over the city and promising a cloudless day.

"The *Belfast* is leaving again on Wednesday," Dan commented casually, as they walked along deserted Wharf Street toward the stables. The *Belfast* had arrived back the day before and they were in full swing getting the boat ready for the next whaling expedition. "This time I have to go with them but we'll all have supper together on Tuesday," he announced.

Nancy frowned at the thought of him leaving but she was relieved he would be here for her birthday at least, even though he had barely mentioned it. She smiled weakly and grasped his hand tighter, looking down at the pavement. Meg and Dan exchanged sly glances and Dan winked secretly at the older woman.

They stopped to admire the gold-lettered signs and classy exterior of Rithet's store and the stately Law Courts Building on Bastion Street. A slight breeze ruffled the flags hanging from the bleak-looking front of the Imperial German Consulate.

Jim Morrison, the blacksmith, was busy in his forge at the corner of Yates, filling the air with the pungent smell of burning fires and hooves. As they approached, Meg held her nose, then hurried across the road to peer in the alluring window of Duncan and Gray, the liquor wholesaler.

The blacksmith glanced up and waved, putting his tools down and wiping his hands on his black apron. Nancy knew old Jim as a customer, coming often for his evening meal and a drink at the Occidental. The old blacksmith walked over, swinging his hammer lightly in his hand. Jim was permanently stooped, the result of many years at his trade, though his great sense of humour still kept him laughing.

"Now, who's this here, young lady?" he asked with a large, friendly grin, pointing his hammer at Dan. "Yer man friend?"

"No," she giggled, clutching Dan's arm possessively. "He's my brother, Dan."

"Pleased to meet ya, lad," Jim chuckled, sticking out a grubby hand. "Must be a hell of a worry having such a beautiful sister!"

Shaking the old man's hand vigorously, Dan smiled. "Not really, sir, I'd kill any man that does her wrong." Nancy's fingers tightened on his arm, shooting a wave of pleasure through his body.

Morrison nodded knowingly, positive it was no idle threat. "We're all missing you, Nancy. I'll be coming to see you at the Balmoral one of these days." Then he waved and returned to his work.

Meg waited for them in front of the Occidental, muttering loudly. "Scotch whisky! Hmmph, most of that stuff's never even seen Scotland!"

As they passed the Chinese Barber at 1619 Store Street, Nancy grabbed Dan's arm. "You need a hair cut, lad!"

"Bossy little devil isn't she?" Meg chuckled, adjusting her bonnet and linking his other arm.

"Not there, I don't," Dan asserted. "We all go to Bill Harrison's just past Pembroke." He raised his arm and pointed further up the street. "Guess I better go see him this week."

Arriving at the livery stable in the Hart Block they found the grey already hitched to the buggy and the stable lad waiting patiently.

"Going far, sir?" the old stableman called, appearing in a doorway.

"Gordon Head, Cordova Bay, then on to Elk Lake," Dan replied, watching the surprised look on his companions' faces.

"Gordon Head," Meg murmured. "That's a long way out of our way."

Dan chuckled softly offering no explanation as he opened the buggy door and invited the ladies to climb in.

The old man turned to Dan and winked. "Everything you need is in the boot, just as you asked, including a sack of feed." Dan tipped his hat and the stableman waved them off.

Trotting gently up Herald, they noticed the different smells of blacksmith's fires, mills, horses, and other undistinguishable scents that mingled together in the calm morning air. Unfettered by the usual weekday traffic and pedestrians, they took Bay Street and turned left onto Cedar Hill. Allowing the grey to rest for a few minutes at the top

81

of the hill, they looked out over the city and marveled at how big it was getting. Carrying on, they reached the rougher, pot-holed surface that took them all the way out to Mount Douglas winding through dark forests and lush farmland where animals of all kinds were seen grazing. Dan was concerned for his passenger's comfort but the women chatted incessantly obviously thinking of it as high adventure.

Finally reaching the base of the tree-enshrouded mountain, they turned left onto Cordova Bay Road for a short distance until they found Cross Road. The familiar sound of squawking seagulls assaulted their ears indicating they were near the ocean. Dan turned another corner and a rough sign indicated they were now on Ash Road. Pulling up to a weathered wooden gate, he jumped out to open it, leading the grey through.

"Where are we?" Meg inquired.

"We could be home," Dan teased mysteriously, tying the horse to a tree. "Come on, let's go take a look."

Puzzled over Dan's comment, Nancy helped Meg from the buggy and taking her arm, they followed him through the trees. It was very rough land and they stepped carefully over fallen branches and around rocks. Soon the trees thinned and they caught the sound of waves beating against unseen rocks.

A clearing came into view and Nancy gasped. Before them lay one of the most beautiful scenes she had ever seen. Walking to the edge of the cliff, she looked cautiously down. A small sandy beach could be seen below and on a collection of large rocks sat three seals and several seagulls who screamed loudly at the intrusion.

"Oh, look at the seals, Aunt Meg, they're playing," Nancy exclaimed delightedly.

"My word it's a beautiful spot, lad" said Meg, breathlessly. "Why have you brought us here?"

Nancy walked over to Dan and slipped her hand into his. "What are you trying to tell me, Danny?" she whispered, squeezing his hand.

Dan tried to speak but the words caught in his throat. Coughing slightly, he began again, staring out to sea with a misty, faraway look in his eyes. "There's twenty-five acres here, Nan, and it's ours ... if you like it." The last words were mumbled as he slipped his arm around her shoulder. Clearing his throat again, he continued. "Just think, a home of our own at last."

Nancy was speechless and turned her head into his shoulder hiding tears that welled in her eyes.

Meg kept back and watched as Nancy and Dan stood on the clifftop outlined against the clear blue sky. Nancy's long hair was blowing gently in the wind that whipped her skirts about her legs. Meg turned and silently walked along the cliff top. The image of the orphans' silhouette burned an indelible picture in her mind. *Those two belong together and I think they are beginning to realize it*, she thought happily.

"Can we afford it, Danny?" Nancy asked, raising her head to see his smile. "Then, let's do it," she said as her heart skipped a beat.

He kissed her cheek and they turned to walk back through the trees to rejoin Meg who was slowly making her way back to the buggy. "Yes, we can, sis, and money to spare," he assured her.

"Better pick a name for it, ladies," he said to them, "because that's going to be our new home!"

"I have a home," said Meg. "Are we going there now, Danny?"

Dan nodded, climbing into the driver's seat. "Hold on tight now, this is going to be a rough ride!"

Going back the way they had come, they now turned right at the Cross and Cordova Bay intersection and found a less travelled, narrow road cut through a forest of tall firs. It was very dark with little light able to penetrate the dense forest. True to his word, they found themselves bouncing violently over very rough ground and Dan slowed the grey as he picked his way over the deeply rutted road often maneuvering through water-filled potholes. Occasionally seeing glimpses of the sea on their right, they realized they were still very close to the ocean.

Reaching the more travelled Cordova Bay Road, the grey happily picked up speed. Almost an hour after leaving Gordon Head, they rounded the sand dunes and arrived at East Saanich Road, the main road to the northern part of the Saanich municipality. A short distance on, they realized they were at the north end of Elk Lake and easily found Brookleigh Lane. It turned out to be a picturesque ride that took them through a little forest between more farmland.

"Should be able to see it soon," Dan called over his shoulder.

Picking their way down the lane, he pulled the horse to a halt at a little stone bridge.

"Which way now?" he asked, steadying the fidgety horse.

"Over there," Meg pointed into the bush. "There's another track, it follows the stream."

Dan turned the horse onto a long-since grown-over track which indicated that nature was reclaiming the precious space. Branches brushed against the buggy as the horse forced his way through. A few minutes later, they came upon a clearing shared by a small log house and two wary deer who watched their noisy approach, then bounded gracefully away.

Dan unhitched the grey and led him over to the stream, returning to see what the women were doing. He heard the creaking of hinges as they forced open the cabin's long unused door. Dan recognized the smell of dampness even before Nancy's nose began twitching. Huge cobwebs hung like curtains everywhere.

Meg located an old broom just inside the door and began carving a way in but stopped when she realized the fruitlessness of the exercise. Her eyes saw the rough table and chairs her brothers had made and sad memories crept into her mind for the first time in months.

"Is there anything you want to take back, Aunt Meg?" Nancy asked sympathetically, from the doorway.

"No, I don't think so. These memories are best left here where they belong, lassie," she sighed. Meg turned and went back outside, took a deep breath of the fresh forest air, and closed the door.

Dan led the horse back from the stream and tethered him to a tree closer to the house. He slipped the foodbag over his neck and returned to the back of the buggy. He now surprised them by extracting a food hamper from the boot box. He walked over to the stream and set it down on a tree stump as the women watched curiously.

"You brought food? How on earth did you manage that?" Nancy asked, opening the lid.

"We're going to have a picnic," Dan declared, explaining how he had ordered it from the obliging stableman.

Meg was smiling again as she joined them. She helped Nancy lay out the lunch of cold meat, pickles and bread, getting some fresh water from the stream. As they did so, Dan talked of his dreams—of how he visualized their new house overlooking the sea and wanted Meg to live with them.

The Scottish lady shook her head. "Nay, laddie," she smiled. "You two will be a married couple by then and you won't want an old lady hanging around."

"We'll be a what?" Nancy laughed. "He's my brother!" She threw a wicked glance at Dan and rubbed her hands together. Scrambling backward, but unable to escape, Dan defended himself from her wild tickling fingers—letting out yelps intermingled with uncontrolled laughter.

"If this is what happens when we feed her Meg ...!" he cried, succumbing once again to her administrations.

Meg giggled like a schoolgirl and shouted encouragement as they rolled happily on the grass, Nancy's skirts flying in all directions. Slowly, the struggling stopped and they lay in each other's arms panting for breath. Nancy sat up first, leaning over to kiss Dan on the nose as his hand reached out to stroke her hair.

"You two young'uns were made for each other," said Meg, "but in my day, we wouldn't dare put on a display like that in public."

"But you're not public, Aunt Meg!" Nancy teased.

"I loved her from the first day I saw her, Aunt Meg," said Dan in a faraway voice, as he slowly sat up. Unashamedly, he pulled Nancy close to him again, gently wrapping his arms around her like protective steel bands. "She was so tiny ... and hurting so badly," he whispered emotionally. "You're mine now, little sister, all mine."

Meg sat watching the young couple as they clung together on the blanket, their bodies gently swaying as one, as their silent memories returned. Dabbing at her eyes with her handkerchief, she muttered softly, "No, it just wouldn't be right." Then, turning to clear up their picnic, she began to put everything back in the basket.

Nancy extracted herself from Dan's arms, stood up, and went over to Meg. Standing in front of her, she reached out and took her gently by the shoulders. "It's not up for discussion, Aunt Meg," she whispered, tenderly. "He made the decision, so you must do what you're told!" She gave the dear old woman a wink and hugged her tenderly.

Travelling back to town via the East Road, they were stopped momentarily as the smoke-puffing V & S Railway engine rattled past pulling five freight cars on its way to Sidney. Minutes later, they were overtaken and passed by several automobiles, tooting their horns and making odd noises as their owners showed off new skills.

"Noisy devilish things," Meg muttered. "They'll never be popular."

Nancy laughed and called to Dan. "Know anything about those contraptions, Dan? Aunt Meg still doesn't believe their popularity will last!"

They got onto Saanich Road and Dan allowed the grey to stretch out into a mile-eating trot. Keeping his eyes on the road, he announced, "I've been learning about engines from Ned."

"You wouldn't drive one of them smelly things, would you, lad?" Meg snapped, looking disgusted as another automobile roared past at a speed of at least twenty miles-an-hour.

"Well, Aunt Meg," he laughed, "yes, I believe I would!"

"Don't you even think of it, Nancy!" the older woman snorted. "A good horse and buggy are good enough for us."

"Everybody's getting them, Aunt Meg," said Nancy. "Haven't you noticed how many are lined up outside Rithet's and the hotels now? They're becoming awfully popular."

Their discussion carried on all the way back into town where they picked up Douglas Street and several blocks later, they reached the Fountain. Stopping briefly to allow the grey a drink from the popular landmark, they continued on carefully negotiating the circle until they found Government Street. Then, Dan let the grey have his head and he made for home.

At the livery stable the old man took the grey's head as he puffed on his foul-smelling pipe. "Good day, lad?" he asked, pleasantly. "Hamper were fine?"

"Yes, yes, everything was very good," Dan assured him with a smile, handing the old man the reins and climbing down.

Nancy nudged Meg and they both started to giggle, watching the stablemen's pipe wobble precariously between missing teeth.

"What is it, ladies?" he asked, just managing to catch the pipe as it slipped from his lips, wiping the spittle with the back of his hand.

Trying to conceal their laughter, the women struggled out of the buggy and staggered into the street leaving the old man scratching his head with the stem of his pipe. Dan watched curiously, looking from one to the other.

"What ails them two females, lad?" the old man asked.

"Sun, I think," Dan muttered, fishing some coins out of his pocket to pay the man, while trying to keep a serious tone in his voice. "Too strong today, musta fried their brains!"

Nodding, the stableman glanced up at the sun, then back at Dan. "Eee, what a shame!" he said, counting the money then putting it into his pocket and shuffling away.

Dan grinned as he set out up Store Street after his companions but soon realized they had disappeared. He was almost to the door of the Occidental when Nancy came out through the swing doors and waved to him.

"Where's Aunt Meg?" he asked.

"At the toilet, silly," Nancy giggled. "We were in a hurry!"

"Oh," Dan muttered, "but what were you two laughing at?"

Meg came out of the hotel door before the girl could answer, took one look at Nancy and began to laugh again.

"It was his pipe," Nancy gasped. "You should watch it sometime."

The whaler shook his head. "Well, I'll be ..., when he asked what you two were laughing at, I told him you'd gone a bit simple in the sun. He seemed to think that was a reasonable explanation!" Slipping his arm around Nancy's shoulder, he whispered in her ear. "And so do I!" getting a sharp elbow in the ribs.

They followed Meg into the office where she made a beeline for the pot-bellied stove, checking to see if there was hot water for tea.

"Is that fire still burning?" Dan asked, in surprise.

"Never been out in the years I've been around here," Meg replied emphatically, looking through one of the openings for glowing embers. She filled the teapot and in a few minutes checked to see if the tea had steeped enough. "Get out the cups, love," she told Nancy.

"I need a pencil and paper," Dan requested, taking a chair at the table. Nancy scuttled away again after placing the cups on the table. Dan began to draw a picture marking the coastline and the property they'd visited. He added Ash Road and the lane leading to the gate, clearly labeling the intersection where Cordova Bay Road met Cedar Hill beneath Mount Douglas.

"We'll build our house here," he said, drawing a square just back from the coastline. "And the boat dock ... here." He marked the spot with a cross before pushing it across the table.

Over dinner their discussion centred on the property. Meg generously offered to sell her cabin and put the money toward the cost of building the new house. Dan, smiling, refused her offer saying they had enough money. He also mentioned that he'd already talked to Jack Duggan about the building. He had offered his help and advice but first they had to finish the deal on the land.

"We'll do that tomorrow," he grinned, "now that my little sister has agreed!"

Preparing to go, Dan gave both ladies a hug. "I'll be waiting for you tomorrow night after work, Nan."

Nancy nodded and watched him stride off toward the *Belfast* feeling Meg's reassuring hand resting lightly on her shoulder.

Next morning, as Nancy hurried up Broughton Street to work, she heard a shouted greeting from a Victoria Baggage Company truck chugging up the incline and saw Waldo waving from the cab.

Arriving at work, word was received that a shipful of tourists was leaving on the early tide and breakfast would have to be handled with speed. Nancy was up to her usual form.

"My verd, you are a vonder," an apparently highborn German gentleman growled.

"Beg pardon, sir?" the puzzled girl replied, as the man jumped to his feet clicking his heels.

"He means you're a wonderful waitress," one of his lady companions interpreted, in perfect English.

"Why, thank you, sir," Nancy smiled pleasantly, giving him a little curtsy.

Harry watched as his dining room staff worked with an efficiency he had always been striving for, but had not quite been able to accomplish before Nancy arrived. *It's her!* he thought to himself. *She ties it all together by example. The others seem eager to follow her.* The Dining Room Manager rubbed his hands together gleefully realizing he'd found a leader at last. There was just one more thing he had to be sure of. As the dining room emptied of guests his mind sought an answer to a question that had been nagging him since hiring Nancy. *Is she as honest as Waldo and Charlotte have portrayed?* Harry was to find his answer sooner than he expected.

The next afternoon, Nancy lined the waitresses up to wish some departing guests 'God speed' and a pleasant trip home. It was another little gesture appreciated by guests who showed their pleasure by the tips they left behind.

Harry Tabour watched from the kitchen as Nancy scooped a substantial pile of money from the tables, putting it into a glass bowl. She put it under the counter and went to wave as the last guest disappeared through the door. Then, the girls eagerly gathered around her, excited to get their share.

Nancy ignored them and instead gave them some brisk orders. The girls, some unhappily, dispersed around the room, clearing and resetting tables. She picked up the bowl of money and went over to where Harry was sitting, setting it down in front of him.

"Will you please divide that evenly six ways, Mr. Tabour," she requested with a wink, turning back to help her staff.

Harry grinned. His question had been answered. Experienced fingers neatly set out six piles of money—whistling through his teeth when he realized there was almost ten dollars for each of the girls. Looking up, he saw Nancy and the girls coming toward him.

"Did you share it evenly, sir?" she asked, loud enough for her girls to hear.

"Just as you requested, lass," he said with a chuckle, pushing back his chair.

"Now, take two dollars from each of our shares," she instructed. One of the waitresses let out an involuntary groan. "That's for the kitchen staff!"

Harry complied, then handed each girl her share. Looking around the dining room and realizing there was only one customer, he made a surprise announcement.

"Stay for a moment, Nancy, but the rest of you are excused for ten minutes." The others quickly dispersed and Harry smiled up at her, pushing her money across the table. "I think you've just taught me something, young lady!" he said, looking at the confident young woman standing in front of him. "But why the kitchen staff?"

"Listen, Harry," she whispered, hands gripping the back of a chair. "If the kitchen knows we appreciate their effort, they'll join the team and make it easier for everyone."

"You're a wise one, Nancy," her boss mused, fingers tapping the table. "It's the first time I've ever heard such a thing being done ... but I like it ... yes, I like it and the kitchen certainly will! Why don't you go deliver it."

"Thanks, I will. There's a first for everything, Mr. Tabour," Nancy flashed back, picking up the extra pile of coins. She turned on her heel and headed for the kitchen, happily jingling the money in her hand.

Nancy had little time to reflect on the date although tomorrow was her birthday. At lunchtime, Dottie and Hannah, two of her girls, decided to treat themselves to chocolates from Rogers'. Returning to the hotel with their little bags of mouth-watering morsels, they announced that the green grocers had been converted to a new candy store. It now sported a wonderful gold-leafed chandelier and many glass-fronted counters in which were stacked the familiar large, round chocolates. They soon had their audience drooling with envy and desire. Then, at the last minute, they produced a gift for each of them and exclamations of delight filled the air.

It was a busy day for the girls and a steady stream of customers kept them on their toes. Tom Ben, from E.A. Morris arrived accompanied by Mr. Richards, the real estate agent, and as always, he was eager to make a sale of his Cuban cigars. Harry came over to sit with them, caressing and sniffing the long brown rolls of tobacco, obviously a customer.

Nancy stopped at the table to take their order. To Harry's surprise, she calmly informed Tom that if Mr. Tabour bought a box of cigars she would expect Tom to give him a special deal. The cigar salesman nodded agreeably.

"How did you do that, Nancy?" Harry asked later.

"Do what?" she replied. "Get you a discount, you mean?"

Harry nodded.

"Easy," she continued, nonchalantly, "you're both friends of mine!" and tossing her head, she walked away.

Harry Tabour just couldn't understand why he felt so elated that this ordinary working girl could make him feel so privileged to be called her friend. Oh, it was true, she was an exceptional worker and had the disposition of an angel. *Some very powerful people readily admit to being her friend, but why?*

At 5:45, Dan walked into the dining room and noticed the manager sitting at his table staring off into space. Pulling out a chair the whaler sat down, bringing Harry back to reality.

"Sorry, Mr. Tabour, did I startle you?"

"Huh ... what?" Harry stammered. "You come to pick up your sister?"

Dan nodded.

The sound of a clock chiming released Harry from his dilemma as Nancy came into the room carrying her hat and coat. She smiled at Dan and bent to kiss his cheek before joining them at the table.

"Have you eaten yet?" she asked, patting Dan's hand.

"Not yet, we've an appointment with Mr. Miller, the barrister and solicitor." Watching the puzzled look on the girl's face, he continued, "He's just up the street in the Times Building. It won't take long."

It was clear to Harry that Dan adored this girl and he felt a twinge of envy. He had never before been witness to such outward affection yet it was very puzzling because they were brother and sister. It was incomprehensible.

"Tell you what," he said, suddenly. "Come back later and have a meal with me, as my guests."

"Oh, no thank you, sir," said Dan, so quietly Nancy strained to hear. "I have other plans, but you could give her the day off tomorrow ... it's her birthday!"

Harry smiled, raising his eyebrows, remembering the promise he'd already made to Charlotte. A look of surprise spread across Nancy's face.

"You don't really mean it?" she asked.

"Yes, we do. You can have the day off tomorrow," he declared. "You've earned it."

"Oh, Mr. Tabour, sir," Nancy gushed, "that's very generous of you. I could kiss you for that!"

"Oh no, you don't!" Harry yelped in alarm, leaping from his chair. "I'm too old for that kind of excitement," he exclaimed, winking at Dan as he backed away and made a hurried retreat toward the kitchen.

"I think you scared him, lass," Dan laughed. "Come on, Nan, it's time we were off."

Outside, they linked arms and walked the short distance to Fort Street easily finding the entrance to the Times Building. Dan said this was the only building in the block to escape the 1910 fire, which was fortuitous because the new building had only recently been completed. They found the stairs and raced each other up to the third floor.

Mr. Miller's secretary introduced herself as Nina and quickly showed them into his office with its massive desk and matching dark bookcases. The blind was drawn to keep out the sunlight and Nancy's first impression of the room was of utter gloom.

Peering over his spectacles, the mustached, deadpan face of Herb Miller watched them enter. He growled a greeting and responded to Dan's introduction with a scowl. Giving the impression of urgency, he quickly shuffled some papers on his desk and pushed the first document toward Dan. A long, bony finger pointed to the place they were to sign. The hovering secretary scurried over with a pen and inkwell, placing each carefully on the desk in front of them.

"You can write, can't you?" Herb Miller rasped, not looking up.

It was an ignorant question and Dan instantly disliked the man, not bothering to answer. Signing the paper, he pushed it toward Nancy and reached for the next. When finished, Nina collected the documents and handed them back to Mr. Miller, who quickly scanned the papers and handed them back to her.

Only then did Mr. Miller seem to relax slightly. He slipped his glasses from his face, tipped back on his chair, and stroked his droopy mustache. "Hard day," he grouched, almost to himself. "You brought a bank draft, boy, like I told you?"

"Yes, sir," Dan replied, extracting a piece of paper from his jacket pocket and handing it across the desk.

"Looks to be in order," the lawyer muttered, inspecting the draft thoroughly before leaning back in his chair and folding his arms across his chest. "Well, folks," he began loudly, fondling his mustache again. "You're the proud owners of the most useless piece of property in Saanich!" Then, in a tone of definite dismissal, he thundered, "I bid you good day."

Nancy and Dan looked at each other and smiled ruefully. The secretary showed them out of the solicitor's office closing his door quietly behind them.

"Don't take any notice of him, he's having a bad day," said Nina. Then, a puzzled look appeared on her face. "What are you going to do way out there?"

"Love each other," Dan answered casually, shaking the lady's hand. Nina's face turned quite red and she quickly ushered them toward the office door, shutting it quickly behind them.

"You devil!" Nancy laughed as they walked arm in arm down Fort Street. "Do you know what that woman thinks?"

"Yes, I do, but it's true! Let them think what they want, we don't care!" he sniggered, slipping his arm through Nancy's and giving it a squeeze.

"Where are we going now?" she asked.

"For a meal … and then the theatre," Dan replied, grinning. "You ever been to the theatre?"

"Don't be silly! Have you?" she giggled.

"No, but tonight we will have," he whispered, "because I've tickets for the Totem."

"The Totem Theatre?" the girl gasped in awe. "That's a bit posh for us, don't you think?"

"A bit what?"

"Posh … that's what Charlotte says."

"Well, then we're going a bit posh tonight," he laughed. "We're going to eat at the Occidental first!"

"Oh no, we're not!" she objected, pulling him to a halt. "I'll feel so silly being a customer after working there so long."

94

The good-natured argument raged as they made their way along Government Street, but there was no budging Dan from his decision. As they entered the lobby, the first person they saw was Joe Simpson, the desk clerk. His mouth drooped open with surprise.

"H - hello, Nancy!" he stammered. "Nice to see you back."

In the dining room, old George Dunn looked up from his paperwork and almost fell off his stool while other staff called out their greetings.

Glancing around the room, she self-consciously said 'hello' to several of her former customers. Eventually, her eyes came to rest on the corner table where, smiling broadly, sat Meg, Waldo, Charlotte, another man and woman … and two empty chairs.

"You're a sneaky little devil!" she laughed, hugging him. "You had this all planned out, didn't you?"

"We thought we'd join you two!" Waldo chuckled, jumping up to hold Nancy's chair before she sat down. "Nancy, this is my wife, Margaret, and that good-looking lad is Charlotte's husband, Edward. We thought it was about time you met our other halves!"

Niceties were exchanged and the waitress, whom Nancy did not know, brought menus.

As they finished the last of their dessert, Mr. Dunn came over.

"Happy birthday, Nancy," he said, smiling. "Any chance of you coming back to work for me?"

"Hold it, George," Charlotte chided. "No business talk allowed tonight!"

The proprietor looked hurt, but managed a smile as Waldo quietly told him to put the meal on his bill.

"Not a chance, lad," George growled. "This one's on me!"

A shocked expression came over Nancy's face, but Dan winked at her, squeezing her hand under the table.

Leaving the hotel, the group moved into the street, walking slowly up Johnson and across Government to the Totem. As they entered the foyer, Charlotte pointed out some of the intricate architectural features of the theatre. Pointing up to the wonderful chandelier hanging like a mountain of light from the high ornate ceiling, she was

95

rewarded by their delighted gasps. Footsteps were silenced as they moved across the plush Oriental carpeting. Over to one side, the highly polished bar was crowded with finely dressed gentlemen, drinking and laughing as they passed the time until the show began. Few women were in sight.

Somewhere a bell began to ring. The foyer cleared quickly as everyone rushed to take their seats, stepping through two huge swing doors held open by uniformed ushers. Dan led the way, easily finding their almost centre seats. Meg lowered herself slowly into the seat, a sigh of delight escaping her lips as she sank into its plushness.

"Try it, Nancy," she whispered, pulling the girl down beside her. "I've never sat in anything like this before … this is real luxury!"

It was barely two minutes later when the lights went down and the strains of *O Canada* filled the room. Few people knew the words of this new National Anthem but many hummed quietly as they stood respectfully to attention. Then, immediately following, the orchestra changed into a lively tune, the curtain opened, and the audience resumed their seats.

For Nancy and Meg, it was a vaudeville night to remember with singers, dancers, musicians, jugglers, and comics in highly imaginative and often hilarious antics. As the show finished and the cast took their bows, the audience rose in a thunderous standing ovation. The clapping brought the artists back many times but just when Nancy thought her hands would fall off, a new quietness settled over the theatre. Everyone stood up again and the orchestra began to play *God Save the King*. The curtain opened and the voices of audience and performers joined together in patriotic tribute.

A few minutes later, the crowd began to slowly shuffle toward the doors, eventually spilling onto Government Street. Nancy noticed the intriguing mixture of buggies and cars waiting in line to pick up their passengers but Meg wasn't impressed, complaining of the noise and smoke. They said hurried goodnights to the Skillings and Townends and headed in the opposite direction.

Dan got himself between Meg and Nancy and extracted them from the crowd who were wandering happily all over the road, making it an almost impossible situation. They could still hear the hum of the crowd as they turned down Yates Street.

It was nearly 11 o'clock when Dan left them at their door. Nancy changed into her night clothes while Meg made a cup of tea. For the next hour they compared notes on their fantastic evening and only when Nancy noticed Meg's eyes beginning to flicker did they realize the time and finally gave in to the call of sleep.

Nancy woke with a start, to the sound of Ned's voice at the door.

"Come on you lazy wenches, get yer rear ends out of them beds!" he shouted jovially. Then, everything was quiet as Nancy sat up in bed, stretched and yawned. "Us lads are going for breakfast up the street!" Ned's voice yelled again just before the door banged and there was silence.

The women were eating breakfast when the three returned. Meg picked up the broom and threw it toward the door as Ned poked his head in.

"Damn it, laddie, yer noisier that a crofter's cockerel. Can't a girl get her beauty sleep around here?"

"Aye, yer can lass," Ned grinned, "but it would take a whole blasted year!"

Ducking as Meg now threw the wet dishrag at him, Tim had to sit down for laughing. At a sign from Dan, the men suddenly moved to stand shoulder to shoulder, watched suspiciously by Meg. Then they began to sing a rousing, rather off-key version of 'Happy Birthday'.

Nancy's face went bright red but she clapped happily.

"Have you three finished with that ruckus?" Meg muttered, grabbing a piece of wood from beside the stove and waving it menacingly as they backed toward the door.

"I surrender," Tim chuckled, going over to Meg and hugging her. "Pour me a pot of tea, love."

"I'll have one, too," Ned muttered, "but I'm not coming near ya!" His eyes twinkled with mischief and he circled the room well out of Meg's reach. "I think you're a lovely little dumpling, but I forgot how damned dangerous you can be!"

They settled down when Dan mentioned business and a delivery of whale oil to one of the coloured families living on Salt Spring Island.

Tim searched the order book and found the entry. Frowning, his finger slowly moved across the page. "You've a good memory, lad." We'll load and deliver it today."

"Not you, Danny, m'boy," Ned intervened, "you get the day off!"

The elder Joyce quickly left the office to arrange the loading of the *Belfast*, leaving Meg and Tim to do the paperwork. Closing the book, Tim glanced up as Nancy re-entered the room, now dressed and pretty as a picture.

"Gorge Hotel," he mumbled thoughtfully, as he stood at the door. "Tram to Eliza's place."

"What the devil are you rambling on about?" Meg asked.

"Oh, I'm thinking on such a special day and a nice one, too, Danny should take Nancy to meet Eliza down at the Gorge."

"Och, too far, that'd take all day," said Meg, dismissing the idea.

"No, it's not," argued Tim. "I was talking to Jim Critchley from the General Store at Sidney. He came for oil Saturday."

"Aye, I saw him," Meg murmured, with a puzzled look.

"Well, he told me all you do is catch the 'Number 5' on Wharf Street and it takes you right there."

Dan and Nancy's eyes met across the room. "You're right, Tim. It would be nice for Nancy to meet the Marshalls."

"Take something to put over your shoulders, lass, and don't forget your hat," Meg suggested. "I'll be expecting you for supper at six."

Nancy dashed back to her room. In a few seconds she returned holding up two recent acquisitions ... a blue and white bonnet with long matching ribbons and a blue shawl.

"Now I'm ready," she announced.

Dan grinned and took his light coat off the hook behind the door, winking at Meg. He loved the way she mothered them. He barely remembered his mother as both of his parents had died before he was five. An uncle had tried to raise him but it became impossible and he'd been sent to the orphanage. From the first day he'd met Meg after her brothers drowned, she had treated him as her own.

98

He turned to Nancy and whispered, "You look lovely, Nan. Let's get going. See you at six, Aunt Meg."

Meg stood at the open door watching as the couple strolled hand-in-hand up the walkway and sighed deeply. All she had ever wanted out of life was a husband and children of her own, but it was not meant to be. Almost all the joy had been taken from her life until that glorious day she had met Nancy and a new door opened allowing her to really care for someone again. Nancy and Dan made her realize that she didn't need to be alone anymore. They loved her and had been insisting she come to live with them. Yes, she wanted to be with them ... needed to be with them. They were discovering their love for each other, at last, and she would give anything to be a part of it.

The open-style sightseeing tram with *Number 5 Victoria Electric Tramways* prominently emblazoned on its exterior, screeched up to its stop in front of the bookstore. Dan and Nancy had just safely sat down in one of the rear seats when the iron monster began to move. Jerking violently into action, the unconcerned conductor staggered down the aisle collecting their seven-cent fare.

They quickly left the city behind, wobbling and jolting as it accelerated. The incessant clanging of the driver's bell rang in their ears but within twenty minutes they were pulling into the terminus.

Elizabeth Marshall, owner of the Gorge Hotel across the street, stood on the wide porch watching the passengers leave the tram. She was a very stylish lady and today she was wearing a long, back dress with blue piping and a black, narrow-brimmed straw hat decorated with spring flowers and tied with a wide blue ribbon under her chin.

A warm smile spread across Eliza's face as she watched the happy, but unfamiliar young couple, walk toward her.

"Lovely day isn't it, folks! I'm Eliza Marshall and welcome to the Gorge Hotel," she called, gliding across the porch to meet them.

"Thank you, ma'am," Nancy replied.

The hotel owner reached out her hands, clasping the girl's in a warm, friendly greeting.

"My, my," she observed, "such pretty hair ...."

"Yes, my sister has always had lovely hair," interrupted Dan.

"Oh, I'm sorry, I thought ...," Eliza began.

"We bring greetings from Ned and Tim Joyce," Dan continued.

Eliza Marshall frowned and putting her hands on her hips studied the young couple for a few seconds. Squinting against the sun, she suddenly smiled. "I remember now. You're Dan ... Dan Brown, aren't you, lad? You were here with the Joyce's last year ... then, you must be Nancy!" she exclaimed. "I should have known by the colour of your hair, dear. It is an usual colour ... quite remarkable. Several people have actually mentioned you in conversation."

Mrs. Marshall opened the door leading into the dining room, insisting they join her. She ushered them to a table next to a window overlooking the picturesque waterway where they could see scores of young people swimming and diving from the rocks overlooking the Gorge Swimming Baths. She ordered tea and cakes and then sat down with them. She was of medium height, solidly built, and Nancy noted that her grey streaked, dark hair must be long for it was rolled into an unusual and attractive style. Plump cheeks and twinkling eyes gave the appearance of humour. Nancy liked her already.

"So, you're the two orphans that the boys talk about."

"We used to be," Dan replied, quietly.

Eliza smiled, she'd heard many tales of these two young people and their determination to be a family and have a home of their own. She noticed they were holding hands under the table, like children unafraid to show their affection for each other.

"Well now, just what did those wild Irishmen send you out here for?" Eliza inquired.

"They didn't send us," Dan replied, "it's Nancy's birthday and we wanted to do something special."

"Bless my soul," Mrs. Marshall clapped her hands gleefully. "How old are you child?"

"Seventeen," Nancy replied, proudly.

"Happy birthday, my dear. I wish I were seventeen again!" Eliza mused, letting her mind wander back through time. "I lived in Nanaimo then. Dad was a coke burner, married at twenty and widowed at twenty-eight." She paused as sad memories flashed past her eyes, then shaking her head almost imperceptibly, she continued. "My, doesn't time fly."

They continued chatting for almost an hour before finally begging their leave. Ignoring Dan, when he requested the bill, Mrs. Marshall called to her brother, Eli Ganner, behind the bar, and introduced him.

"Eli runs the bar and dairy," she explained. "He and his family live just behind the hotel." Eli was of medium build but Dan couldn't help but notice the size and strength of his handshake which told him he was accustomed to hard work.

Eli laughed when the Joyce brothers were mentioned. "Damned wild Irishmen, they should be locked up!"

Leaving their new friends waving from the porch, Dan and Nancy headed off across the tracks to explore the City Gorge Park, with its many attractions. Reading a sign that pointed the way to a whale skeleton, Nancy picked up her pace along the cinder trail never having seen one of the great mammals before. She tugged at Dan's hand pulling him along, then stopped in wonder as they came upon the creature with the huge white bones.

"That's only a small whale, Nan. They're much bigger by the time we take them."

They found a lion trapped in a cage with its eyes dull and pleading. Nancy couldn't bare to look in the rest of the cages, truly understanding how they felt. Farther along the path, they bumped into Frank Merryfield, a former city fireman, known to Nancy from the Occidental.

"Having a day out, Mr. Merryfield?" she asked pleasantly, after introducing Dan.

"Oh no, love, I work here now," he laughed. "I'm the magician!"

"What does a magician do?" she asked.

Frank Merryfield pulled a large coin from his pocket and balanced it on the fingers of his upturned hand. He rolled the coin first one way up his arm, then back to his hand. Tossing it into the air he caught it, then clapped his hands to show it wasn't there anymore.

"But where did it go?" she asked in amazement.

"That's magic!" Frank exclaimed, grinning. Then he tipped his hat, bid them good day, and carried on up the path.

As they strolled arm-in-arm under flowering trees and through walkways graced with multi-coloured blooms and shrubs, they often bent to partake of the fabulous aromas. They heard the happy screams of children and discovered an area with mechanical rides, full of youngsters. After watching their fascinating antics for a while, they moved down to the water and found the refreshments pavilion, the House of Sweets, where they bought five-cent strawberry flavoured ice-cream cones.

Slipping their shoes off they paddled in the cool waters of the Gorge, splashing and laughing like happy children ... the children they had never been.

It was a little past three when they made their way back to the hotel for something to eat. The dining room was very busy with afternoon tea, but they managed to find a table right in the centre area. They spotted some familiar faces, mostly businessmen, one of the city councillors, and a minister. But the one face that stood out from the others was the man at a corner table surrounded by a group of soft-spoken men in business suits.

Suddenly, Nancy realized she knew him. "Look Danny," she whispered, "there's Premier McBride."

Just at that moment, McBride looked up and noticed the familiar-looking auburn-haired girl. Their eyes met for a fleeting second and each nodded a silent greeting. Two of his companions noticed and swung their heads around to see who McBride had acknowledged, nudging the others and displaying evil grins.

Dan was watching and suddenly his chair squeaked as it moved backwards on the polished floor ... his face set in a hard line of displeasure as he came to his feet. Then, he heard the soft voice of Eliza Marshall at his shoulder.

"Don't do it, lad, it isn't worth it," she whispered, laying her hand gently on his arm. "Let me deal with them."

"Damn," Dan growled under his breath, returning to his seat and easing his chair quietly back into place.

Eliza made a suggestion for some light refreshment and they readily agreed. Calling the waitress over to their table, Eliza gave her their order. As she turned to speak to the couple, her attention was disturbed by an arrogant voice calling her over to the Premier's table.

She strode purposefully over to the corner table. This was her house, and she quickly made that plain to the offender by ordering him out of the hotel until he found better manners. There was no argument offered and even the Premier rose from his seat and spoke fiercely to the man. The offender looked at the girl, snickering to himself, and then left the building.

Richard McBride stayed on his feet, offering Eliza a quiet apology, then totally startling everyone by calling out a greeting to Nancy before sitting down.

"Do you know that man?" Eliza asked.

"Yes, I do," she answered, offering no further explanation.

The waitress arrived with their lunch, destroying any further chance for a now very curious Eliza to question Nancy.

Their meal was delicious, as Eliza had predicted. The fresh salmon sandwiches were very tasty, and the fruit pie they shared, was liberally covered with the most delicious cream sauce … a speciality of the chef, they were told. When they finished, Dan called for the server and requested the bill. The girl looked puzzled and admitted that the bill had mysteriously disappeared.

"I'll ask Mrs. Marshall, sir," she said apologetically, then rushed off to find the owner.

Ten minutes later Eliza appeared, grinning from ear to ear, and sat down with them. "I believe you now, Nancy," she whispered. "The Premier paid your bill!"

"That was awfully nice of him," Nancy giggled, looking at Dan, "and he's gone so we can't even thank him." Then changing the subject, she added, "I'm afraid we must be going, Mrs. Marshall. It's almost time to catch the tram."

Eliza enjoyed this young couple and would have liked to spend more time with them. "We'll meet again soon. I do hope your visit was something special for your birthday, dear."

"It certainly was and we will be back, of that you can be sure," answered Dan.

As they left the hotel, Eli called to them from behind the bar.

"They're awfully nice people, Dan," Nancy said happily, clutching his arm as they walked across the street.

At the tram terminus, they met up with a small group waiting to return to Victoria. They discovered they were visitors to the city, horseracing enthusiasts and their wives, here for the big 60-day racing calendar at the Willows Racetrack. They talked of horses and pedigrees, races and feed, showering praise on the beauty of the half-mile Willows track and the wonderful exhibition hall.

"The original hall was a real work of art but it burnt down some years ago," Dan explained. "What you have seen is only a few years old. The original would have been much too expensive to duplicate now with rising costs, so this one is far less grand."

One of the men asked Dan what he did for a living and when he told them he was a whaler a serious expression clouded the man's face.

"That's awfully dangerous work," said one of the women.

"Yes, sometimes," Dan replied, "but the sea is all I know."

They heard the tram in the distance and it arrived a few minutes later. It spewed its load of passengers before moving into the loop and turning, ready for its return to the city. There was a ten minute stopover allowing time for the driver and conductor to take a quick break and have a much-needed drink.

"James Bay via the City," the conductor called ten minutes later and the open-topped tram jerked into motion.

There were only twenty people aboard as the conductor came to collect their fares. Dan described points of interest along the route, much to the delight of the visitors until just before crossing the Ellice Street Bridge, he told of the disaster many years before when this same bridge had collapsed killing scores of people. Seeing the shocked look on the lady's faces, he realized this piece of history had not been in the best taste and he quickly changed the subject pointing to the whaler's dock down the inlet.

Enjoying the interesting information, one of the men offered an invitation to the young couple for a day at the racetrack as their guests. Dan graciously declined, saying he would be out at sea.

"Your wife can join us then," said one of the women, looking inquiringly from one to the other. "My name is Beth Jorgensen and that's my husband, Gus," she continued, pointing to the pleasant-looking man across the aisle who had issued the first invitation. "We're from Seattle and we get terribly lonely after the racing day is over. Perhaps you could join us one evening while your husband is away, Nancy."

Dan's eyes flashed toward Nancy catching the amused twinkle in her eyes. They were obviously thinking the same thing. "That's twice today," he laughed, "Nancy is my sister!"

The group joined in the laughter and Beth tittered at her easy mistake. "I'm so sorry, why don't you join us for supper tonight."

"Sorry again, Mrs. Jorgensen," Dan chuckled. "It's Nancy's birthday and I have something else arranged for tonight."

Led by Gus Jorgensen, they spontaneously burst into a loud rendition of *Happy Birthday*, with other passengers joining in.

"I'm a waitress at the Balmoral Hotel," said Nancy. "You should try us for supper one evening. I'm there until six o'clock.. I'm sure my aunt would love to come to the races, but my day off is Sunday."

"We should be able to work something out, Nancy," said Mr. Jorgensen. "We'll drop by the hotel to see you in a few days."

Reaching their stop, Dan and Nancy disembarked and waved to the others.

"What do you mean you've got something arranged for tonight?" she asked after the tram had gone.

Dan just grinned, his ears picking up the soft hum of nearby voices. Jerking his arm, she repeated her question but he grabbed her hand and they ran down the boardwalk.

Reaching the door, he turned the handle then suddenly spun around and swept her off her feet. Clasping her arms around his neck in surprise, he nudged the door with his foot ...

"HAPPY BIRTHDAY!" came the chorus of voices.

Nancy was stunned and stared disbelieving at the group.

Setting her back onto her feet, Dan grasped her shoulders from behind and kissed her on the cheek. "Surprise," he whispered into her ear, "I love you."

The merriment continued all evening as they partook of the refreshments supplied by Meg and the kitchen staff of the Balmoral. When Nancy cut her very first birthday cake, sharing the first piece with Dan, there were tears in many eyes.

It was still light when the guests began to leave at 9:30. The Skillings and Townends walked with Harry toward the Balmoral, leaving the younger men trying to start Irish Jack's automobile that was refusing to turn over. Taking it in turns, Dan and Tim cranked the handle at the front. Finally, after a great deal of cracking and popping, the engine sputtered into life, much to Nellie's relief. Waving, she quickly climbed aboard and Jack sheepishly drove the chugging monster away.

Dan put his hands through Nancy and Meg's arms and led them back toward the office.

"Thanks for a wonderful birthday. I shall never forget this day as long as I live! The *Belfast* leaves in the morning ... and time has gone by so quickly."

"I know, love, but we're going to share a lot more birthdays and other days in the years to come. I promise each one will be better than the last."

"I just might hold you to that one!"

"You do that and see if I'm not right," Dan replied, winking at Meg.

Chapter 9

At 4:30 the next morning, the ships of the whaling fleet were quietly being readied for their pre-dawn departure. The crew had slept aboard, and now the *Belfast*, always the leader, was first to slip her mooring. With the powerful engine on low throttle, she pulled smoothly away from the dock.

There was a nip in the air as a stiff breeze blew off the water. Rounding the mouth of the harbour, the line of whaling boats faced the open sea and Ned opened the throttle. The signal lights of a navy vessel standing off Esquimalt winked a salute as the first light of dawn began to creep silently along the coastline. Soon, the last glimpses of the city slipped from view and the *Belfast* turned westward into the fogbank while the other boats skirted the coast. An hour later, they were well into the Strait and heading toward the Pacific Ocean.

Ned, directing operations, frowned, and raising his nose, sniffed the air. "THERE ... OUT YONDER ... YES, SIREE, I CAN SMELL 'EM!" he shouted eagerly, over the wind and engine noise, his arm pointing due west.

Dumpy turned the vessel onto a new bearing, trusting the instincts of Ned and his nose.

"GET THE CANNON READY, DANNY," the canny old whaler, yelled. "THEY'RE JUST UP AHEAD."

Dan charged his weapon with powder, setting the long harpoon in the barrel before joining Ned at the rail.

"THERE!" Ned pointed to a spot between the fog and the waves about 500 feet off the bow where he had seen the familiar shadow ripple the surface.

Dan's eyes fastened on the spot, tense with anticipation, his cannon at the ready.

"SHE'S COMING!" Ned just managed to say as the great grey shape burst though the surface, spouting water before it dove again.

The cannon boomed, sending the harpoon swooshing through the air—landing with a thud as it slid deeply into the whale's body. A second thud followed as the bomb tip exploded turning the water instantly red. The *Belfast* gave a mighty lurch as the great mammal in its last throes of life, dove for the deep. The lines twanged tight with the strain, pulling the boat with it for mere seconds before settling back again.

"Good shot, Danny," Ned grunted. "You got him good."

Tim and his crew belowdecks appeared topside having shut the engines down. All hands worked with practiced precision securing the ninety-foot monster while Tim and Dan pumped the carcass full of air. The whale rose to the surface and was soon floating behind the boat secured by its tail.

"GOOD WORK, LADS," Ned called, when they had finished. "LET'S HEAD FOR SECHART."

Sechart, Mackenzie and Mann's westcoast whale processing station, was built deep in the sheltered waters of Barkley Sound. A place the Joyce brothers often deposited their whales. They enjoyed good relations with manager, Willis Balcom, a nephew of the legendary seaman, Sprott Balcom, an old friend of theirs.

With the engines pounding, they made their run for Sechart, hampered by the enormous weight. The fog lifted and away in the distance they could see the last of the whaling fleet making their way up the coast. More than an hour slipped by before they passed Cape Beale and slowly eased the *Belfast* into the dock.

Willis Balcom stood with hands in his pockets watching them tie the whale to the tow ring on the dock.

"That was a damned quick kill!" the manager grunted, as Ned jumped down onto the wooden planking beside him.

Ned smiled, tapping his finger on his nose.

Willis shook his head and laughed. "Don't tell me, smelled it again did ya!" he sniggered.

Pulling out his notebook, the skipper slapped it into Willis' open hand.

"Sign that, lad, it's a Blue," Ned growled, measuring the whale by striding along the dock. When he reached the end, he shouted, "NINETY FEET."

Striding back, he took the book from his friend, leaping back over the rail and onto the ship, winking at his grinning brother. Balcom's men released the whale from the *Belfast* and Tim scuttled away below. In a moment, the engines burst back into life.

"CAST HER OFF!" the skipper yelled, watching Dan untie the lines then leap across the ever-widening gap.

Dumpy eased the *Belfast* around, pointing her bow out of the bay, glancing at Ned for direction.

"STRAIGHT OUT ABOUT FIVE MILES," called Ned, his eyes searching the water ahead. "WE'LL BRING 'EM ANOTHER BEFORE SUPPER!"

Nancy awoke early, dressed quickly, and ran outside onto the dock. The great empty space of the *Belfast*'s berth caused a lump in her throat as she ran to the end of the dock and peered fruitlessly into the distance.

The mocking cry of a score of seagulls and the steady beat of ship's engines moving up and down the inlet brought her back to reality. Finally, a smile brushed her face as she heard Meg calling her to breakfast.

"There's always an emptiness when the men go away," the older woman muttered, sensing the girl's pain, "but we'll get back to normal in a day or two. Ned promised they would be back before winter set in."

Having no desire or time to enter into a conversation about the missing boats, Nancy simply nodded and wriggled into her coat. Giving Meg a quick, affectionate kiss on the cheek, she was gone.

There were very few people stirring in Broughton Street that morning, but those that were, all eagerly waved a greeting to the auburn-haired girl. Dick, the newspaper vendor at the corner of

Douglas and Fort, loudly shouted the headlines as he paced back and forth in his territory.

"TUNNEL THROUGH MOUNTAIN!" he screamed, limping about on his lame leg. Then changing his tone abruptly, he called, "Morning, Miss Nancy."

Entering the side door of the Balmoral ten minutes early, she was greeted by a frowning cook. Putting on the long apron that almost covered her mid-calf length dress, she asked, "Why the frown, Mary, what's wrong?"

"It's Mr. Tabour, lass," she whined. "He's not here yet."

Nancy laughed, filling her hands with cutlery as she prepared to set tables. Hearing this news, she handed them to Dottie, who had just come through the door. "Right, my dear. I'll take over until Mr. Tabour arrives. What do you need to know?"

Mary's face dropped in surprise. "It - it's the lunch menu," she stammered. "Shall we do salmon or lamb?"

"Lamb, Mary, lamb … but make sure you've enough of it," Nancy reminded her. "And do a little salmon, too."

The cook turned back to her kitchen much happier that a decision had been made. Charles Redfern's clock in Government Street rang its half-hour bell as the hotel opened its doors and the early morning patrons streamed in.

At 8:30, as the dining room cleared of the early morning crowd and hotel guests began arriving, Harry Tabour rushed through the door looking flustered and worried. His eyes darted about the room.

Nancy, passing with a tray full of food, snapped, "Go in your office and have a cup of coffee, Harry. Everything's under control."

Harry sheepishly obeyed, glad to be relieved of the responsibility while he nursed his aching head. Passing through the kitchen, he noticed the staff were working efficiently. He went into his office and flopped into the chair. His hand reached into a drawer and removed a bottle. Placing it on the desk, he was removing the cork when Nancy appeared at his door with a tray and a fresh pot of coffee. She slid it on the desk right under his nose, the familiar aroma bringing a wane smile to the manager's lips.

She reached for the bottle of liquor, replaced the cork, and tucking it under her apron backed out of the office. "You've had enough of this for one day, my lad," she admonished him, disappearing around the corner.

Harry reappeared an hour later. He stepped into the dining room and just stood watching. Nancy was chatting with the Wilson brothers, the high-class clothiers who owned W & J Wilson in Trounce Alley. When she noticed Harry, she quickly excused herself and went to join him.

"Food," she whispered, noticing his pallor, "that's what you need!"

"Just toast!" Harry pleaded.

"Come sit down," Nancy ordered, pulling out a chair.

Harry tried to smile as he followed the girl's instructions taking the fresh cup of coffee she offered. The Wilson's were just leaving and stopped for a moment at Harry's table, causing the manager to jump respectfully to his feet.

"That's a smart girl you've got there, Tabour. You'd do well to keep her!" old Mr. Wilson growled, pointing his walking stick at Nancy before slowly and painfully moving away.

Nancy skillfully avoided Harry's questions returning soon with a plate of bacon, eggs, and toast, placing it in front of him. He groaned and looked up to give her an argument, but she had already gone to another table. Smiling guiltily, he changed his mind and picked up the fork.

Later, with a clear head, he knew he should be extremely grateful to Nancy for the understanding she had displayed during his indiscretion. Being an intelligent man, he realized she'd no doubt saved his job from the wrath of the owners who would never tolerate such behaviour.

On the 25th, Nancy got a nice surprise when the Jorgensens called at the Balmoral for lunch. They told her their racehorse *Broom Queen* was racing at the Willows Racetrack on Saturday afternoon and they hoped Nancy and her aunt would be able to attend as their guests.

Confident that Harry would give her the afternoon off, Nancy accepted.

"Our car will come for you at one o'clock," Beth announced, getting directions to the office.

Excusing herself, Nancy returned to work, her head spinning with thoughts of a new adventure. Meanwhile, Gus Jorgensen noticed Harry enter the room and finding out he was the manager, beckoned him over to their table. He introduced himself and his wife, explaining he was a racehorse owner from Seattle and why they were in town. This had the desired effect, obviously impressing Harry.

"You a racing man?" the American asked, already sure of the answer.

"Yes, sir," Harry chuckled. "A punter, but never very lucky!"

"It's nothing to do with luck," snapped Gus. "Sit down and I'll make you a winner."

Gus now had Harry's total attention. He eagerly slipped into a chair at their table, leaning closer to catch every word.

"There's a horse running in the two o'clock race that's a sure winner," Gus whispered

The manager leaned further over the table in his eagerness, hands shaking with excitement as he clasped them in front of him.

"Gus, no!" Beth reprimanded her husband. "Don't tell everyone." Then she reached out to pat her husband's hand, a mischievous twinkle in her eyes. "Weren't you going to ask him if Nancy could have Saturday afternoon off, to go with us to the races?"

Harry's eyes swung from one to the other, hardly able to contain himself. He wiped his mouth catching a drop of saliva before it escaped. He wasn't going to miss this opportunity. "Yes, of course, she can go," Harry whimpered, "just tell me the name of that winner!"

"Be careful, Gus," Beth whispered guardedly, extending the manager's anxiety to breaking point.

"It's alright, sweetheart," her husband chuckled. "If he calls Nancy over and tells her, I'll give him the name of the horse."

Harry almost fell off his chair in his eagerness. Wiping the sweat from his brow with a napkin, he beckoned Nancy over.

112

"Sit down, Harry," she said in a concerned voice, noticing the strain on his face. "What's the matter?"

"I - I ...," he stammered, "you can have Saturday afternoon off!"

Taking the napkin from his hand, Nancy gently brushed the sweat from his eyes, glancing suspiciously at the Jorgensens who were displaying looks of complete innocence.

"Thank you, sir," she whispered. "Now, please calm down."

Not having the time to stay, she tried to keep her eye on Harry from across the room. However, she failed to notice Mr. Jorgensen lean towards him and whisper something in his ear.

"*Bold Ruler* in the 2 o'clock Saturday."

Leaping from his chair, Harry strode across the dining room with long loping strides, quickly disappearing out of the hotel door. Back at the table, the Jorgensen's burst into laughter.

"I sure hope *Bold Ruler* wins on Saturday, dear!"

"Oh, it will!" her husband assured her, "but he won't be getting long odds."

After making sure Nancy understood the arrangements, the still laughing couple left the hotel giving the girl an uncomfortable feeling they'd played some joke on poor Harry.

On Saturday morning, Harry was sitting in his office working on the day's menu when Nancy arrived, humming as she entered the kitchen.

"You sound awfully happy, Nancy!" he called, with a chuckle.

"Isn't she always?" Mary added, walking by.

Going into the staff room, Nancy looked at herself in the mirror and realized he was right ... she was happy today and with good cause. She had never been to a horse race and neither had Meg.

Jessie arrived and standing with Mary and Harry at the kitchen door, watched as the redhead skipped from table to table, setting tables with remarkable speed.

"She's a one-man army!" Harry exclaimed.

"What's she so happy about?" Mary asked.

113

"She's going to the horse races at the Willows," he laughed. "I've given her the afternoon off."

"Nancy, going to the races?" asked Jessie, surprise in her voice.

"Yeah," Mary explained. "It seems those Americans who were in the other day gave her a special invitation. She sure meets some people!"

At noon, Nancy raced out of the side door and into Fort Street. She dodged traffic at Douglas and impatiently waited for the streetcar to rumble by on Government. Turning down the hill to Wharf Street, she easily dodged slow moving traffic but had to jump out of the way when the Metchosin-bound stagecoach barrelled past.

"What took you so long, love!" a grinning Meg asked, as she burst into the office. "I've laid your clothes out on your bed."

Nancy changed quickly, her excited fingers struggling with buttons and ribbon. Carefully smoothing out the wrinkles from her dress, she finally walked out of her room carrying the new, wide-brimmed hat Meg had decorated especially for this occasion.

"Come and relax with a cup of tea while I brush your hair, dear."

With every stroke of the brush, Meg sighed quietly, her eyes misting over as she thought of her affection for this young girl. A few minutes later, a sharp knock on the door quickly brought Meg back to the present and she went to the door. Nancy leapt out of the chair flushed with excitement.

The smiling, neatly uniformed man standing in the doorway was holding a peak cap under his arm. He bowed slightly as he greeted them. "Miss Nancy, Miss MacDonald, I'm Peter, your driver."

"We'll be out in just a moment," Meg replied, peering over her spectacles at the young man who nodded politely.

Nancy picked up her shawl and hat and waited while Meg tidied her own hair, reverently setting her tartan bonnet in place and wrapping a matching shawl around her shoulders before they went out the door. A large, shiny green automobile with its top folded down, stood near the door. Peter was waiting, holding the half-door open. Climbing in, with his assistance, they sank into the luxurious leather seats, looking around them in awe. Several passersby even stopped to watch. Peter climbed in and started the engine which purred into life immediately. Going up to Wharf, he skillfully manoeuvred through the maze of traffic before turning into Fort Street. It wasn't long before they'd left the bustle of the city behind as they headed towards Oak Bay.

He was a talkative young man, full of enthusiasm for the automobile he was driving. He said it was a Dodge Tourer made in Michigan ... Mr. Jorgensen's favourite car.

"You mean he has more than one car?" asked Nancy.

"Oh yes, Mr. and Mrs. Jorgensen own several cars, but this is the one they always travel with."

"Who is Mr. Jorgensen?" Meg asked. "What does he do?"

"He's a shipping line owner, ma'am, but he loves his horses!"

Slowing, they now joined a long line of carriages and automobiles all heading up Cadboro Bay Road. A few blocks further on, they turned into Willows Drive and saw a gate marked *Owners and Trainers*. They were the third in a line of shiny, rather large motors.

"Who's that up ahead of us?" Nancy asked, peering around the driver.

"Some of Victoria's well-known citizens, I grant you, but I'm afraid I don't know their names," Peter answered diplomatically, saluting the gateman as he passed through without question.

The loud speakers were booming out the list of runners in the two o'clock race as he escorted them to the Jorgensen's private box. There were six people there ahead of them and the men rose as Beth made the introductions. There was Terry O'Reilly, an Irish-American with laughing eyes and a wonderful smile, and Bob Leighton, the track manager. They recognized John Bryant, the flyer they had earlier met at The Empress.

"Nice to see you again, ladies. This is my wife, Alys. She's also a flyer," said John, obviously proud of her accomplishment.

"You know each other?" asked Gus.

"Yes, we've met briefly once before," Bryant replied.

"That was the night you were meeting Richard McBride and Charlotte at the Occidental wasn't it, dear?" Alys inquired. "They were very impressed with you, Nancy."

Gus Jorgensen looked puzzled by the conversation relating to the Premier and muttered something under his breath. His thoughts were interrupted by the loud speakers booming out a call for the horses to go to the starting post. A few minutes later, a hunting horn sounded sharply over the buzz of the crowd as a player on horseback led the contestants in a parade past the stands. Bob Leighton excused himself, and O'Reilly quietly slipped away at the same time.

The noise of the crowd settled to a whisper as they watched the racers approach the starting line. Suddenly, the starter's flag dropped and the crowd burst into an ear-slitting roar as the loud speakers boomed, "AND THEY'RE OFF!"

The horses pounded frantically down the track ... jockey's colourful shirts billowing in the wind. The roar of the crowd grew louder and louder as the horses came back to pass in front of the stands ... and then out around the bend once again.

Terry returned, joining Gus and Beth already on their feet, craning their necks for a better view as they shouted excitedly. Two horses were now labouring out in front of the others vying for the lead as they turned into the straightaway. Moisture flying from its nostrils, *Bold Ruler* was still pulling ahead even as he flashed past the winning post.

"*BOLD RULER* BY A HEAD!" the loudspeaker boomed, almost drowned out by the noise of the crowd. "WE HAVE A CLEAR WINNER AND NO OBJECTION FLAG!"

There was a slight pause as the crowd suddenly went quiet, waiting for the official result.

"NUMBER FIVE, *BOLD RULER* WINS THE TWO O'CLOCK RACE!" the voice announced and the crowd again erupted.

"Popular winner," John Bryant exclaimed.

"We won, we won," Alys squeaked excitedly, hugging Meg who stood next to her.

Beth Jorgensen slipped her hand through her husband's arm. "Mr. Jorgensen, you're a marvel at picking winners!"

"Sometimes it's not what you know, my love, but rather *who* you know!" Gus laughed, then turned to Nancy. "How did you like your first horse race, my girl?"

Nancy carefully considered her answer. She had been closely watching people's reactions to *Bold Ruler* being declared winner. "It's terribly disappointing if you don't pick the winner. Look at all those torn up tickets floating in the air," she observed. "Not the way I would choose to spend my hard-earned money."

"It's gambling, lassie, not for us poor folks," Meg enjoined, "but terribly exciting."

"Well, it's about to get more exciting, Aunt Meg," Gus laughed, as he saw Terry hurrying toward them.

John Bryant and his wife left to cash in their winning tickets and stretch their legs, promising to be back for the next race. O'Reilly entered the box, handing Beth two small brown envelopes then left again as quickly as he had arrived.

"Well, my dears, this is what it feels like to win," she laughed, handing each of her guests an envelope.

With surprise, and fumbling fingers Nancy and Meg opened their envelopes to discover they contained some money.

"But how?" Meg asked.

"Gus put a ten dollar bet for each of you on *Bold Ruler* to win at two to one. There should be thirty dollars in each of those envelopes."

"But you shouldn't have …," Nancy began, but was interrupted by the sound of a familiar voice behind her.

"We need you, sir."

Nancy swung around to face Jebediah Judd.

"You too, Nancy!" Jeb snapped. "Bring her along to the stables, Gus." Without waiting for a reply, he turned and hurried back up the aisle. The Jorgensen's seemed surprised at Jebediah's order, but Gus quickly reached for Nancy's arm.

"Come on, and don't lose me," he said, urgently.

For an older man, Gus moved through the crowd very quickly, never once looking back. Nancy clutched the back of his shirt as they dashed out to the stable area.

Jeb was already waiting at the corner and he took Nancy by the arm and spoke urgently to her. "I need you right here," he said. "Somebody's going to try to walk out of this area hiding something that may be quite small. We can use your sharp eyes. There are two lads in the box behind you, they'll help you when you need 'em."

Jebediah left quickly, going out of sight into another box. She heard a gruff voice behind her.

"Hello Nancy, don't look around. It's Sgt. Walker and I have two constables in here. Just call if you need us."

Still mystified, yet remaining calm, Nancy stood absolutely-still hearing Jeb's words rattle in her brain. She was now beginning to deduce some small fragment of sense. *Jeb said someone was going to try to walk out with something ... then it must be small enough to hide on their person. Someone will be nervous and it may be obvious,"* she thought, her eyes wandering up and down the stable block.

She caught the movement of a stable worker carrying a bucket out of a loose box. He passed another man who suddenly slipped his hand into the bucket but kept on walking.

"Now!" Nancy hissed, her heel kicking the door behind her.

Sgt. Walker and his constables emerged, dressed as stablemen.

"Stop the man coming toward us!" she ordered, her eyes following the movements of the stableman who had put his bucket down and was now sauntering nonchalantly toward her. He became very nervous upon seeing the police officers. "And this one, too!" she exclaimed, pointing to a man now only four feet away. The police moved quickly and soon had the two suspects out of sight.

"Go find Mr. Judd, lass," Sgt. Walker urged.

Nancy went up the stable block and quickly found Jebediah talking to Gus. Jeb's eyes were cold and worried as he saw Nancy.

"Nothing?" he asked, his voice almost pleading.

Nancy's smile flashed as brightly as her auburn hair. "We've got them!"

Jebediah yelped with joy, jumping forward to hug the girl. Gus had that look of complete disbelief again.

"You two obviously know each other!" he said, as they hurried down the stable block.

"You might say yes to that," Jeb said, in a serious tone. "Nancy seems to be able to solve mysteries that have me beat!" At the sound of running feet, he turned away to look over his shoulder.

"Damn it, they beat us again!" Terry gasped.

"Not this time, sonny," Jeb laughed. "I brought out my secret weapon!" He watched the confused look on O'Reilly's face with amusement.

"You'll need that bucket," Nancy suggested, nudging it with her toe as they passed. "That's what they used to move whatever it is they're hiding ... look's innocent enough doesn't it?"

Terry stooped to pick up the bucket as the voice of the loud speaker began reading off the names of the horses running in the three o'clock race.

"Damn, if we don't hurry we're going to miss our race!" Gus exclaimed. "Come on, Nancy."

Spinning around, the racehorse owner hurried off towards the grandstand not waiting for a reply. The smiling girl watched him go but made no move to follow.

"Coming with *me* are you?" Jeb asked, winking at the girl.

Entering the last box of the row, they found Sgt. Walker and the constables guarding the two men, one of whom was expounding about justice and being held without reason. He also made it plain that there was going to be a complaint made to the appropriate authorities if he was not released immediately.

Nancy stood just inside the door watching the man, noticing his expensive suit and fancy shirt, but there was something odd about him that her mind couldn't quite grasp. There it was again—the man's left elbow seemed to stay well away from his body, all the time. The only thing that could cause that was pain ... or something held under his arm.

Sgt. Walker threatened them both with jail if they didn't come clean and tell the whole story. Jebediah tried a different approach ... to no avail.

"Any ideas, lass?" he asked, quietly.

"Yes, sir," the redhead purred. "Take that one out of here," she said loudly enough for them all to hear, pointing at the stablehand. "This one is ready to talk."

The well-dressed man gave a vicious laugh of defiance, accompanied by a string of cuss words as the constables removed his partner, whose eyes twitched nervously.

"Now," said the redhead, smiling wickedly at the remaining suspect, "give me your coat, sir."

"No damned way, girl!" he hissed, stepping back against the wall.

Sgt. Walker's body moved threateningly forward. His hands were knotted convincingly into tight fists. The man slowly took off his coat and flung it at the officer's feet.

"Go through it, Jeb," Nancy suggested, "and watch for extra padding in the left armpit." Her eyes never leaving the man's face, she watched as he became noticeably more agitated.

"Nothing!" Jeb muttered. "But yer right about that padding."

"Waistcoat and shirt, please," the girl demanded, calmly. She quickly took a step backwards as the suspect took them off. He flung them past her into the corner, sending a vicious threat in her direction.

Terry O'Reilly, who was quietly watching, recovered the garments and handed them to Jeb. His fingers quickly located the small bottle in the secret pocket under the armpit of the fancy waistcoat.

"Got it, Nancy!" he cried, holding up a small brown bottle. "How the hell did ya know?"

Before she could give him an answer, they heard the loud speaker announce the result of the three o'clock race.

"We've missed it, Nancy," Terry grinned wryly, straining for the name of the winner.

"*Broom Queen* by five lengths," came the announcement, this time barely audible with the noise in the background.

120

Sgt. Walker's handcuffs snapped onto the now much-subdued felon's wrists as he pleaded for leniency, reeling off a string of names apparently involved in the doping of racehorses.

"Take me back to the Jorgensen's box please, Mr. O'Reilly. My aunt will be worried about me," she said, smiling at Jebediah who was holding his bottle of evidence tightly in his hand.

"Do it, lad," the Pinkerton man ordered.

As Nancy and Terry went to leave, she turned to Jeb. "You'll come see me before you leave won't you?"

Jebediah winked.

Returning to the grandstand, they found Meg and the Bryants sitting, but excitedly staring down the track. The Jorgensens were missing.

"There they are!" Terry called above the noise, pointing to the presentation area in front of the stands.

At that moment, Gus and Beth were accepting the winner's trophy from Doctor Kerr, the president of the track. Then, the trainer led *Broom Queen* away, a purple sash now gracing the victorious horse's withers.

"Where have you been?" Meg asked, when she saw Nancy. "I was getting worried about you."

The Bryants, with Meg adding her excited observations, related in great detail how the race had been won.

Terry sat by quietly, trying to work out the connection between Jeb and Nancy. The more he thought about it the less sense it made. *This beautiful young woman is only a waitress, what made old Jebediah think she could catch the horse dopers when they'd eluded capture for so long? Sgt. Walker seemed to have a great respect for her, too.* He was still puzzling it out when the Jorgensens returned.

Beth was giggling excitedly when she and Gus returned to the box. Behind her, Gus' eyes asked Terry a question ... his eyebrows shooting up when Terry answered with a smile and a slight nod.

"Go find Judd," Gus whispered. "Tell him to come to our room at six."

Watching the 4 o'clock race was something of an anticlimax after all the earlier excitement, one horse outclassing the others by such a great distance it was hardly a race at all.

"Shall we go, Gus dear?" Beth suggested, her voice sounding tired.

"Yes, I think we've had enough excitement for one day. You coming with us, Johnny boy? There's plenty of room," he said, turning to the Bryants.

"Thanks, Gus, but we're meeting a flyer from Seattle. Bert Munter … do you know him?"

"Know of him," Gus smiled. "He's a wild one I'm told, but then you're all crazy, you flyers!"

John laughed, fully aware this was a widely held view. "Come back on August 6th, that's the day I fly my demonstration over Victoria."

All the way back into the city Meg chatted incessantly. Her day at the races would remain in her memory for years to come.

"We'd like you both to join us for supper later," Gus announced. Come to our suite at six o'clock. It's just a little private affair, but you have earned it!"

"Oh, please come, it's our last day in Victoria," Beth urged, seeing their hesitation.

"What is your room number?" Nancy asked.

"241," said Beth, sighing as she fell tiredly back against the leather seats.

Back at the Joyce Bros. office, Peter opened the car door and assisted the women as they alighted. Then, he quickly climbed in behind the Tourer's steering wheel and drove away.

A note pinned to their door, fluttered in the breeze, drawing Nancy's attention. Removing the paper, she read it aloud, BIG CATCH FOR BELFAST STOP NEED MANY ORDERS FOR OIL STOP. It's signed, CG … who's CG?" she asked.

Chuckling, Meg unlocked the door and they stepped inside. "Why love, it's the Coast Guard. They must have received a radio message from the boys."

122

"They want more orders for oil … how will we do that?"

"Sit down, dear, and we'll have a cup of tea while we plan it out." Rattling the poker in the still-hot embers, she loaded the stove with wood and coal and the flames soon crackled back into life. She placed the cast iron kettle over the hole to boil while Nancy set cups on the table.

"I shall have to try to get pre-delivery orders," Meg muttered, "a ten-percent discount for paying half now and half on delivery."

"But that means you'll get less money," said Nancy, coming out of her bedroom. She wasn't quite able to grasp Meg's reasoning.

"Not really," Meg smiled. "They must have an awful lot of oil, that's what they're telling me. If that's true the price will drop in October." Nancy looked blank. "By getting the orders locked in now at today's prices, less ten-percent, we will more than likely end up with a better price than the other suppliers."

"Golly, that's clever!" the girl chortled.

The kettle lid began it's incessant rattling as the water started to boil furiously and Meg got up to make the tea.

"It's fairly simple, lass, when everybody's chasing a limited market, the price could drop twenty-five percent, but if ours is pre-sold at a fixed price … we win."

"And if it doesn't?" Nancy asked, thoughtfully.

"They wouldn't have sent that message so soon, it's only June you know," Meg laughed.

At 5:45 pm, they walked toward the harbour noticing there were several large passenger ships tied up at nearby wharves. Crossing the street, they stood in front of the massive stone expanse of the city's premier hotel. Set amid neatly manicured lawns and flower beds brimming with flowers, it was an impressive display for locals and tourists alike. The James Bay streetcar trundled by causing them to momentarily raise their voices as they walked along the pathway and up the stairs of the grand entranceway.

Inside, the smartly uniformed porter showed them to the elevator, although Meg declined and asked for the stairs. Making no sound on

123

the red, thickly carpeted hallway, they moved up the stairs to the second floor. It didn't take long to find Suite 241 and a light knock brought Beth to the door.

Already seated in two deeply upholstered armchairs were Jebediah and Terry O'Reilly, who leapt to their feet to greet them. Two unfamiliar faces were introduced as Bertha Landes, a Washington politician and Mayor George Cotterill of Seattle.

During the meal, Terry and Jeb told the story of their exciting afternoon at the racetrack. They made quite sure everyone knew it was due to Nancy's quick observations that the rascals were finally foiled. Gus and Beth, who hadn't heard the whole story before, listened in amazement.

"I've heard about you twice today, young lady," Bertha Landes said quietly, "once from Charlotte Townend and now from Mr. Judd."

Jebediah slowly laid down his cutlery. Folding his arms across his chest, he said, "Bertha, you have no idea what we owe this young lady. If she ever needs my help, I'd offer it freely."

"Here, here," Gus agreed.

Meg's eyes glowed with pride as she listened to these strangers talking of her Nancy. The room became quiet as if they were waiting for the girl to say something.

"You know, we do have a little problem ... that is if you really want to help," Nancy said, blushing slightly. "We need to sell whale oil ... lots of it!"

"Whale oil!" Gus laughed. "Are you serious, lass?"

The solemn note that had descended on the party was swept away in the burst of laughter that followed. Even Meg smiled at the manner in which Nancy had announced her strange request.

"You heard her," Jebediah growled across the table. "Let's hear your solutions, gentlemen."

"Easy ... ," Gus laughed, "I'll take it all, if you like! How much have you got, lass?"

"We're not sure yet," Meg intervened. "Maybe a thousand barrels, but it's not necessary for you to take them all. However, we will give you a discount, sir."

"Oh no you won't!" Beth laughed. "He'll get rid of them for you. Just tell him how many and the price. Gus can sell snow to the Eskimos!"

After supper, Jebediah finished his story about the men caught at the racetrack. Evidently, they had been sought all over America by the racing association and federal police. The prisoners were already aboard a ship bound for Seattle in the morning and he had been assured there would be no story in the Victoria press. The local police were content to let the Americans deal with their own criminals, thereby saving the city and the racetrack any embarrassment.

When Meg and Nancy finally said their goodbyes, Terry insisted on walking them home. Outside Meg's dimly lit door, he produced an envelope and handed it to Nancy.

"Here's all the information you need on how to contact the Jorgensen's, … telephone numbers, both personal and business, and his home address," Terry explained. Then giving her a wink, he added, "My number is also there, if the need should arise!"

Chapter 10

As the Sunday morning sun began warming the bitter sea breeze, church bells rang through the air, calling worshipers to morning service.

"Would you like to go to church, love?" Meg asked.

"Not really," the girl answered, her mind flashing back to the orphanage. "But please don't let me stop you, Aunt Meg."

"Just for me, Nancy. I really don't want to go alone!"

Nancy looked puzzled, wondering why Meg would suddenly get the urge to attend a service amongst all those miserably serious faces that people seemed to wear when attending church. She remembered well how she'd been forced to go as a child and those fierce-looking clergy still frightened her. The orphanage had been run by church people and a shudder ran through her body just to think about it.

"We've such a lot to be thankful for," Meg whispered. "I think we should go."

"If you really want to," the girl said, showing little enthusiasm. "I suppose we could thank the Joyces ... and my Danny, too."

"You're right, lass. We'll visit St. Andrews ... you'll need a hat."

Still not sure she liked the idea, Nancy dutifully followed along with Meg. They walked up Broughton Street toward Douglas. As they came closer, she hung back a little to observe the congregation filing in through the three large doors of the Presbyterian church. A strange chill went through her body which she tried to ignore.

"Look at them," she whispered, "they don't look happy at all!"

"Then you smile for everybody," Meg said sharply, steering the girl through the imposing entrance.

Nancy noticed an empty pew near the back and headed for it. "I'm not going any closer," she whispered defiantly, a note of panic in her voice.

The centre area was almost filled when someone closed the doors causing Nancy to swing around nervously as the daylight disappeared. As the first hymn was announced, Meg opened the hymn book they were sharing and the organist touched the keys bringing the instrument to life.

Voices rose from the congregation and a now more-relaxed Nancy began to sing, losing herself in the tune and the words. The auburn-haired girl's voice soon rose above all the others—crystal clear and sweet. Meg listened in amazement, never having heard Nancy sing before. The minister smiled over his hymn book, looking in their direction, and many heads turned to follow his gaze.

Later, as the minister delivered his sermon, she found herself agreeing with this fierce-looking man of the cloth and his notions of how good Christians should behave toward their fellow man. A wry smile danced about her lips as she listened to the minister's strong Scottish accent. *Maybe Aunt Meg feels more at home here.*

As the strains of the last hymn drifted away, a hushed murmur went through the audience as the organist rose and turned slowly toward the congregation. Gazing out past the faces to the back of the church, he smiled and bowed slightly. He'd played this hymn hundreds of times before but had never enjoyed it as much as today.

The minister stepped back into his pulpit and smiling through his neatly trimmed beard looked out into the audience. He spoke slowly and his voice thundered around the stark columns. "It appears we have a visitor today and we sincerely hope she will come and sing with us again."

A murmur ran through the congregation as everyone turned … just in time to catch the flash of red hair as the visitors quickly left through the door behind them. Nancy, blushing with embarrassment, grasped Meg's arm and hurried her up the street.

"Where in heaven's name did you learn to sing like that?"

"I don't know, I just sing. I knew those hymns from going to the Iron Church as a youngster, but I've never had a reaction like this before! I'm sorry I spoiled it for you, Aunt Meg."

"Lassie, it was worth it just to hear you sing!"

127

That afternoon, Meg had some contracts to work on and suggested to her young companion that it would be an opportune time for her to begin learning about business ... learning contract work might help her find a better job one day. She explained the legality and binding factors on each of the parties involved and where the advantages lay for the Joyce's in pre-selling their whale oil production. She also remembered to emphasize the importance of the agreement Gus Jorgensen had offered.

Nancy learned quickly and once she grasped the principal of writing a contract, Meg went on to explain how their accounts were kept—expenses and orders all in separate books. The girl watched with interest, her eyes darting over the long columns of figures. She suddenly pointed to an entry in the expenses book.

"Irish whisky!" she exclaimed. "That's a business expense?"

"Gets cold out on the water!" Meg laughed at the eagle-eyed youngster.

After supper, they decided to go for a walk up Fort Street.

"I like window shopping, don't you, Aunt Meg?

"Window shopping ... I've never heard that expression before!"

"I just made it up. It seems appropriate, don't you think? The stores are closed so we can only pretend we're shopping!"

As they walked, they chatted about the property at Gordon Head and what it would be like to live in the country, in their own home.

"I don't remember ever living in a real house," Nancy sighed. "I wonder if I ever did? I so wish I could remember my life before the orphanage." They were now walking along a residential street and Nancy stopped in front of a recently completed larger home, studying it carefully.

"Someday, you and Dan will build a fine house at Gordon Head, lassie," reminded Meg. "Don't you fret about the past, it's the future that matters now."

As they turned for home, a buggy drew into the curb and stopped beside them.

"Good evening, ladies," Jack Duggan addressed them. "Can we give you a ride somewhere?"

"Hello, Nellie," Meg responded. "Nice to see you again."

The Duggan's had soon coaxed Meg and Nancy into the buggy and as the horse pulled away from the curb, he asked about the whalers and wondered when the *Belfast* was returning. The conversation eventually led to the races at the Willows. Nellie was spellbound when Meg told them of being invited there by an owner who won the big race of the day.

"We were there, too," Jack muttered, "watching from the terrace."

"You mean ...," Nellie interrupted, enviously, "you were there with Mr. Jorgensen, the owner of *Broom Queen?*"

Meg nodded, and slipping her arm around Nancy's waist, she said proudly, "We had supper with them in their room at The Empress afterwards. They're friends of Nancy and Dan's."

"Whoa, Dolly!" Jack called to the horse, pulling back on the reins until the buggy stopped.

"You mean you know him that well, Nancy?"

"Oh yes, they're just nice ordinary people."

"Ordinary, my foot!" Jack chuckled. "He's a multi-millionaire!"

"We should call over at Harry Maynard's and tell him," his wife chortled. "He'll be green with envy!"

"Right," Jack muttered, clucking to the horse to start moving again. "Are you girls in a hurry?"

Settling back in the comfortable seats, the buggy picked up speed, slowing slightly to pass an oncoming streetcar before turning onto Ellice Street and the bridge. Silver Spring Brewery's five-storied building quickly came into sight with its four-foot-high letters painted on the front. Jack swung the buggy into the brewery yard and past the main building, coming to a stop in front of a well-hidden, private home. He jumped down to tie the horse to the hitching post and then offered a hand to the women.

"Go ring the bell, Nellie," he ordered his wife.

"You don't need to Jack Duggan, we know you're here!" Harry called, from the corner of the building. "Bit late for visiting, isn't it?" he asked, his eyes twinkling with fun. "You're always welcome though Nellie, come on in … and who are these lovely ladies? What a pleasant surprise. Come in and meet our Millie."

The door swung open and a small women stepped outside greeting Nellie with a warm hug. Once inside, Jack introduced them, explaining how they had come upon their friends while out riding.

"It seems like I've seen you before," Millie commented, showing them into a large sitting room with many comfortable chairs.

"I work in the Dining Room at the Balmoral," Nancy offered.

"No," Millie murmured, "didn't I see you at the Willows Racetrack on Saturday?"

"That's very possible," Meg intervened, knowing why they were there. "We were guests of the Jorgensens."

Harry Maynard sat bolt upright in his chair. "They're friends of yours?" he inquired reverently, his attention riveted on Meg.

"They're Nancy's friends," Meg laughed. "We were there to see their horse *Broom Queen* win the big race."

Conversation centred on the races for a while as Harry showed off his love and knowledge of the sport, enthusiastically telling them that he, too, owned a horse.

Suddenly his wife burst into the conversation. "You wouldn't be the girl who sang in the Presbyterian Church this morning, would you, Nancy?" she asked. "You know, Harry, the one Mary Osborne described to us."

Harry Maynard stared at Nancy. "Red hair … and beautiful, too!" he mumbled. "Was it you, lass?"

A blush of embarrassment crept over Nancy's face as Meg's hand patted her leg.

"Yes, it was my girl who sang this morning. She does have a lovely voice," Meg answered, proudly.

"Don't be embarrassed, love," Nellie consoled her. "You possess a wonderful gift."

"But I've never sung before. I mean, except as a child in church," Nancy explained, softly. "I don't know what came over me."

"Will you sing for us … now?" Millie begged. "I can accompany you on the piano. Let's just ignore the rest of them and have some fun

… just you and me!" Moving across the room, she swept a lace cover from a magnificent grand piano standing in the far corner of the spacious room, one which no doubt had seen many a concert. She sat down and began to play a few bars of a well-known ballad.

"Do you know this one?" she asked, as the melodic strains of the popular Irish song *Danny Boy* floated through the room. Jack went to stand beside the piano and his rich tenor voice began to hum the tune.

"Do you have the words?" Nancy asked, moving toward the piano.

Mrs. Maynard handed her the music and began to play the song from memory. When Nancy began to sing, it was as if they were being transported to another time and place. Her voice rose majestically, yet gently above Jack's, and all eyes were on the girl as her clear, sweet voice filled the room.

Nellie rose slowly from her chair, dabbed the moisture from her eyes and walked over to her husband who had stopped singing and was now staring at Nancy in disbelief. Slipping her arm around his waist, Nellie gently hugged him, assuming he was thinking of his homeland.

When the song finished, Harry was the only one able to speak. "By golly, lass, you sure can sing!" he exclaimed. "I don't make any wonder the churchgoers were surprised." Then noticing his wife was still facing the piano, he asked, "You alright Millie, love?"

His wife slowly turned around and he could see that her face was flushed. "I have never heard that song sung so beautifully," she whispered, emotionally. "If that comes naturally, Nancy Wilson, what a marvelous gift you possess!"

The emotion in the room was so strong no one else spoke for what seemed an eternity.

"Would anyone like a drink?" Harry asked, breaking the silence.

"A big one!" Jack muttered, watching his wife and Millie nod their heads.

"And what would you ladies like to drink?" Harry inquired, turning to Nancy and Meg.

"A scotch for me, please," said Meg, "and tea for Nancy."

"Tea?" the host grimaced.

After refreshments were served and their drinks finished, Nellie reminded her husband that it was time for them to go if they were to get home while there was still daylight.

"You will come again won't you ladies. You're always welcome in our home," Millie said, with a warm smile, as they collected their wraps.

"Yes, ma'am, we will," replied Nancy. "We need to sell you some oil."

"What sort of oil," Harry asked. "Is this another surprise?"

"Whale oil, sir, from the Joyce's," Nancy replied, seriously. "You own the brewery don't you?"

"Yes," Harry's voice faltered, "and we do use a lot of oil."

"Then we have a deal for you," Nancy announced, confidently. "If you order now and pay for half of it, we'll give you ten-percent off today's price ... with final payment and delivery in November."

"My goodness!" Harry muttered. "What a salesman ... pardon me, I mean saleswomen! Come see me tomorrow, lass, we'll take forty barrels and I've a job for you ... ever tried selling beer?"

"No, no!" Nancy laughed. "I don't need a job, but my aunt will write up the contract if you come down to the Joyce Bros. office on Wharf Street."

"I'll be there tomorrow morning," Harry assured them.

Jack and Nellie Duggan sat patiently in the buggy noting the manner in which Nancy handled her sale. Nancy helped Meg climb into the conveyance but hesitating, she turned back to Millie and gave her a hug, thanking her for her hospitality and her piano playing. Then aided by Harry, she climbed aboard.

"NANCY!" he shouted, as the horse began to pull away. "Come and visit us again ... soon."

It only took ten minutes to reach the office.

"You certainly made an impression on the Maynard's dear, though it doesn't surprise me a bit,"Nellie said softly. She pulled the carriage door closed and they began to move off.

132

"Come sing for *me* sometime, Nancy," Jack called over his shoulder, but the sound of the horse's hooves was all the women heard as the carriage disappeared up the street.

Lights were beginning to glow on the ships anchored in the harbour creating an almost fairy-like scene with reflections dancing off the calm water.

"My goodness, what a weekend we've had," Meg murmured tiredly, turning the key in the lock.

"Evening, ladies," a voice came from the shadows, startling them.

"Jeb!" Nancy exclaimed, in shocked surprise, as the familiar shape appeared. "What are you doing here?"

"Bad news, I'm afraid," he growled. "Let's step inside."

Once inside, Jeb stood with his back to the door. Solemn faced, he tilted his hat to the back of his head and told them one of his prisoners had escaped. Seems he had jumped overboard as the ship left port that morning.

"But he'll drown, it's cold in these waters," Meg predicted.

"We don't think so," Jeb said, shaking his head in a worried manner. "I've learned this chap is quite a swimmer and this was the closest shore."

"So," Nancy said, slipping off her coat, "you think I'm in some sort of danger from this man?"

"Don't know that for sure," he growled, "but I can't take a chance."

Meg sighed and flopped into a chair, holding her head in her hands. "You have to protect her, Mr. Judd," she moaned, "or Danny will kill somebody."

"Don't worry, Miss MacDonald. You'll both be guarded night and day until we catch him."

With his hand on the door, he suddenly turned back to face the women, a smile playing about the corners of his mouth.

"He should be easy to spot," he said, gruffly, "he's missing the little finger and half the next one from his right hand and covers it up by wearing a glove." He paused, watching Nancy's reaction. "So keep your wits about you, girl. I know you can do it ... and remember there

133

will be someone close by if you need him." Pulling his hat down, Jeb opened the door and stepped out into the evening's fast fading light.

"Lock that door, Nancy!" Meg snapped, urgency in her tone. "We're not taking any chances starting from now."

Just before six the next morning, they were eating breakfast when Nancy realized her aunt was already dressed and acting very edgy.

"What's the matter, Aunt Meg?"

"I'm going to walk you to work!"

"No, you're not," the girl said gently, going to stand behind the older woman's chair. She wrapped her arms around Meg's neck and hugged her. "Aunt Meg, I love you," she whispered, gently kissing her wrinkled cheek, "you're the closest thing to a mother I'll ever know, but you have to stop worrying. Jeb promised to take care of us." Then, with another quick kiss on Meg's now tear-stained cheek, she swept up her coat and ran out the door.

The week thankfully passed uneventfully, except for Harry Tabour talking about his big win at the racetrack. He seemed to find great delight in telling everyone he was a friend of Gus Jorgensen's, the American owner of *Broom Queen*. It was harmless chatter and Nancy paid him no heed, as he impressed friends and patrons with the story. Jebediah appeared many times during that week, always watching from a distance but letting Nancy know he was nearby.

On Sunday, Meg decided the sunshine gave them a good excuse to begin a cleanup of the office. This had been neglected as she spent her time compiling lists of whale oil orders. In the meantime, Nancy was having great success selling the product to many of her acquaintances and admirers.

Waldo had been a tremendous help, bringing in many orders for them and Harry Maynard, true to his word, had given them a large order also informing his fellow brewers of the good deal to be had at the Joyce Bros. wharf. This resulted in another large order from the Victoria Phoenix brewery.

By eleven o'clock in the morning, both the inner harbour and Victoria Arm were alive with swimmers and boaters enjoying the lovely summer weather. Meg finished cleaning the floors and together they wrung out the big mop laying it neatly on the dock to dry in the sun. Then, each holding onto the handle of the heavy steel bucket, they threw the dirty water into the sea. Setting down the bucket, they stood to watch as a team of rowers went by, gliding gracefully through a light ripple on the waters of the Arm.

Suddenly, a silent hand reached up and grabbed the side of the dock a short distance away. The other hand quickly followed and a man's wet, but fully clothed, body slowly materialized behind them.

Catching the movement out of the corner of her eye, Nancy grabbed the heavy steel bucket and quickly moved a step closer to the intruder. Swinging it with all her strength, it crashed against the side of the man's head as he rose to his feet. A rush of air escaped his lips as he went sprawling, lifeless, onto the dock, bleeding from a wicked cut on his forehead. Grabbing a nearby rope, Nancy quickly tied his hands behind his back, then trussed up his feet as best she could.

By this time, Meg was coming to her senses. "My Lord, what are you doing? Do you know this man?" she asked in alarm.

"Look at his right hand," the girl said, breathlessly. "It's Jeb's missing prisoner!"

Peering closely at the unconscious man's hand and trying not to notice the blood, the older lady gasped. "Now what do we do? He's bleeding badly," Meg asked frantically, totally confused by the sudden turn of events.

"First, you calm down, Aunt Meg! He'll live," Nancy assured her. "Go to the office and find something big and red, a piece of cloth or something."

"What am I going to do with it?"

"You're going to wave it to attract attention and get us some help!"

"Attract whose attention?"

"Just do it, Aunt Meg. Do it now, please!"

Shaking her head in confusion, the Scottish woman hurried to the office, found a red cloth and going to the corner of the building began waving it wildly in all directions. She was surprised by the instant

135

reaction it invoked from two nearby figures as a city policeman and a stranger ran across Wharf Street toward them. She pointed to the end of the dock where Nancy stood and the men tore past her. Skidding to a halt in front of the prone swimmer, the policeman looked at Nancy inquiringly.

"Look at his right hand," she said, excitedly. "It's the missing prisoner."

Meanwhile, the second man quickly produced his wallet showing the constable his identification. Just then, the prisoner began to groan. Together, the two men untied him, fastening handcuffs to his wrists before roughly dragging the bleeding and dazed criminal to his feet.

"Well done, lass!" the policeman commented, admiringly.

"I'll tell my boss, Mr. Judd, that *you* caught him single-handed!" the American drawled.

Picking up the rope, the Pinkerton man threw a loop around the stumbling swimmer's neck.

"No, no sir, you can't do that!" the constable objected.

"Oh yes, I can," he growled. "I'll hang the dog if he tries to run! This one has caused us enough trouble already." Still arguing, the officers led the man away.

Nancy gently put her arm around her aunt. "There, there, it's all over, Aunt Meg. You can stop worrying now. Come on, I'll make you a nice cup of tea and you'll feel better."

Knowing the cup of tea would do the trick, Meg began to relax, laughing as she told Nancy how determined she had looked when she hit the man. "I should have realized what was happening but when you hit him I was so shocked I couldn't move!"

"There was hardly time to explain!" Nancy giggled.

The Scot sipped her tea then setting the cup slowly onto its saucer, she sighed. "I'm certainly glad you were alert to the danger. Jack Duggan was right, you are full of surprises!"

"Let's get changed and go for a walk in the park. We deserve it!" Nancy suggested. "The city workers have finished putting up the new streetlights this week ... the ones with the five globe clusters. Folks are calling them Morley's folly but I quite like them. They give the city an old-fashioned look."

It was almost mid-afternoon before they stepped out into the summer heat. Their wide-brimmed straw hats with flowers all around made them look quite the ladies of fashion. They picked up their parasols and went out the door. As they started up the boardwalk, a small automobile pulled up to the curb and sounded its horn. Jebediah waved to them. After extracting his long legs from the small Ford, he leaned against the car smoking his pipe and waiting for them.

"Well, you did it again, lass!" he laughed.

"Did what?" Meg asked, cautiously.

"Got me out of trouble by doing my job for me ... and this time with a bucket! You know, that rogue still can't focus his eyes straight, you must have hit him awfully hard!" he laughed, banging his fist on the side of the car. "You had the whole damned city police force howling with laughter when my man told them how you captured him with a mop bucket! They even forgot to confiscate it as evidence!"

Jeb's laugh was infectious and soon Nancy and Meg had joined in.

"I just had to come and see that you were both alright, and to thank you again, love. You really are my good luck charm!" He hugged both women, kissing Nancy on the cheek, then climbed back into his car and noisily drove away.

"Now that's a man who knows how to have a good laugh," Meg said thoughtfully, watching the car disappear.

Still chuckling, they walked up Fort Street turning south at Government and going past The Empress, noting the steady stream of cars and horse-drawn carriages entering and leaving both doors of the now-famous hotel. They continued on to Beacon Hill Park stopping for a rest under a willow tree beside beautiful Goodacre Lake. Many of the sleepy-eyed ducks were already out of sight seeking whatever shade they could find from the hot sun.

In the distance, they heard the roar and clapping of a crowd. Deciding to investigate, they made their way toward the noise, coming to a grassy field down toward Dallas Road. Standing out in the middle of this field were a group of men dressed completely in white.

"What are they doing, Aunt Meg?"

"Cricket," came a voice behind them. "There's been a man out, caught by square leg."

"Did he say, there's a man out there with a square leg?" Nancy laughed, turning again to Meg.

"No, no!" the voice replied, sharply. "He doesn't *have* a square leg, he *is* a square leg! Look, there he is talking to the silly-mid-on."

The women's eyes met and Nancy stifled another giggle. Off to one side, another man in white carrying a flat, wooden bat, came out of a small building and walked out into the middle of the field. He went to stand in front of three, tall wooden sticks sticking out of the ground. He stood still for a moment, looking all around him, then shouted something that sounded like, "TWO LEGS, UMPIRE."

"He says he's got two legs!" Nancy said, growing more puzzled.

"Well, I can see he's got two legs!" Meg grunted in frustration.

Suddenly, one of the men on the field began to run toward the man with the bat, flailing his arms about as he did so. Then he stopped sharply and hurled a ball at him, knocking one of the three sticks clean out of the ground. They could hear a voice yell from out on the field but couldn't make out what was said. Then, the batsman walked back to the little building.

"Oh, my," Meg whispered. "That wasn't very nice of him was it? He's not going to play now. Come on, love, we don't want any part of this silly game."

"That's cricket, madam!" came the sharp voice again.

Meg had had just about enough. She spun around and faced the speaker, a well-dressed man of about 45 years, threatening him with her raised parasol. In surprise, the man jumped back, losing his straw hat. But the undaunted Scottish woman confronted him fiercely.

"Young man, if you say one more word, I'll cricket you! If you had any sense at all you'd go out there and stop that man throwing balls at people, he's going to hurt someone!" Finished her tirade, she

138

glared up at him, picked up her skirts and hurried past with Nancy close behind, grinning foolishly.

"Slow down, Aunt Meg," she called, grabbing her by the arm.

"I won't be watching that silly game again," she declared. "It's worse than that tennis game where they call each other love, even the men!"

Nancy wasn't about to tackle this subject so she merely took Meg's arm and led her back towards the city. At the harbour, an open-topped Model A honked its horn going in the opposite direction. The driver waved madly at them.

"Who was that?" Meg asked, waving the fumes away.

"It was Waldo, I think."

A church bell began ringing its announcement of a six o'clock service.

"Shall we go to church tonight?" Meg asked, casting a hopeful glance at the girl.

"Alright, if you like. Can you manage waiting for supper?" Nancy asked, thoughtfully.

"Oh yes, I'm not hungry yet. We can have a light supper later on and we won't be late."

"Let's take a quick walk to The Empress' greenhouse. The flowers will be marvelous right now."

In a few minutes, they were resting on a low wall at the rear of the hotel and peering though the glass of a large glass structure. It was a wondrous sight and Nancy told her that many people came specifically to see this impressive display with its hundreds of tropical blooms.

Meg gasped at the beauty, but the peeling church bells seemed to be beckoning. "Time to go," she announced.

They found the pathway that took them quickly to Douglas Street and headed up the hill to St. Andrews.

They were last through the doors before they thudded to a close. They quietly took a seat near where they had sat on their earlier visit. The minister, behind his pulpit, peered through his spectacles desperately trying to adjust to the dim light and see who sat at the

139

back. As the organist began to play the opening hymn and the congregation began singing, a smile crossed the minister's face as he heard the familiar sounds that told him she had returned.

Returning to his pulpit after the hymn, he introduced a guest minister from Seattle who was giving the sermon tonight. The Reverend Mark Mathews was a powerful speaker, full of fire and brimstone as his voice thundered off the walls and pillars, denouncing the demon drink ... alcohol.

"Prohibition, that's what we need!" he ranted, working himself into a frenzy by the end of his monologue. He climbed down from the pulpit sweating profusely, but not before announcing the next hymn.

The organ's thick tones began to fill the church but the congregation only murmured the words, waiting for Nancy's voice to again take up the tune. But her lips remained closed, not a sound escaped as she stared blankly ahead. Closing the service with a prayer, the resident minister was now appearing quite perplexed and when he looked up again, the girl had disappeared.

Rushing Meg out onto the sidewalk, Nancy hurried up the street not turning to look back until she reached Gordon Street.

"Whatever is wrong, lass?" Meg asked, catching her breath.

"I had the strangest feeling of doom, Aunt Meg. That man spells trouble and I didn't like him at all!"

"Is that why you wouldn't sing?" Meg chuckled, slipping an arm around the girl's shoulders and watching her nod. Meg had her own thoughts about this Rev. Mathews. She was pretty sure she had read something about him in the newspaper recently.

Surprisingly, they walked the rest of the way home in silence. Meg wondered how good a judge of character Nancy was and vowed to herself that when she heard the name Rev. Mark Mathews the next time, she would not forget it.

Chapter 11

Weeks flew by and the orders for oil just kept increasing. Meg was beginning to worry that they had over-sold and wouldn't be able to fill the orders that took up page after page in her book. But Nancy had confidence in her aunt's original plan and over Sunday dinner at the beginning of August, they voted to continue.

At the Balmoral, excitement had been mounting over John Bryant's scheduled flying demonstration on the 6th, and now the day had finally arrived. From about 4:30 in the afternoon, people abandoned whatever they were doing and poured into the streets until a huge crowd had gathered around the harbour to watch the Curtiss biplane take off. At 5 o'clock, word arrived that Mr. Bryant was checking out his plane for takeoff. Then, at 5:20, someone ran into the street and shouted, "He's ready!"

Instantly, the hotel cleared and everyone rushed out into the street to watch. In the distance, they could hear the roar of an engine in the harbour. The crowd went silent and everyone knew Bryant was trying to lift his plane off the water. Then, the crowd went wild as the small plane lifted higher and higher. Visible to all, it swept out over Victoria West gaining altitude as it turned back, circling the city and the enthusiastic crowd. The crowd now watched with bated breath as the little plane went into a steep dive. From Nancy's vantage spot it seemed to be right over City Hall and the crowds again yelled their encouragement.

Suddenly, disaster struck. The tiny plane wasn't coming out of its dive. It kept plummeting toward the rooftops. First, one wing crumbled, sending pieces floating through the air as if in slow motion. The now hushed crowd watched in shocked disbelief as the plane began to spin uncontrollably. The horror of the situation now gripped the spectators and many prayed out loud. When they heard the terrible sound of the plane ripping through the roof of a building, a thousand sighs left the lips of the watchers and they stood silent in their agony. A scream caught in Nancy's throat as John's fate became clear and she covered her face with her hands as tears stung her eyes.

Harry checked his watch, a nervous habit he always had when his mind was disturbed. It was a little after six o'clock and everyone knew John Bryant was dead.

August 6th would be recorded as a sad day in Victoria's history and there were many moist eyes among the witnesses. The crowd slowly dissipated as people returned to their businesses and Nancy wiped her tears and went slowly back inside the hotel.

News came shortly before she left for home ... the plane had plunged into the roof of the Lee Dye Building in Chinatown, a soap factory, killing the 26-year-old pilot ... a pleasant young man she had known so briefly.

The next day, the local newspapers were full of the story of the tragedy blaming the mayor and council for allowing the flight to take place. Arguments raged all over the city, in bars, and on street corners.

"Unnatural," said Meg sadly, "it should never have been allowed."

Harry Maynard called in a few evenings later while out delivering some orders. He expressed his views on the merits of flying and the conversation naturally turned to John Bryant.

"You know, John used to say that someday we'll see those flying machines all over the sky. Hard to believe, but perhaps he was right. Look at the automobile. Soon everybody will own one. The days of the horse and buggy appear to be numbered."

Harry Maynard intrigued Nancy. Never timid to expound his visions of the future, his views were always interesting and made Nancy think of the years ahead. It had been Harry, in part, who had encouraged them to continue taking oil orders. His thoughts on whaling were controversial ... he always said they were taking too many, just as Ned did. Each year he predicted it would be their last good year. Meg, forever loyal to the Joyce boys, had laughed at the brewer's comments as she quietly sipped her tea, dismissing them as impossible.

But Nancy now listened thoughtfully to this man who had built Silver Springs Brewery with skill and integrity, gaining the respect of the city's most successful businessmen. An unseen bond had grown between Harry and this young girl ever since the night she sang at his home. He had become very fatherly as he talked of his own start in business. He told her that as a young man he had worked for Joe Loewen and Ludwig Erb, at the Victoria Brewery on Government Street. They were now his good friends and competitors. Hard work always paid off, he said. He had heard about Nancy's work and knew that this girl was going to be a success at whatever she did.

Out on the Pacific, the crew of the *Belfast* worked the sea for nearly three months as only the Joyce crew could. They took whales with startling efficiency, always patrolling the outer limits of the fleet. Using Ned's instinct and his powerful nose, they amassed a record total of kills in the 1912-13 season. This was the best year the *Belfast* had ever had on the westcoast and the Joyces put much of their success down to their skilled gunner, Dan Brown.

Then, in a wild September storm, they turned northward after completing arrangements with the Pacific Whaling Company agent in Rose Harbour. Ned, always concerned with the speed at which they were killing off the whales, suggested to his friend, Bill Grant, a company executive, that they should limit the kill to preserve the numbers for other years.

Bill merely laughed. "Make hay while the sun shines lad ... it won't always be so good."

Meg and Nancy often rented the horse and buggy and visited the Gordon Head property that summer. They loved to sit near the edge of the cliff and look out at the sea trying to imagine what it would be like to live there and have this wonderful view every day.

They also enjoyed the ride through Beacon Hill Park and around Dallas Road to the borders of Oak Bay returning to James Bay to check on the building of the massive 2,500 foot dock and breakwater at Ogden Point. It was a huge project and the local newspapers reported it would take three to four years to complete. The building of a deepwater dock was the brainchild of Senator Harry Barnard, the newspapers loudly proclaimed. Victorians chuckled when they read this knowing the Daily Colonist and Victoria Times weren't always so kind to the dear old senator.

City elections were coming soon and many would-be politicians were trying to excite their supporters. As usual, Charlotte Townend was in the centre of things. She often called to visit Nancy attempting to persuade her into promoting her candidates among the hotel patrons.

Much to the amusement of Waldo Skillings and Harry Tabour, Nancy resisted Charlotte's attempts to involve her in the political scene. However, she did agree to sing at a rally Charlotte was holding in aid of Alexander Stewart and two other candidates. They were all patrons of the Balmoral and according to Charlotte, Mr. Stewart was highly regarded as an upstanding citizen. Nancy made only two conditions ... that Millie Maynard play the piano and Meg be invited to attend.

On the evening of Friday, October 24th, Charlotte's rally was held in the Odd Fellows Hall on Douglas Street. Nancy and Meg were asked to arrive at nine o'clock when the politics and speeches would be finished and everyone would be ready for some socializing.

"Are you nervous?" Meg asked, as they walked along Douglas.

"No, all I'm going to do is sing," she chuckled, "and sell whale oil!"

"Don't you dare!" Meg cried.

They were interrupted when two male figures stepped from the shadows in front of them. "Spare a copper for a hungry miner, Miss Nancy?" asked one of the dark figures.

"Now then you two!" the authoritative voice of Sgt. Walker boomed from further up the street as he came running to their assistance. The dark figures turned away but the big city policeman managed to grasp them by their collars.

"Wait a minute, please Sergeant," Nancy cried. "Who spoke my name?"

Moving closer, she peered into the dirty, whiskered face of the old man. "Is that you, English Jack?" she gasped, "or am I dreaming?"

Wriggling, he tried unsuccessfully to escape the strong hand of the Sergeant.

In desperation, Jack pulled off his cap. "It's me, lass. It's Jack. Tell 'im to let us go," he pleaded.

"Let them go please, Sgt. Walker. I know this one."

Reluctantly, the policeman released his grip on English Jack's coat collar allowing the old man to face them ... none too steadily. He continued his hold on the second man.

Moving closer, she whispered, "Are you alright, Jack?"

"We haven't eaten for four days, lass," the other one moaned.

Nancy reached into her bag, pulled out her purse, and extracted a ten dollar bill.

"Whatever are you doing, love?" Meg asked. "Don't give them your money."

"Hush, Aunt Meg, I'll explain later," said Nancy, holding out the ten dollar bill to the policeman. "Can you see they get some food, Sergeant, then lock them up for a day. You can send them back to me at seven tomorrow night," she giggled, watching the dismayed look on the old man's face.

"Humph," Sgt. Walker growled. "This is highly irregular, Miss Nancy." Scowling fiercely, the city policeman looked at the men and then back to Nancy before continuing. "But for you, Miss, I'll do it!" Reaching for the ten dollar bill, he slipped his hat off, dropped the ten dollars into it and set it firmly back on his head. "Come on, you two scallywags," he muttered, catching hold of Jack's collar again.

Across the street, Charlotte stood in the doorway of the Odd Fellows Hall with a group of her followers, watching the fascinating scene across the street.

"What was that all about?" Charlotte inquired suspiciously, when they arrived.

"Oh, just an old friend saying hello," Nancy answered, lightly.

145

Charlotte smiled, disbelieving, yet knowing when to stop prying, and she hurried them up the stairs to the waiting group. A sudden quiet fell over the meeting room when they walked in. Millie Maynard waved from the raised stage, already sitting at the piano. She was very eager to hear Nancy sing again.

"Give me your coat, love," said Meg, hanging it over her arm. Then she found a chair near the back of the hall and watched proudly as the auburn-haired girl tossed her head confidently and followed Charlotte up to the stage, waiting as she held up her arms for silence.

"Ladies and gentlemen," she began. "Most of you know Nancy Wilson from the dining room at the Balmoral. Well, tonight she is going to show us another of her talents and sing for us. Let's give her a nice welcome."

Light applause sounded as she stepped forward, her eyes searching the crowd and finding Meg.

"Good people," Nancy addressed them confidently, "would you allow my Aunt Meg to come and sit up here with me?"

Instantly, an older gentleman handed his chair onto the stage, while another escorted the blushing Scottish lady to her new seat. Nancy's eye caught sight of Harry Maynard sitting half-hidden in the back corner while his wife's fingers lightly caressed the keyboard.

"Good evening, Millie, so nice to see you again," Nancy whispered, accepting the sheet music the pianist handed to her. Nancy quickly looked at the music. The words were familiar and she trusted Millie explicitly. Millie played a lengthy introduction and then nodded at Nancy.

Nancy took a deep breath and began to sing … the sweet, clear tones filling the silent hall with the strains of *Beautiful Dreamer*. Millie marvelled at the girl's ability, never missing a word. As their first song ended, the hall erupted in applause.

"BRAVO, NANCY, sing us a song of the sea," called someone near the back.

Through misty eyes, Millie shuffled through her papers, finally coming up with a single sheet of music which she handed to the girl. She waited for Nancy's signal and then fingers raised she closed her

146

eyes and began to play the introduction. Well-trained fingers easily found the notes for this was one of her favourites and she'd played it hundreds of times. Nancy recognized the *Skye Boat Song* as one Meg often hummed at home. The haunting melody soon had the audience mesmerized. When it was over, Meg and many others, dabbed at their eyes. Bowing to the grateful crowd, Nancy accepted their thunderous applause.

Millie stood up and clapped, too. Hugging her affectionately, she spoke softly into her ear. "You have a gift from heaven, my dear. Thank you for sharing it."

Charlotte sat at the back of the hall watching the audience reaction to her guest. *My gosh, what a drawing card I've found*, she thought, dreaming of political rallies with Nancy singing her heart out.

Nancy walked to the edge of the stage and held up her hand for silence. "Ladies and gentlemen, thank you for inviting me to sing for you tonight." Going over to stand beside Meg, she continued. "My aunt, Meg MacDonald, represents the Joyce brothers and their whale oil business. She would be happy to take any of your orders at her office in Wharf Street during business hours." She walked back to the piano. "Now, if I can persuade Mrs. Maynard, I'll sing you one more song!"

As the enthusiastic clapping subsided, Millie sat down at the piano and quickly selected the perfect song to round off a memorable evening. When it was over, Charlotte dabbed her eyes with her handkerchief and looked around to see many ladies doing the same. Not only was this girl's voice remarkable, but her knowledge of music told her Nancy didn't even know how to read music.

"When are the boys home, Meg?" Harry asked, as they walked outside later.

"Tuesday," said Nancy, with obvious excitement in her voice.

"I'll walk you home," Waldo called, coming up from behind them.

"Thanks for singing, Nancy. It was wonderful," Charlotte gushed, then lowering her voice to a whisper, "will you do it again for me sometime?"

"Of course I will," Nancy replied, giving the woman a hug before turning to her aunt. "Come on, Aunt Meg, I've got to work tomorrow.

Dawn's heavy mist followed the chill of an early October evening, but the bright autumn sun soon filtered through the clouds showing promise of another lovely Indian Summer day. Nancy was glad to be alive. She waved to Meg framed in the doorway and hurried up the street to the hotel. Glancing out past the lighthouse, her pulse began to race as she envisioned Dan aboard the *Belfast* on his way home. Her long auburn hair streaming behind her as she hurried, she returned the greetings of several deliverymen and then caught the shrill cry of the newspaper vendor.

"SING FER ME, NANCY ... YER SO LOVE-LY!"

Waving her fist good-naturedly at the boy, she crossed the road, wondering how Dick had known about her singing. At the hotel, her attention was taken up immediately by the mess left from the night before. *A late party*, she thought to herself, as she grabbed her apron from her locker, pulled her hair up in a knot at the back of her head, and hurried out to the dining room. After she set the last place for breakfast, she returned to the kitchen where cook was waiting for her.

"Didn't tell us you were a singer, did you?" Mary asked.

Puzzled as to how the cook knew, she had no time to answer as the first customer entered the dining room ... whistling one of the songs she'd sung last night. *It's a conspiracy, how do they all know?* she thought, as she placed an order of toast and coffee in front of young Mr. Davis, of Spencer's Store.

"You must have enjoyed yourself last night," he commented, giving her a broad smile.

Puzzled, she followed his glance to the headline of the Daily Colonist laid on the table in front of him. "MINER STRIKE GETS UNRULY" it said in big bold headlines.

"I don't understand, Mr. Davis," she said, frowning. "How do you know?"

"Why everyone knows, my dear," he chuckled, turning the newspaper to the inside sheet.

There, prominently surrounded by thick black lines was this heading: "WAITRESS TURNS SINGER AT RALLY".

"Oh no!" she gasped, covering her mouth with her hand.

"Nancy, don't be embarrassed," Mr. Davis said kindly, "it says you were a joy to hear." He paused, his eyes examining Nancy in a completely new light this morning. "And I believe them."

Thanking him profusely, Nancy moved away. During the day, many mentioned the newspaper article making her cheeks go pink with each comment. Harry arrived, a little late as usual, and motioned that he wanted to see her in his office. Ten minutes later, when Jessie arrived, Nancy popped her head around the doorway. He sat smiling—the newspaper open at the article about the rally.

"You're a very popular girl this morning, young lady," he chuckled. "This should be good for business today!"

"Is that all you wanted me for?" she muttered, slightly annoyed but knowing Harry really meant it in jest. He shook his head and she hurried off to her chores.

All day the comments were centred on Nancy's singing with many regular patrons expressing their surprise at the newspaper report. Strangers had no trouble recognizing the waitress after the reporter's description that referred to her as the beautiful girl with the flaming red hair. Harry Tabour smiled continually as the crowds filled the Balmoral Dining Room that day, all wanting a glimpse of the singer.

Nancy breathed a sigh of relief at the end of her shift. Weary from lack of sleep the night before and a long day on her feet she headed for home. Walking slowly, her thoughts on Dan as she looked out the harbour, she suddenly remembered English Jack. Meg, standing outside the office talking to a friend, noticed Nancy quicken her pace.

"Did you remember something?" she asked, when the girl arrived.

"English Jack," Nancy murmured. "He's coming tonight."

A frown passed across the Scottish lady's face. Nancy still hadn't explained to her why she was bothering to help the old miners. She was certainly going to find out now, she resolved, as she finished her conversation and followed Nancy into the office.

Chapter 12

After supper they were relaxing with one of Meg's delicious sugar cookies and a cup of tea when Nancy jumped up from the table. She went to her room and returned quickly with English Jack's bag, dropping it onto the table with a thud. Meg's eyes widened as she opened it, recognizing the contents immediately.

"Where in heaven's name did you get all that gold?"

"It's Jack's," Nancy whispered. "Me and Dan found it in the alley behind the Occidental, a long time ago."

"And you didn't give it back?"

"Couldn't ... he disappeared. That was why we were trying to find him."

"Hmm, didn't want to tell me the real reason, eh? And now what are you going to do? He'll be here in ten minutes."

"That's my problem, isn't it?" Nancy chuckled. "If I give it back to him, he'll just blow it on drink."

"But you can't just keep it!"

A knock sounded at the door interrupting their discussion. Nancy quickly put the bag into her apron pocket and went to open it. Sure enough, there stood Sgt. Walker with the two miners, all cleaned up and looking remarkably decent.

"Now, don't they look better?" Sgt. Walker laughed. "I had 'em cleaned up and the Salvation Army provided the clothes. This one's on me, lass," he stated, proudly handing her back her ten-dollar bill. "Just make sure I don't get 'em back!"

She thanked the Sergeant profusely before he left and invited the men to sit down at the table. Totally sober and looking a bit sheepish after his stay in the city jail, English Jack tried to apologize for the trouble he'd caused vowing it would never happen again.

Nancy gave her aunt a mischievous wink. "Look here, Jack," she said seriously. "If I was to give you a job, could you do it?"

"I'd try, Miss Nancy," began the whisker-faced old man, but then he hesitated, "but to be honest, it would be a hard one."

Meg clucked her tongue in disgust, but Nancy just smiled knowingly.

"Well then, how much money would you need for a grub stake, and would you go back to the goldfield?"

"Two hundred dollars," Jack replied, instantly. "And we'd be off to Alaska like a shot."

"Alaska?" she asked, looking at him with a questioning frown. "That's an awfully long way." But seeing him nod expectantly, she decided not to ask anymore questions. "Then it's a deal, Jack," she said, "regular terms?"

Pushing her chair back from the table, Meg shook her head as she watched Nancy disappear into her room. She returned with some bills in her hand and two blankets over her arm.

"You can sleep in the shed on our dock tonight. We'll feed you breakfast at first light then off you go ... and I get half the gold."

"Yer an angel, Nancy, m'love, just like Nellie Cashman," Jack announced passionately, leaping from his chair. "I won't let yer down, lass," he insisted. "I'll make ya rich!"

Meg hung back a little as Nancy, still clutching the two hundred dollars in her hand, took the miners out to the shed.

"You'll get this in the morning," she announced, slapping the money on her free hand. Returning to the office, she sat down with Meg. "I wonder who Nellie Cashman is?" she asked.

"Isn't she the woman who went over that Chilicot Pass to the Yukon goldrush?" said Meg.

"You mean the Chilkoot Pass. I studied that in school at the orphanage. Those poor people ... what they didn't do for gold in those days! Not many women went to the Yukon did they?"

"Enough of them did!" Meg snorted. "But this Nellie Cashman, she was something else, it seems. She had restaurants and gave money to the church and hospitals. You know, she gave money to the

Sisters of St. Ann right here in Victoria for their new hospital. That was even before she went to the Yukon."

"And Jack likens me to her, my goodness!"

The next morning, the men ate a hearty breakfast and prepared to leave. Nancy handed Jack the money and he quickly tucked it inside his coat out of sight—a quick goodbye and they were on their way.

"That's the last we'll see of them," Meg grouched. "That was a smart bit of thinking, lassie."

Nancy gave her a quick hug. "Now, let's get back to work, Aunt Meg. How many orders do we have now?"

"It seems we have about triple the normal amount, I do hope we can fill them all. Do you think we could have misunderstood the note?"

"Everything will be fine. We'd better go check the dock, they'll be home in two days," said Nancy, changing the subject.

They went outside together, first checking the heavy equipment needed for unloading the barrels of oil when the *Belfast* arrived. Opening the shed door where the miners had slept, Meg noticed a note pinned on a nail behind the door.

"Well, I'll be darned, wouldn't have thought they could write!"

"What is it?" Nancy asked.

"It's a thank-you note from English Jack," said Meg, pulling the note carefully from the nail. "It says, THANK YOU NANCY FOR HELPING US. WE HEREBY AGREE TO GIVE YOU HALF OF OUR GOLD. It's signed by Jack with an X beside it. Do you think he means it?"

"I wasn't sure he understood our agreement last night, but he obviously did," Nancy sighed, "but I won't hold my breath! That X must be his friend's signature. Jack is a lot smarter than I realized."

The sound of feet on the boardwalk brought the women scurrying back to the front of the building to find Billy knocking on the office door. He was still growing and had filled out a bit, being taller than most of the other natives. His dark skin seemed even browner, no doubt from long hours in the sun. When he saw them, he flashed a wary smile.

"Hello, Billy," she shouted, walking toward him. "Good to see you, come on in." Noticing his serious face, she asked, "Is there a problem?"

Leading the way, Meg soon had the young man sitting at the table and explaining the reason for his visit. Yes, there did seem to be a problem and he needed Nancy's help, but he was talking so fast it was difficult for them to catch all the words. His eyes were pleading with her and she held up her hand for him to stop.

"Tell me again, slowly," Nancy said, patiently.

"Farmer shot at Tom Two-Feathers ... just missed him, too!" Billy said, more slowly.

"But why?" Nancy asked, sharply.

"No reason," said Billy, shrugging his shoulders.

Trying not to smile, Nancy glanced at Meg. She could tell Meg shared her own thoughts as Billy displayed a too innocent expression. She stood up, trying not to smile. "If you did nothing and he shot at you for nothing, then that sounds like you're about even!"

"No, no, Miss Nancy. You tell him to stop," Billy insisted.

"Then tell me the truth or I won't help you."

Questions and answers flew back and forth until Billy sheepishly admitted they were trying to steal Farmer Irvine's chickens. Meg was fascinated by the manner in which Nancy managed to extract the story from her old friend.

"Are you going to do it again?" Nancy asked.

"No!" the lad exclaimed, fear dancing in his dark brown eyes, which seemed to grow larger as he talked. "He shoot at us every time he see us!"

"He can't be trying to hit you or you'd be dead by now!" Meg interceded.

"I wouldn't like to be dead, Miss Nancy," he whispered through trembling lips.

"Hush up, Billy, you're not going to be dead, but we have to find some way of appeasing Mr. Irvine," said Nancy.

By the time they finished their discussion it was lunchtime and Nancy realized she would have to talk to the farmer herself—Billy being adamant that he wouldn't go near him. A quick meal was eaten and then they hurried over to the livery stable. Managing to get the familiar grey, they were soon on their way. Going via the old Rock Bay Bridge and Bay Street, they were soon on their way to Esquimalt with Meg in command and Billy's horse tied behind. She drove confidently following the boy's directions going along several dust tracks in the direction of the reservation.

"Which way to the Irvine farm, Billy?" she asked, a while later.

"I not go there!" he protested, loudly. "He shoot me!"

"Oh yes, you are, my lad," Nancy snapped. "You're going to face him like a man and apologize."

Visibly shaken, Billy sank into the corner of the seat fearful of the consequences but realized Nancy had her mind made up. Arriving at the open farmer's gate, they saw a dray coming towards them and Meg slowed the horse to a walk. By the whimpering sounds, emanating from Billy, Nancy assumed that the tall, rangy man who was now stopping his horse alongside, was Farmer Irvine.

"Ladies," he said, pleasantly, tipping his hat slightly and removing the pipe from his mouth.

It was then he saw the Indian lad cowering in the back corner. Letting out an oath, Tom Irvine quickly produced a rifle from under his seat, jumped down, and ran around to the other side of the buggy.

"Now I've got yer!" he snarled, raising the gun to his shoulder and aiming it at the boy.

Billy, now shaking with fear, closed his eyes. Meg was speechless but Nancy leapt out of the buggy, placing herself directly into the line of fire. With her long red hair blowing in the wind and a determined look on her face, she was a fearsome and unexpected vision as she stood with hands on hips glaring up at him.

A strange expression crept over the farmer's face as he slowly lowered his rifle. "You could have got hurt, Miss," he growled.

"Put the gun down, Mr. Irvine," she said calmly, "that lad wants to apologize for the trouble he's caused you."

"Apologize ... an Indian?" he snorted. "That'll be a first!"

"Well, let's see," she said, looking over her shoulder. "Come here, Billy."

Meg gave the boy a little shove, but he shuffled over on his seat to hide behind the girl.

"Get down, Billy, right here in front of me!" she ordered, watching his slow movements as he came to her side. "And stand up straight like a man!"

Realizing Nancy meant business, Billy squared his shoulders... then looked down at the ground. He stood silent for a full minute while everyone waited. Then, he suddenly looked up at the farmer, swallowing hard. "I - I'm sorry ... sir," he said, almost in a whisper.

Totally shocked, the farmer pushed back his cap. "Well, I'll be damned!"

"Now," she continued, "let's solve this problem once and for all. I've got an idea." She paused watching the two men eye each other cautiously. "You two could be friends if you learned to work together."

Tom Irvine's eyes flashed. "Work together!" he growled.

"Yes," Nancy continued. "If you employ him to patrol your fence line, you'll never get anything stolen!"

"Impossible," he muttered, "can't afford to pay him."

"Not for money, for friendship and a meal, or a helping hand now and then."

"He wouldn't do it," grouched the man, walking over to the dray and sliding the gun back under the seat.

"I would!" the boy interceded, having finally found courage to talk. "If you teach Billy ... how to farm," he said, haltingly.

Ever so slowly, a smile appeared on the farmer's face, as he puffed thoughtfully on his pipe thinking about the work he could get done if he had the use of some stronger hands.

Meg chuckled quietly to herself. *This is pure magic. What a miracle worker is my Nancy!* "Come on, lass," she called. "I think we can go now."

155

"Just a minute," said the farmer. "Who are you and what's the Indian's name?"

"His name is Billy," replied Nancy. "I'm Nancy Wilson and this is my aunt, Meg MacDonald, who works for the Joyce Bros. ... selling whale oil."

"Billy!" barked the old man. "Turn that buggy round for the ladies."

Billy quickly did as he was told, standing by the horse's head while Nancy climbed up beside Meg.

"Don't go yet!" called the old man, following behind her. "You said ... oil. I'll be needin lamp oil for winter. Two barrels should do it, are you takin orders?"

"Yes, we are," Nancy nodded. "Half the money now, the other half when you pick it up, for a ten-percent discount."

"But I haven't any money until I sell my crops," he said, disappointment showing on his face as his smoking pipe drooped between slack lips.

"What do you grow?" Meg asked.

"Potatoes. I'm picking them now but it's a slow job on my own."

"Not on yer own now," Billy called, from the front of the horse. "I get women from village to help."

"See!" Nancy laughed, patting the old man's knurled hand as it rested on the buggy. "This friendship is working already. What about a market for your produce?"

"Got one," he muttered. "Chinaman usually buy 'em."

"Then consider your order taken. If your customer doesn't want them, we'll take them. Billy can show you where our office is," Nancy answered brightly, nudging her aunt to start the horse moving.

It was well into the afternoon when Meg turned the buggy onto Craigflower Road. Eagerly the grey picked up speed with Meg skillfully avoiding most of the deep ruts in the road. Passing Lampson Street in a swirl of dust, in the distance they could hear the whistle of the train. They couldn't see it for the trees but when they came to the crossing Meg slowed the horse to a walk, according to regulations.

156

They crossed the old Rock Bay Bridge, shivering when they felt the cool breeze blowing up the inlet. Streetcars moved noisily along Store Street as the grey headed for home, almost without direction.

"Had a good day, ladies?" the stableman asked, as the grey pulled to a halt beside him.

The stable lad shot across the yard, quickly touching his cap to the ladies as he reached out to grab hold of the horse's head.

"We've had a lovely afternoon," Meg said, beaming. Just goes to show doesn't it ... we're never too old to learn!"

"I'm sure you're right, lady," he replied, looking at her vaguely.

Pulling the shawl around her shoulders, Nancy shivered in the cool air as they hurried along Wharf Street.

Later, it was almost bedtime before Meg mentioned the afternoon events. "You certainly surprised me this afternoon by the way you solved young Billy's problem."

"It wasn't me that solved it really," the girl said, yawning. "I just helped them talk to each other and they did the rest."

"Well, it was terribly brave to stand in front of that farmer's gun like you did. It fair made me quake."

"Sold another two barrels of oil, didn't I?" Nancy laughed, mischievously.

"That you did, lass," her aunt chuckled, also stifling a yawn.

"We are a good team, you and me, and now I think it's time for bed."

Meg busied herself as Nancy went to her room, changed into her nightclothes and slid into bed. In a little while, she went into the girl's room and sat down on the bed beside her, kissing Nancy's forehead. "Nancy Wilson, I think God sent me an angel when he sent you, lassie!" she whispered, her voice barely audible as she gently stroked the girl's hair.

"I love you, Aunt Meg," Nancy whispered, wrapping her arms around Meg's neck. "I am so lucky to have found you and Danny. You are the best family a girl could ever have."

She lay back on her pillow and contentedly closed her eyes. Meg covered her lily-white arms with the patchwork quilt she had made for one of her brothers so long ago. She gazed down at the beautiful girl and said a little prayer of thanks. If she needed a new family, she couldn't have done any better.

During the night, Nancy was awakened by the sound of the wind whistling through cracks in the walls. She momentarily thought of Dan and the *Belfast* plying their way homeward through high seas and then fell back into a fitful sleep.

As daylight lit up the harbour, people were seen scurrying about to keep warm or cleaning up the mess left by the storm. Nancy instantly felt the welcome warmth of the kitchen as she burst through the back door of the Balmoral. She was greeted by Mary, who at that moment, was removing something that smelled awfully good from the oven. She checked the dining room and then went to open the front doors, standing inside, out of the cold, as she welcomed their first customers. She heard the sound of a train whistle in the distance and Redfern's clock chime its melodious half-hour. The city was indeed waking up.

Harry came hurrying around the corner, his face pale and drawn. He muttered a greeting to Nancy in the doorway.

Mr. Jenkins, a porter at The Empress, waved to them from the corner, as he paid Dick for his morning paper. "JUST HEARD THERE'S A SHIP IN TROUBLE ON THE ROCKS OUT METCHOSIN WAY," he called, then hurried away.

Couldn't be the Belfast, Nancy thought to herself, *it's a day too early.* But the news bothered her all morning. Confirmation came as the lunch crowd filled the dining room and word spread of the disaster at Albert Head.

Nancy breathed a sigh of relief when she heard it was a freighter and no lives had been lost. It was the middle of the afternoon when Waldo arrived accompanied by another couple.

"You heard the news?" he asked, glancing up as Nancy arrived to take their order.

"Yes, I heard. I was worried it might be the *Belfast*, they're due back tomorrow."

"No, it's not the *Belfast*. It's a small freighter owned by Jorgensens, out of Seattle," explained the young woman seated opposite Waldo.

"Let me introduce you, Nancy," Waldo offered. "Meet Annie Duke; she lives at Albert Head. And this fellow is Lee Field, also from Metchosin. And this lovely waitress is a very special person to me. Her name is Nancy Wilson and I'm hopelessly in love with her!"

"Oh, Mr. Skillings!" Nancy objected, blushing. "Now what can I get you folks to eat?" she continued, quickly.

"It's all right, love," Annie laughed. "I've known the Skillings family since I was knee high to a grasshopper!"

Taking their order, Nancy excused herself and returned to the kitchen. She saw Harry heading toward her, his face now set in a scowl.

"What's wrong?" she asked.

"Have you heard anything about the ship that's gone down during the night? No one seems to know much about it."

Nancy's eyes sparkled with amusement knowing how important gossip was to Harry. She flashed him a grin and turned to go, calling over her shoulder, "I'll see what I can find out, boss, anything to keep you happy!"

"How the devil can you do that?" he snapped.

A wicked chuckle from his head waitress brought a laugh from Mary who was listening from the other side of the kitchen.

"You just wait, Harry, you know that girl has her ways!"

Returning to Waldo's table, she emptied her tray. "How do you know about the ship wreck, Miss Duke?"

Fork poised in mid-air, Annie smiled. "Why love, we were there. That's where we live. It's beached just south of Tower Point on the Witty property." The women's eyes met and held their gaze for a moment. "Come and join us when we've eaten, and we'll tell you all about it."

"That will be difficult," Nancy explained. "Hotel rules don't allow it but thank you for offering." Returning to the kitchen, she suddenly had a thought. "I'm due for a break in a few minutes, Harry. I'm going to put my coat on over my apron and go out to the dining room." It was a daring statement even though she was aware the owners forbade it.

Harry was speechless, but he knew Nancy well enough now to know that when she was on a mission no one could stop her.

"Don't do it, lass, you'll get into trouble," whispered Mary.

"Hush, Mary. It's quiet, nobody will even notice."

Harry went out to the dining room and began to pace back and forth from a position where he could watch the door. Nervously, he waited for Nancy's entrance. In the staff room, Nancy found Mary's snug-fitting woolen hat and pulled it onto her head hiding her hair. Then she slipped into the cook's large coat and quietly left through the back door.

Harry was so engrossed in his own thoughts, he totally missed her entrance. She walked right past him and joined Waldo and his guests.

"Why are you dressed like that?" Annie whispered.

"Something wrong, lass?" Waldo frowned, looking past her toward the door as he pulled her up a chair.

"I'm not supposed to sit with hotel guests," Nancy said softly, "but I want to know about that shipwreck."

"Apparently the wind came up about midnight," Annie began, "pushing the *Southern Bell* onto the rocks. When she began to take on water the Captain made the decision to abandon ship. He and his eight crewmen managed to scramble off safely before she went down. They were soaking wet, but none the worse for wear when they came upon our farmhouse in the dark. The storm pulled the ship back into deeper water and by daybreak much of its deck cargo was found strewn along the shore. The ship is now sitting precariously on the rocks but high tide will change that soon enough!"

"Oh my," Nancy gasped, "that's terrible."

"Your husband is a sailor?" Lee asked.

"No," Waldo interjected, "her brother. Danny will be alright, love, he's on a whaler and the Joyce boys know this coast like the back of their hand."

"You said it was a Jorgensen ship, didn't you?" asked Nancy.

160

"That's right, the Captain told us," Annie replied. "Jorgensen Shipping from Seattle."

Standing up, Nancy prepared to leave. "I have to go now but thanks for the information, Miss Duke. I feel gratefully relieved knowing it couldn't be my brother's ship."

Watching the redhead leave, Waldo smiled. He explained to his friends how he knew Nancy and her brother, telling them of their unusual relationship and their complete devotion to each other.

"They sound like nice people," Annie commented, her hand creeping across the table to touch Lee's fingers. "I know what it's like to have a special friend."

At six o'clock, Nancy deposited her last tray of dishes on the sink just as Harry appeared.

"You didn't join Waldo, lass. I'm glad," he said. "I noticed they had someone else join them for awhile but she was a stranger to me."

"Harry, that ship is the *Southern Bell* and it's floating helplessly somewhere off Witty's Beach. It belongs to your friend, Gus Jorgensen. Apparently, no lives were lost and the crew made it safely to the Duke Farm in Metchosin." Nancy paused to slip on her coat. "Does that satisfy your curiosity, Mr. Tabour?"

Heels clicking on the pavement and head bent against the wind, she hurried toward home, not even looking at the grey, cold waters of the harbour. The boardwalk rattled under her feet.

"Whew, it's cold out there," she exclaimed, slamming the door behind her and moving quickly to the stove.

"There's a note on the table you should read," Meg said, brightly.

Nancy went over to the table and picked up the piece of paper. It read, "BELFAST OFF TOWER POINT TAKING SALVAGE STOP BE HOME TONIGHT STOP"

"They're home, lass," Meg sighed. "They're home, safe and sound."

"Hurrah!" Nancy exclaimed, flopping into a chair. "What does taking salvage mean, Aunt Meg?"

161

As they ate, they kept one ear tuned to the harbour listening for the familiar sounds of the *Belfast*'s engine. Nancy filled her in on what she had heard at the hotel about the downed ship and Meg answered her question.

Spending all her life as part of a seafaring family, constantly waiting for ships and loved ones to come home, Meg was well versed in salvage operations. "When a ship's abandoned at sea it's free for the taking ... to any ship that's brave enough to get a towline aboard." She sighed deeply before adding, "It can be terribly dangerous."

"You mean if the *Belfast* tows it into port, it's theirs to keep along with the cargo? It's high tide now ... the boys must think they'll be able to get it off the rocks," she mused.

Meg nodded, but the thought of winds and danger on the seas had caused her mind to drift back in time. She couldn't help but remember the searing pain she had felt as a child when that wild Atlantic storm had stolen the lives of her father and brother. She turned away as a tear found its way down her cheek and then she thought of that day only a few years before when the *Belfast* had returned with the bodies of her two remaining brothers. Her shoulders sagged visibly and Nancy, now realizing something was wrong, went to stand behind her.

Wrapping her arms around the older lady, she spoke in a soft, soothing voice. "Please don't be sad, Aunt Meg."

"You and Danny are all I have left," Meg whispered, covering her face with her hand and speaking in a voice laced with emotion.

Nancy held her tightly for a moment and then knelt down in front of her. Taking her hands gently in hers, she tried to find some soothing words of comfort. "I know you have your sad memories, Aunt Meg, but we're a family now ... you, Dan, and me. We're bound together by something much stronger than blood ... we love you, and you'll always be a part of our lives."

Chapter 13

Three hours later, the dull pounding of toiling engines caused both women to stand up, straining their ears.

"They're here!" Nancy squealed, jumping to her feet and dashing for the door, grabbing her coat on the way. She was just in time to see Dan and several others leap from the moving whaler onto the dock. Spinning around, Dan dashed to the bow as one of the crew sent another rope flying through the air over his head. The others disappeared into the darkness at the end of the dock.

"TURN HER LOOSE, DUMPY," Ned screamed over the wind.

The engines burst back into life, churning the water into foam as the stern of the whaler moved closer to the dock. When he was finished, Dan noticed the women and with a yelp ran to greet them.

"Doggone it, I missed you two!" he called, scooping the girl into his arms.

"Hmpph! Missed me, my eye! What have you brought? What's this about salvage, Ned?" Meg called, ignoring Dan and squinting through the darkness. By the dim light on the wharf she could just make out the large, dark shape of another ship behind the *Belfast* and curiously began to walk toward it.

Laughing, the Joyces converged on her, affectionately hugging her before leading her toward the office.

"See you tomorrow," Dumpy called as he scooted past them, heading for the nearest bar with the rest of the crew.

"We've been dry for a week," Ned chuckled. "They'll be feeling no pain within the hour! Now, you ladies go on in and make us something to eat. We're right starved. We've got a few things to attend to and we need to unload some of the salvage so we can find enough room to sleep. We'll be there in about twenty minutes and then we'll tell you all about it.

163

Going inside, Meg and Nancy put on some fresh tea as they chattered excitedly. Meg told Nancy what she had seen and they wondered how the *Belfast* had managed to bring in such a large vessel.

"Maybe they had help. I thought the engines sounded awfully loud," said Nancy.

By the time they had a heaping plate of sandwiches prepared, the three men filed into the warm kitchen, washed their hands at the sink, and pulled their chairs up to the table. In no time, the mound of sandwiches had almost disappeared as Meg and Nancy caught them up on the local news including the death of John Bryant. None of the men had met him, but they had heard about the planned flight and were shocked at the sad news.

Then relaxing at last with a cup of tea, Tim changed the subject, telling of their tremendous catch and explaining why they had sent the message about oil orders.

"We're all taking too many whales," Ned growled, shaking his head sadly. "I keep warning them but they won't listen!"

"Come on, don't keep us in suspense," begged Nancy, going over to sit on Dan's lap. "Tell us about the salvage operation."

"We heard about it on the radio at first light as we were pulling into the strait. We decided to try for the salvage and when we reached Pedder Bay, the Coast Guard was already there. Fred Barrett told us we were the first so we checked it out," Tim explained.

"It was a big sucker and we had no idea how we were going to do it on our own when the rest of the whalers came up behind us and offered to help," Dan reiterated, kissing Nan's cheek then moving her off his lap and getting another cup of tea.

"Thought it were awful neighbourly of them. Guess we'll have to take them out to the Saloon and get 'em all drunk!" Ned laughed.

It was almost 11:30 when Nancy yawned uncontrollably and went to hug Dan and the others. "I just can't keep my eyes open anymore... goodnight!" she said, through another yawn.

As soon as she had disappeared, Meg jumped up from her chair and went to her desk. "We haven't told you all our news! You should see the order books, lads," she whispered, conspiratorially, "they're full, and it's all due to that girl!" She lay three books on the table and each reached for one and began to flip through the pages.

"Whew, will you take a look at the final figures!" Dan muttered, pushing his book across the table to Ned.

Ned scanned the numbers at the bottom of the last page. "Wow!" he gasped. "We're rich, that is, if the price doesn't go down!"

"Doesn't matter," Meg snapped. "We gave ten-percent discount on this year's price for half the cash now and the rest when they pick it up. Half the money's in the bank already, gathering interest!"

"And who's idea was that Miss MacDonald ... I wonder!" Tim laughed as his fingers ran up the list of orders. "There's some big orders here," he whispered. "How in heaven did Nancy meet all these people?"

"Oh ho, me lad," Meg said, proudly, "you've never seen our Nancy when she starts selling whale oil. Why, one night at Charlotte Townend's rally...," she had to stop for a moment as memories flooded back and she began to laugh. "It was a political meeting Charlotte was holding at the Odd Fellows Hall and Nancy sang for them."

"Singing ... our Nancy, and at a political meeting?" Ned frowned.

Meg ignored him and continued. "Afterwards with the audience still screaming for more, that little redhead began selling whale oil. It was unbelievable, you have no idea. The next day, I was taking orders left and right."

Dan's eyes danced with amusement. "Didn't know she could sing, did you?"

"No, did you?" asked Tim, throwing a quizzical look at his friend.

"I sure did!" Dan replied, leaning back in his chair. "She sang to me down at the beach one night."

"You never told me!" Meg scolded.

"Or us!" Ned added.

"It was my secret! She sang it just for me," said Dan getting a faraway look in his eyes.

The men were already up and eating breakfast when Nancy got up next morning. She had heard the sounds of their heavy boots moving about outside and glancing out the back window, she saw mounds of wooden boxes and bales stacked on the jetty.

"What're all those boxes?" she asked Meg.

"Salvage from the wreck," she answered, putting the girl's breakfast on the table in front of her. "Come on, lass, you'll be late."

After breakfast, Nancy slipped into her coat, kissed her aunt, and hurried outside to greet the men. Dan saw her and jumped over one of the wet bales to land beside her. His hands were dirty, so he planted a kiss on her nose.

"I'll be here when you get home tonight," he said, turning away.

"Hey, brother," she called, with a twinkle in her eye. Running up to him, she put her hands on his shoulders and standing on tip toe, kissed him quickly on the cheek. Then, she turned and ran up the walkway, not stopping until she heard Redfern's clock begin its seven chimes.

"Is the devil chasing you, Nancy?" Dick called, as she hurried by.

"Want some tea, lass?" Mary asked, indicating a steaming cup she had just poured as Nancy came through the door.

"Thanks, Mary! A piece of toast would be nice, too, if you have the time!"

"Question is, are you going to stay still long enough to eat it?"

Warming her hands over the big stove as she passed, she reached for the cup and headed for the staff room. When she came out, she glanced into the dining room and saw that most of the tables were in a mess. Darn," she muttered, "don't those girls ever clean up at night!"

"Easy, love," Mary soothed. "I heard they were really busy right up to closing last night."

Her comment fell on deaf ears as Nancy grabbed a tray and cloth and disappeared into the dining room. At that moment, Harry came through the back door rubbing his hands.

"Nancy not here yet?" he groaned.

Blowing a wisp of hair from her face, Mary pointed toward the dining room. A relieved smile appeared on Harry's face as he went into his office.

"Hear anymore about the wreck?" he shouted through the open door, as Nancy went by.

"Didn't you get enough information yesterday?" she asked cheekily, emptying her tray of dirty dishes on the counter.

The manager's chair made a loud scraping sound as he pushed it away from his desk. Walking out to the kitchen, he was just in time to see Nancy disappear again as the door swung behind her.

"Damn, she's elusive," he said to Mary. "Doesn't she ever keep still?"

"We open in five minutes," Mary reminded him. "And she'll be ready, never seen anybody who moves as fast as her on a morning."

At that moment, the redhead did reappear, grabbing her now cold, hard toast, biting off a mouthful sending crumbs everywhere.

"Eating all the hotel profit, I see!" Harry teased.

"That wreck," she said, having to stop to take a sip of her cold tea, "is tied up at the end of our dock." But that was all she had time to say before she hurried off to open the door.

The disaster in Parry Bay was certainly the main topic of conversation that day, though no one seemed to know the whole story. As the day went by, Nancy learned many bits of information that would come in handy as the men sorted the salvage.

Joseph Wilson was telling Mr. Boggs, his breakfast partner, he'd lost a hundred bolts of high-quality worsted and other cloth in the wreck. Mr. Davis had a list of Spencer's Store goods that were aboard, proclaiming he would buy all the salvage if he could find out who had it. No one see
med aware, as yet, that the wreck was tied up at the Joyce Bros. dock.

Just before quitting time, Nancy felt a hand on her shoulder and turned to find Gus Jorgensen standing behind her.

"Got a minute, Nancy? I need to speak with you," he whispered, moving toward a table in the corner.

167

When she joined him a few minutes later, there were a group of men sitting with him. They looked tired and terribly serious, although Gus didn't appear to share their concern. His grin was as friendly as ever.

"Anybody hurt in that wreck last night?" he asked her quietly, as she took the food order.

"No one," she replied, just as quietly. "Come around to the Joyce's office at 7:30, Gus. I'm just leaving, but I have some information you'll want."

Harry hadn't noticed the Jorgensen group and when Nancy finished her shift, she slipped out of the backdoor and made her way home clasping her coat tightly about her neck to keep warm.

"Paper and pencil quick, before I forget!" she gasped, bursting through the door.

Meg quickly produced the items and watching over her shoulder, read the words as Nancy wrote all the tidbits of information she'd gathered throughout the day.

"My word," she chuckled, "you've had some busy ears today!"

"Had a visitor, too," Nancy smiled, as she set the table. "A friend of yours."

"A friend of mine?" Meg asked, setting some plates on the table and ladling out steaming spoonfuls of tasty-smelling stew. Just then the three whalers entered, their shirt sleeves rolled up over their elbows. They sniffed the air and smiled.

"Aren't you cold?" Nancy asked, shivering a little as the cool air from the open door struck her.

"Thought it were warm out there ... sure smells good in here!" Ned exclaimed, leading the men to the sink.

When Dan pulled his chair up beside Nancy, he lightly brushed the back of his hand against her face.

"WHOA!" she cried, "you feel like a block of frozen codfish!"

"Stop it you two," Meg scolded. "Supper's getting cold!"

Under the table, Dan and Nancy squeezed each other's hand and grinned.

The men were sitting around the fire and the women were washing up the dishes when they heard someone else arrive. Dan went to answer the door and in stepped Gus Jorgensen and another man.

"Hello Dan, nice to see you again … Nancy, Miss MacDonald," said Gus in his usual, friendly manner. "I took the liberty of bringing my lawyer, William Foster. I thought we might have need of him."

"These are my employers, sir," said Dan. "Ned and Tim Joyce … meet Mr. Jorgensen of Jorgensen Shipping in Seattle."

A smile began to spread across Gus' face. "You're the whalers," he laughed, turning to the redhead. "So this is the source of the whale oil you've been selling!"

Two more chairs were found and pulled up to the table.

"Nancy," Gus began, "we're here tonight because you told me you had some information for me and I assumed it was about my ship. Jeb said if anybody knew what had happened to it, you would be the one to ask! I'd like it back if it's worth repairing. Can you help me?"

"It is my opinion," Mr. Foster interrupted, "that we should go to the harbour authorities."

"It would be a wasted trip," Nancy quipped, coyly.

Ned raised an eyebrow as he glanced across at the redhead, wondering where this conversation was leading but deciding that Nancy probably knew what she was doing.

"If I knew who had the vessel, do I understand correctly, you'd be willing to buy it back, Mr. Jorgensen?" she asked.

Before Gus could answer, Bill Foster banged the table with the flat of his hand, staring fiercely at Nancy. "Look here, young lady," he snapped. "Mr. Jorgensen's question was simple enough for even you to understand!"

Meg dropped the silverware she was drying with a clatter and turned toward them, her eyes blazing with anger.

"It's all right, Aunt Meg," Dan quickly intervened. Pushing his chair back from the table, the young whaler rose and walked slowly over to stand protectively behind Nancy, his hands lightly resting on her shoulders.

"Mister," he whispered, forcing a smile. "If you open your mouth once more and speak to my sister like that again, I'll throw you off the dock!"

Startled by the quiet menace in Dan's voice, the lawyer recoiled slightly, his face turning red with embarrassment

"Bill, don't be such an idiot!" said Gus, glaring at his lawyer. "These people are my friends. Now apologize to that girl or I'll *tell* Dan to drown you!"

Bill Foster began to stutter an apology, his urge to dominate the meeting totally extinguished. He had never felt so low or dejected and now the humiliation was about to become complete.

"Please, Mr. Jorgensen," said Nancy, softly. "Mr. Foster was only doing what he thought you wanted."

A grin began to ease its way onto the wealthy American's face, as he turned again to his lawyer, now totally humiliated. "You see, Bill, you could have got killed by every man in this room for being nasty to that little redhead. Then what happens, damn it if she doesn't come to your defence!"

"I'm really sorry, Miss Nancy," Bill mumbled.

Dan returned to his seat and winked at Nancy. "Right, sis, now you carry on."

"You asked if I knew where the ship is and who has it. Do you want to buy it back?" she asked.

"Yes, if it can be repaired," Gus answered, guardedly. "It would be cheaper than trying to replace it."

"And the salvaged goods?"

"The salvage company can have them. She was fully insured, ship and cargo."

Sharp glances passed quickly between the Joyce's.

"Then you won't suffer any losses?" Nancy ventured, as the room went quiet and everyone held their breath awaiting the answer.

"Not a nickel, sweetheart," Gus laughed.

"And the price you'll pay?"

"It would depend on the extent of the damage, but not less than $30,000."

The intake of air from several pair of lips was obvious.

"Oh my," Meg gasped, "that's a fortune."

"I would want it brought in and delivered to the shipyard for repair," Gus continued, his eyes still not leaving Nancy's face.

"Have we heard a commitment here, Mr. Lawyer?" she asked.

"Yes, ma'am," Bill Foster affirmed. "Loud and clear."

"Then you've come to the right place, Mr. Jorgensen," Nancy announced, a smile tickling at the corners of her mouth. "Your ship is tied up at the end of our dock."

"WHAT!" Gus boomed in surprise, almost leaping out of his chair. "You already have it?"

When the laughter died down the still-smiling Seattle millionaire began to explain that someone from Lloyds of London, the insurers, would be in contact with them very soon to try and buy the ship.

"They'll offer you pennies, fix it up, and send it back to us saving their company thousands on the insurance," he explained.

Dan, who had been listening intently, smiled knowingly as he made some simple observations. "Now you've made a deal with us, Mr. Jorgensen, am I correct in thinking that Lloyds can't touch it and will have to pay you the full insured cost?" When the shipowner nodded, Dan continued. "Jorgensen Shipping will do the repairs using the insurance money, and pocket what's left over."

"Smart lad," Gus exclaimed. "It's called using an opportunity, all legal, fair, and good business."

"We keep the salvage goods ... all of them?" Nancy asked, her eyes focused on the lawyer.

Bill Foster smiled, glancing at his employer for an answer. He was beginning to like this unusual girl.

The shipowner nodded again. "Write it up, Bill, and we'll handle all the legal work. I'm buying a bare ship."

Taking some papers from his leather satchel, Bill Foster began to work feverishly to prepare the Documents of Commitment. For thirty minutes the group talked quietly amongst themselves, interrupted only by intermittent hushed consultation with the lawyer.

171

"There's a movement afoot to make booze illegal in Washington State," Gus announced. "It's being stirred up by the Reverend Mathews, a Presbyterian Minister."

"Never," pronounced Meg, "or he's noo a Scot! Och, we've heard that man ...."

"Right," Foster interrupted, pushing his laboriously handwritten documents across the table to the Joyces. "Check these out gentlemen. I'll need you both to sign at the bottom."

Tim Joyce read the papers out loud to his brother while the others listened intently. Dan and Nancy's eyes locked in silent understanding.

"Sounds just fine, don't it Tim?" asked Ned.

"No, it does not!" said Nancy, frowning gravelly.

"Why?" the lawyer asked, his face turning crimson again. He quickly reached for the documents, scanning them one more time as his employer watched curiously.

"What is it, Nancy love?" Tim asked, frowning.

Bill Foster's hands were noticeably shaking as he rifled through the papers once more.

"Leave them!" Gus growled. "Come Nancy, tell us what's wrong."

"There's no completion date," she announced, slowly and deliberately. "You could have us on a string forever ... if you wanted!"

Tim and Ned passed startled looks between them as Dan and Gus began to laugh.

"I - I didn't do it on purpose, Miss Nancy," Bill stammered.

"No doubt an honest mistake, Mr. Foster."

"My word," said Meg, "you'll stand some watching, lad!"

"Easy, Aunt Meg," Nancy chuckled. "We'll fix it up right now. He can write it on the bottom of the document ... *payment of $15,000 at signing, balance upon possession by Jorgensen Shipping.*"

Do it, Bill," Gus ordered. "And you, young lady, should come and work for me!"

"Not a chance!" Dan retorted. "She belongs here with me." Opening his arms, she came to sit on his lap. Folding them

172

protectively around her, their bodies melded together and he kissed her proudly on the cheek. The others watched fascinated, leaving no doubt in anyone's mind that these two were much more than siblings.

Finishing with the papers, Bill Foster handed one copy to his employer and one to Nancy. Gus nodded as he read the note on the bottom. He glanced at Nancy who passed her copy over to the Joyce's ... just as a knock sounded at the door.

Meg looked startled and glanced at the clock. "It's late for callers," she muttered, going to the door.

"Tom Westin, ma'am," said the stranger framed in the outside light. "Insurers, ma'am, representing Lloyds of London ... regarding the wreck you have tied up at your dock."

"Tomorrow, lad," Ned shouted.

"But sir, this is urgent business. I'm with Findley, Durham and Brodie," the man said importantly, stepping into the room uninvited and holding the door open. "There could be a windfall of cash for the person responsible."

"How much cash?" Ned asked.

"Substantial, sir, substantial," the Lloyd's representative assured him, still holding the door.

"Shut the door, man. Don't you know it's winter! Danny, help your Aunt Meg," demanded Ned.

Nancy leapt up and Dan moved to the door pushing it out of the man's reach causing him to lose his balance.

"How much cash?" Ned asked again.

"Five thousand," Westin replied, desperately trying to keep his composure.

"Throw him out, Danny!" Ned grunted, as Dan spun the man around and pushed him back through the doorway.

"Ten thousand!" came a bleating cry from out of the darkness as Dan closed the door.

"You treat all your late callers this way?" asked Gus, with a twinkle in his eye.

"No," Ned laughed, "we only turn the kid loose on special occasions!"

Three days later, Jorgensen Shipping deposited $15,000 into the Joyce Bros. bank account and word was received that the Americans had left town. Gus, however, demonstrating his trust in the young Canadians, had sent papers authorizing Nancy, with Dan's assistance, to make decisions regarding the repairs to the salvaged vessel on behalf of his company.

Work on the *Southern Bell* began immediately. Pumps were set in place to right the badly listing vessel to enable its cargo to be removed from the submerged hold. Ned and Dumpy had taken the *Belfast* to Sechart Harbour towing a barge leased from the C.P. Railway. They would pick up another load of oil from the whale processing plant and return immediately. Activity on the dock now became hectic as oil customers lined up and dock space became scarce as the piles of salvaged cargo grew higher each day.

An assortment of vehicles appeared keeping Dan, Tim, and the rest of the crew busy loading oil barrels. Meanwhile, in the office, Meg was coping well with the steady stream of people and the large amounts of cash filling the steel box under her desk.

Many inquiries had already been received regarding the salvage stacked on the dock. The feisty Scot kept a carefully documented list of names and items of interest, informing them that Nancy would be dealing with the goods on the weekend.

On November 1st, a heavy frost touched Victoria streets, forming ice on roadways and puddles. Nancy clutched her scarf around her face and walked carefully up Broughton, barely conscious of the muffled greetings being sent her way.

"Cold enough, Miss Nancy!" called Dick, sending up a white cloud of steam as his words evaporated in the cold air.

Waving to the boy, she cautiously crossed the slippery street and almost ran the last steps to the warm refuge of the hotel.

"Teapot's full, love, it's just been made," Mary called.

Nancy poured herself a cup of tea and was just coming out of the staff room as Harry came puffing and blowing through the door.

"Pour me one too, lass," he gasped, rushing over to the stove to warm his hands. "It's damned cold out there!"

Knowing exactly how he liked his first cup of tea, Nancy placed the cup and saucer on a tray and added one of Mary's fresh scones. She carried it into his office and set it on the desk in front of him.

"Thanks!" he called, as she scurried away.

Messrs. Wilson, Davis and Ben were first though the door as they hurried in and sat down at a table together, loosening coats and scarves as they chatted.

"Have the Joyce's emptied that vessel yet?" Davis asked.

"I don't know, but they're apparently waiting for another oil shipment," Ben offered.

"What's that?" Wilson replied, his eyebrows arching in surprise. "They've already sold a full load of that oil? I'd better order some before they run out."

"I'll have to talk to them. We were expecting some prime full-leaf tobacco in airtight containers on that ship," Tom muttered, not realizing Nancy was listening. "They should still be good as new once it's salvaged. It'll take too long to get another shipment here, but we should be able to pick them up at half price from the salvage."

Smiling, Nancy moved away, surprised that a man of business would speak so freely of such pertinent information! Mr. Wilson, also, seemed to be in a nervous state, constantly drumming his fingers on the table.

"All that beautiful cloth," she heard him moan, as she went by their table a few minutes later, "ruined by a trick of fate and we're needing it desperately."

"Depends how it was packed," suggested Tom.

Listening to the snatches of conversation, Nancy began to formulate a plan. It seemed that almost every person in the dining room, knew someone who'd told them something about the list of goods that were aboard the *Southern Bell*.

By the middle of the afternoon when Harry went uptown to meet with friends, Nancy went into his office and telephoned E.A.Morris, asking the price of a bale of prime full-leaf tobacco. *One hundred and twenty-five dollars*, the voice on the other end of the line stated without hesitation. Nancy thanked him and put down the telephone.

My plan will work just fine, she thought to herself as she wrote the figures down. Her next call was to W & J Wilson, and just as easily they gave her the price of a bolt of fine English worsted. Chuckling at the simplicity of her plan, Nancy picked up her paper, tucked it carefully up her sleeve, and went back to work.

Arriving home just after six o'clock, she entered the warm kitchen finding Tim and Dan already at the sink vying for space.

"Sit straight down, lass, everything's ready," Meg greeted her.

Dan joined her at the table as Tim dried his hands and expectantly watched Meg fill four plates with food. Nancy smiled as their fingers touched under the table and Dan squeezed them lightly.

"Have you got all the cargo off the *Bell* yet?" she asked.

"About half," Tim mumbled, through a mouthful of food, "but all the water's out now."

"You have a list of the goods, don't you?" Nancy asked eagerly, laying down her cutlery.

"Yes, we have," Meg said, sharply. "Now eat, your supper's getting cold. There's time for business when we've finished."

The rebuke brought a chuckle from the men as Nancy made a face and followed the instructions in silence. It wasn't until the dishes were cleared away and Meg motioned to Nancy to sit back down at the table, that the subject was mentioned again.

"Now, young lady let me show you what we know," she said, looking sideways at her and frowning. Picking up her account book and a sheet of paper, she slid the paper toward Nancy. Meg calmly sipped her tea as Nancy's eyes flashed over the page searching for the tobacco and cloth. She smiled when she found them.

"These two," she said, pointing to the list. "Did you notice their condition … were they packed in waterproof wrapping or are they full of water?" Her pencil checked off two items on the list and she pushed it back across the table to Meg.

Meg looked at the paper, then handed it to Dan.

176

"Both wrapped tight, sis. I'd say waterproof, but we haven't opened them yet."

Tim also took a look. "Can't say I remember. Why so interested, Nancy?"

"Because I have customers for both those items ... and at a good price!" she quipped, winking at the older man. "If we could get hold of the shipping manifest, we'd know who was taking delivery of every bit of that cargo—like handing us a list of prospective customers!"

"That should be easy," Tim ventured, "the Captain will have them or know where they are."

Suddenly, Dan stood up and went to the door. He silently slipped into his coat and turned to face them as he put on his cap.

"Where are you going, Danny?" asked Nancy.

"For a walk onto the Harbour Master's office," he replied.

"What good will that do?" she asked, tapping her pencil on the table.

"You tell 'em Tim. I'll be back in half an hour," the young whaler called over his shoulder, slamming the door behind him.

"The Captain would have filed a report with the Coast Guard and other authorities, before leaving the area," explained Tim. "Them's the rules of the sea, and Danny's counting on it."

Walking quickly to the Harbour Master's office just a few doors away, Dan opened a door and entered a small barely lit room. The bell hanging over the door jingled a greeting and a warning.

"Who's there?" rasped a voice from another room, as heavy feet sounded on the bare wooden floor.

"Oh it's you, Danny," Fred Barrett growled when he saw the familiar figure. "What can I do for you, lad?"

"Has the Captain of the *Southern Bell* made his report yet, Fred?" Dan came straight to the point, watching Fred flip through the pages of the report book laying on the counter.

"Not yet ... but," the Coast Guard officer hissed when his eyes caught an entry in the book, "he has an appointment at nine on

177

Monday." Pausing, he looked up with a grin. "That what you wanted to know, son?" he asked, slamming the book closed.

"Will the documents be available to the public?"

"Nope!" Fred Barrett snapped. "Not until after the inquiry."

Dan pursed his lips in frustration, shook his head and turned to go.

"What is it you want, lad?" Fred muttered. "You know I'll help if I can."

"We need the cargo manifest," said Dan, hopefully.

Scowling, the Coast Guard officer rubbed his chin. "I'll get it for you; they won't need it for the inquiry. It'll cost you a meal, Danny boy! Tell Nancy I'll bring it to her at the Balmoral at lunch on Monday. Now get the hell out of here ... it's past my bedtime!"

Smiling, the young whaler watched his friend stomp out of the room. He remembered the day, many years back when Fred had helped fish him out of the harbour unconscious after an accident on the *Belfast*. Ned told him afterwards that Fred had said something about a life saved from the sea made the rescuer responsible for that life ever after. As he walked back to the office, Dan thought back on Fred's actions ever since that day. It was true he had always been a good friend, helping and advising whenever he could. This set Dan to wondering if Fred had really taken that old saying to heart.

"Well?" Nancy asked as Dan arrived and hung up his coat.

"You'll have your list at lunchtime on Monday. Fred's going to bring it to the Balmoral and we owe him lunch!"

"Hmm ... had to resort to bribery, did you!" Nancy laughed. "That's just solved all our problems, Aunt Meg."

"Fancy a drink, Dan?" Tim asked, as he picked up his coat.

"Me, too!" Nancy giggled, jumping to her feet.

"Oh no you don't, me girl," Dan barked. "You can't go where we're going, and anyway, it's time you were in bed! We obviously need you wide awake if you're going to be any good to us as a spy!"

Pouting, Nancy's shoulders sagged as she pretended to be disappointed. Dan put his coat back on then walked over and picked her up in his arms like a doll. She wrapped her arms around his neck and whispered, "You're going, Danny?"

178

"Yes, I am. I'll see you in the morning," he said tenderly, planting a kiss on her nose. Then he carried her over to Meg and sat her down in the chair next to the older woman. "Here, Aunt Meg," he chuckled. "You look after our little spy and make sure she gets to bed soon!"

As the door banged shut, Nancy jumped up excitedly and gave Meg a hug. "I love him so, Aunt Meg. He really belongs to me doesn't he?"

"Aye, lassie, and you to him!" The words caught in her throat as she wound her arms about the girl. "And you both belong to me!"

Chapter 14

Mayor Morley's new fangled streetlights cast an eerie glow as the whalers hunched their shoulders against the wind and happily made their way up the street to the door of the Occidental Bar. Pulling it open, the noise that assaulted their ears was deafening.

The men took their beers to a table well away from the bar. Shortly afterwards, they were joined by two more seamen who seemed to want to talk about the *Southern Bell*.

"We stood on the headland and watched the salvagers," Tom Jolly said loudly. "That ship were bobbing like a cork in them giant waves."

"Some idiot harpooned it then leapt on board," interrupted Matt Downs, his partner. "That was a death trap, he'd more courage than brains!"

Tim drained his bottle, banging it on the table before wiping the froth from his lips. Dan rose, scowling at the two fishermen as he left the table to push his way back to the bar.

"For your information, we're those whalers!" Tim hissed, "and that lad's the best gunner on this whole damned coast."

The fishermen looked stunned.

"Ya mean ...," Downs whispered in awe, as Dan arrived back at the table with two more beer, "he harpooned it like a whale!"

"Well, I'll be damned," Jolly interjected. "He'd hafta be crazy, I reckon!"

Tim and Dan's eyes locked for a moment as a sly smile passed between them. Then, roaring with laughter, they clinked glasses.

Early next morning, Tim and a gang of labourers were busy clearing the rest of the cargo from the hold of the *Bell*; Dan was arranging the bales and crates in neat rows along the dock. Nancy and

Meg had identified the bales of tobacco leaf and the crates of fine Yorkshire worsted cloth meant for Wilsons. Both were waterproof wrapped and showed no outward sign of damage.

Meg brewed some strong coffee for the men, putting it in a large pot set on a glowing brazier at the end of the dock. At break time, the men simply dipped their tin cups into the steaming black brew. *If this doesn't warm their innards, nothing would,* Meg often said.

The women were taking their tea in the office when a knock sounded on the door. Meg opened it, revealing Sid Johnston, one of the E.A. Morris buyers.

"It's the salvage ma'am," he smiled self-consciously, clenching his hat to his chest. "I'm here to inquire if you've recovered some tobacco leaf and if we might buy it. Oh, hello Nancy," he greeted the girl in surprise. "What are you doing here?"

"I live here, you just met my Aunt Meg … she'll show you the bales of tobacco."

Sid followed Meg out onto the jetty. Indicating the bales, he took a few minutes to inspect them thoroughly.

"Water damage minimal," he said, stoically. "I could be generous and offer you fifteen dollars a bale."

"Write it down, Aunt Meg," Nancy's voice came from behind them. "We'll let you know when the other offers come in, Sid."

"Other offers?" he said meekly, raising his eyebrows in alarm.

"Yes, there's McKillop and Griffiths, and several others who have shown an interest," Nancy replied.

"W - w - well," he stammered, shaken by the news of competition, "I could offer a little more."

"Like seventy-five dollars a bale!" Nancy suggested, sharply. "And you could take them all!"

"No … no, I couldn't do that," he quivered. "It's salvage and should be cheap."

"Then forget it, because here comes McKillop," she said, turning away.

"Damn it … I'll take it all!" Sid groaned, furtively glancing over his shoulder.

181

"Write it up, Aunt Meg," Nancy ordered, a smile of devilment on her lips as she marveled at the ease she was able to deal with these supposedly astute businessmen. "And have him sign an offer to purchase." As she watched them walk toward the office, she called after them. "We'll need it paid for and off the dock by noon tomorrow, Sid!"

At 2 pm that same afternoon, old Mr. Wilson, sporting a silver-topped cane, arrived at the dock accompanied by two finely dressed young men. He quickly inquired after his shipment of cloth and Meg directed them to it's location, where they found Nancy. His critical eye watched carefully while his companions checked the crates. They spent a few minutes in discussion and then he turned to Nancy.

"We'll take them all ... at thirty-percent off my invoice price," he said at last, in a formal manner. "Any water damage and you take it back."

"Twenty-five ... and it's a deal!" Nancy replied. "No doubt you've brought the invoice with you."

Her remark obviously surprised the clothier giving him the uncomfortable feeling of being outwitted. His cane tapped nervously on the boards of the dock as he beckoned to one of his companions.

"Write it up, Aunt Meg."

Watching the men from a distance as they followed Meg back to her office, she noticed Mr. Wilson's puzzled expression, but she also noticed he now had the invoice in his hand.

All the cargo had now been removed from the *Bell* and the ship was made ready for towing up the inlet to the William Turpel drydock at Point Hope. Emerson Turpel, the son of the owner, had agreed to do a survey of damage and provide an estimate of repair costs.

The Turpel's were eastcoasters and very good friends of the Joyces. The two groups were often heard swapping yarns of the Atlantic Coast when they socialized together.

That evening, with supper over, the four of them sat around the kitchen table, talking to the accompaniment of Meg's clicking

182

knitting needles. It had been a long, but satisfying day. They each had a story to tell but it was the sales that the women had completed that the men were most eager to hear about.

"How did you know what price to ask, Meg?" Tim inquired. "Seems odd you'd know the cost of tobacco when you've never smoked in your life!"

"Easy," Meg retorted, "it's Nancy who knows the prices."

"Yes, and it'll get easier after tomorrow when I get the *Bell's* cargo manifest from Fred Barrett," she confirmed.

"That won't tell you the price of anything," Tim snorted.

Leaning forward, Nancy's eyes sparkled with mischief. "It'll tell me, what's in each crate and who owns it!"

"And then what?" asked Dan.

"Why, I'll simply pick up the telephone and ask them how much they sell it for," Nancy laughed. "Take off their 40% mark up and we have a pretty accurate wholesale price."

Meg's teacup rattled on the saucer as she giggled involuntarily. Her face couldn't hide the admiration she felt for her young protégée who had learnt her lessons so well.

"I like it," Tim chuckled, "there's just enough devilment in it for an old Irisher like me. Twas a fateful day when Danny brought you to us, girl."

"Amen!" said Meg.

A rush of air escaped Dan's lips as he locked eyes with Nancy. Reaching out, his powerful hand consumed hers.

"What I want to know, young lady, is where did you learn to deal with people like you do?" asked Meg. "That man from Morris' was still talking to himself when he left here."

"Dear Aunt Meg," Nancy laughed, letting go of Dan's hand. "I've been dealing with pompous men in restaurants for a long time. Often, they are just like children. You've no idea what tricks they get up to and I hear it all!"

Tim sat bolt upright in his chair and scowled at Dan as if he was waiting for him to present an argument. But Dan merely laughed,

183

nodding his head in agreement. Tim finally objected to Nancy's statement but this was only met with more laughter.

Slowly and deliberately, Nancy rose from the table and went over to Tim. She sat down on his knee putting her arms affectionately around his neck. As his face grew redder, she hugged him tenderly and planted a kiss on his nose, finally ending his tirade.

Resignedly, Tim's arms reached up to hold her. "My word, lass, you are so damned honest it's perplexing!"

"I know what'll cheer him up, Nancy," said Meg. "We haven't told him how much he and Ned made on our sales."

"Aye, that'd do it!" Tim said eagerly, easing the girl off his knee and sitting up in his chair. "How much?"

"Seven hundred for the tobacco," Meg announced, watching the pleasure begin to sparkle in his eyes. "And ...," she emphasized, "one thousand, four hundred and forty for the cloth!"

Tim and Dan were obviously impressed ... and momentarily speechless. "So much?" was all Tim could manage.

"It wasn't all my doing," Nancy laughed. "Yes, I meddled with the tobacco man's brain because he was trying to be slick, but Mr. Wilson is an honest man and easy to do business with." She paused, yawning tiredly. "That was a good day's work and if you'll all excuse me, I'm off to bed."

Sleep came easy to Nancy that night. It seemed but a moment before she felt Meg's gentle hand shaking her shoulder disturbing her dream of a house overlooking the sea.

"But I just came to bed!" she mumbled, sleepily.

"It's almost six-thirty," Meg said, gently. "Tea's made. Come on, love, you'll soon be wide awake."

As she left the jetty, her pace quickened as freezing winds nipped at her face and the rain dampened her feet.

The Balmoral's early morning ritual was interrupted by the delivery truck from Queen's Market bringing supplies. Mary checked the boxes as Nat, the big, bearded driver, dropped them inside the door and handed Nancy the delivery slip for a signature.

184

"Why don't you let her sign it?" he growled, nodding at Mary.

"She can't write," Nancy replied, smiling at the bear of a man. "Can you?"

"Yes, ah can … and ah can read, too," he announced, proudly.

The sound of whistling alerted them to get out of the way as Harry burst through the door, a huge smile on his face.

"Have you dealt with it, lass?" he asked, swishing by them. "Then give the man a coffee, Mary," Harry called over his shoulder. "I need to see Nancy in my office."

"Now what's up?" Mary winced, fearing the worst as Nat waved goodby, obviously declining the coffee.

"Stop worrying, he's in a good mood, isn't he?" Nancy replied, putting his usual tray together with tea and a fresh raisin scone.

"You got your own mailing system going, lass?" he asked, looking up as she entered and slid the tray onto his desk. He dropped a small parcel onto his desk in front of her, then pulled the tray toward him. "That came for you via C.P. Railway to The Empress," he said, obviously curious of the contents. "Jenkins gave it to Joe Simpson at the Occidental who passed it on to me. What the hell is it?"

"I don't know," said Nancy, turning the parcel over in her hands, curious herself but not letting it show. She glanced at the clock. "I'll find out later, it's time we opened the doors." Spinning around, she hurried out of the room and quickly put the parcel into her locker, grinning to herself as she heard a disappointed Harry shout after her.

Within five minutes the dining room was buzzing, giving Nancy no time whatsoever to think of her parcel for several hours. Catching snatches of conversations, she quickly realized that a number of the patrons were discussing the salvage.

Tom Mund, from the neighbouring Horseshoe Bar, loudly expounded his theory that the Joyces were merely whalers and wouldn't know the price of anything except rope.

"Don't you believe it," one of Morris' men loudly declared. "Someone down there knows business!"

185

"Well, who is it then?" the tavern-keeper yelled across the dining room, jumping to his feet so quickly his chair crashed to the floor. "It can't be that old Scotty who runs their office?"

Nancy's blood began to boil at Mund's insulting reference, but fortunately, Harry heard the commotion and came running from the kitchen. He pleaded with the tavern-keeper to be quiet and sit down. The redhead moved quickly to pick up the chair but as she stooped the man pushed her roughly out of the way sending her onto her knees. A sudden hush came over the dining room.

"Pick her up you oaf ... or you'll wish you had!" a menacing voice snarled from the doorway.

Someone's coffee cup rattled nervously as all heads swung toward the door. Terry O'Reilly, looking every inch the gangster, stepped into the room. Standing up straight and flexing his broad shoulders, he glared through the tension-filled air at Tom Mund. Then, with a menacing fire in his eyes, O'Reilly took another step forward.

Mund quickly offered Nancy his hand and helped her onto her feet. "Sorry," he mumbled, making a speedy detour around the outside tables as he made for the door.

Terry's eyes watched his every step until the door closed behind him. A low murmur now began to run through the room which Terry ignored. "Good day to you, folks ... ma'am," he said pleasantly, tipping his hat and winking at Nancy before disappearing back the way he had come.

"Who was that?" the whispered question ran from table to table as the dining room resumed its normal buzz, but Nancy wasn't about to spoil the mystery.

As the morning wore on, the general topic of conversation turned back to the salvage. Fred Barrett walked in at lunchtime and found a table. He handed Nancy an envelope as he gave his food order.

"The *Belfast* came in this morning," he informed her, opening his newspaper.

"Loaded?" Nancy asked, eagerly.

"Aye, towing a barge," Fred chuckled.

Knowing that the return of the *Belfast* meant they could finish their oil orders, Nancy happily put the letter away in her locker as she waited for Fred's order. Her eyes came to rest on the little parcel. "I wonder what that is?" she mused, picking it up to feel its weight again. But it offered her no clue.

"Order's ready, Nancy," Mary called, and she hastily put the parcel back on the shelf.

"Danny said he'd pay for this," Fred muttered, glancing up at the girl as she put his lunch in front of him.

"I know," she whispered, "there won't be any bill, Fred."

A look of gratitude swept over his face and Nancy smiled warmly at him, throwing his heart in a whirl. "Thanks Nancy," he replied, surprised at how this girl could send an old man's heart a flutter.

The afternoon went quickly and it was almost six o'clock when several patrons arrived looking bedraggled and asking for a hot drink. An unexpected windstorm had blown down a scaffold on Yates Street and it seemed there was a possibility of the streetcars shutting down as shingles and hoardings were being torn loose everywhere. It sounded mighty dangerous to be out on the streets.

Putting on her coat an hour later, Nancy could hear the wind as it whistled through the poorly fitting windows of the staff room and she wished she didn't have to go out.

"Want me to take you home, lass?" Harry called, although his voice seemed to have a reluctant edge.

"Oh please, Harry, if you don't mind ..." she replied, just as the crash of a slamming door echoed through the building.

"Yer brother's here for you, Nancy!" shouted one of the girls, as she whipped into the kitchen.

Relief was apparent on Harry's face as he slipped off his coat. He had a terrible fear of storms, though he tried not to let it be known.

Dan, dressed in rain gear dripping with water, appeared. Grinning, he held out an extra raincoat to Nancy and helped her into it. "We decided I'd better come get you," he laughed. "Meg was afraid a little thing like you would get drowned or blown away and we'd never see you again!"

Arms around each other's waists, they struggled down Broughton Street as the relentless wind and rain pounded their bodies. Enjoying the closeness, they tried to run but it was impossible and they broke into giggles and held each other tighter as water dripped from their noses and hair.

At Wharf Street, a hoarding came loose and Dan pulled her to safety as it crashed into the heavy stone corner of the Pither and Leiser Building, showering the sidewalk with flying debris. Stumbling across the deserted street and down the boardwalk, Dan hurriedly opened the door and pushed Nancy inside, pulling it shut behind her. Meg jumped to her feet and rushed to Nancy's assistance.

"Where's Dan gone?" Nancy croaked, when she realized he was not behind her.

"Probably checking the dock. Oh my, I'm so glad Dan went for you, lassie!" exclaimed Meg, helping her remove her wet clothes, sending a shower of water onto the floor. Then she pulled Nancy over toward the warm stove where she had a blanket waiting. "Come on, love," she implored, "let's get you warm, Dan will be back in a minute." Seeing Nancy was settled, she found a mop and cleaned up the floor.

A noise at the door alerted them as Dan returned forcing the door shut with an effort that visibly surprised him. Meg's eyes inquired if the salvage was tied down securely on the jetty. Nodding to set her mind at rest, Dan, still breathless from his efforts, hung his coat up behind the door and drew a chair up beside Nancy.

"*Belfast* came in today," he announced. "We should be able to fill more of your orders tomorrow."

"I know, Fred came in today. I haven't looked at his papers yet. They're in my coat pocket. Oh, I almost forgot ... I got a mystery parcel today." Jumping up with the blanket still around her, she went to her coat and produced the envelope Fred had given her at lunchtime. She handed it to Meg.

"A mystery parcel from who?" asked Dan.

"I don't know yet, silly," she giggled, putting the blanket to one side and retrieving the little box from her other pocket. "It's a mystery

188

to me, too. What does the manifest say we've got in those boxes on the dock, Aunt Meg?"

Reaching for her glasses, Meg moved to the table, spreading the papers out flat as they all gathered around. As Dan scanned them over her shoulder, Nancy's eager fingers played with the wax seal on her box.

"This is what you wanted, sis," Dan announced, jubilantly. "Now we know what's in them boxes and who it's for! What's in your parcel?"

"Let's find out, shall we?" she said eagerly, as nimble fingers quickly stripped away the wrapping to reveal a beautiful little box with the initials "NW" carved delicately into the wood.

"That's a fine piece of carving," Dan murmured appreciatively, staring at the little box.

"It's stuck tight," she groaned, trying to pull the lid off.

Dan produced his knife from its sheath on his belt, took the box from Nancy and began to pry the lid off.

"Careful, Danny!" she admonished, gasping as the lid dropped on the table and a glint of gold was seen through the paper packing. Nancy pulled away the covering and several shiny nuggets were found nestled in the bottom of the little box.

"Gold!" Meg whispered.

"My God," Dan exclaimed, "who sent that … and why? You must have an admirer, girl!"

As she emptied the misshaped pieces of varying sizes onto the table, a small, tattered piece of paper also appeared. Unfolding it carefully, Nancy haltingly read the crudely written words aloud. "WE HIT IT GOOD. YOUR SHARE. JACK."

A tear ran down Nancy's cheek as she stared at the note. Dan put his arm around her shoulder and took it from her. "Your share? What's that all about, sis?" Kneeling beside her chair, he forcibly turned her chair around to face him. Suddenly, it was if all the cares in the world were on her shoulders and she began to sob. Puzzled, Dan took her into his arms.

189

"It's old English Jack," Meg answered, her own voice quivering with emotion. "He's hit it big and agreed to share it with Nancy."

"But why would he share it with you, love?"

"Remember the two man who were fighting in the alley outside the Occidental last year, Danny," Nancy haltingly began, as she tried to gather her composure. "That little sack I tripped on was Jack's gold." Dan nodded. "He disappeared for a long time and I tried to find him. Well, he finally turned up again while you were away, and I grub staked him with his own money without telling him."

"So," the whaler laughed. "Be happy, he's hit it big."

"But now I've got more of his gold. He thinks he owes me."

"Hey, it's alright, love. He doesn't need it now," Dan chuckled. "But if he ever comes back again, we'll take care of him, I promise you that."

Knowing Dan would be true to his word, Nancy picked up the gold and placed it carefully back into the box and replaced the lid. Reaching for the list of cargo, she scanned it through tearful eyes.

"It's going to be easy now. Those boxes are all branded with numbers." She looked up at the waiting faces. "We'll give them all twenty-five percent discount on their original order, that way we all win. It's already worked for Morris' and Wilson's."

Sometime later, Dan went to the window and looked out into the darkness. "Wind's dropped and I see some stars. I think it's going to be a lovely day tomorrow."

"Och, you've a hope, lad!" said Meg.

"That's the way of Victoria weather, Aunt Meg," Dan laughed. "One day it can be hell and the next one heaven."

During the night the storm did blow itself out, leaving the litter-strewn streets to city workers urgently attempting to clean up the mess for early morning traffic. Dan watched from the end of the boardwalk as Nancy waved, then disappeared up Broughton Street. Turning toward the jetty, he knew he had a full day ahead of him. It would now be an easier task identifying the crates and boxes, now that they had the cargo list to work from.

190

By the time Meg came out with the coffee, they were well into the job with many of the crates already open and their contents checked. She was amazed at the packing skills of the factory workers. When Tim pried open a crate of fine English Bone China, not a single piece was broken.

"Some of these pieces are staying right here!" she exclaimed, excitedly holding up several decorative pieces putting them into a small wooden box.

Oil customers began arriving telling the men their stories of how Nancy had convinced them to buy the oil. The last customer of the day was the Silver Springs Brewery truck, which almost cleaned them out. The two hefty brewery workers made short work of the loading before handing a sealed envelope to Meg, marked as full payment. As she emptied the contents onto her desk, a note appeared. Neatly written on the outside of the folded paper were the words, *To The Attention of Nancy*. Meg counted the money and wrote the receipt handing it to the men who hurried off.

She picked up the note turning it over in her hands wondering what it could mean. Then the distinctive sound of horse's hooves and iron-rimmed wheels could be heard arriving on the jetty. Sliding the note into her ledger, Meg rushed out to see who it was. Billy was talking to Dan while four of his friends sat waiting in a heavily loaded dray.

"Hello Miss MacDonald," Billy greeted her. "I come for oil. We brought potatoes to pay you."

"I thought Mr. Irvine sold the potatoes to the Chinaman," said Meg.

"Mr. Irvine say Chinaman had enough potatoes!" Billy explained.

"Alright, have them stack the potatoes by the office wall. Dan, you can give him two barrels."

The young whaler scratched his head but carried out his instructions and soon the boys had two tons of potatoes stacked neatly against the office wall.

Ned strolled over to see what was happening. He burst into laughter when he saw the potatoes. "I'll bet this is another of Nancy's deals!"

"Danny," Meg snapped, "put the two barrels of oil on the dray and stop looking so daft."

Spurred into action by the Scot's sharp tone, the barrels were quickly loaded and Billy turned to shake hands with Dan and Ned. He thanked Meg profusely and said he had a message for Nancy from Farmer Irvine.

"Mr. Irvine tell me to say thank you to Nancy," he said, smiling broadly. "He say she always welcome at his farm. He likes way she do business."

Ned shook his head in puzzled amusement as they watched the dray leave. "Our Nancy's a bundle of surprises, but what on earth are we going to do with all these potatoes?"

"Frankly, I don't know yet. Wash up, Danny, and go meet your sister," Meg ordered, as she headed into the office. "She'll know what to do. Ned can cover the potatoes."

"Go on, lad," Ned chuckled. "You heard the boss! I'll finish up."

When Nancy noticed Danny sitting at a table in the corner of the Balmoral Dining Room, a frown crossed her tired face. Knowing it was not the end of her shift for another hour, she was more than a bit concerned why he had come. "Is there a problem at home, Danny?"

"Just a little one," he grinned, hand mimicking the size of a potato.

Frowning again, but interrupted by a customer, she told him she'd be back. Her mind was a whirl trying to imagine what Dan could be referring to, when she noticed Waldo had also entered and was sitting by himself reading some papers.

"Are you expecting someone, Mr. Skillings?"

"Wilson and a visitor," he grunted, not looking up.

Returning a few minutes later with three cups and saucers and a pot of coffee, she found William Wilson and another well-dressed man had already arrived.

192

The old clothing merchant looked up at the girl. "There was no damage in those crates, my dear," he told her in a secretive voice.

Indicating how pleased she was to hear the news, she poured a cup of coffee for each of them then moved off to quickly deliver a cup to Dan. It wasn't until sometime later, and almost six o'clock, when she finally had time to talk to Dan.

"Now, what's the problem, Danny?"

"Potatoes … two tons of them!"

"Potatoes!" she mumbled to herself, repeating it over and over again as she made her way into the kitchen.

"Time you went home," Harry called from his office.

"I'm going soon," Nancy called back, "but I've got a problem with potatoes to sort out."

Harry's face turned ashen white and he jumped up, chair grating on the floor, as he rushed to the door.

"Mary, you did order the potatoes, didn't you?"

"No, Mr. Tabour, I did not!" she called back, as she dropped what she was doing and headed into the storeroom. "You said you were going to order them this morning."

"Damn!" the manager cried in frustration. "I forgot all about it."

A smile played on Nancy's lips as she stood watching the developing scene.

"We're almost out, Harry," Mary called from the door of the storeroom. "We'll need some tonight."

Shoulders sagging, the manager turned back to his office, knowing it would be impossible to get a delivery so late in the day. As he slumped into his chair, Nancy casually slipped out of the kitchen to find Dan.

"Where are the potatoes?" she asked, finding him waiting in the hall. "I seem to remember something about potatoes, but I didn't realize…."

"They're stacked against our office wall, all two tons of them! We assumed you knew about them. Billy brought them in."

"Oh my gosh! Go back to the dining room and wait for me," she whispered, hurrying back to the kitchen.

Puzzled, Dan went back into the dining room but before he sat down, he let his eyes wander around the room. Waldo was now alone and waving to get his attention so Dan went over to his table.

"Hello Dan," Waldo greeted the whaler, indicating he should sit down. "Waiting for Nancy?"

"Yes," Dan admitted, thoughtfully, "but she's busy with something."

Meanwhile, Nancy walked into Harry's office and found him sitting despondently at his desk.

"Now what?" he asked, gloomily.

"I've got the potatoes you need," she announced, coyly. "Two tons of them ... but you'll have to take them all!"

Harry sat bolt upright in his chair, a look of astonishment on his face. "Can I get them tonight?"

"Yes, if we agree on a price."

"Top price ... just bring me the bill," said Harry, sitting back in his chair and sighing with relief. He couldn't believe his luck that the problem had been solved so easily.

Nodding, she quickly left his office, hung her apron up, and with a grin brightening her face she went over to Dan and Waldo.

"This couldn't be better," she mumbled under her breath. Cautiously looking around the nearly empty room, she sat down at their table. "Can you move two ton of potatoes tonight, Waldo?"

"Depends ... from where to where?"

"From our dock to the Balmoral!"

"I'll get on it right now," Waldo replied. "I don't see a problem."

"Have you sold them already?" Dan whispered, incredulously, as Waldo left the room.

Nancy just had time to explain what was happening when Waldo returned, grinning. "It's as good as done! I managed to catch the boys and they'll be down at the dock within the half-hour."

Thanking Waldo profusely, Nancy went to find Harry. Instead, she talked to an elated Mary, asking her to relay the news to Harry if she saw him.

194

Ten minutes later, she and Dan were on their way home. Streetcars could be heard in the distance although the streets were almost deserted. Crossing Wharf Street, they peered down the hill into the eerie glow of the poorly lit dock, trying to see if Waldo's men had arrived. Then they noticed several swinging lanterns lighting the way for one of the Victoria Cartage trucks which was backing up near the office. They ran down the boards and Dan said he would deal with it.

"Where have you been?" Meg called worriedly, as she came through the door.

"I've sold the potatoes! They're loading them for the Balmoral as we speak!" Nancy announced, smugly.

"Doesn't surprise me one little bit," muttered the Scot, placing their steaming dinners on the table as Dan entered. "She has a gift lad, she could sell snow to the Eskimos!" Then a thought struck Meg and going over to her ledger, she produced the note from Crystal Springs. "This came for you today, lassie."

Nancy opened the letter, reading it aloud. *Dear Nancy, We dearly hope you will accept our invitation to come for Christmas Dinner on December 25th. Please bring your family and come sing for us. Kindest regards, Harry and Millie Maynard.*

"That's the second invitation to a party we've had today," Nancy chuckled, before hungrily shoveling in another mouthful. "Charlotte was at the hotel today and asked us all to her Christmas Party for December 23rd. She said she wanted to be the first to book us."

"That was nice of her. Oh, there's something else happened this afternoon while you were away, Dan," announced Meg. "Tim and Ned had a visit from an agent for William Schupp, an American of German decent. He wants to buy their boat and the business."

Dan's knife and fork clattered onto the table and he gaped at Meg. "They wouldn't sell the old *Belfast*, would they?"

I'm sure Ned and Tim wouldn't do anything without talking to us," Nancy suggested.

"They're getting older, lad," Meg interjected, "and you know how Ned feels about the dearth of whales. We'll see them in the morning and I grant you they'll mention it, just you wait and see."

Next morning, just as Nancy was leaving for work, the Joyces arrived and Ned, somehow anticipating the question on all their minds, came straight to the point.

"No, we're not selling, but this will be our last season. Tim and I have decided to take the *Belfast* home."

"To Newfoundland?" asked Nancy, not sure if she had understood. "That's such a long way. Are you sure the boat will be alright?"

"Don't you worry, that boat has a lot of miles left in her old hull yet," Ned assured them all.

Breathing a sigh of relief, Nancy quickly gave Meg and Dan a hug and left for work, turning to cast her eyes over the familiar grey shape of the *Belfast* as it sat tied to the jetty. *One more season,* she thought to herself, thankful her world was not going to change for a while.

Dick called out his weather forecast as she passed. "Going to be a hot one today, Miss Nancy," he yelled, sarcastically.

"Yes, I can feel it already," she shouted back, shivering playfully.

Harry was sat at his desk when she arrived, sniffing the wonderful aroma of Mary's fresh baking.

"Did you bring me the bill for those potatoes?" he called.

"Sure did," she replied, poking her head into his office and waving a piece of paper. "Why are you so early?"

Smiling, Harry flicked the pages of his newspaper over nonchalantly, and held out his hand for the bill. "Alex Stewart's running for mayor," he announced, letting his eyes run over the bill. "Have you met Alex Stewart yet, Nancy?" he asked, counting out some money onto his desk.

"Charlotte introduced us at her meeting," she replied. "Oh, and by the way, Harry, you will need to pay Waldo for the late delivery of those potatoes."

The manager nodded, pushing the pile of money across his desk. Before she could pick it up, he threw another five-dollar bill on top.

"You pay Waldo, Nancy, you'll see him before I do."

196

Chapter 15

As November came to a close, oil sales boomed and the last of the salvage was sold, clearing the way for the *Belfast* to sail up the coast to replenish the oil stock again. With orders still on the books, Ned had been forced into buying oil from the Balcom's at Sechart. They were overstocked anyway, due to the tremendous catch of the past season.

Nancy and Meg became regulars at some of the city's better clothing stores. They enjoyed keeping an eye on the fashion changes filtering through from England. Quality shops like Wilson's or Gordon's in Yates, were usually the first to see the new fashions, although Nancy often heard tourists complain that shopping in Victoria was useless because it was so far behind everywhere else. Meg had also taken a definite liking to Campbell's on Government because of their good Scottish name.

Alex Stewart was voted the new mayor in the municipal elections and Charlotte was delighted when George Bell and Walter Sergeant, the other two candidates she and her husband had supported, also succeeded onto council.

Even colder winds, now coupled with sleet-filled rain, whipped the streets in early December as winter put its icy grip on the city. There was a happy sense of Christmas in the air when the papers blared the disturbing news of the ominous threat of war in Europe. Naturally, this now became the new topic for discussion, although Nancy couldn't understand why people were so concerned, after all England and Europe were a long way away.

Charlotte and Jane Newcomb walked into the dining room one day greeting Nancy warmly as they took her usual table in the corner.

"There will be two more joining us, Nancy," Charlotte announced, loudly. "Oh, here they are now!"

A nun in long black robes, holding the arm of a slim, older woman, slowly made their way to the table. Nancy watched with interest, never having seen a nun in the hotel before. The whole room fell strangely quiet as people talked in whispers and watched the lady in black and her companions as they went over to Charlotte's table.

"Can I get you ladies something?" Nancy asked as the newcomers sat down. It was then she noticed the colour of the older woman's hair. Like her own it had once been the colour of copper though now mostly grey. Looking up, the woman caught the girl watching her.

"You must be Nancy," she said, with twinkling eyes.

"Yes, ma'am, I am," she answered, trying not to look as puzzled as she felt, wondering how she knew.

"Bring tea for Sister Mary and coffee for the rest of us, Nancy," instructed Charlotte, chuckling as the nun flicked her eyes up sharply. "Oh yes, and do bring some sweet cakes too, please!"

In the kitchen, Harry was talking to Mary when Nancy came through the doors.

"Take a look in the dining room," she suggested, "and tell me who those ladies are with Charlotte Townend."

Harry straightened his tie, put on his nicest smile, and walked out through the swinging door, his eyes quickly scanning the room. Slowly threading his way through the tables, acknowledging other guests, he nonchalantly arrived at Charlotte's table.

"Good day, ladies, is everything to your liking?" he asked, with obvious concern.

"Yes, thank you, Mr. Tabour," Charlotte answered. Knowing Nancy as well as she did, she sensed he'd been sent on a mission, so she introduced him to her friends. "Mr. Tabour, I'd like you to meet my good friends, Sister Mary, of the Sister's of St. Ann, Jane Newcolm, who was a dear friend of John Bryant ... "

"God rest his soul," interrupted Sister Mary, making the sign of the Cross.

"And our famous Nellie Cashman. You wouldn't guess she was a goldminer way up in the Arctic Circle, would you!" laughed Charlotte.

"My goodness, ladies, I am utterly enthralled with the company you keep, Charlotte. We are certainly honoured to have you all with us today," he said, in his most charming European manner. "If there is anything I can do to make your visit more pleasant, please tell Nancy."

Making his way back to the kitchen, Harry couldn't help but feel very proud of himself. *Mission accomplished,* he thought with a grin. Nancy was waiting with her tray just inside the door as he quickly recited the information to her.

"Oh my goodness," she said, putting her hand to her forehead and looking like she was going to swoon.

"Nancy, whatever is the matter?" Harry asked.

"Nellie Cashman ... in *my* dining room! Do you know who *she* is, Harry? She's a very famous lady ... I hope I don't dump the plate of cakes in her lap!"

"I'm sure she's had worse experiences in the places she's been. Now get out there, girl!" Harry said, giving her a little push.

Making her way over to their table, she took a deep breath and began to empty her tray sliding the cup and saucer in front of the nun and distributing the three cups of coffee to the others.

"I hope you will enjoy the cakes, Sister Mary. Our wonderful cook, Mary, makes them fresh each day," Nancy purred, gaining back her confidence but not daring to look at Nellie Cashman. She placed the plate of sweet cakes close to the nun and quickly moved on to another table.

Sister Mary's cheeks glowed a faint pink and a smile parted her lips as she reached for one of the cakes. Nellie Cashman began to giggle at her side.

"Oh, do be quiet, Nellie!" Sister Mary chided. "Sweet cakes are my only weakness."

"How did you know our waitresses name, Nellie?" Charlotte asked.

"English Jack described her in great detail to me, when I saw him some time ago up north." Pausing to sip on her coffee, she smiled at her companions and then added, "She has a quick mind and a confident air about her ... beautiful, too. I surprised her a little when I called her by name, but in the time it takes to pour a coffee she knew who I was, and that surprises me. Jack thinks she's an angel and perhaps he's right."

"A good girl, I pray," Sister Mary quietly interjected. Turning her head, the nun followed Nancy's movements studying her intently as she moved about the room.

Charlotte jumped to Nancy's defence. "That girl is one of the sweetest woman you could ever meet. She's an orphan and lives with a woman she calls her aunt," Charlotte declared sharply, emphasizing her point by tapping her finger on the table. "They're devoted to each other, really nice people, and good friends of mine, I'm proud to say."

"Here, here," Jane agreed.

"It was merely a question, not a criticism," the nun said haughtily, realizing she had spoken out of turn.

Eyes flashing, the friends stared at each other across the table. Nellie cleared her throat to get their attention. "Come, come, girls," she chided, good naturedly. "Your comment *was* out of order, Sister Mary!"

"I'm sorry, my dear, please forgive the rambling's of a silly old lady," Sister Mary whispered, obviously sincere as she reached for Charlotte's hand and squeezed it affectionately.

In the meantime, at another table, Nancy was talking to one of the Turpel shipyard foremen, unaware of the disturbance she'd caused.

"How are repairs to the *Southern Bell* coming along?" she asked.

"They should start in the first week of January. Dan just authorized the work," he said, pointing to the neatly folded papers on the table.

"Foresee any big problems?" Nancy inquired, watching him shake his head as he bit into his sandwich.

Finishing her shift, Nancy left for home, stopping only briefly to gaze in the well-lit window of Victoria Book and Stationary. The books were stacked neatly amongst the nativity figures giving it a welcome Christmas flavour. The art shop of the Shaw Brothers next door, held an equally fascinating display of pictures painted by local artists, each with its tiny price tag written so small it was impossible to make out unless one viewed it up close from inside the store.

A horse and dray, out unusually late for such a night, plodded along Wharf Street it's driver bundled up so tightly against the wind Nancy could not tell who it was although he touched his hat as he passed.

Dan smiled when she entered. Laying down the newspaper, he watched as she quickly took off her coat and headed for the stove.

"Signed the papers for the repairs to the Jorgensen freighter today," he announced.

"I know," she grinned, turning to face him. "One of Turpel's men told me."

"Can't I find anything to tell you that you don't already know?" he grouched, giving her a wink.

"Oh, that could be a difficult order," Meg agreed. "Not much our Nancy doesn't find out one way or another!"

Over supper they talked of the new house at Gordon Head. They had been discussing it from time to time and it had already been settled that there would be two stories and a partial basement cut into the rock for cold storage. An addition would be built on the back at ground level for Meg, so she would have no stairs to climb. Meg was now more comfortable with their decision to have her come live with them and she was becoming quite content to share in the excitement of planning their future.

With Christmas looming, they received another party invitation. This one from the Duggan's for the 20th. As expected, it was to be a small dinner party at their home in Fernwood.

It was a quiet time for everyone except Nancy. Tim and Ned had already gone up Island to visit relatives, possibly for the last time before they headed eastward. With all their oil supplies sold, there wasn't much for Dan or Meg to do either. So on Tuesday, realizing it was going to be a nice day for a ride, Dan hired a horse and rode out to the property alone. He had already talked to Jack Duggan about the house, but now they were ready to talk details. Before they did that, he wanted to check the location one more time.

Dan sat down on a fallen tree near the edge of the cliff, a forest of majestic Douglas Firs—so plentiful in this area—at his back. He marvelled at the clear view of snow-capped Mount Baker across the expanse of dark blue water. He had not realized how magnificent the view really was. Taking the time now to survey the outlook, he noted the many islands just off their coastline. There was a slight fog this morning and it hung around and between the islands causing each one to stand out like a majestic barren land.

When one takes the time to enjoy nature, it is amazing what you can see, he thought. Loving the sea since his first job on a boat as a 16-year-old, he had decided that he would spend the rest of his life here surrounded by the water and natural beauty. "Well, Danny-boy, you have certainly kept your promise," he mumbled aloud.

The pounding of the white-capped waves on the rocks below must have beckoned him for he suddenly stood up and moved to the cliff edge. Looking below, he hesitated for only a moment and then he was scrambling through the brush and over the rocks as he descended the steep cliff face … sliding … falling, grasping branches to slow his movement. Finally, he found himself at the hightide mark, clearly indicated by seaweed-strewn rocks.

As he landed, he was just in time to see a large buck with almost a full set of antlers, bound away. It's graceful agility, as it leapt from one small foothold to another, kept Dan's attention until the animal disappeared into the bushes that grew tenaciously to the rocks lining the little cove.

"Now where's he gone," Dan whispered, waiting for the animal to reappear. But nothing moved so he carefully made his way toward the place where the deer had disappeared. Suddenly, the animal came crashing through the bushes, hurtling toward him. He sunk onto his knees clinging to the rocks as the animal sailed over him disappearing quickly into the thick foliage.

Dan moved forward and parted the thick underbrush at the exact spot where it had burst into view. Behind the screen of heavy branches and shaded by an overhang of rock was the opening to a large cave. It was over four feet high and about five feet wide, stretching further back into the rock than the daylight would allow him to see.

As he forced his way into the cave entrance, a huge swarm of bats flew past his head and the pungent stench of droppings filled his nostrils. Realizing his eyes could not pierce the gloom and finding breathing difficult, he quickly turned, exiting the dank room. Emerging, he filled his lungs with the clean ocean air. *An interesting bonus,* he thought. *I hope we never want to use it cause I'll not want to be the one to have to clean it out!*

He went down to the water's edge and sat on a rock thinking it would be nice to have a boat but the clear water looked too shallow. He washed his cut hands in the salt water, feeling the familiar sting. Ten minutes later, he decided it was time to go back. He found it slightly more difficult clawing his way up the cliff and his hands were soon cut and his clothes covered with nettles. By the time he was at the top, he had determined that one of the first things they would need was a stairway to the beach.

When his head cleared the top of the rocks, he noticed the two men standing by his horse. They were dressed in work clothes and must have walked in from the road. Standing up and brushing himself off, he walked toward them.

"Hello. Can I help you?" he asked.

"Are you the owner of this land, sir?" one of the men asked politely.

"Yes, I am," he replied curtly, "and what is your interest?"

"We're loggers, sir … buyers of good quality standing timber," the man explained. "Are you interested in selling these trees?"

The thought of selling the trees hadn't even entered Dan's head so he was at a loss for words. Having no idea of prices, he asked them to make him an offer. The older man looked at his companion and grinned slyly as he walked over to some trees and studied them. He walked around for a minute or two looking up, occasionally shielding his eyes from the sun that managed to penetrate the thick foliage.

"Two hundred dollars, sir, for all of them," he announced, stroking his beard. "We'll remove them and clean up the mess."

"Submit your price in writing to the Joyce Bros. office on Wharf Street and I'll give it my consideration," Dan announced sternly, not having a good feeling about these men. "Now I shall have to insist you leave my property."

Reaching for the reins of his mount, he watched the men walk away speaking in low tones to each other. Dan smiled inwardly as he realized the men had given him an idea.

Riding back along the valley in the cool winter sunshine, he stopped several times to admire other properties visualizing how their market gardens and orchards would look in the peek of summer. *Could we make a living doing this?* he wondered thinking how pleasant it would be to get out in this warm sunshine and work his own land. *Twenty-five acres could make a nice little farm.* Then he spurred his mount into a gallop, swinging down a lane that took him onto Cedar Hill Road.

Arriving back before Nancy got home, he was bubbling over with enthusiasm by the time she came through the door. Hardly giving her time to remove her coat, he began spilling out his idea.

"Easy love," Nancy said, patiently. "You're a seaman, not a farmer!"

Meg laughed as she set their plates down on the table and joined them, listening as they made their plans for a large vegetable and flower garden in the logged off area.

"What do you think, Aunt Meg?" he asked, pushing his empty plate away from him and sitting back in his chair.

"Oh Danny," she sighed. "I'm just happy to be part of whatever you two decide to do."

"Not good enough, young lady," Nancy chided. "We want your opinion ... you have more experience than us in these matters."

"Sometimes I wonder," Meg retorted, shaking her head. "But why don't you wait and talk to Jack Duggan on Saturday. He has more knowledge of the area and could advise you much better than I can."

"She's right, Dan," Nancy yawned. "We'll have the perfect opportunity at their Christmas dinner.

The next morning, Dick was shouting loudly about the forecast of snow when one of Rithet's trucks skidded around the corner on the frosty surface banging into a lamppost nearby. Contents spilled into the street but the driver and the lamppost appeared unhurt. Watching the driver climb out and kick his tires, Nancy assumed his pride had suffered the worst damage. Chuckling to herself, she entered the hotel kitchen and was surprised to see Harry there ahead of her.

"What's wrong, Harry, couldn't you sleep?" she teased.

"It's the cold that wakes him," Mary laughed. "He's always crying poor. He probably can't afford glass for his windows!

"It might help his bankbook," suggested Nancy, " if he stopped entertaining the ladies."

"And going out on the town in the middle of the week," added Mary, winking at Nancy.

They could hear him chuckling as he listened to their silly conversation. Nancy, checking the dining room, was surprised to find everything in order leaving her plenty of time to have her tea and toast as she chattered to Mary before opening the doors.

Redfern's clock was chiming as the first customer pushed through the doors. Tom Ben waddled in, his nose as red as a beacon.

"Coffee quick, Nancy, I must be chilled to the bone," he muttered, finding a seat far from the door.

Filling quickly, the dining room was soon a hive of activity. Harry pitched in to help Mary while Nancy hurriedly served the tables. A sigh of relief escaped her lips when she saw Hannah come through the door early.

Sgt. Walker arrived, sauntering up to Tom Ben's table where Jim Waites, the locksmith, and Frank West, a shoemaker in the adjoining shop on Fort Street, had already joined him.

205

"Mind if I sit here, lads?" Walker asked, pulling out a chair.

"Sit yourself down," Ben replied, moving a box of cigars out of the way as Nancy brought another cup of coffee.

"We need your services, Jim," the Sergeant addressed the locksmith. "Somebody tried to kick in the door at Fred Foster's and bent his lock last night." He paused to take a sip of his hot coffee.

"Hmm, that's the furriers, ain't it?" asked Waites, with a smile. "Well, it were so cold, maybe they needed a warm coat!"

"That's not all of it," Walker continued, still trying to be serious. "Just for spite, they bust into John Thompson, the dentist's next door at 1214, and broke his door right off its hinges!"

"Solving that's easy, just look for somebody with new teeth in their face!" Frank West laughed, liking his own joke.

Nancy was bringing fresh coffee as the group again broke into loud laughter attracting the curious eyes of other patrons.

"More coffee, children?" she asked, smiling brightly.

"Not for me," said Sgt. Walker, coming to his feet. "But do me a favour, girl. Let me know if you see a chap with brand new teeth!" Not being able to contain himself any longer, the Sergeant burst into laughter and headed for the door leaving Nancy frowning behind him. The other two men also left, leaving Tom Ben alone at the table.

"You want more coffee, Mr. Ben?" Nancy asked, noticing the three cigar boxes on the table. "Got a customer for some cigars this morning?"

"Long Gun … he'll be here in a minute."

"Who?"

"Jack Irvine," the salesman explained, hardly lifting his eyes from his cup. "It's his nickname."

"I wonder if he's any relation to Tom Irvine, a farmer in Esquimalt," she commented. Receiving only a nod indicating he didn't know, she shrugged her shoulders and filled his cup. As she moved on to the next customer, she remembered she'd heard the name a long time back when she worked at the Occidental. He was the man who hunted down the cougar that was killing sheep in Oak Bay … ending its life with a single shot, it was said. She saw him when he arrived a bit later and besides his odd mode of dress, he looked like any other man to her.

Saturday finally arrived and after a busy shift Nancy dragged her weary legs toward home almost wishing she didn't have to go out to a party tonight. As she came down the broadwalk, she recognized Jack Duggan's horse and buggy tied at the office and her step brightened. She enjoyed Jack and Nellie's company and reminded herself how much she'd been looking forward to seeing them again.

Jack was in the office talking to Dan and Meg and she was surprised with the new surge of energy that rushed through her body when the old bricklayer greeted her with his familiar hug. Changing quickly into the new green dress Dan had bought her for Christmas, they were soon away and trotting up Johnson Street. They were met at the door by a delighted Nellie who escorted them quickly into the warm parlour with its roaring fire. They heard the sound of an automobile and Jack's voice shouting to someone.

"That's Harry and Millie," she exclaimed, happily.

"You're right, love," Nellie chuckled. "When they heard you were coming tonight we couldn't keep them away!"

The door banged and Millie's tinkling laughter filled the hallway as her footsteps came rushing down the passage. She had already hugged everyone by the time Jack and Harry arrived. Harry greeted everyone formally until his eyes fell on Nancy, turning soft and gentle as he held out his arms.

"Gracious child, it's so good to see you again. I think we should adopt her, Millie, so we can see her more often!"

Dan reacted immediately by pulling Nancy gently backwards until she sat on his knee, his arm wrapped protectively around her waist.

"Can't sir, because I already done it. She's mine!"

"Right, let's eat, Mother," Jack said quickly, breaking the uncomfortable silence that followed Dan's comment.

"It's all right, Dan, we wouldn't take her away from you, but you'll need to get used to sharing!" Millie scolded.

As supper progressed, Dan and Nancy began to talk about the new house and Dan brought up the issues they had with the Gordon Head property. Everyone listened patiently and then Jack made a stunning announcement.

"Well Danny, although we've been awfully busy of late, things are tapering off for winter. I'll take on the job of organizing the clearing of your land and building the foundations provided you come and work at the site when you're able." Receiving a silent reaction of surprise from Dan, he took it to be a 'yes' and continued, "We'll start straight after the new year. I'll also check around and find you a good framer and finishing carpenter. Victoria is experiencing such a building boom there are lots of men around seeking work. It shouldn't be hard to find workers. We'll have the house up in no time."

"That's wonderful, Jack, we can't thank you enough," said Nancy.

"What about the well?" Harry asked. "I know an Indian who can witch for water."

"Send him down to Dan," the builder replied. "You can take him out to the property can't you, Danny?"

The women who had sat listening to the conversation, now followed Nellie's lead and began clearing the table.

"You men go sit in the parlour and light your pipes while we clean up," she suggested, gathering up some of the dirty dishes.

"Wait a minute," Nancy cried. "I want to know what that was about the Indian that can ... which what?"

Holding up his hand to quell the ripple of laughter that ran through the room, Harry began to explain that witching is a term used by people who are sensitive to the vibrations of underground water. Holding a forked willow twig in their hands, these witchers could apparently find water as they walked slowly over a piece of land. The stick would often seem to become possessed and actually point to the ground, sometimes causing the person's hand to bleed, the force being so strong.

Nancy and Dan listened intently, trying to make some sense of it.

"And does it work?" she asked doubtfully.

"Yes, it does," Jack confirmed. "I've seen it done many times."

The men moved off into the parlour settling into the comfortable chairs facing the log fire and filling their pipes from the bowl supplied by their host. Dan kept throwing question after question at Jack who patiently explained the details of building a house.

Finally, just as the ladies rejoined them, Jack removed his pipe. "Look, lad," he growled, "we'll build that house and have money left over when we sell that big timber to Cameron or Jim Leigh, so stop your worrying. As far as what you should do with the land, well, I don't know, I think you should stick to the sea. There are too many farmers around her already."

Nellie walked across the room and removed a lace cover from the piano. Millie looked through the pile of music on the small table next to the piano, selected several pieces and set them up on the rack in front of her. Then she sat down and flexed her fingers several times turning to talk to Nancy. Meg found a comfortable chair and Nellie went to sit beside her husband on the settee.

Nancy and Millie discussed their selections for a few minutes then the pianist handed Nancy several sheets of music. She studied them while Millie's fingers skimmed lightly over the keys in an unknown ditty.

"Play the first bit of this one for me, please Millie," Nancy whispered stepping back from the piano and closing her eyes.

Millie's fingers flew over the keys, instantly bringing the instrument to life. Nellie inched closer to her husband as she recognized one of their favourite songs and Dan moved his chair back a little. Nancy's eyes flashed open when she heard his chair squeak.

"Ready," Millie murmured, glancing up at the girl.

The first song, a haunting melody from Ireland titled, *If I Ever See My Ireland Again*, was especially for Jack and Nellie, and had the desired effect almost moving them to tears as Nancy sang it to perfection. With hardly a pause the pianist moved straight into the Christmas classic, *Oh Holy Night*. As she played, Millie had an uncanny feeling that she was accompanying the voice of an angel. In the many years she had played for the Victoria School of Music, not many singers had impressed her as much as this girl. Between songs,

209

the silence in the room was broken only by the soft sniffling of Meg and Nellie as their fingers quietly sought out their delicate handkerchiefs.

"Thank you, dear friends," Nancy murmured, reacting to their applause. Glancing around the room, she asked, "Now may I sing one just for me?"

"Of course you can, dear," said Nellie.

"I'm ready, Millie," she whispered.

As the haunting notes drifted through the house, the audience instantly recognized the longtime favourite, *I'll Never Love Anyone As Much As I Love You*. Someone gasped as Nancy walked over to kneel at Dan's feet. She sang to him with such passion that Millie began missing notes. As the song came to an end, she lowered her head onto the lap of the man she called brother, sobbing quietly as he affectionately stroked her hair.

The room remained quiet, stunned by the outpouring of emotion from this girl whom they had come to call their own, yet suddenly realizing they hardly knew her.

Finally, Harry spoke. "You're a treasure, lass. In my entire life I've never heard singing like that before," he said softly, grasping his pipe tightly in his shaking hand. "I find it mighty disturbing when someone is able to reach out and touch my soul."

"You're right, Mr. Maynard," his wife whispered, wiping away a tear, then rising and closing the piano lid. "Now folks, it's very late. It's been a wonderful evening and it's been lovely seeing you all again but we should be getting these good people home."

Christmas greetings with the inevitable hugs went around, thanking the hosts for the lovely evening, as they got into their coats. The Duggan's waved goodbye from the doorway as Harry drove the Packard out onto the dark street and headed for the lights of the city.

There was barely any conversation until they entered the city and the strains of a German band at the Kaiserhof Hotel at the corner of Blanshard and Johnson were heard in the distance. Bringing the car to a stop at the curb, they wound their windows down and listened to the pleasant sounds of Christmas carols being sung loudly in German.

"Great voices," he chuckled, must be some of the Arion Choir members here tonight. Come on, Nancy, let's go join them!"

"No, Harry," his wife objected. "It's far too late."

But Harry wasn't listening. He leapt out of the car, opening Dan's door and dashing around to open Millie's.

"I can't sing in German!" Nancy called, as Dan helped her from the car.

"You won't have to," Harry laughed, "they're friends of mine. They speak English, too!"

Millie was obviously cross with her husband as he ushered them into the hotel and found them a table. He ordered five glasses of Crystal Springs brew from the waiter as soon as the band took a break.

"If you want to sing in English," Harry assured her, "you can. We'll all join in."

Nancy smiled, now warming to Harry's mischievous behaviour as the drinks arrived at the table, at which time she quietly asked the waiter for a glass of water. It wasn't long before the band began to play again. It was the popular yuletide song, *Joy To The World*, and they all joined in the singing.

Dan and Harry persuaded her to stand and within seconds glasses stopped their clinking, voices throughout the room became suddenly quiet, and the only sound that was heard was the voice of an angel. As the song came to an end, Nancy sat down. The bandleader bowed to her graciously and the hotel patrons erupted in clapping.

"Well done, love," Meg called, clapping as hard as she could.

"Are you satisfied now, you old devil?" Millie snapped at her grinning husband.

"More!" a lone voice called in English, quickly followed by more clapping and calling. Seeing they were not going to stop any too soon, Nancy turned helplessly to Harry.

"I guess you'll just have to sing another one!" he said, with a grin.

"I thought you were going to sing with me, Harry?" Nancy reminded him.

"Ah, Nancy, you know you do much better by yourself, and you like it that way anyway," said Harry, pretending to whine.

She shook her finger at him and rose to her feet, looking over at the waiting bandleader who was gesturing for her to come to the front. "Do you know *Oh Holy Night?*" she asked, but his answer was drowned out by the approval of the crowd.

A hush fell over the room as the band played the introduction to the well-loved song. As the sound of her voice again filled the room, the effect on the German audience was dramatic this time. Harry couldn't believe their reaction and finally felt some remorse for having brought Nancy. These hardheaded German businessmen had gone strangely silent hearing this beloved old song. Bowing their heads, they simply stared into their glasses. At the end of the song, they cheered again, but this time it was without the enthusiasm they had shown minutes before. Something was wrong, and Harry didn't know how to explain it.

It took a long time to extract themselves from the group as each of the men personally presented their thanks to the singer and said their goodnights, albeit slightly subdued. However, when Harry's car pulled away from the sidewalk, a goodly number of them stood on the street and held their glasses high in salute.

"You were wonderful, Nancy. That's given the Arion Choir something to think about!" Harry commented, glancing at his wife.

"Harry Maynard," Millie snapped, "don't you ever subject her to anything like that again ... sometimes you still act like a little boy who wants his own way!"

"Sorry, dear," the brewer whispered, attempting to be humble but in the dark he grinned mischievously, totally forgetting his earlier feeling of remorse. Arriving at the Joyce's, he pulled the Packard to a stop in front of the office. Dan jumped out, shaking hands with Harry and calling his thanks as he moved toward the door, key in hand.

Meg, taking Nancy's arm, turned to face the brewer and his wife. "It's been a pleasant evening and thank you for the ride," she said. Then the Scot paused as an ominous look came over her face. "But I won't have you using my girl!"

"He won't. I promise you, Meg," Millie assured her. "Thanks again, Nancy, you thrill me every time you sing, dear, and Merry Christmas to all of you."

"Merry Christmas and thanks for the ride!" called Nancy, as the car began to move away.

They silently watched as the car sped away and then they carefully negotiated the frosty planks to the open door. Dan had already thrown a new log onto the fire and the kettle was beginning to steam.

Nancy was surprised to hear the strains of the distant clock strike eight as she yawned and sat up in bed the next morning. She rose and peeked through the steamed-up window toward the dock where the boats sat snug and dry under their canvas coverings. Snow was falling lightly and as it painted the streets with whiteness, the muffled church bells began calling to each other across the city.

Sitting down to a breakfast of salt-cured ham and fresh eggs, bartered from a farmer on Burnside for a small pail of oil, Meg moved to the window and pulled the curtain aside.

"Fancy a walk … window shopping?" she asked Nancy, returning to her seat to finish her breakfast by mopping up the bacon fat with a slab of rye bread.

"Hmm … thought me and Dan would draw up some ideas for the house," Nancy answered, through a mouthful of food.

"Not this morning, honey," Dan announced. "I've work to get done on the *Belfast* in case it snows more."

"Well, I guess that settles that. Sure, Aunt Meg, it's fun to walk in the snow and we don't get many opportunities. We'll have to be careful though. It will be slippery underfoot."

When Dan had left, the women began making a list of things they would need for the new place, and decided which shops had the biggest windows. Wrapping up warmly, complete with cozy and soft handmuffs made by Meg from rabbit hides given to her by one of Billy's friends, they prepared to brave the weather.

They were surprised by the number of folk out on the streets, many on their way to church. They walked up Fort Street, past

Douglas and found B.C. Hardware. Peering through the large window, Meg pointed out one of the new stoves, a Lorain Campaign, which she had seen featured in their recent advertisement in the newspaper. It was a gleaming monster with cast iron decorations.

"Wouldn't it be marvelous to have one of these, Aunt Meg?" Nancy asked, excitement in her voice.

"Can you afford it?" she whispered.

"Dan says we can have whatever we want," Nancy giggled. "Between our pay cheques, and Jack's gold, we have a lot more money than we dreamed possible. And we still have all those trees which will help defray costs on the house. Come on, we've got lots to see. On the way home we'll look in Weiler's and see if we can see any interesting furniture, and Spencer's will have a pretty window, too," she continued, wound up like an excited toy. "They're all so lovely right now with Christmas decorations everywhere."

"Oh no, Weiler's is much too expensive, lass," Meg objected.

All morning Nancy coaxed Meg from store to store. They were having a wonderful time lining up their future shopping spree.

Finally, as it began to snow harder, Meg suggested it was time to go home. I think that's enough for one day, love, my feet are fair aching … it's a wonder yours aren't!"

"I'm sorry, Aunt Meg. Actually, now that I think on it, it would be nice to sit down. Let's go home, love," she said affectionately. "I'll make *you* a cup of tea. This has been so much fun, hasn't it! I can hardly wait until the house is built and we can really go shopping!"

"Nancy, let's go to church tonight. There'll be a special Christmas service, which you would like because of the singing."

To Meg's surprise, the girl offered no argument. "I think that would be a nice idea, Aunt Meg. I promise to sing quietly and not disturb the congregation!"

"Lassie, you sing however your heart wants, as long as you don't mind the attention, I somehow think this time everyone will want to sing with you."

Chapter 16

Charlotte's party on the 23rd became the highlight of the pre-Christmas celebrations. It was a festive occasion with a houseful of influential people, including Premier McBride, the new Mayor, and their wives. Dan found he could intrigue the guests with tales of his whaling experiences—the danger appealing to their sense of adventure no doubt, though few would have dared to follow his path.

Meg was sitting on the settee quietly sipping her scotch whisky when the Premier sat down beside her, admiring the highland tartan skirt she was wearing.

"My folks were Irish," he murmured, opening the conversation.

"McBride is it not, sir?" Meg asked, watching his eyes twinkle as he nodded in agreement. "Then it's more than likely your ancestors were Scottish, a way back."

"Maybe we're related," he whispered, warming to her instantly.

"Och no, laddie," she laughed, "I'm a MacLeod and a MacDonald, an ah'll noo be needing anymore relations!"

McBride looked carefully at her knowing they had met before, but where? Then suddenly it came to him. "You're Meg MacDonald, Nancy's aunt, aren't you?"

"Sort of," Meg replied, evasively. "They're both mine."

"Oh, you mean you're aunt to both Dan and Nancy?" L a u g h i n g again, the Scot explained how the three of them had became a family … by their choice.

He soon realized he hadn't changed his earlier opinion about this lady with the down to earth humour, twinkling eyes, and sharp wit. When she offered him a challenge, she was not surprised at all with his reply.

"Now tell me, sir," she ventured. "How many relatives would you have, if you could choose your own family?"

"Not too damned many!" Premier McBride admitted, sharply. Then, interrupted by party revelers, he was dragged away.

Alex Stewart, the new Mayor of Victoria took his place on the couch, flopping down beside Meg, red-faced and eager for a moment of relaxation.

"Hello, Miss MacDonald, can I get you another drink?"

"No, thank you, Mr. Stewart," Meg replied quietly, "but there is something you can do for Dan and Nancy."

"Anything," he whispered, now curious of this harmless-looking woman's intentions. "I owe Nancy a big favour after that night at the Odd Fellows Hall."

"Well," she began, "they're going to build a house at Gordon Head and might need a bit of help with the paperwork."

Alex smiled and held up his hand for her to stop.

"That's in Saanich and out of my jurisdiction," he murmured. "Who's building it for them?"

"Jack Duggan."

"Won't be a minute's bother, my dear," Alex assured her. "Jack knows everybody and will make certain everything is done right."

Charlotte and Nancy were talking quietly with the Maynards when the pleading voice of the Premier came loudly from the corner.

"Nancy, how about a song!"

Nancy felt a hand take her elbow as Millie led her toward the piano, whispering her own private request as she sat down and her fingers began to caress the keys.

"Just lively Christmas songs, love!" she whispered.

A hush fell over the group as Millie began to play the first few bars of *Joy to The World* and Nancy's lovely voice filled the house. She motioned for them to join her on the second verse and the sound was deafening. For the next half hour they sang their hearts out touching on both old and new Christmas hymns and favourites like, *I Heard The Bells On Christmas Day*, *Silent Night*, *What Child is This*, *Hark the Herald Angels Sing* and *Deck the Halls* as Millie went through her Christmas repertoire. Then, Nancy motioned for quiet.

"This has been a wonderful evening, thank you for sharing your voices!" There was a happy round of applause, then Nancy raised her hand again. "I would like to leave you with one of my favourites, *O Holy Night*."

As the party came to an end, she had many offers to attend Christmas Day celebrations but declined graciously, looking over at Millie.

"Sorry friends," Millie said smugly, winking at the girl. "Nancy and her family will be guests at our home this Christmas!"

Soon afterward, in the gently falling snow, Harry Maynard eased his Packard up to the sidewalk above the Joyce's office. Exchanging goodnights, he watched Dan assist them along the slippery boards to the door before he drove away.

On Christmas Eve morning, Nancy stepped out into six inches of fresh snow that covered the city, glad for her new, warm winter boots. Dan had seen them in the window at Frank West's, the shoemaker around the corner on Fort Street. Frank had stayed open one day the previous week, as a special favour, and Dan had taken her there after work. The delivery men were all back to using their horses this morning, and Dick, hunched over at his corner, jumped to his feet and threw a snowball, yelling a lively greeting as she passed.

"Come in, lovey," Mary called, as she entered the hotel kitchen. It didn't sound like Mary though, the voice was too loud and slurred, and she'd never called her lovey before.

"Mary, you've been drinking!" Nancy groaned, as she watched her friend grab for the counter, almost falling.

Pulling up a chair, she forcibly sat Mary down and proceeded to fill her with several cups of black coffee. In between, she got herself ready and made things more orderly in the kitchen.

Finally, Mary pushed the cup away in frustration. "If I don't go pee, I'm going to burst!" she wailed, standing up and demonstrating that she was already noticeably steadier on her feet.

With a sad frown, Nancy assisted her down the hallway. She waited for her outside the toilet, sighing when she heard the cook heaving as she deposited both coffee and spirits into the bowl. Emerging red-faced and wheezing, Nancy took her back to her chair making some toast and a nice cup of tea before going in to check the dining room and open the doors. By the time Nancy returned, Mary had made a miraculous recovery and both of them were extremely grateful that Harry was late.

Stamping snow from their feet in the hallway, the happy guests didn't seem to mind the inconvenience as the occurrence of a white Christmas was most unusual in Victoria. There was more than the usual number of people for breakfast that day and many businessmen were opening their stores early for the last day of shopping before Christmas.

Tom Ben seized the opportunity, like the true salesman he was, selling box after box of cigars. Nancy noticed what was happening and was puzzled, he seemed to have a never ending supply as he scooted between the tables. Harry Tabour solved her puzzle when he arrived for work with a box of cigars tucked under his own arm.

"How'd you get them?" she asked bluntly, pointing to the box. "I'd swear Tom's never left the dining room."

"Met him in the doorway," Harry chuckled. "He's a man outside with them loaded on a handcart!"

"Well, blow me down, now that's what I call being prepared!"

All day the hectic pace carried on and Nancy's girls were heard to comment that the patrons were being unusually generous with their gratuities this year. Nancy herself collected personal gifts from Mr. Davies, the Wilsons, Waldo and several more of the regulars.

Just before six, Harry asked her to divide the gratuities between the girls. Counting everything equally, according to the hours each waitress had worked, Nancy divided the coins on the table before taking ten-percent from each girl, for the kitchen staff.

Mary looked up when Nancy called to her and Harry, who was just leaving his office, watched curiously through the open door.

"How many youngsters have you got at home, Mary?"

"Why, love, you know I have five," Mary chided. "Six, if you count my Jim!"

"Then you take this," Nancy whispered, adding her stack of coins to cook's and pushing it across the table. Nancy knew full well that Jim was her husband who had lost a leg in a boating accident the year before and hadn't been able to work since. "And you have a good Christmas, Mary," she said, with sincerity, giving the woman a hug.

Mary, stammering for words and with tears in her eyes, tried to object. However, Nancy quickly slipped into her coat, blew her a kiss from the door and calling a Happy Christmas to Harry and the others, and hurriedly went out the door.

Harry was taken aback, but not particularly surprised, by Nancy's unselfish action. He felt both privileged and embarrassed to have witnessed the little scene which demonstrated the true meaning of Christmas. Moving back into his office and sitting down heavily, with elbows on the desk cradling his chin in his hands, he began to think of what it would be like to be totally alone in this world—nobody to care for, or to care for him. Oh, he had friends and acquaintances, drinking pals by the score, and a lady or two, but no family at all and nobody really close. As the realization struck home, he envied Mary with her children and one-legged husband. She had both a loving family and a special friend who really cared ... Nancy Wilson.

Half an hour later, he went out to say goodnight to his staff who had locked the doors and were getting ready to go home, earlier than usual. He had tried to get into a better mood but he was feeling quite low. *Damn that Nancy, she always makes me wish I was someone I'm not!*

He put his coat on and felt in his pocket for his gloves. When his hand came out he found he had a five dollar bill in it. *Oh yeah, change from the cigars. Well, that's a fiver I didn't think I had. I think I'll go have a Christmas drink with the boys.* With the money scrunched up in his hand, he went toward the back door, meeting Mary coming out of the staff room. She stopped and looked at his sad face and came over to give him a hug. Without even thinking, Harry dropped the fiver into her coat pocket and hugged her back.

"Have a nice Christmas, Mary," he said, opening the back door. As he walked up the street, he began to whistle a Christmas Carol and couldn't help but wonder what had gotten into him.

Heavy slush created by the extra Christmas traffic crackled under Nancy's feet as she hurried down Broughton Street and through the throng of shoppers. She waved to a workman in the lighted interior of Brayshaw's carriageworks, calling out a Christmas greeting.

Streetcars were laden with people trying to get everywhere in a hurry—last minute shoppers wrapped up warmly against the cold—as the ungainly vehicles with their now muffled sounds, moved even more slowly than usual toward their destinations.

Turning into Wharf Street, she noticed a horse tied under the light, outside the office. *I wonder who that could be,* she thought to herself as she opened the door.

Billy was sitting at the table wiping his mouth when Nancy stepped into the room. Grinning, he jumped up and came over to shake hands in a friendly but formal manner.

"Nancy look good," he chuckled, "red cheeks ... happy eyes!"

"What brings you out in this terrible weather, Billy?"

"This ...," Dan laughed, turning around slowly from his position at the sink. He was holding up a huge turkey, half naked of feathers.

Meg chuckled as she saw Nancy's reaction. Billy was obviously glowing with pride as he waited for Nancy to say something.

"It's a lovely bird, Billy, but who is it from?" she asked.

"From me," he smiled thumping his chest with a fist, "and Farmer Irvine."

"And for what reason are we getting this wonderful gift?"

"Mr. Irvine say you fine girl and very brave."

"Aunt Meg," Dan whispered, "can you find those two large cups I got for Tim and Ned and give them to Billy, please."

Meg opened a cupboard door producing two unusually large china cups, setting them on the table. Billy's eyes widened, never having seen such colourful items before. His fingers gently caressed the china.

"For me?" he whispered, picking up one of them and cradling it carefully in his hands.

"Yes, Billy, and you can give one to your father. They are very fragile so you must treat them with care. We'd better wrap them up extra carefully," she suggested, finding some newspaper. "We don't want them to get broken on the bumpy ride home."

Putting their coats on, they all went outside and Dan packed the precious parcel into a leather bag hanging from his saddle. Billy waved as he set his mount in motion, picking its way carefully up to the street.

Back inside, Meg posed a question in her usual blunt Scottish manner. "Right, you two!" she said standing with hands on hips. "What the devil are we going to do with that monster bird?"

Dan and Nancy's eyes met across the stove, as they warmed their hands. Meg patiently stood waiting when Dan suddenly reached out and drew Nancy close to him, speaking so softly Meg had to strain to hear. "It's not there anymore, sweetheart," he said, then seeing Meg's puzzled frown, he explained. "She wanted to give the turkey to the orphanage for the children, but it's not there anymore and the new one is too far away."

"Salvation Army then," Nancy suggested, snuggling closer to him. "They feed the poor people."

"You knew what she was thinking?" Meg asked.

"That was easy, Aunt Meg!" he admitted.

It was agreed that Dan would deliver the turkey to the Salvation Army Barracks in Broad Street, early the next morning. They were holding a special Christmas dinner for the poor so would no doubt appreciate it. Though tired, they all stayed up to hear the church bells ring for midnight mass. Standing on the quiet dock as a light dusting of snow fell, they huddled together for warmth. Looking up into the darkness, Dan noticed a small hole appear in the clouds, giving a view of faraway stars.

"Sing for us, Nancy," he said softly, releasing her from his grasp.

She walked a few feet ahead and looked up into the beautiful sky as the clouds began to peel away and more stars appeared. *What a perfect place for a concert*, she thought looking out over the quiet waters. Her first notes cut through the sharp frosty air bathing the dock with an invisible warm glow. Dan looked at Meg and put his arm around her shoulder. Mesmerized, they savoured each moment as the crystal clear sounds of *O Holy Night* drifted through the air.

Christmas at the Maynard's was a day Nancy and Dan would long cherish in their memories. The guest list was filled with many notable people eager to meet the red haired singer Millie had so often talked about. Nancy had seen many of them before but had never met them socially.

One of the highlights of the day was Harry dressed up as Saint Nicholas handing out bottles of wine to his guests just before supper. They were all prettily wrapped and tied in pink ribbon and caused many cryptic comments. On the side of Nancy's bottle was a small box fastened securely to the wrapping.

Dan led her to a quiet corner where Nellie and Meg were talking. He held her bottle of wine while she opened her mystery box. Pushing back the lid, she audibly sighed when she saw the gold ring nestled inside on its blue velvet pad. It was a plain band with a heart and some words engraved inside … *H and M, to Nancy*. Nancy tried it on and found it fit her finger perfectly, showing Dan and the others. Taking her hand gently, he lifted it to his lips and lightly kissed her fingers.

"It's beautiful … like you, my darling," he whispered.

Dinner was a sumptuous affair from the exquisitely decorated table and the perfectly carved goose, to the piping hot Christmas pudding heavily soaked in rum and set ablaze by Harry. A toast was proposed to the hosts, as everyone finished the delightful meal.

"The best is yet to come friends … shall we retire to the sitting room?" Harry replied, with an impish grin.

Taking their wine glasses with them and all chatting at once, they soon found their seats. Millie walked over to her piano, sat down, and began to play Christmas songs while the group settled down, some of them singing aloud. A few minutes later, she stood to face her guests.

Motioning for quiet, she announced, "Friends, yes, we have a very special treat for you." She held out her hand and beckoned to Nancy. "Let me introduce the special young lady you have all come to hear tonight … Nancy Wilson."

Leaving her seat beside Dan and Meg, and amid a ripple of whispers, Nancy made her way toward the piano. Then, all went quiet. Taking the girl's hand, Millie sat back down on her stool, pulling Nancy down beside her.

"Your choice tonight, love, sing whatever you like."

"Thanks for my ring," Nancy whispered back, kissing Millie's cheek. "We'll do a couple of Christmas songs, then do you know the one Aunt Meg is always singing?"

"*My Bonnie Scotland*, you mean," Millie chuckled. "Yes, yes, of course I do."

"Right then, two carols, Aunt Meg's and an Irish song."

Harry stood by the fire grinning as he puffed silently on his cigar.

As the carols finished and the haunting Scottish melody filled the room, Meg took Dan's arm. "She's singing that for me!" she whispered, her eyes misting over.

"I know, love," said Dan, taking her hand and squeezing it affectionately.

"Bless her," Nellie whispered to her husband, though Jack's eyes never left the singer.

As the song finished, appreciative applause rang out and more than one sigh was heard from a Scots in the room.

Millie's fingers danced across the keyboard moving quickly into the last song. Jack came to life as he recognized the tune of an old Irish ditty. His feet began to tap and when Nancy playfully added some heel and toe steps she beckoned him to join her. Jack whooped happily and everyone began to clap their hands encouraging them on. As the song finished the guests cheered and Jack swept the redhead into his arms spinning her around and around until he was dizzy and Dan rushed to save them from disaster. The music stopped, the room quieted and Harry stepped forward, his glass raised.

"Nancy, you're marvellous, love. Here's to your health and Merry Christmas everyone!" he exclaimed, emptying his glass.

It was near midnight when Harry dropped them at the foot of Fort Street, not wanting to chance the steep drive. Goodnights were exchanged and Dan shook hands with the brewer thanking him for a wonderful time.

Nancy leaned in the Packard's open window and kissed Harry lightly on the cheek. "That's for my ring and our dance, you old softie," she giggled, grabbing Dan's arm for balance as she slipped about precariously.

As Harry drove slowly away, Dan took the women's arms and they carefully navigated the slippery walkway together.

223

The streets were deserted Friday morning when Nancy made her way toward the Balmoral. A couple broken bottles sparkling with frost in the streetlight's glow, gave proof of late night revellers. Dick was missing from the corner as there was no paper today, leaving Nancy with a twinge of emptiness.

"Better have a look in there, lass," Mary growled, as she arrived. "It's a hell of a mess!"

Nancy pushed open one of the swinging doors, smiled ruefully at the chaos, and went to change. Returning in a few minutes, she grabbed a cloth and a tray and went to work, finishing with just four minutes to spare before opening.

"Have your tea, dear," Mary urged, handing Nancy a cup and noticing the ring on her finger. "Wow, that's a beauty!" she exclaimed, reaching for the girl's hand to look at it more closely. "Danny bought you a ring, did he?"

Nancy pulled her hand away and quickly moved up the hall to the front door. "No, not Dan!" she called back, causing the puzzled cook to stare after her. Redfern's clock was still striking as the big doors of the Balmoral swung open.

Down at the police station, Sgt. Walker glanced at the clock on the wall then dropped his gaze back to the telegram. It was a puzzling message from the mainland police force. He read the paper over and over, frowning until his forehead had deep furrows. On the pad beside him, he wrote a quick message. NANCY WILSON KNOWN TO THIS FORCE STOP SHE IS A FINE YOUNG LADY STOP.

"Send this straight back, Tom, and sign it with my name," he said, to the young telegraph operator.

"Wonder why they want a report on Nancy, Sarg?" Tom asked, taking the message and returning to his desk.

Walker lapsed into silence, ignoring the constable's question completely. He picked up the telegram once more and studied it, reading it aloud again in disbelief. FULL REPORT REQUIRED URGENTLY ON NANCY WILSON CITIZEN OF VICTORIA STOP BELIEVED TO RESIDE AT JOYCE BROS OFFICE ON WHARF STREET STOP. It made no sense at all.

Tap, tap tap, went the striker on the telegraph as Tom began sending the reply. The jingling telephone stirred the Sergeant back into action, jamming the receiver into his ear. His eyebrows climbed up his forehead in surprise when he heard Nancy's calm voice on the other end.

"Can you send a constable down to the Balmoral right away, please. We're having some trouble."

"Be right there!" he replied, dropping the receiver back onto its cradle. Leaping from his desk, Walker grabbed his coat calling over his shoulder to his startled telegraph operator. "Stay there, Tom! Tell the next one in Nancy's got trouble at the Balmoral!"

Nancy's first customers that morning were four sea captains, obviously far away from home and celebrating Christmas in the only manner they knew how. Staggering into the dining room, they loudly demanded more rum. Nancy fearlessly tried to reason with them, explaining she simply couldn't serve drinks this early in the day.

Things went from bad to worse as the seamen became louder and more abusive, making Mary very nervous wishing aloud that Harry would arrive. It was about that time Nancy rang the police station.

Cursing weather that forced him to walk, the Sergeant ran down Douglas Street slipping and sliding on the icy, but luckily almost deserted, pavement. Crashing through the doors of the Balmoral, he entered the lobby. He stood for a moment to catch his breath, then moved determinedly forward as he heard loud voices.

"What's going on here!" he snapped, with fierce authority.

"She," said one of the seamen, pointing a wavering finger at Nancy, "won't give us a drink!"

Harry Tabour arrived unnoticed and eager to be in on the action hurried forward.

"Lock them up, Sergeant," he demanded, aggressively.

"Wait," Nancy implored. "I've a suggestion. If we rent them a room and sell them a bottle, they can drink all they want!"

The seamen smiled drunkenly.

Sgt. Walker realized this was probably the best course of action with the least trouble, and not wanting his station full of drunks in the festive season, agreed immediately.

Harry began to object but Walker would have none of it.

"I expect you'll be able to deal with this situation now, Mr. Tabour. I'll help you get them to their room."

Harry, realizing his objections were useless, scurried away for a key, grumbling under his breath. Escorting the tipsy sailors to their room proved to be quite a humorous ordeal, even causing the hard-nosed Sergeant to laugh. By the time Nancy had acquired them a bottle, two of the seamen were already asleep on the floor. Holding his finger to his lips, Walker shepherded Nancy and Harry quietly out of the room.. They sat down in a quiet corner of the dining room and the policeman complimented Nancy for her quick thinking.

"Were you born in Victoria, lass?" he asked, innocently.

"No," Nancy replied, "I think I was four when we came here."

"Your folks live in the city?"

Harry had heard enough and leapt from his chair. "What the hell are you doing, Walker? Why all the questions?"

Taken by surprise, Walker forced himself to stay calm as Nancy slipped out from behind the table and went to look after a customer. "Because she's a friend, Tabour, and a mighty fine girl. I just wanted to get to know her a bit better."

"Well Mr. Nosy, let me fill you in," Harry growled, warming to his task. "She was brought up at the orphanage then worked for the temperance ladies. She bought her damned freedom by working at the Occidental for George Dunn, then I stole her ... best blasted decision I ever made! Any more you want to know?" Receiving no reply, he thundered, "Then go to hell!" and stormed off into the kitchen.

Walker watched Harry depart, puzzled by his outburst. Then he heard a softspoken voice behind him.

"Sergeant," said Tom Ben, having arrived unnoticed during the manager's outburst and found his own table. "Nancy's a good girl. Ask anyone who comes in here."

"I'm sorry, Mr. Ben, I didn't see you," Nancy called, hearing the new voice and heading toward the kitchen for his coffee. The men were talking quietly when she returned carrying two cups and a pot of steaming coffee.

"Relax, Sergeant, and have a coffee ... on the house," she smiled. "I'm not offended, but you sure touched Harry on the raw."

226

Sighing, Walker sat back in his chair glancing sideways at Nancy as she poured him a coffee. "I would like you to consider me your friend, lass," he whispered. "And so, obviously, is Harry Tabour! If you ever have a problem, love, you can be sure you have no shortage of friends who will want to help you."

Nancy was puzzled by the policeman's sudden outpouring, but she had no time to ponder his reasons as more customers were arriving.

She was so busy she totally forgot the four seamen until they trouped sheepishly into the dining room during the last hour of her shift. They were tidy, sober and well mannered, too.

"Can we apologize, young lady ...," one of the men muttered gruffly, "for causing you such trouble this morning?"

"Think nothing of it," she replied. "What you men now need is a good meal, so what will you have? We have a tasty turkey dinner with all the trimmings, if you are so inclined."

They turned to each other and as if conjuring up a picture in their minds, quickly handed the menus back to her, nodding in agreement. But before she moved away, the man nearest to her reached out and touched her arm. "We owe you, lass," he murmured. "You kept us out of the brig this morning. We won't forget it."

"What's a brig?" Nancy inquired, frowning.

"Lock up ... jail," one of the others said with a grunt. "The desk clerk told us what you did."

Blushing, Nancy smiled, telling them she would have their supper on the table in a few minutes. Later, they waved as they left and when she cleared their table, she was shocked to find a folded ten dollar bill neatly tucked under one of the plates.

The last days of 1913 were warmer but uneventful. Meg seemed to be singing Scottish songs all the time. When asked, she explained it was coming time for the Scots traditional feast in commemoration to the bard, Robbie Burns. In a deep Scottish brogue she entertained them, giggling as she finished each line. They had a difficult time understanding what she was saying, begging her to explain what the strange words meant but still being none the wiser when she did!

Arriving back in town early in January, Tim and Ned announced the *Belfast* would be leaving on the 15th of March, heading south this time for Oregon. They reminded everyone it would be their last season and they would be leaving soon after. They had a lot of work ahead of them before the *Belfast* was ready to face the sea again.

Encouraged by sunny weather the Joyces pulled the *Belfast* out of the water and began the arduous task of scrapping barnacles and repairing the hull. Dan was given the more pleasant job of painting topside. He also visited the Turpel shipyards, working out final details of the repairs to the *Southern Bell*.

By the middle of January, Jim Leigh, owner of the Rock Bay sawmill, had come to satisfactory terms with Jack Duggan with regards to the removal of timber from the Gordon Head property. Jim had agreed to cut and clear a portion of the land, returning a sufficient amount of cut lumber to the property for building the house, with no extra cost to the owners.

On January 25th, Meg brought out her surprise ... an unusual-looking, spicy roast of meat, she called *haggis*. She claimed it was cooked to perfection but it was mighty strange-tasting meat, they decided. After supper, she kept them laughing as she related the tall tales and legends of Scotland's mystery creature.

On the 1st of February, Dan rented a buggy and took them out to see the progress on the house, promising to make it a weekly event, weather permitting, until he went away. On one such visit, they were standing by the still-glowing embers of the logger's brushfire when a visitor arrived, suddenly appearing at the top of the cliff.

Dressed in traditional regalia, complete with facepaint, and carrying an enormous bunch of feathers, he stood at the edge of the cleared area. When Dan went to speak to him, he announced in broken English that he was the 'waterman' and had been sent by Harry Maynard. Dan found him to be an amusing old native but the women chose to remain by the fire and watch from a safe distance.

The tall, lanky Indian, with long grey hair hanging loose about his shoulders, wasted no time. Donning his feathered headdress, he sniffed the breeze and began to dance, chanting softly. Dan decided to follow him as he moved easily amongst the fallen boughs and tree stumps, watching the man's fascinating movements with great interest. Then, without warning, there was complete silence as he stood absolutely still and stared at the ground. Fumbling under his robe, he produced a forked stick, which he clutched in both hands and held stiffly out in front of him. He shuffled forward, swinging the stick slowly from side to side. Suddenly, the stick swung downward and the native let out a deep groan.

"WATER!" he cried, marking the place with a rock.

"Well, I'll be damned!" exclaimed Dan, scratching his head. He ran toward the native, piling several more rocks onto the spot to mark it well. The Indian took off his robe and headdress, carefully wrapping them up together. Without another word, he walked off along the cliff the same way he had come.

The next week, Dan began what he thought might be the arduous task of digging their well. The still very firm ground would be a challenge and he hoped to hit water before he had to leave in March ... still six weeks away. However, much to his delight, just as the Indian had predicted, within the first week of digging he was rewarded when clear fresh water filled the hole.

Two weeks later, Jack Duggan had completed the paperwork with the municipal council and had his permissions to begin building the foundations on the second day of March. Dan brought home the good news that Jack was already putting his crew of workman together and weather permitting, the house would be finished before the end of summer. Their home was becoming a reality.

Chapter 17

A few days before the end of February, Nancy had two visitors who arrived just as they were finishing supper. Sgt. Walker was accompanied by a young man carrying what appeared to be a large, and very weathered, wooden box. Setting it down heavily on the floor just inside the doorway, the man quickly departed.

"Come in out of the rain, Sergeant," Meg clucked.

Removing his wet hat, he stuffed it under his arm as he remained by the door. "Nancy," he said, in an unusually serious tone, taking some papers from his pocket. "I have some bad news."

"Bad news, Sergeant?" Dan asked sharply, springing to his feet.

Leaving the box on the floor, the Sergeant drew out a chair and sat down at the table, inviting the serious-faced group to join him. Laying the papers on the table, he reached into his pocket and brought out a large key which he placed beside them.

"Jack Cunningham has been killed in a rock slide in Alaska," he announced, without mincing words. Hearing no comment, he glanced from one to the other noting their blank faces. "You probably knew him as English Jack."

"Oh no!" Nancy gasped, feeling a hard lump in her throat and tears sting her eyes.

"Was he family?" he asked, watching Nancy shake her head in disbelief as the colour drained from her face.

"Just an old man she was kind to," Meg explained, going to stand behind her and placing her hands on the girl's shoulders.

"Well, it seems as if he has left you all his worldly possessions and they are in the box," Walker stated, picking up the key. "That's all there is left I'm told, everything else is buried with Jack and his partner under the mountain where he had his claim!" He paused, still holding the key. Nancy sat quietly, as if in a daze, and a silent tear rolled down her cheek. Dan looked at Nancy and took the key from the policeman, turning it over and examining it.

230

"What else can you tell us, Sergeant?" he asked, going over to the box and running his hand slowly across the rough surface.

"Evidentially, it happened just before Christmas. The magistrate found his will in that box back at his camp." Walker sighed deeply. "They've been investigating you to see who you are, Nancy. The city police have been helping them."

Dan's head jerked up, glaring at the Sergeant as he hissed, "You've been doing what … was that why you were asking questions that day at the hotel?"

"Don't worry your head, lad," said Walker, ignoring his question. "I personally vouched for Nancy … as did everyone else we talked to. Just sign these papers, lass," he said gently, "and I'll be on my way."

Meg brought a pen and inkpot, talking to herself as she placed them on the table. Reading each paper carefully before signing, Nancy silently handed them back to the Sergeant. Dan, who had been trying the key in the padlock, suddenly snapped it open.

"Don't look in there yet!" Walker snapped, rising from the table and slipping the papers back into his pocket. "Wait until I've gone."

Dan frowned but left the lid closed, his eyes following the policeman as he went to the door and put his hand on the latch.

Turning back just before stepping out into the rain, Walker looked back at Nancy. "Sorry, lass," he whispered. "It's all part of my job."

The door banged shut and the sound of his heavy footsteps faded in the distance. Nancy wiped the tears from her cheek with the back of her hand and knelt down beside Dan in front of the box. He looked at her questioningly and she nodded solemnly. Slowly, he lifted the lid. On top was a crumpled piece of paper that had been smoothed out flat and appeared to be a note containing only one line. Dan picked it up and read it silently before handing it to Nancy.

She recognized Jack's unusual scrawled handwriting. It said, EVERYTHING BELONGS TO NANCY WILSON OF VICTORIA. It was signed, JACK CUNNINGHAM, below it was a crude cross and the name of his partner as the witness.

"And that bit of paper is a legal document," Meg muttered in amazement, looking over their shoulders.

Dan began to remove the dusty items from the prospector's box ... papers, a pair of old boots, cracked spectacles, and a small flat package neatly folded and wrapped in water-stained paper.

"This looks like it was something special to him," said Dan, handing it to Nancy.

Unfolding it carefully, Nancy gasped, for embroidered neatly in the corner of what appeared to be a discoloured ladies handkerchief was the word, NANCY. "Why, that's mine," she whispered. "I sewed it while I worked at the Occidental. I lost it one day and had no idea where it had gone."

"Jack must have pinched it for a keepsake," said Meg, sitting down at the table. "You've been someone special to him for awhile."

The box seemed to be almost empty when Dan carefully removed a dirty and torn shirt, whistling with surprise as he peered into the bottom.

"What is it, Dan?" asked Meg, jumping up to join them again.

"Just look at that!" he exclaimed, barely able to speak. In the bottom of the old prospector's box was a layer of gold nuggets of various sizes ... the largest about the size of a robin's egg.

Nancy picked up the biggest one and held it up for Meg to see. "It's really heavy!" she said in surprise, noticing how the precious metal sparkled in the dim light.

"Why there's a fortune in there!" Meg exclaimed, staggering back to her chair and resting her hand on her chest. Dan took the nugget from Nancy and returned the items to the box.

"We had better take these to the bank in the morning, love."

Safely stowed away, they tried to settle down with a cup of tea as they talked about Jack, giving Dan a clearer picture of all that had happened.

"That old man obviously thought the world of you," said Dan.

"He's right, Nancy," added Meg. "You were probably the closest thing to a daughter he ever had."

It was still dark when Nancy and Meg stood on the wharf to wave goodbye to Dan and the boys on the morning of March 15th. Nancy felt sad and empty as the whaler went out of sight around the bend, leaving the Joyce Bros. jetty looking lonely and bare.

232

During the week, talk at the hotel was again of the impending war in Europe, as it had often been of late. Men spoke of forming militia groups ready for the call to arms from the King. Even Meg noticed the talk in the stores. She mentioned one evening that she was beginning to feel a strange tension grip the city.

Jack Duggan called at the office one evening to tell them about the progress on the house and to inform them that the roof would be on by the first of May. Then with a grin, he slyly mentioned he'd done something neither Dan nor Nancy had asked for. He didn't want to tell them but without too much persuasion he finally admitted one of his skilled stonemasons had built a tidy stairway down the cliff face.

"Oh, I can hardly wait to see them," Nancy cried. "We'll just have to go out on Sunday now."

"I doubt if I'll ever be inclined to use them," snorted Meg.

As he was about to leave, Jack turned back scratching his head as a puzzled look came onto his face. "Do you want a boathouse, Nancy? We'll have a lot of lumber left."

"Dan thought it was too shallow for a boat."

"No, it ain't," Jack assured her. "Drops right off. Water is so clear, it fools you."

Pondering for a moment, Nancy remembered that Dan had told her of a cave in the face of the cliff. "Alright then, build it right below the cave, Jack, I think that's where Dan would want it. But won't it be underwater when the tide comes in?"

"Oh no, lass, it'll float! Just leave it to me," the builder laughed, opening the door and stepping outside, but he stopped before he had gone two steps and came back. "Did you say cave?"

Nancy was surprised that Jack wasn't aware of the cave. "Yes, Dan says it's well-hidden in the thick brush below that great cedar tree that stands on the clifftop."

"That tree's gone now!" Jack exclaimed. "That was a big one and we didn't like its precarious angle. Dan and I were afraid it might come down in a storm and take the whole cliff with it. The stump's still there, you can plant flowers around it! Why don't you let me drive you out to the house on the weekend so you can have a look?"

"That's awfully nice of you to offer Jack, but Meg and I'll take the buggy out on Sunday if it's nice. We enjoy the trip."

233

Jack waved his understanding, tipping his hat.

May arrived bringing beautiful sunshine, encouraging hundreds of spring flowers to show their glorious blooms. Gardeners had been busy since the first warm rays hit the city in March and already there were some beautiful displays in Beacon Hill Park, The Empress Hotel, and gardens all over the city.

The women hired the grey and buggy and drove out to their new home. They marvelled at the sight of freshly tilled farmlands and the multitude of colours that Spring had brought to Saanich. Market gardens were springing up all along the route and Meg said they'd have to remember where they were so they could get some fruit and vegetables when they came in season.

Everything looked so different when they turned into Ash Road— they had to look again to be sure they had the right property. The workmen had erected a fine wooden fence that went as far as the eye could see into the trees. Pulling up in front of their gate Nancy leapt from the buggy, excitedly unlatching it and pushing it open. It swung easily on a rope and after Meg moved the buggy forward, she swung it closed again.

Their nostrils recognized the smell of still-burning wood even before they saw the great pile of stumps smoldering in front of them. Through the trees that remained they could see the shape of the new house. They hadn't been out for a few weeks and much had changed. Jack had been true to his word and they could see the roof was on. A sudden thrill ran through Nancy's body wishing Dan could be here.

Meg drove the grey slowly down the dirt track. New lumber smells permeated the air as they reached the house. Nancy couldn't contain herself as she stood up in the buggy and gazed in disbelief. It was actually looking like a house already and only the framing was finished! This was her first real home. It was a dream she'd had forever, and now it was actually coming true. She jumped down and taking Meg's hands helped her from the buggy.

First they walked around the perimeter of the house, then Nancy ran with excited energy into the partly-finished building. Panting for breath as she tried to keep pace with the girl, Meg finally had to stop.

"Slow down, lass. You're wearing this old women out!" she laughed, finding a barrel of nails and sitting down heavily.

"Oh, but isn't it marvelous, Aunt Meg!" cried Nancy. "I'm going to have a look at the stairs and walk down to the boathouse."

"Be careful, lass!" Meg called after her.

Jack was right, the stone stairway was wide and well-made. The men had done an excellent job, some of the steps had been carved right out of the rock face itself. Nancy began her descent, taking her time as she looked about her. Stopping about halfway down, she noticed a walkway being built about ten feet above the waterline. It was set into the hillside and straddled two of the giant boulders. Big iron rings had been set into them with concrete.

"That must be for the boathouse," she mused, aloud. Then she heard a splash and two seals surfaced nearby. *They're probably the ones we saw before when we first came here.* She sat down to watch them for a few minutes, laughing at their antics, then she hurried back up the stairs before Meg got worried.

Cutting over to Cedar Hill Road, Meg gave the grey his head and he soon ate up the miles until they reached the Fernwood hill. Being extra cautious Meg held him back until they reached the bottom and turned onto Bay Street. In no time, the grey had them home and the sound of iron-shod hooves alerted the stableboy who dashed out to help them.

"Been out to a farm?" inquired the old man.

"How'd you know that?" Nancy asked.

"Good rich soil on the horses feathers," grunted the stableman, turning to walk away.

"Hey mister!" Nancy called. "It's a horse not a chicken, what are feathers?"

Grinning through black teeth, the old man turned around. "Feathers, lass," he said, "are the long hairs around a horse's ankle ... everybody knows that!"

Newspapers carried stories of impending war from England and excerpts of speeches made in Ottawa by Prime Minister Borden. Preparation was the byword on the community's lips as Richard

235

McBride gave orders to form militia units and proceed with rigorous training.

The Bay Street Armoury was pushed to completion and staffed with officers and soldiers from the regular army, many of whom had already served with the British forces overseas. There was also a rumour that McBride, sorely afraid of a seaward attack on Victoria or BC's coast, was considering other action to protect the province.

Harry Tabour was no longer seen regularly at the hotel, leaving more and more of the responsibility to Nancy. He'd lived in Victoria for many years as a well-respected citizen but being of German decent he was now finding it difficult to avoid confrontation. Unfortunately, these situations were becoming more common as the inevitability of war grew. He had also stopped going to the Kaiserhof Hotel where the German nationals liked to socialize.

Nancy and Meg were searching the newspaper for furniture advertisements when Fred Barrett called at the office one afternoon in mid-May. He had news from the *Belfast* that the boys were on their way home. Turpel's shipyard also rang to inform them that the *Bell* would be finished before the middle of June.

"Everything's happening at the same time," said Nancy.

"You'd better telephone the Jorgensens," Meg suggested.

Nancy picked up the receiver and cranked the handle a few times. Hearing the operator's voice on the other end, she gave her the Seattle number and waited.

After three rings Beth answered, squealing happily when she heard Nancy's voice. "Pick up the telephone, darling," Nancy heard her call to her husband. "We've got Nancy on the line from Victoria!"

Gus dropped his newspaper and reached for the telephone but all he could hear was his wife's voice.

"Is Gus there?" Nancy asked, when Beth stopped for a breath.

"Yes, I am, sweetheart," replied Gus, calmly. "Be quiet, Beth, let the girl talk. It's so nice to hear her voice."

"The shipyard says the *Southern Bell* could be finished before the middle of June," Nancy informed them.

"Well that's just fine, honey," the millionaire chuckled. "We're booked into The Empress from the fifth. We're coming up for your birthday!"

"Oh good!" she giggled. "I'd forgotten all about my birthday!"

"We'll have a little party," Gus announced, "and you can give me the bill. Now say good-bye, Beth, and put the telephone down. She'll tell you all the news when you see her."

Down the coast, Dan was standing the night watch as the *Belfast* slowly chugged its way northward. This trip had been fraught with disaster from the start and finding no whales they had decided to seek the next best thing ... seals, their precious skins so popular in coats and warm winter clothing. Dan looked at the bundles of sealskins lashed to both sides of the outer deck and sighed. *The boys will certainly be glad to call it quits after this trip*, he thought sadly.

Three days before, they had barely cleared the wild Oregon coastline, still being at the mouth of the Columbia, when a squall struck about mid-afternoon. This area was well-known for its disastrous tides and they valiantly fought five to eight-foot swells desperately inching northeastward. Knowing they were close to the rocky shoreline and whirling seas of Cape Disappointment, a well-known graveyard of unfortunate ships and sailors, they used every ounce of energy to keep the ship afloat.

Hampered by a rudder damaged several days before, when pounded against a small island near Astoria, they had been forced to stop to make temporary repairs. Now, once again the sea boiled and the foaming waves heaved the *Belfast* treacherously close to the rocks. Unseen disaster lurked all about them ruining their chances of outmaneuvering the storm. Finally, just before darkness set in, with the North Head Lighthouse and its rocky shore behind them, they dropped anchor, hoping to ride out the storm.

Several hours later, the wind and waves finally abated and again they continued their slow journey ... limping northward. With most of the crew asleep below, Dan stared through the darkness, using only the moon to light their path. The dark sea pushed them northward and with time on his hands, troubled thoughts now brought Nancy to mind. He had not wanted to think about the future, there had been enough to deal with planning the house, but what about after that?

With the Joyces' departure now eminent, he knew his decisions would affect the lives of two other people. Was he going to stay with the whaling fleet or become a farmer, or was there something else he could do? He had almost ruled out whaling, although he loved the sea so much. If Ned was right, the fleet wouldn't be around much longer and the governments were beginning to regulate what the public perceived as inhumane methods of killing seals. The clouds began to clear away and a myriad of stars came out giving him hope that they had seen the worst.

It's a good thing our bank account is in such good shape, he thought. *The economy sure isn't and jobs will be hard to find. What if war breaks out in Europe? Everyone says its coming and yet no one wants to even think about it. Nancy would be frantic if I joined the service ...what would happen to them if I was injured or ...*

WRRAAACKK!! Suddenly, a disconcerting tearing sound rent the silence as the *Belfast* lurched to one side throwing Dan against the cabin wall.

"Damn, now we're in trouble!" he said aloud, realizing by the dead silence that the engine had stopped. He spun round, hurrying down the ladder into the darkness.

"Don't panic, lad," Ned's amazingly calm voice came from beside him. "I'll have a look, you get back on deck and drop anchor."

The others quickly appeared pulling coats and boots on as they gathered round, all peering over the stern where Dan was now dangling in water up to his armpits.

"IT'S THE BLOODY RUDDER, IT'S GONE, knew it wouldn't last!" he yelled.

"Come on up, lad," called Ned. "Nothin any of us can do until we have some light."

"I'll make a pot of tea," Tim announced. "And now that we're all up, may as well have something to eat. Dumpy, come and help. There might not be time to eat later!"

Daylight brought realization of just how close they had come to total disaster. The battered rudder would take them no further. Actually, they were amazed it had lasted as long as it had. Knowing there was a whaling station at Gray's Harbour at least a day and a half away, they rigged a small wooden door to the broken, rudder stem lashing it together as best they could.

Unfortunately though, the rudder was not their only problem. Other damage had been sustained and they would have to operate the makeshift rudder by rope. Dan, being the strongest volunteered for the job, but they soon realized it would be a two-man effort. Ned, despite Tim's argument, agreed to join Dan in what was to become a desperate and exhausting task to keep the ship on course.

As soon as first light crept over the horizon, they were underway again. Even at a slow speed, fighting even minimal tides became the job from hell. Two of the crew rigged up a tent-like apparatus to give them some protection from the elements. However, it seemed nothing could protect their hands. After several hours of pulling, the ropes had ripped their heavy gloves to shreds. Wracked with pain from their bleeding hands, the men did not dare take more than short breaks for fear the boat would drift off course. They held on, desperately waiting for word that Gray's Harbour was near. The sea seemed determined to break them, but they weren't giving in yet.

Dan peered outside barely able to focus, he was so tired. They tried talking to keep awake, but soon decided they needed to conserve energy. One of the crew fed him a drink of sweet tea and it cleared Dan's head a little. He realized the sun was out, but fortunately cloud-cover was keeping the heat to a minimum. He noticed they were edging dangerously close to land again and his heart sank as he mustered hidden strength to make the adjustment.

Sometime later, although he had no concept of time, he imagined he recognized the familiar landscape south of the protected harbour. Suddenly, Dumpy came screaming through the ship with the most welcome words they had ever heard.

"GRAY'S HARBOUR! WE'VE MADE IT!"

With Dumpy's help, they gave one more excruciatingly painful pull on the ropes, easing the *Belfast* into the calmer waters of the naturally protected harbour. Exhausted, they collapsed on the floor, the ropes still fast in their bloody hands.

"Hold on, boys, help is close at hand," he assured them gently, before returning to his post.

239

"HOQUIAM, DEAD AHEAD!" Tim called, as he eased off the power allowing the *Belfast* to limp into the Whaling Station at the Indian settlement.

Dumpy took over and Tim rushed to the stern to check on his brother and Dan. Bearing witness to the heartbreaking, bloody scene and the near-frozen mangled hands still wrapped around bloody ropes, brought tears to the seasoned sailor's eyes. Knowing he could do little until they reached land, he gave them both a stiff drink and tried to make them more comfortable. Then he went back on deck to join the others, allowing the fresh air to clear his head as he prepared for landing.

A small crowd had gathered on the whaling station's dock as the *Belfast* limped into port. Eager hands from the Village of Hoquiam caught the ropes and pulled the ship into the jetty, tying her fast. Joe, the station manager, upon hearing Tim's quick description of the men's injuries, called several of his men and they leapt aboard. An immediate call went through the village and in a few minutes a native woman rushed to the dock carrying a large bag. They were told she was a healer and would have them feeling better in no time.

Later, the villagers fed the *Belfast*'s crew, two of the native women spooning food into Ned and Dan's mouths ... their heavily bandaged hands resting in their laps. Barely able to find the energy to swallow, they were taken to makeshift beds in the whaling station office. They didn't awaken until two days later when the Belfast was almost seaworthy again. Stripped of her broken rudder, the men had built the *Belfast* a new one, and in two days had it installed and working.

Refusing any payment, Joe exclaimed, "We're all brothers of the sea, we might need your help some day."

Lining the dock early the next morning, the villagers called out their farewells as the *Belfast* made her way slowly out to sea. Dumpy blew the horn in a final tribute and they picked up speed. In open water, they rounded the point and set a course north by northwest.

Later that day, sniffing the air, Ned stared out to sea shielding his eyes with his bandaged hand. "Told you, lad," he muttered to the young whaler standing beside him. "We've ruined the whaling, took far too many last year!"

"You're definitely going, aren't you?" said Dan sadly, already knowing the answer. "Meg's going to live with us, you know?"

"Hell, son!" Ned chuckled. "Meg MacDonald thinks she's your mother. It would break her heart to be parted from you and Nancy. She's happiest here and she has no family where we're going."

Late afternoon of the third day out of Gray's Harbour, they came within sight of the familiar tree-covered hills of Vancouver Island. Ned raised his bandaged hand and pointed toward the cliffs of Cape Flattery close on their starboard side.

Dumpy, at the helm, yelled down the speaking tube to Tim, calling for more power to combat the tide as they entered the strait. Within the hour they were rounding the point and knew Metchosin ... and Victoria, were not far ahead.

They crossed the Strait and spent the night in familiar Canadian waters off Pedder Bay before pulling anchor at first light. They entered Victoria Harbour to a small chorus of welcome home blasts from ships along the harbour.

As Dumpy gently eased them toward the jetty, Meg's trained senses heard the sound of the familiar engine and hurried outside. She was just in time to see them pull up to the dock.

She knew something was wrong the instant she saw Dumpy and Tim leap from the rail. A puzzled expression flashed across her face as her eyes searched for Dan and Ned. Her breath came in short bursts and her heart began to pound. Then to her relief, the missing men appeared. She saw their bandaged hands and rushed forward to meet them.

"Oh, lads! Whatever have ye done?" she asked, sympathetically.

"Just rope burns, Aunt Meg," Dan explained, hugging her carefully. "Stop your worrying. We'll take the bandages off when we get inside and you can check them out for us."

"Call the sealskin buyers, Meg," Ned ordered. "Tell 'em we've got about three hundred."

Meg hurried into the office and quickly made a telephone call to Rithet's who agreed to send a buyer right away. Tim followed her, asking for the cash box so he could pay Dumpy and the boys.

"Sorry, lads, wish it didn't have to end like this," Tim said sadly, as he handed the crew their pay. "We're sure going to miss you all."

Shaking Tim's hand and slapping Ned affectionately on the back, the men said their goodbyes and began to walk away ... except for Dumpy who stopped to talk to Dan.

"What are you going to do, Danny?" he asked, hopefully.

Shrugging his shoulders, Dan's tired mind couldn't even think straight and he looked forlornly at his longtime friend.

"You can still come and visit us, lad. You know you can find us out at Gordon Head if we're not here!" announced Meg, as Jack turned to go. He acknowledged her comment with a half-hearted wave.

"Why wouldn't you be here?" Ned snapped. "You'll still have your job, Meg. I know you're going to live with the youngun's, but we're giving the office and dock to Dan ... or haven't we mentioned that!" he said, suddenly grinning.

Dan looked up in surprise. *Giving it to him? This could change everything,* he thought. "No you hadn't mentioned it, Ned. I'd like to talk about it, but later ... I think I'll go meet Nancy," Dan muttered.

"No you won't, m'lad," Meg scolded, as a knock came at the door. "Not until I've dressed those hands!"

Roland Houseman from Rithet's stood in the open doorway.

Tim leapt from his chair and quickly led the buyer down to the dock, pointing to the bundles of skins still lashed tightly to the deck. Houseman climbed aboard and checked the skins with experienced hands before making an offer.

"Eight-fifty a skin," he grunted, peering over his thick spectacles to cock an eyebrow at the whaler.

"You telling me they're worth less than last year?" Tim snapped, scowling at the buyer as he returned to his side.

"Yes, sir," he said, without hesitation, his eyes darting back to the skins.

Suddenly, a scream from the direction of Wharf Street, interrupted their conversation. Turning to see what the problem was, they saw Nancy tearing down the boardwalk toward them. She ran past the office, not seeing Dan inside the open door, dropped her bag and flew into Tim's arms. "You're home at last!" she cried, jubilantly.

"Your daughter, sir?" Houseman asked, surprised at the intrusion.

Tim returned her hug, totally ignoring the question.

Hearing the visitor's tone of voice, Nancy freed herself. Recognizing him as a customer, she smiled wickedly at the visitor.

"And who might you be, young man?" she asked, sweetly.

"I - I - I'm, Roland Houseman, sealskin buyer from Rithet's. I'd like to get on with this if your father has time!" he said tersely.

"Hold on there, lad," Tim rasped. "We don't have a deal, you only offered me eight-fifty a skin."

"What!" cried Nancy, moving toward the buyer.

In his urgency to move away from the girl, he stumbled, knocking his glasses to the deck.

"Robber!" she said loudly, leaning closer so she was within inches of his face. "Hudson's Bay told me yesterday they'd pay twelve-fifty!"

Tim raised his hand to his mouth and coughed slightly. It was interesting to watch Houseman's reaction as Nancy played with him, not allowing him to pick up his glasses.

"I can match their offer, Miss," he whimpered, obviously nervous as his eyes darted to his precious glasses lying on the ground.

"Then, put these on," said the girl, picking up his spectacles and handing them back to him, "and write out a purchase order for twelve-fifty, please."

Tim turned his back on the buyer who fumbled in his briefcase for his papers and then with trembling hand wrote out something in a small book. He glanced fearfully up at the girl before tearing the page from his book and handing it to her. Tim could hardly contain his urge to laugh, not daring to turn around as Nancy dismissed the befuddled young man.

The rapidly retreating footsteps were the signal Tim needed as he burst into laughter. "You knew Houseman?" he asked, as they walked arm in arm toward the office.

"I've seen him at the Balmoral with some of his cronies, always talks big about taking advantage of some poor little trapper or farmer." Pausing for a moment, Nancy smiled, "That's why I attacked him, he was trying it on with you."

"But you didn't really know the price of sealskins, did you?"

243

Steps from the office, she stopped and turn to face him. "Look Tim," she said, "I knew where you'd gone and with Ned's comments about whales I knew it was a possibility you would bring back skins. So, I've been keeping my eye on the prices. You'd be surprised what I hear at the hotel!"

Tim threw up his arms in submission, then remembering Danny, he took her arm gently. "Nancy, there's something you should know," the whaler whispered. "Danny and Ned have been hurt ... "

Nancy eyes flashed and she pulled away from him and dashed into the office. Meg looked up, startled by Nancy's sudden entry as she applied new bandages to Dan's wounds.

"Gracious, what have you done, Danny!"

"It's alright, sis, just some rope burns and they're feeling better already. An Indian women put some mysterious herbs on them at Hoquiam and now that Aunt Meg's added her magic, they'll be better in no time!"

Nancy stood behind him and wrapped her arms around his neck, planting a kiss on his cheek. When Meg finished, Dan turned and held his arms out ... Nancy needed no more of an invitation.

Nancy felt a warm contented feeling as she watched Dan wave from the boardwalk, his bandaged hand high in the air. They had had a lovely weekend despite his injury and all of them had gone up town to see the May Day Parade the morning before. It was always fun to see the bands and decorations but the addition of so many motorized vehicles had completely changed the look of the parade in the past few years and allowed for more complicated trimmings. Meg would have liked to have seen the Gorge Regatta but said there was always next year.

From the front of his shop, Waldo hailed Nancy as he stood watching Hagenbuch, the sign writer, and his men loading some large signs onto one of his company trucks. "Mornin' Nancy! I see the *Belfast*'s been home for a few days. I'll be in to see you later on."

Waving, Nancy carried on up to Douglas where young Dick's cheeky voice came ringing through the still morning air.

"Nancy's happy ... Danny's home!" he chanted .

"Brat," she called over her shoulder.

Mary called to her through the open door as she heard the familiar quick footsteps. "Bring that milk in with ya, love!"

Stooping for the milk can, Nancy was glad to hear Harry's distinctive whistling and hurried inside to change. She checked the restaurant—surprised when she found it unusually clean and tidy.

"How do you like that?" Harry chuckled, surprising everyone with his happy mood. "That new girl is great, Nancy! She took over your shift and worked all weekend. Now all you have to do is show her how to open ...." Harry suddenly realized he wasn't talking to Nancy anymore as she had left the kitchen.

"Not too fast, Harry," Mary intervened. "We'll be lost without Nancy. Did you hear about Dan's accident? Word is, he and Ned got some ugly rope burns on their hands this trip."

"No, haven't heard anything. All the more reason she needs time off, lass," Harry sighed. "Their house is almost finished, too."

"And don't forget, it's her 18th birthday in two weeks!" Mary whispered.

Chapter 18

The new topic of gossip circulating around the city and the Balmoral Dining Room was that the price of petroleum oil was coming onto the market much lower than that of whale oil. *Our timing worked out perfectly, just as Aunt Meg had said*, thought Nancy. She already knew from her eavesdropping that many of the traders were feeling the pinch of hard times as coal exports were down and fishery plants were closing. Large employers were now stooping to the use of cheaper Oriental or East Indian labour causing violent friction around the city. There had already been one riot after several white men had been thrown out of work. There was also mounting discontent with Richard McBride and his provincial government. Nancy was feeling bad that her friend had been blamed for many of the province's woes. So many of these conversations had become doom and gloom she often wished they could find something more pleasant to talk about.

At 1:30 that afternoon, Waldo and Charlotte arrived, taking a large table. Soon after, the Maynards also appeared, followed by Dan, who winked at her as he, too, joined the others.

Nancy noticed a sixth chair had been pulled up. *Who else is coming?* she wondered as she realized her friends were unusually quiet and whispering across the table to each other. "Are you waiting for someone?" she asked.

"Yes ... me!" a male voice rasped behind her. Startled, she leapt to one side, her eyes flashing. "Easy girl," he laughed. "It's only me, yer Uncle Jeb!"

He hugged Nancy warmly and shook hands with the men inquiring about Dan's bandaged hands. As he sat down, he laughingly requested a coffee with two fat fingers of whisky.

"Leave the whisky out, love, he's cheeky enough without it!" Charlotte called after her.

Awhile later, Harry Tabour joined the group momentarily. Listening carefully as Millie quietly listed off the refreshments they would need for Nancy's surprise birthday party, being cautious that she wasn't within hearing distance.

Returning to his office, he called to Nancy as he passed. "Come see me before you leave, Nancy. I've something to tell you."

A few minutes later, the group called their goodbyes and Nancy joined them at the door.

"I'll be back at six to walk you home," Dan assured her. "Seems I have nothing else to do these days," he added ruefully.

Just before six, the new waitress arrived. Katherine Flounder was a year older than Nancy. Although born in Seattle where her father worked on the docks for one of the shipping companies, her parents were Canadian. She had come to Victoria to take care of her aging grandparents who lived on Cook Street near the garbage dump.

Kate was tall and slim with an impish smile and blond curls that bounced about when she moved. A ready smile and pleasant disposition, coupled with her eagerness to learn, had endeared her to Nancy from their first meeting. People said they looked so much alike, except for their hair, they could be sisters, and their friendship was flourishing.

"Nancy," Harry called, "bring Kate in with you."

"You, too!" Nancy giggled, linking arms with her as they made their way into Harry's office.

"I want you to train Kate to open in the morning," said Harry, watching the redhead's expression turn into a frown. Folding his arms on the desk, he leaned toward her and whispered, "Then, you can have some time off!"

"Oh, when?" Nancy asked, smiling eagerly.

"How about from the 6th to the 15th," Harry laughed. "You can start training her on Monday morning when I've put you on the same shift. Five days should be enough time."

"This month? Oh my!" Nancy squealed, when he nodded his affirmation. Dashing around the desk, she planted a kiss on his cheek.

"Get her out of here, Kate!" he cried, winking at the new girl.

At six o'clock, Dan returned and he announced that under Meg's orders he had to take her for a walk in the sunshine before dinner.

247

Going down Fort to Government Street, they turned left and saw Leah Rogers standing outside the grocery store where she and her husband, Charles, sold their fresh chocolates. She was looking across the street at Shakespeare's Jewellers, one of the shops in the two-storey building they had purchased in 1903. Their plan had included opening a chocolate factory but so far it hadn't happened.

Leah recognized Nancy instantly. She and her husband arrived for work very early and had often seen the girl walking to work, impressed by her cheerfulness. Leah had spoken with the couple many times before and she waved to catch their attention.

"Feel like a chocolate today, Nancy?" she asked, knowing Dan would decline, as he had often done in the past. Nancy's beaming face gave Leah her answer. She enjoyed seeing the happy looks on people's faces when they thought of these unusual chocolates they had named, Victoria Creams. She reached into a box on the counter and handed one of the popular, large chocolates to Dan, standing closest to her. Extending his bandaged hand, she gasped.

"Oh my, Danny, whatever have you done to yourself?"

"Just a little rope burn, ma'am, nothing to worry about. Sorry, I didn't mean to shock you. I've become so accustomed to these bandages," Dan grinned weakly, as the candymaker's wife handed the chocolate into Nancy's now outstretched hand. Thanking her, they made their way back outside. As they carried on toward the harbour, they laughingly shared Nancy's chocolate ... taking small bites to make it last longer.

Near the corner of Government and Wharf they stopped to check out the ships in the inner harbour before turning right at the Post Office and starting down Wharf to home. They peered in the windows of Harper and Wells car showroom, admiring the shiny new vehicles.

The voice of Fred Barrett rang across the street from the steps of the Harbour Master's Office. "You all right, Danny?" he asked, a tinge of concern in his voice.

"Yes, I'm fine, Fred," Dan replied, raising one bandaged hand in salute. "It keeps Aunt Meg and Nancy happy being doctor and nurse to me and Ned ... and thinking we're totally helpless! I may leave these bandages on forever," he teased, josselling Nancy playfully, but grunting in surprise as her elbow jabbed at him.

Meg heard them coming as she set the table, calling Dan over to her desk when they entered. "We'll try taking them bandages off tonight, Danny. Let's kill two birds with a stone by getting these hands some exercise and air!" she said "You'll need to be careful though, and wrap them up again before bed."

Nancy watched intently as Meg began unwinding the bandages, wincing as some raw flesh appeared. She automatically slid her arm around him in sympathy. Dan slowly flexed his stiff fingers, gritting his teeth as the pain shot through his body. Meg handed Dan the jar of petroleum jelly and he gingerly applied some to the scabs that were beginning to form, helping his fingers move more freely.

"That's better, Aunt Meg," he whispered. "I think I can manage a spoon, if it doesn't slip out of my fingers!"

With his food cut into small portions, the whaler managed quite well, enjoying the feel of independence for the first time in over a week.

"Harry's giving me nine days off ...," announced Nancy excitedly through a mouthful of food, "from the 6th to the 15th."

"Great," Dan grunted, "we can spend some of it out at the house. They're so far ahead of schedule, we'll be able to start moving in soon. They can easily work around us to complete the finishing touches. Jack was sure right about how easy it was to find labour."

Meg made a clucking sound as she reached into her apron pocket and produced a key. "Jack Duggan called and left this for you. He says Waldo has the other one ... he still has a few things to deliver."

Footsteps sounded on the boardwalk and Meg lay the key on the table and moved toward the door. Opening it just before their visitor knocked, revealed a broadly smiling Jebediah.

"Come on in, Jeb," Nancy called. "What brings you back to Victoria this time? Do you have anymore crooks for me to catch!"

"Want some apple pie, Mr. Judd?" Meg asked. Smiling, he made himself at home pulling up a chair and then looked up at her, running his tongue over his lips.

"Gus sent me up to help you with the *Southern Bell* and to book him and Beth into The Empress from the 5th," he began, taking a mouthful of apple pie and custard.

"She'll be ready at the middle of June. I hope you've brought some money," laughed Nancy, as the craggy-faced detective extracted some papers from his breast pocket.

These, young lady, are for you," he said, smoothing out the folds and pushing them toward her. "Payment for the shipyard by bank draft ... that only you can release!" He paused as she exhaled loudly. "That hard-nosed old Swede really trusts you, lass," he muttered. "And this one gives Dan the authority to hire a crew to sail the *Bell* to Seattle in June ... if you need any of his Seattle men just let him know."

Jebediah handed the top two papers to Nancy and the last one to Dan. "Feast your eyes on that one, lad," he whispered, a smile crinkling the corners of his mouth. "That's *your* boat ... Gus called it a little bonus! It's waiting at the Jorgensen's private dock in Seattle. You'll be bringing it back with you ... that is, if those battered hands of yours are working by then!"

"*My* boat?" Dan gasped, ignoring Jeb's comment.

The women crowded around Dan's chair, staring wide-eyed at an artist's impression of a long, sleek, blue motorboat.

"But why would he give it to me?" Dan asked, incredulously.

Resting his elbows on the table and cradling his chin, Jeb gazed at them across the table, enjoying the impact of his message.

Meg broke the silence. "Never look a gift horse in the mouth, laddie!"

"I suppose you're right, Aunt Meg. It looks awfully fast!" he said, glancing up at the redhead now draped over his shoulder.

"Just what we need out at Gordon Head," Nancy declared. "And the boathouse is nearly ready, too!"

"What boathouse?" asked Dan.

"The one Jack built because they had extra lumber. He said the water is much deeper than you thought."

"Well, sounds like you don't need my help planning things at all, you've done just fine on your own," Dan replied. "And to think that we'll actually have a boat to go in it. That's great!"

At 9:30, Nancy stood up and yawned. She gave each of them an affectionate hug and headed into her room.

"Coming for a drink, lad?" Jebediah invited the whaler.

"Hmm, that's a good idea!" Dan replied, glancing across at the frowning Scot. "I'll bandage my hands later, Aunt Meg."

"You be careful, son," she warned.

A pleasant breeze came off the water, as they turned their backs on the harbour. It gently rustled the colourful British flags hanging from several nearby buildings, remnants of Victoria Day Celebrations.

Jeb, with Dan following close behind, entered the noisy Ship Inn and pushed their way through the crowd to stand at the bar. Peter Jones, one of McQuade's men from the ship's chandlers across the street, and a known busybody that Dan had no use for, called to him as he came through the crowd.

"You just missed the Joyces, Danny. They left not more than ten minutes ago. How are the hands?"

"They'll be up at the Lighthouse," Dan replied, ignoring his question. "That's where the whalers go."

"What crew will you be joining now, Dan?" Peter pressed on, eagerly searching for information to pass onto customers.

"I'm finished with whaling," Dan replied, picking up his beer gingerly in both hands. "Maybe I'll go farming or logging, who knows."

"No, you won't," Jones insisted. "You're the best gunner on this coast. Look what you did to that freighter, you don't want to waste that talent!"

Standing off to one side, an army captain in uniform interrupted their conversation. "Are you the man that shot a line into the nose of that floundering freighter out at Parry Bay?" he asked, watching for but receiving no answer. "Quite a feat in a wild storm!"

Jeb had noticed Dan's growing agitation with Jones and now with the soldier. He feared a confrontation. He knew he should let Dan deal with the situation in his own way, nevertheless, he kept a close eye on the proceedings.

"Luck!" growled Dan, finishing his beer in one gulp and heading for the door.

"Wait," called the Captain. "I have need of you!"

Jebediah chuckled as he increased the length of his step to keep up with Dan. "Where are we going?"

"Lighthouse ... to find the boys."

251

Peter Jones was making the most of his newfound friend, an army officer in the Royal Artillery training battalion. Captain Percy Neville had announced rather loudly that he was here from England as an expert on the highly mobile but very erratic field guns. Admitting he was the third son of a titled gentry, his commission as a Captain had been granted by the King. Secretly knowing his only chance at glory was the army, he had become a dutiful and eventually, highly successful soldier. Having never married, he had chosen instead, devotion to his regiment, winning many honours for his light artillery marksmanship. He had been sent from England to train a militia battalion in Victoria and the story of the skilled whaler and his cannon had intrigued him. Evidently, this whaler had captured the freighter by harpooning it high in the bow ... and now, meeting the man in the flesh and letting him slip through his grasp, agitated him.

"Damn!" he exclaimed, turning to Peter Jones. "I need to talk with that man."

"No problem, buy me a drink an I'll take you to him!"

Arriving at the Lighthouse Saloon at the corner of Store and Cormorant, Dan and Jeb found themselves stepping over the legs of sailors sat drinking on the sidewalk outside. Dan could hear Tim Joyce laughing and found him with Emerson Turpel at a table crowded with men. Pushing his way through a group near the bar with his elbows, Dan opened a path to their table, kicked a chair in place, and sat down.

Dan introduced Jeb as a friend of Nancy's visiting from Seattle.

"You folks in Seattle gearing up for the war?" an old pipe-smoking seaman, bluntly asked.

"Don't really know," Jebediah lied. "I have no interest in politics."

"THERE HE IS!" was heard over the din and as Dan turned to face the commotion, he came face to face with the persistent Peter Jones, who was leading the army captain toward their table.

Dan, frowning, slowly slid his beer bottle toward the centre of the table and rose to his feet. A quietness descended on the saloon as all eyes watched the two men enter and push toward the Joyce table.

Tim Joyce's voice cracked though the stillness. "Not with those hands, lad!"

Percy Neville stood his ground but Peter Jones, sensing danger, made a hasty exit. Jebediah stood up and smiled at the Captain, flexing his shoulders menacingly.

"Wait, sir, I beg of you. My name is Captain Percy Neville and I apologize for this intrusion but I need to speak to that young man on a matter of business."

"Then say it and be gone!" Jebediah growled.

"Are you the man who harpooned the freighter?" he asked, as Dan sat down again. "If you are, I could use your help."

"Yes, he is," Ned offered. "Leave him be, Jeb. Let him sit down."

Percy breathed a sigh of relief, the men relaxed, and the saloon resumed its noisy chatter. He quickly found a chair and placing it close to Dan, began to explain his dilemma. "I need an experienced gunner to give my unit a demonstration," he began, a note of desperation in his voice. "Would you come out to the firing range and show us what you can do."

After some discussion of the situation, it was agreed that Dan would go out to the firing range the following Monday at 10 a.m. Jeb was staying in town and said he would see he got there. With appreciation written all over his face, the Captain offered to buy the table a drink.

"That's not the way we do things," Ned stated, noting the Captain's surprised expression. "You're our guest, we pay for the drinks!"

Later, on their way home, Jebediah seemed to want to discuss Percy and the demonstration. "These new fangled guns are not like shooting a whaling cannon, Dan."

"Same principle basically," Dan muttered. "If you know the distance and amount of powder in the shot, should be easy. The trajectory only varies according to weather."

"Where in the devil did you learn all about shooting?"

"From Ned, he's a hell of a teacher ... and Tim taught me all about engines."

"I suppose you can steer by the stars, too!"

"Stars or compass, sail or engine, whatever you fancy!" Dan retorted proudly. The American waved as he left the whaler at the end of the boardwalk and carried on towards The Empress.

The next morning, Nancy kept hearing Dan's name bantered about as she moved about the tables in the dining room of the Balmoral. They seemed to be linking him to an English army officer and the Lighthouse Saloon. She wondered what he and Jeb had gotten up to the night before. It was beginning to drive her crazy when, in mid-afternoon, Emerson Turpel appeared.

"We should be finished with the *Bell* by the 9th of June," he announced, as Nancy filled his cup. "I told Dan last night."

"You saw Danny last night?"

"Had a drink with him and that American friend of yours in the Lighthouse Saloon."

Between customers, Nancy finally extracted the story from the shipbuilder, putting her mind at ease.

On Friday, as they left the Balmoral, she thought Dan seemed agitated about something. She linked arms, snuggled closer, and waited, noticing he had chosen a different route home.

"We're calling at Harper and Wells …," he declared, finally.

She knew this was one of the many car dealerships in town and she glanced suspiciously up at him.

"We're going to pick out our new automobile!" he announced.

"But we can't drive a car!" Nancy exclaimed, as he pulled her along.

He turned abruptly and led her through the side door of the showroom, almost colliding with Waldo Skillings who was talking to the owner. Brian Harper beckoned them toward a fancy-looking Model T truck with shiny dark-blue paintwork and a rear box with fancy wood trim. Nancy stood beside Waldo, wide-eyed at the array of shiny new cars.

"Is this the colour, Mr. Brown?" Harper asked.

"Do you like it, Nan?" he asked, a note of eagerness in his voice. "Waldo says it's just what we need out at Gordon Head."

Nancy went over to the truck and walked around it surveying it carefully. The men waited patiently, looking from one to the other.

"Well, young lady, what do you think?" asked Waldo.

"There's no room for Aunt Meg!" she retorted.

The men glanced in alarm at each other.

"B - b - but it's a standard vehicle, M - M - Miss Nancy," Harper stammered, as visions of losing a sale flashed though his mind.

"Well, you'll just have to make one with a wider cab!" she said, flatly, not even sure why she had said such a thing. *Surely it's not possible to make it wider.*

"Now look here," Harper replied, trying a more forceful approach.

"Whoa back, lad," Waldo intervened, taking Brian aside. "Take my advice and don't try to bully that girl or you'll get a real surprise. Work with them and see what happens."

Nancy moved closer to Dan and his hand reached for her shoulder.

Harper, meanwhile, clasped his hands behind his back and despite his agitation, tried to follow his friend's advice. Displaying a genial exterior, he began to walk around the truck, silently studying it and considering his options. Earlier in the day, he'd had no trouble whatsoever convincing the young whaler that this was the truck he needed. *Women! Why do some men insist on involving them?* he chuntered. *It usually only causes more problems!*

"If you extended the cab or made it wider so three could sit ...," Waldo interjected.

"No, no, it cannot be done," Harper resisted.

"Then we'll get what we want in Seattle, Mr. Harper," replied Nancy in a matter-of-fact tone, turning towards the door.

"Wait," he bleated, in desperation beginning to walk away from them. "I'll get Willie, our coach builder, to come out," he called over his shoulder.

William Jackson was a tall, skinny man of about 30 years. His clothes were covered in dust and paint but he trotted out obediently behind his employer. His dark, but sparkling eyes, searched their faces and he moved to the side of the blue truck. His hand lovingly stroked the paintwork.

"That cab can't be widened can it, Willie?" Harper inquired.

"It's possible, sir," Willie drawled, "but it would make the gasoline tank mighty awkward to fill, being under the seat." Pausing, he scratched his head, then turned to the young couple. "How much wider do you need?"

"So three of us can ride," said Dan, watching as the young man climbed up to have a better look.

"Could split the seat in the middle and add a removable section," he said, talking more to himself than anyone else. "Then it would be no trouble at all getting to the fuel tank. All it needs," he continued, his voice growing louder, "is some darned fine coach work. Oh yes, Mr. Harper it can be done!"

"Thank you, Willie," Nancy purred, spinning around to face the owner. "You have fourteen days to complete it or the sale is off, Mr. Harper," she stated sharply. "Yes or no?"

Harper began to splutter. Thrown completely off guard but remembering Waldo's warning, he calmed himself and merely nodded.

"We'll pay cash,," Nancy announced, taking Dan's arm, "when we take delivery by the 13th of June. Good day, gentleman."

Dan waved as Nancy dragged him quickly away ... the bewildered owner leaned against the truck mopping his brow. Through the large, plate glass window, Waldo watched them walk up the street, now holding hands as they disappeared around a corner.

"Well, now you know who makes the decisions for them two," Waldo laughed. "Be warned, that girl usually gets what she wants!"

Meg had the door open and heard their laughing long before they arrived. It was so nice to hear Dan having fun again. She had been amazed with the speed the boy's hands had healed, with only the deepest cuts still giving them any pause. She couldn't help wondering what the Indian women had used on them.

"Did you order that buggy for Sunday, Dan?" she asked.

"I sure did. I pick it up at 7:30. We'll be away from here by eight."

Over supper they told Meg about the truck and giggled at the astounded look on her face.

"Oh no, not one of those noisy, smelly things!" she protested, playfully. "Are we going to have one of them in the family, too!"

Chapter 19

Dan noticed a sleeping drunk in the doorway of the Royal Arms Hotel as he passed, but otherwise the streets were deserted as he made his way up Store Street to the stables. The Chinese laundries were eerily quiet without their usual chattering workers, and the wooden shacks, some on stilts, were reminiscent of old gold towns he had seen in his younger days. In the background, the gentle hum of a lathe at Hafer's, the German machinist, told him someone was already at work.

Turning right at Herald Street, he heard the sound of horse's hooves and the pungent smell of manure hung in the air. The grey, already harnessed to a buggy, was ready and waiting. Its ears flicked with anticipation as Dan entered the yard greeted warmly by the old stableman.

Removing his pipe and spitting a stream of tobacco-stained saliva onto the ground, the old man informed him that a nosebag for the grey, had already been loaded.

"How are the hands, lad? Heard you had an accident."

"Almost as good as new!" Dan replied, climbing aboard and holding up his hands. Then he flicked the reins urging the horse forward.

Returning home, he hurriedly ate his breakfast while the women loaded the buggy with the hamper and other necessary items. In fifteen minutes they were on their way. Snorting with pleasure, the long-striding horse soon had the buggy out of the city and onto Hillside Avenue. At the top of the hill, they turned left onto Cedar Hill Road and for the next couple miles found themselves bouncing over the dry, rutted surface as the slightly hilly path ran its course along the side of the valley. Meg breathed deeply, smelling the heavily fruit-scented air as her eyes roamed across the sparsely populated area of farms and fields. This was pure heaven to the Scot who didn't mind the lack of people in the least.

Galloping hooves warned of company and Meg looked back to see a single horse and rider gaining on them. Tapping Dan on the back to alert him, he slowed the grey giving the horseman room to pass. The horse slowed as it came alongside, however, and recognizing the rider, they laughed as Jebediah doffed his hat gallantly to the ladies.

"Good morning ladies … Dan. I thought I'd take a ride out to see this new house of yours. Thought I might run into you!"

"Well, this is a surprise, we'll meet you there. I assume you know the way," said Dan, urging the grey back onto the road.

When they reached the gate, Jeb was waiting. Dan jumped out to swing it open, leading the grey through. Jebediah pulled ahead, stopping when he came within sight of the grand-looking house, now almost completed. As the buggy pulled in behind, Jeb remained in the saddle, turning in all directions as the others came to join him.

"Oh my," Nancy said, excitedly, "I love it even more each time we come. Do you like it, Jeb?"

"Do I like it, you must be joking!" the American replied. "This is one of the most awe-inspiring properties I've ever seen!"

Dan, helping Meg over the rough ground, watched as Nancy raced up the wide steps to the front door. Finding it locked, she moved along the veranda peering in each of the windows. Dan unlocked the door and she came up beside him. Their eyes met and he scooped her casually up into his arms. Kissing her nose, she giggled and he stepped over the threshold.

"A home of our own …," Nancy whispered into his ear, as Dan set her down on the polished wooden floor. For the next half-hour she moved from room to room, dragging Meg with her, squealing with delight at everything she saw. Looking out of an upstairs windows, she saw the men crossing the open ground toward the clifftop.

Turning the latch and lifting the window, she shouted. "DAN BROWN, I LOVE YOU!"

Jeb looked around in amazement as they descended the new stairs to the beach. *These young people today have no pride whatsoever,* he thought. Reaching the bottom, Dan's eyes glowed as he absorbed every detail of the new dock. Jebediah stroked his chin, frowning, as he looked back up the shear cliff.

"How will you get anything down to a boat, lad?" he asked, doubtfully.

"Through the cave," replied Dan, with a straight face.

A look of fascinated interest, flashed across the American's face. "You have a cave, too? But I still don't see how that helps the loading."

Dan, motioning for him to follow, parted the bushes behind the boathouse, revealing an opening into the face of the rock.

"If I clean this out," he said, pulling the bushes aside, "and build a chute from the opening at the top of the cliff ...."

"Well I'll be a monkey's uncle! Don't say anymore," Jebediah gasped. "It's a natural for easy loading and a perfect place for your new speedboat."

The men slowly retraced their steps as Jebediah's eyes darted about trying to keep up with his thoughts.

"I think," he began, slowly, "that Gus will want to talk to you!"

"About the *Bell*?" asked Dan, as they neared the top.

"No ...," Jeb muttered, "about Prohibition!"

The women's voices calling them interrupted their conversation and Dan hurried up the remaining stairs leaving Jeb to come at his own speed.

"Aren't those stairs perfect?"said Nancy, walking across the clearing to meet them.

"More perfect than you know," said Jeb, arriving at the top obviously out of breath.

"We can even take Aunt Meg down these stairs," said Nancy.

"Not on your life, girl! Those steep stairs are for young'uns only!" Meg rejoined. "Look at Jeb, it's even too much for him!" she laughed, as Dan reached out a hand to help Jeb over the top.

"Boy, the going down was a lot easier than the coming up!" Jeb gasped.

"You'll feel a lot better with some of Aunt Meg's food under your belt, Jeb," Nancy declared. "Come up and sit on the veranda in one of our new chairs ... enjoy the view from a safe distance!

Inside, a meal from their picnic basket was soon set out on the new dining room table. Smiling, Nancy stood back and marveled at how nice everything looked. Meg had given them a beautiful linen

259

tablecloth she had embroidered many years before, when her eyesight was better she said. It was now laid out on the shiny new table covered with an array of fine china cups and saucers, and dishes of food.

The dining room was large and looked quite elegant with the dark-stained furniture. There was plenty of room for the china cupboard and sideboard made of the same wood as the table and chairs. The heavy, but colourful, lined damask curtains, were pulled back on either side of the windows. Underneath, elegant lace sheers, found by Nancy at Spencer's, allowed one to easily see outside.

Tramping noisily down the hallway, the men were halted by Meg's fierce command. "Wipe your feet, boys," she called, in a voice not to be ignored.

Nancy directed Dan to one side of the table and Jebediah to the other beside Meg. Eating in their own house for the first time seemed to create a momentary somber moment for the two young people and instinctively, they joined hands under the table.

"Aunt Meg, will you say Grace, please?" Dan asked, quietly.

Jeb fidgeted nervously, rarely having been exposed to religion in his adult years. His suspicious nature coupled with sad memories made him view men of the cloth with mistrust and derision. These memories now flooded back into his mind remembering that black day when his mother had died. Of how, as a child of 12, he had held her hand and watched the hard-working, hard-drinking women die without the Lord's blessing because the minister had refused to see her. Giving his head a violent shake, he pushed his festering memories back to another time, as Meg's recitation ended.

Later, hunger satisfied and sitting alone with Dan on the veranda quietly smoking their pipes, the American broached a new subject. "We're heading into a dry spell in Seattle," he began, staring off in the distance. "Maybe you'd like the job of delivering our liquor, using that boat waiting for you at the Jorgensen jetty."

"Sounds illegal," muttered Dan, glancing up at the women who had just joined them.

"Sort of," Jeb growled, lapsing into silence.

Meg broke into their thoughts, relating a tale of her father and brothers transporting Scottish whisky to the ports of England from an illegal distillery set in the wild hills of Skye.

Jebediah smiled. "It wouldn't be illegal in Canadian waters ... only when you crossed the line," he explained, with a chuckle. "We've only one Coast Guard boat, that should be easy to avoid ... for an experienced seaman like you!"

Nancy rose and began pacing the veranda, frowning as her supple young mind wrestled with Jeb's idea. They watched her expectantly until suddenly she stopped in front of Dan, held out her hand and suggested they go for a stroll. She led him to the stairway at the edge of the cliff.

"We'd need fuel tanks down there on the dock," she pointed, "and how would we load all that stuff?"

"Easy!" Dan chuckled, having already warmed to the adventure. "I could build a chute into the cave from up here."

"Can I be your crew?"

"We'd need one other and I bet Dumpy would do it."

It was the jaunty spring in their step that gave away their decision to the eagle-eyed American as they walked across the clearing to the house. Jeb stood alone as they approached him on the veranda and. Nancy's eyes searched for Meg.

"Meg said she was tired so she went to lie down," Jeb informed them.

"Right, if Gus wants us to, we'll do it," Dan stated, "but it will take a lot of planning."

The old detective smiled at his thoughts. *Gus was right. Both of these young people have a sense of adventure. He already knew Nancy's capabilities. Together they'll make an unbeatable team.*

He had agreed that with Dan's knowledge of the coast and Nancy's quick brain it had every possibility of working. He also realized there would be an element of danger when breaking the law and he'd move heaven and earth to protect Nancy, who'd become a very special person to him. So, for the time being, he pushed away the sense of foreboding.

"Yes, it will, lad," he agreed. "Gus will talk to you himself. He and Beth will be here Friday."

261

Nancy disappeared inside to check on Meg. Quietly opening her bedroom door a crack, she looked in. She heard the distinctive sound of Meg's heavy breathing and smiled, blowing a kiss to the sleeping figure. Returning to the veranda, Nancy was just in time to wave goodbye to Jebediah, as he mounted his horse.

"Was Jeb in a hurry?" she asked, as the American disappeared into the trees.

"No," Dan replied, "but he had his question answered—let's get a light and take a look at that cave."

Going into the kitchen, he fetched the oil lamp and some matches. As they walked down the steps, Dan warned her of the bats in the cave telling her to stay well back. Trying not to disturb the bushes that concealed the entrance, they peered into the darkness. Dan lit the lamp and hundreds of bats awakened from slumber, screeching loudly as they flew around in confused circles and past their heads.

Nancy screamed, leaping back onto the rocks, covering her face. Dan set the lamp down on a ledge just inside the cave and quickly ducked as the remaining bats flew past him. Slowly, the dust-filled air cleared and he picked up the lamp and they ventured inside.

"What a horrible smell!" declared Nancy, pinching her nose and retreating a step as Dan went on ahead.

"T H E R E ' S — T H E R E ' S — T H e r e ' s   A — A — A L I G H T — L I G H T — L I g h t   B A C K — B A C K — B a c k HERE—HERE—Here!" came Dan's voice echoing from inside the cave. In a few minutes, he emerged. "Let's get some dry grass and sticks. I think we can find another opening!"

The brush on the hillside was tinder dry and in no time they had enough fuel for a fire. With Nancy carrying the lamp, they went back inside. As Dan set the grass and sticks into an organized pile, he explained his plan and gave her some instructions.

"Go up to the top of the stairs and watch for the smoke," he ordered. "When you see it, find the hole it's coming out of and mark the spot. Hopefully it will be close to the house." He watched her back as she picked her way carefully outside and up the stairs.

An eerie glow spread through the cave as the flames took hold. With the aid of the dry grass, the flames were soon lighting up more of the cave's interior than Dan had seen before. He was prepared to escape from the smoke, but soon realized it wasn't necessary as it was pulled deeper into the cavernous interior as if by an unseen hand. He took the opportunity to look around. He now realized that the smaller entrance opened into a spacious room. The high granite walls and roof sparkled as the light from the flames reached the specks of silica embedded in the rock.

Dashing out of the cave, he raced up the stairs, calling her.

"OVER HERE, DAN!" she shouted. "I FOUND IT!"

He followed her voice and found her waving from the west side of the house. He ran toward her and discovered a tiny wisp of smoke curling upward from a pile of rubble left by the workmen.

"That hole must slope all the way down into the cave!" he said excitedly, pulling some of the debris aside. "The builders probably uncovered it for us. If we erected a workshop over this end, we could build a slide down into the cave. Nobody will be able to see a thing!"

Laughing at their good fortune, they hugged and made their way arm in arm back to the house. Meg was up and had already made tea.

"What have you two been up to?" she asked coyly, cocking an eyebrow at them. She was not at all surprised when she merely received a grin and shrugged shoulders in reply.

After tea, they decided they should get back to the city. The sun had dipped well below the tops of the trees already. Dan went to check on the fire, then returned quickly and hitched up the horse. Meg and Nancy felt a tinge of longing as they locked the door, wishing they could stay, yet knowing they'd soon be here forever.

As Dan came into the office for breakfast on Monday morning, he proclaimed that the glorious sunrise was a good omen for his visit to the shooting range that day. He walked Nancy to work and continued up to Fernwood, intent on catching Jack Duggan before he left for work.

Jack was surprised when Dan walked into the yard as he was loading his truck for going out to Gordon Head.

"Morning, Danny. What brings you out so early. Is there a problem?"

"No, no, everything is just fine ... great, in fact. Nancy loved the stairway to the beach and is very excited about the house. The boathouse was a great idea, and we'll soon have a boat to put in it! Actually, that's what I've come about."

Jack laughed when Dan explained the new project and his Irish blood surged more quickly through his veins at the suggestion of adventure. He willingly expressed his desire to help with the chute.

"Leave it to me, lad," he chuckled. "I know just what you need."

"Say hello to Nellie," said Dan, turning toward the gate.

"Hold on, son. I'll save you the walk. I have to stop at Prior's Hardware on Johnson before I go out to the house anyway."

"That would be much appreciated, Jack. I'm in a bit of a hurry."

Dan had never driven with Jack before and had to admit that he was quite a good driver. He laughed when the builder told him that he rarely made it to his destination without crashing into something.

"Never very serious though," he growled, "just a blasted nuisance! Where would you like me to let you off, Dan?"

"I'll go on to the store with you, Jack. I can walk the rest of the way from there," said Dan as they turned into Johnson Street and passed the Colonial Hotel.

Upon reaching Jack's destination, Dan jumped out and headed up Wharf Street past the Occidental and the many warehouses that lined the harbour area.

Jeb's car was already sitting outside the office door. Stepping inside, he was confronted by Ned, Tim, and Jeb, all grinning broadly.

"We're going with you!" Ned informed him. "Damn it, I taught you. I don't want to miss this!"

All four of them piled into the car and with Jeb driving and Ned in front giving directions, they were off. They left the city by the Pt. Ellice bridge, travelling at a mere walking speed as the law directed, and then down Craigflower Road past Craigflower School. As with most roads in the summer, the going was rough due to the ruts and within the hour they were on the less-travelled road to Langford. Here, they negotiated even deeper holes and exposed rocks played havoc with the car's thin rubber tires.

"This road must be impassible after a rain," said Jeb, easing the car around another large hole.

"Well, it would be in one of these motorized contraptions!" said Ned laughing. "Give me a horse any day."

In another half hour, they came to a sign showing the government insignia, nailed to a tree. It pointed up a track that took them some distance through a thick forest. It ended in a large meadow at the base of a small mountain where groups of uniformed soldiers on horseback raced back and forth, pulling small cannons behind them. During the exercise, each group stopped, prepared their cannon then fired at the mountain.

Capt. Percy Neville, mounted on a fine bay, saw the car enter the meadow and shouting orders to his Sergeant raced across the grass to meet them. Dismounting, he barked at the visitors, "Leave the vehicle there, men. I'll send mounts for you all," Then he was off again, this time at a full gallop.

"What the hell ...?" Jebediah began, reacting to the soldier's curt manner.

"Leave it, Jeb," Tim said, solemnly. "There's a war coming, the lad's just doing his job. You do ride, don't you?"

"Only when I'm forced into it!" Jeb replied.

Four horses arrived and the men mounted, their degree of horsemanship, or lack of same, being readily seen! A soldier led them to the far end of the meadow where they found two large upright guns set on wheels pointed at the mountain. Capt. Neville stepped forward as they dismounted. Shaking hands, he greeted them warmly.

"Sergeant!" he called, loudly. "Show Mr. Brown how to aim and fire that 13-pounder."

"Yes, sir," came the instant, snapped reply.

Dan followed the Sergeant, listening intently to his instructions. Two soldiers stood waiting beside the gun. Percy took his position at the second gun.

"Ready, Dan?" he asked, watching as the whaler nodded. "See that red flag over yonder?" He pointed to the far end of the meadow to where a tiny red flag fluttered against the mountain backdrop. "Can you hit it?" Percy asked, smiling.

"He sure can!" Ned answered boldly.

"You first," Dan murmured, glancing at the tree tops and noticing how much they were bending in the wind.

Thirty seconds later, Percy had his gun aimed and ready. BANG! The gun recoiled violently, first backwards and then forward on its wheels. A shell whistled though the air, landing with a thud close to the target. A rider galloped across the meadow toward them, sliding his steaming horse to a halt in front of the Captain and saluting smartly.

"Forty feet short. Twenty feet to the right, sir," he barked, before saluting again and galloping back in the direction he had come.

"Your turn, m'boy," Percy said gently. "Can you do any better?"

Dan quietly gave instructions to the two soldiers to load his gun. Looking down the barrel, he made his final adjustment.

BANG! went the second explosion and all eyes focused on the distant target.

Suddenly, the target disappeared and the rider came tearing full gallop back toward them. Leaping from his horse, he stood breathless before the Captain and saluted.

"Hit plumb centre, sir," he gasped.

"My god, you are good!" Percy exclaimed.

"Hey, soldier boy!" Ned interrupted again. "You see that large boulder up on that ridge, Capt. Neville." He pointed high up on the mountain. "If some of your men would like to go up there and dislodge it, setting it rolling down the hill, we'll give you another demonstration. Tell them to wave when they are ready and we will wave back when they are to let it go.

Percy nodded, more than a bit interested to see if Dan could hit a moving target. He gave orders to his messenger to delegate three soldiers to climb up to the ridge. They were to receive explicit instructions before beginning their climb. Meanwhile, he had the remaining men strip one of the guns of its gears, allowing it to swivel freely. Then he ordered it reloaded. Twenty minutes passed before the soldiers appeared on the rim and signalled they were ready. Ned glanced at Dan who winked, then nodded his readiness.

Ned waved his arms and the soldiers eased the boulder into motion. As it began moving down the hill, Dan took his line down the barrel, easing it gently into the direction he needed. The boulder was quickly picking up speed.

BANG! The free recoil almost knocked Dan right off his feet and all eyes watched spellbound. The shell smashed squarely into the moving boulder and it disintegrated before their eyes.

"Whew!" Percy gasped.

Jebediah smiled in disbelief. *And I was worried this lad couldn't take care of himself!*

"Can you show us how you did that, Dan? We'd be mighty grateful," said Percy.

"Sure, but you should really talk to my teacher, Ned Joyce," Dan replied. "He's standing right beside you."

"You taught him?" Percy asked, turning to Ned. "Will you stay and give my men some instruction?"

A surge of patriotism surged through the old whaler's body. Like nearly everyone in Victoria, he felt war was inevitable. This turn of events now presented him with a small opportunity to help his country.

"We certainly will!" Ned declared proudly, his eyes making contact with his brother, who nodded in agreement.

"How will you get back?" asked Dan.

"I'll see they get home," Percy declared.

"Great shooting, lad," Jeb congratulated Dan, as they walked back to the car. "Are all whaleboat gunners that good?"

Dan smiled to himself, knowing full well that this man so experienced in measuring the truth of a situation, had an ulterior motive. "No," he said, slowly, "but that old man's the best of 'em all."

On their way back toward the city, Dan gave Jeb directions to the Gorge Hotel. They arrived as a streetcar was leaving with a full load a passengers and Elizabeth Marshall was standing on the veranda. When she saw Dan, she came eagerly forward to greet them.

"Hello Dan, what a nice surprise. Where's Nancy?" she asked.

"She's at work, but I'd like you to meet Jebediah Judd, a good friend of ours … and we're mighty hungry, Mrs. Marshall," Dan laughed as Jeb and Eliza shook hands.

She showed them to a window table from where they had a wonderful view down The Arm toward town, and of the swimming area, busy with picnickers despite the day of the week. Over a cold plate of ham, pickles, and fresh baked bread, the men sipped on a cooling beer and talked of their impending adventure. It soon became obvious to Dan that Jeb had grown more apprehensive, worrying about the dangers and especially of Nancy's involvement.

"The problem doesn't exist here in Victoria from what I have seen, but around the Seattle docks there is a huge underworld element. They are always seeking easy gains to fund their activities." He carefully watched Dan's facial expressions for any sign of fear. Seeing none, he continued. "You've met Terry O'Reilly, haven't you, lad?"

"No, but Nancy has spoken of him. Who is he?" asked Dan cautiously.

"In Seattle, it's well known that he is part of an underworld Irish-American group paid to keep the Jorgensen enterprises free of interference ... I think you get my meaning," Jeb said quietly, leaning forward to keep his voice down. Jeb knew he had now earned Dan's rapt attention.

"Nancy speaks highly of him, does she know all this?"

"I don't believe so, but he is totally loyal to Gus Jorgensen and thinks the world of Nancy," Jeb assured him.

Dan frowned, his forehead wrinkling. "I'll kill any man who tries to hurt my sister," he said, fiercely.

Surprised by the intensity of the lad's statement, Jebediah knew without any doubt that Dan Brown would die to protect his redhead. Changing the subject, Jeb asked about the freighter and the arrangements to deliver it to Seattle, pleased when he heard that the Joyces had agreed to crew, along with Fred Barrett and Dumpy aided by several of Gus' own men.

"All you need now is a Captain," the American jested. "Then you're set for a cruise."

"Oh, we've got a Captain," Dan laughed. "She's got red hair and a temper to match!"

"Nancy's going with us?" Jebediah's eyebrow lifted in surprise. "Well then, I'm going, too. It should be quite a party!"

As they left the hotel, Eliza cornered Dan inquiring what his plans were after the *Belfast* left Victoria.

Dan shrugged his shoulders. "Might join the army," he replied, as Jeb got in behind the wheel.

"I hope you don't have to do that, Danny," Eliza whispered, reaching for the whaler's arm as they moved down the steps to the car. "Nancy couldn't bare it if she lost you."

Dan was considering her comment when he heard his name being called and turned to see Eli waving from the doorway. Jeb started the engine and it became quite impossible to exchange words over the engine noise, so Dan merely waved back.

"Let's go, boy," Jeb yelled.

Dan quickly shook Eliza's hand and jumped aboard. The car lurched forward spewing a huge cloud of smoke and Eliza retreated coughing, up the steps to join Eli who was waving from the doorway.

Chapter 20

Jack Duggan found the hole and scratched his head, wondering how best to determine the angle to the cave. A dog whined from the edge of the trees, drawing his attention to a shadowy figure that was silently watching him.

"Step out and state your business!" Jack growled.

A tattered figure with a small terrier dog moved out of the trees and slowly came toward him. Sam Smith, a well-known rabbit and small game hunter, was a hermit who lived in the forests of Saanich and moved freely through the area clearing vermin and small game with his dog and several ferrets. He was tolerated by the local landowners though never made welcome.

"What are you doing?" Sam inquired, lifting his battered hat and rubbing his head, ignoring Jack's question.

"Trying to find out where this hole goes," Jack muttered, pointing with the toe of his boot to an almost hidden six-inch hole amongst a pile of rubble."

"Cave," grunted Sam. "It's been there for years."

"You know about it?"

"Know every hole fer miles around here," Sam muttered. "Damn near lost me dog down that one, a few years back!"

"Tell me about it."

A twinkle of light appeared in the hermit's eyes. His dark-brown face remained stern and unsmiling as his mind folded the pages of his memory back to that day when his dog had followed a rabbit into the hole. "Couldn't get old Flash out this way," he said, reaching down with a dirty hand to fondle the terrier. "Hole drops nearly straight down for five or six feet. There's a tunnel that comes out down there," he said pointing to the exact location of the entrance to the cave. Then he turned without a backward glance and ambled away, disappearing into the trees.

Jack watched the man go and thought of the rumours he had often heard. Thought to be more than half Indian, it was said he roamed the area asking for nothing, disappearing for weeks though no one knew to where. Turning back to his hole, Jack now realized he had all the information he needed to fulfil his promise to Dan.

On their way back to town, Dan and Jeb stopped at the Point Hope shipyard. As the car pulled up, Kenneth Macpherson, the yard superintendent, greeted them from the door. A smile spread across his face when he recognized Dan.

"Yer a wee bit early, lad," he called, jovially. "The *Bell* won't be ready 'till the ninth."

"Thought I'd show it to this old fella," replied Dan, grinning broadly. "If that's alright with you."

"You cheeky young whelp!" Jeb retorted.

Laughing, Macpherson invited them to accompany him onto the dock. The *Southern Bell* looked big and beautiful with its new coat of paint displaying the blue and white of the Jorgensen colours. An unusual three-cornered hole high in the bow, framed in brass and gleaming in the sun, caught Jeb's attention.

"What's that for?" Jeb asked, noticing Dan's face turn red.

"It's where *he* shot the old lady," Macpherson explained, grinning as he motioned with his head to Dan. "Nancy wanted us to preserve the spot!"

"From the deck of a pitching ship ...," Jeb muttered. "Why, that rock rolling down the hill was child's play to you!"

The superintendent displayed a blank expression, but receiving no explanation, asked, "Want to go aboard, Dan?"

"Might as well, now we're here."

Nodding, the superintendent led the way over the drydock gangway and onto the deck of the *Bell*. They walked through the ship checking out the officer's cabins and galley, and lastly, the wheelhouse and bridge.

"It's like new!" exclaimed Jebediah, impressed by the quality workmanship. "Gus will be pleased."

"We did it all under budget, too," Macpherson boasted, as they arrived back at the car. "Even put our new patented, locking watertight hatch covers on her."

"That sounds impressive," said Dan, climbing in beside Jeb. "Thanks for the tour. See you on the ninth."

Dan was relieved when the car stopped in front of the Balmoral. The old detective had never stopped talking all the way into the city. He had expounded his admiration of the Canadian shipyard until Dan's ears were ringing and he longed for quiet. Nancy found him sitting alone in the dining room sipping on a coffee while he waited patiently to walk her home.

"Who's the new girl?" he asked.

"Katherine Flounder from Seattle," she said, suddenly feeling a twinge of jealousy. "Hold on, I'll introduce you."

Leaving her bag on the chair, Nancy returned to the kitchen catching Katherine just she was leaving through the back door.

"Come and meet my brother, Kate."

Delighted by the invitation, having heard many veiled comments about this unusual couple, Katherine followed Nancy back into the dining room.

"So you're from Seattle, Kate," said Dan, smiling pleasantly. "Did you live there long?"

"All my life. I was born there!" she laughed. "Dad works on the docks, but he and mother are Canadian by birth." Her mood changed noticeably and a sad expression crept across her face. Her voice softened. "My grandma's really sick. I had to come here to look after her and grandfather."

"Do you have other family in Victoria?" Dan asked.

"Yes and no," Kate sighed. "My ma's cousins, the Schnarr's, are around here somewhere, but they're always moving and I haven't been able to locate them yet. We haven't heard from them in years."

"Do you know the docks in Seattle?" Dan asked, a curious light springing to his eyes.

"Yes, of course, why do you ask?"

Ignoring her question, Dan posed another. "Do you know the Joyce Bros. dock down below Wharf Street?"

The girl shook her head.

"If you have time, why don't you come down with us, then you'll know how to find us if you ever need anything."

As they walked, Kate noted with interest that her companions were holding hands. She smiled at their childish behaviour, but nevertheless, felt a strange touch of envy pass over her heart.

"Tell me," she begged curiously. "Are you two really brother and sister?"

"Only by choice," Nancy laughed, "Not by nature."

"Now you've really got me puzzled!" she laughed, stopping at the curb as the Metchosin stagecoach rumbled through.

Dan pointed out the Post Office, Roger's Chocolates and a few other prominent businesses as they went by. "We're orphans," he explained. "We adopted each other ... and then there's Aunt Meg.

"Oh, now I see," Kate said, smiling. "You have a common aunt. Well, that would make you cousins."

"No," Dan chuckled. "We adopted her, too!"

Kate stopped dead in her tracks and stood with her hands on her hips glowering at him. "You're pulling my leg ... aren't you?"

"No, we aren't. It's all very true," he said, slipping his arm around Nancy and giving her an affectionate squeeze. Turning his eyes softly upon his sister, he met her gaze, noting the sudden glazed look in her eyes. He brushed her cheek with his lips and Nancy grinned, grabbing his arm.

"Come on, we'll introduce you to Aunt Meg," she said, pulling Dan along.

Nancy's words shook Kate out of her trance. Her heart had begun to race as she watched her new friends displaying their affection; she had often dreamed of experiencing the love of a special man like Dan Brown. She couldn't help but think how lucky Nancy was. She also had some of the answers that Mary had refused to divulge when she'd asked about Nancy, curtly being told to mind her own business.

Meg stood at the office door watching for their return, pleased when she saw they'd brought home a guest. They went inside and sat down at the table. Ten minutes later, Kate rose as if to leave.

"You'll stay for supper, won't you, Kate?" Meg asked.

"Thank you, no, I must get supper for my grandparents," she explained.

As they opened the door, they heard the sound of an automobile screeching to a halt nearby. Looking around the corner, Nancy saw Jebediah hurrying towards them.

"I have to leave town tonight," he gasped, short of breath. Gus needs me in Seattle. You can use it while I'm gone," he said, throwing a car key at Dan.

"Tonight, but how?" asked Nancy.

Jeb sat down, breathlessly telling of arrangements he'd made with someone at The Empress boathouse. "I'll be back before Wednesday," he assured them. Noticing Kate for the first time, the American's eyebrows raised. "Who's this pretty young thing?"

Introducing Katherine, Jeb's interest immediately heightened when he heard of her dockyard connection.

"Can I give you a ride home, Kate?" he asked. Kate drew back almost imperceptibly. "I need to give Dan a quick lesson in driving that damned automobile!"

More at ease knowing Dan was coming, Kate thanked him and they all walked up to the car. The men climbed into the front with Dan at the wheel. Katherine settled comfortably into the backseat and Jeb began giving instructions.

Meg and Nancy watched as the engine roared into life. Gears crunched, offending their ears and the car took off with a great leap. Kate smiled nervously. She had often ridden in her father's cars but riding with a new driver was a totally new experience. She gripped the seat for dear life as they gathered speed, bouncing and jolting along as Dan learned the gears.

"Do you think they'll be alright?" Meg asked, wringing her hands as they went around the corner out of sight.

Nancy couldn't answer for laughing, though she was glad they'd left her behind. Wiping her eyes, Nancy moved toward the office.

"Cheer up Aunt Meg, they'll be alright, although I'm not so sure about Kate," she tittered. "I'll bet she has a tale to tell tomorrow … if she survives!"

They were just finishing supper when they heard the car returning, and dashed outside. Dumbfounded, they watched the automobile creep sedately to a halt at the curb.

"Well done, lad," Jeb shouted, jumping out. "Now you've got it."

Dan sat staring through the window, a smile creasing his lips. He wondered if he'd remember it all tomorrow.

Nancy went over to him and tapped on his arm. "You going to sit there forever?" she laughed, feeling a swell of pride.

Later, they all sat in the office and Jeb went into hysterics as he and Dan told of Kate and her terror-stricken pleading, begging them to stop and let her walk.

"Poor Kate!" Dan chuckled. "I don't think she'll ride with me again for a long time!"

"Oh you'll get better with practice," said Jeb, winking at the women. "I'll get my bag out of the boot. I think I'll walk from here; we've both had enough driving for one day!"

When Kate arrived at the Balmoral next morning, Nancy was already at work. With time to spare before opening, they sipped their tea and discussed her wild ride.

"Frightened the living daylight out of me!" she admitted. "What a terrible driver! He just missed crashing into a streetcar, then he drove straight at a light pole!" she shuddered. "I closed my eyes after that."

"And what did Mr. Judd do through all this," Nancy whispered sympathetically, hardly able to contain her laughter.

"He whooped like a cowboy," Kate smiled, beginning to see the funny side. "I think he enjoyed it!"

Soon Kate had the whole staff laughing over her escapade. Harry came in through the back door, coming to a dead stop when he found his staff laughing. His mustache twitched nervously as he pompously watched the group.

"Now then," he said loudly, "do you think we can get on with some work!"

"Oh shut up, Harry!" Nancy admonished. "Get a coffee and go read your newspaper."

Totally deflated, the manager slipped into his office, banging the door behind him. The last of the laughter subsided as Kate went out to open the doors.

Sgt. Walker was first in, hurrying over to a table. Seeing Nancy wiping her eyes on her apron, he asked gently, "Are you alright, lass?"

"Oh, quite alright thanks, Sergeant … just laughing at a funny story. What brings you out so early?"

Pursing his lips, the policeman glanced around the room. "Somebody," he growled, haughtily, "drove a car like a maniac through the city last night and I want to know who it was." He paused to glance around the room again. "So, if you hear anything, you just call me, lass."

Sgt. Walker drank his coffee, nodded curtly to a few of the patrons and left. A call for service from one of the impatient Brackman-Ker buyers took Nancy over to refill their coffee cups, but her mind was still turning over what the Sergeant had said. *This is one time I won't hear a thing, Sgt. Walker*!

Over the next two days, with practice and some pointers from Waldo and one of his drivers, Dan's driving improved remarkably. Waldo told him he was lucky to have smaller feet because he knew some men with large feet who had a terrible time driving. Seems their foot was always touching the gas pedal instead of the brake, sometimes with dire consequences!

The car, whom Nancy had nicknamed, *Nellie*, was a boon getting him quickly out to Gordon Head to help Jack with the chute.

"Perfect!" Jack chortled after they had tried it out with a boxful of rocks for the first time. The shed now going up over the hole would serve nicely as a garage for the truck. With lots of room for out-of-sight storage, it would also reduce the risk of prying eyes.

"Does Nancy know about the party yet?" Jack asked, finishing up one afternoon.

"No," grinned Dan. "I don't think she has a clue about it."

At six o'clock, Dan pulled the car smoothly up to the curb in front of the Balmoral. Entering the dining room, he couldn't see Nancy but

Dottie told him she was in Harry's office giving Kate her last minute instructions. He sat down at a corner table and waited.

"Dan's here," called Dottie, as she went by the office.

Harry watched Nancy jump to her feet. "Sit still and finish what you're doing," he ordered, gently. "You look good in this office, Nancy, it might be yours one of these days."

"I think we've finished," she announced, handing Kate a list of the things they had discussed. Kate returned to work and Nancy turned back to face her manager. She had noticed his veiled comment and wondered if it had anything to do with why he had been so glum of late. "What's wrong, Harry?" she asked, her eyes full of concern. "You haven't been yourself lately."

"Oh, it's this blasted war thing. Everybody's talking about it, Nancy. I'm a German by birth, you know." Harry's eyes got misty as he talked of his fears. "Some fool will do something stupid over there," he predicted, "and Europe will explode in flames. But don't you give it a thought, girl. You go and have a nice holiday and we'll be just fine. Kate's a good girl."

Nancy nodded and tried to smile. She didn't understand his fears about the war because she had tried not to think about it and really knew nothing about it, save what she heard from customers. Putting facts together, however, and now hearing Harry's comment, she suspected he was thinking seriously about leaving Victoria.

Mary looked up from her worktable muttering unintelligible sentences as Kate came out of Harry's office.

"What did you say, Mary?" Kate asked.

"Oh, it's just that I am going to miss her terribly," she sighed, dropping her eyes.

"Don't be silly," Nancy laughed, joining them. "I'm only going for a little holiday!"

"Well, be off with you, girl! Go and enjoy your holiday and that wonderful new house," Mary said flippantly, affectionately hugging Nancy before she headed into the backroom to change her clothes.

There were dancing lights of devilment in the redhead's eyes when Dan told her he had Jeb's car and was taking her for a ride before supper. They took the long way, along Dallas Road past the luxurious

Dallas Hotel and around to Beacon Hill Park. Flushed by the thrill of the ride and knowing she didn't have to go back to work for nine whole days, Nancy was beginning to feel like a real lady.

Meg met them at the door and told them Brian Harper had called and wanted to see them at the auto showroom. "I'll keep supper warm," she assured them, as they quickly parked the car and ran back up to the street.

"I wonder what the matter is," Dan called as he grabbed her arm, pulling her out of the path of a bicycle.

Entering the showroom, Brian saw them immediately.

"Come, look what our Willie has done for you," he said, excitedly leading them out to the body shop.

The little blue Ford truck stood in the middle of the workshop. It was certainly wider, though it was impossible to tell that Willie had added a piece in the middle. Its dark blue paintwork shone like a highly polished mirror. Glancing inside, Nancy cast a frown at the dealer, who chuckled on seeing her expression. He explained grandly that the seats were being specially made. She'll be ready Monday afternoon," he announced.

"That early?" Nancy asked, knowing she had given them until the following Saturday.

"We aim to please, Miss Nancy. We aim to please!"

Over supper, they told Meg about the new truck, the developments at Gordon Head, and the pending trip to Seattle. She quickly declined the offer to sail in the freighter saying she was much too old for that kind of adventure. She hadn't looked too pleased about the truck either, but they knew she was trying to understand that it was going to be impossible to fight the existence of motorized vehicles forever.

The women talked about their first shopping trip which was planned for the next day. "We've been doing a lot of window shopping and planning while you've been away, Danny. Finally, I'll have some time to actually go buy our furniture," Nancy exclaimed, excitedly.

"Waldo said he would personally see to delivery of any large items for us and he still has our key," said Dan.

It was almost bedtime when Meg suddenly broke into their conversation. "In all this excitement, we've forgotten something very important."

"What's that?" they asked in unison.

"We don't have a name for the house. A special house like ours should definitely have a name."

Nancy looking wistfully off into space. Finally, she broke the silence. "*Cunningham Manor* ... yes, that's what we'll call it. *Cunningham Manor!*"

Dan noticed the puzzled expression on Meg's face. "In memory of old English Jack Cunningham," he explained. "His gold will help to furnish the house and do future improvements."

For the first morning of her holiday, Nancy tried fruitlessly to sleep in, but habit and the call of nature woke her at the usual time. Lolling in bed for awhile, she soon felt restless and got up. Dressing slowly, she heard Meg humming a lively Scottish tune while she made breakfast. Nancy combed her hair, greeted Meg, telling her she'd be back in a few minutes, and went outside to find Dan.

"You missed a beautiful sunrise, my girl," he announced, putting his arm around her waist and pulling her close. "Decided to lay about, did you? I thought you and Aunt Meg had a shopping trip planned."

"I decided to spoil myself for one morning. The stores don't open until 9:30 anyway," she retorted, defensively.

Sauntering along the dock, they laughed at the antics of the perpetually voracious seagulls as they swooped into the water for tidbits at the cannery. The whaler's eyes rested on the *Belfast*, sloshing gently at her mooring.

"I'll miss you, old girl," he muttered, walking over to pat the whaling ship's rail.

Nancy's thoughts turned to the *Belfast*, too, knowing the ship would soon be just a memory. Sad thoughts tightened her fingers in Dan's palm. Glancing down at the top of her head shimmering in the sunlight, he slipped his arm around her shoulder again.

"I know, love, I feel it, too," he whispered, gently.

Nancy had breakfast and by 9:30 she and Meg were on their way up town. Dan said he was taking the car and going to check on the *Bell*. This was a prearranged rouse between Meg and Dan ... his real purpose was making sure all Nancy's birthday arrangements were ready for Wednesday and he was beginning to get very nervous that something would go wrong. So many people knew about the party, it was going to be a miracle if she didn't find out about it.

Harry Maynard was crossing the brewery yard when the car skidded to a halt and Dan jumped out.

"Stop worrying," said Harry, seeing his furrowed brow. "You just keep her away from Gordon Head until two on Wednesday." He paused watching as Dan fidgeted uncomfortably. "Tell you what, go talk to Emerson and ask him to call Nancy."

"W-what for?"

"He can have her come to his office on Wednesday morning to sign the papers for the freighter. That way it all sounds legitimate and she'll be tied up until lunchtime," Harry laughed. "You know Gus and Beth Jorgensen are here?" he said. "And Jebediah is expected back later this morning. They're all staying at The Empress."

Emerson Turpel saw no harm in complying with Dan's request, promising to call Nancy on Monday morning. *Next stop, The Empress,* Dan moaned to himself, as he became more agitated, sending the car roaring out of the shipyard gates. Saturday shoppers and tourists waiting for taxis and trams, milled in the streets making progress almost impossible. Frustrated by the traffic, Dan parked Jeb's car in front of the office, jumped out and ran the rest of the way.

Gus, Beth, and Terry O'Reilly, were standing in front of The Empress talking as Dan ran down the hill. Beth saw him first.

"Hello Dan ... is something wrong?" Beth inquired, noticing his haggard appearance.

"No!" he retorted, looking at Gus. "I just need to talk to you."

"Let's go inside and sit down," Beth suggested, calmly.

"Leave the lad alone, Beth," Gus laughed, watching Dan closely. "He's scared to death Nancy's going to find out what we're all up to. Just leave it to me. We'll come down after lunch and I'll talk to her. She won't suspect a thing."

At two o'clock, the Americans, including Jeb, arrived at the Joyce Bros. dock and were talking to Dan, when Meg and Nancy were spotted returning home. They appeared to be loaded down with parcels.

"Time for you two to go tend to that little business matter," Gus reminded Jeb and Terry, glancing at his watch.

The men turned to go, almost colliding with Nancy and Meg as they hurried around the corner. Putting down her parcels, Nancy hugged Jeb, but merely greeted Terry.

"What about me? Don't I get a hug, too!" the gangster pouted, until a puzzled Nancy obliged, never seeing Terry act this way before.

"Danny, have you given Jeb his car key back?" she asked.

"Oops!" His hand dove into his pocket. "I forgot!"

Offering the key to the American, Jeb pushed it away. "No, no lad, you use it if you need it." Then saying that he and Terry had some business to attend to the two men started toward the road. Jeb suddenly turned back and shouted over his shoulder in a teasing voice. "You'll soon be a woman, Nancy!"

"I'm a woman now!" she called back. "Just ask my brother!"

Gus and Beth looked at each other and laughed as Nancy came over to give them each a hug before slipping under Dan's protective arm.

While making tea, Beth helped Meg empty the shopping bags as they waited for the others to come in. Meg was obviously delighted with the bargains they had found, telling Beth about their successful shopping trip and the wonderful furniture and stove they had picked out. Before long the table was covered with dusters and brooms, a bucket and mop, pot holders and kitchen linens, bedroom and bathroom linens and a beautiful, lace edged white tablecloth.

"I've always dreamed of having one of these," the Scot said lovingly, her hands caressing the soft material as it lay on the battered old table.

"What's this?" Beth asked, examining a small, neatly wrapped parcel.

The tiny parcel was from Spencer's Store and to Beth Jorgensen, trying to guess its contents, it presented quite a mystery. Meg was silent not wanting to spoil Beth's fun as she turned the package over and over in her hand and shook it gently. She watched the door as footsteps sounded outside and Nancy arrived with the two men.

"Whatever are you two up to?" Nancy chided the pair, seeing the wrappings all over the table.

"Beth's helping me sort out our shopping and she's trying to guess what's in your big parcel," Meg chuckled.

Dan's hand flashed out, as Beth gently tossed him the small package. First, he shook it, frowning when he heard a rattle. Shaking his head he tossed it to Gus, who repeated the process.

"Damnit," he said. "There's an easy way to solve this puzzle ... open it, Nancy!"

"You can open it, Gus. It won't bite you!"

Meg and Nancy laughed as the Seattle millionaire's large fingers fussed with the delicate wrapping, revealing a small box. Gus, now enthralled by the mystery, carefully grasped the box and removed its lid.

"Well, I'll be rubbed!" he exclaimed, using an old southern saying, as he removed the shiny brass whistle. "Whatever are you going to use this for?"

A knowing smile lit up Dan's face, recalling a conversation with Meg two days before as they stood on the dock watching a navy ship go though a drill. He had explained to Meg how the piper whistled his orders to the crew and Meg had been enthralled.

"Bless your soul, Aunt Meg," he said, "but that's not the right kind of whistle."

"Tell him, Nancy," the old lady chuckled.

"It's like this," Nancy began, as she produced two more identical whistles out of her pocket. "If we work out our own code, we can talk to each other," she explained excitedly. "It won't matter if we're in the house or at the bottom of the cliff, in the workshop, or in the boat out on the water. The possibilities are endless."

"It's brilliant," Beth whispered.

"I'm sure it'll work at Gordon Head," said Gus, "but that rough crowd on the Seattle docks will soon catch onto your game if that's what you had in mind. The idea's a good one though, if you could only disguise the sound of the whistle."

"We can," said Dan turning to face Nancy. "You told me that your friend Billy had some hollow sticks and when he blew them they sounded like a duck or a loon."

"Yes, I saw them," said Nancy, pensively. "We'll go find him tomorrow."

Gus' face broke into a grin and taking his wife's arm led her toward the door. "You folks are busy now, so we'll just get on our way. We old folks need our afternoon nap, you know!"

Over a bite to eat, Nancy decided to solve the problem of the whistles immediately. It would be good to see Billy again and she was confident they would find him out at the Irvine farm.

"Are you coming with us, Aunt Meg?"

"No, I think I like Gus' idea of a nap. You've fair worn me out today, love," she admitted.

"That's alright. You have a nice rest and we'll be back for supper," Dan called, as he moved to the door.

Traffic was thick along Wharf and Store Streets and Dan grumbled quietly to himself until they were out of the city. When they arrived at Irvine's farm and turned up the road that led to the house, deep ruts in the dusty road made the car bounce about wildly.

Two very large horses were straining on ropes tied around a large tree stump, urged on by Billy's shouting. As they stepped out of the car, the soil nearby heaved and the massive tree root violently tore from the ground and was dragged away by the sweating horses.

"Drag it over yonder, Billy," Tom Irvine called, indicating a pile of brush and stumps some distance away. He looked pleased when he finally noticed the young couple and walked over to greet them. "Hello Nancy," he said, mopping sweat from his brow as he cocked an eyebrow at Dan.

Nancy introduced Dan and the men shook hands warmly as the farmer politely, yet bluntly, inquired why they were there. Nancy explained about the whistles mentioning the ones Billy used to make.

"They're not whistles, lass," Tom chuckled. "They're callers, come and I'll show you. He turned and walked toward a log cabin.

They had never seen a log house up close and Nancy was fascinated. As they looked up they could see the top of a rough fieldstone chimney rising above the single roof which sloped slightly toward the rear.

"Did you built this house yourself?" she asked.

"Yep, took me the better part of a year when I moved here in '85," said the old farmer. "See how these peeled cedar logs are notched on the corners and squared by an axe. With patience, they fit together snugly to hold the walls in place. Those windows were the hardest part," he said, indicating two small windows on the front of the house neatly cut into the walls. "Come on in," he said, bending down as he stepped through the low doorway.

As they entered, the dimly lit interior smelt strongly of cedar. However, its tidiness surprised them having been told by Jackie that the farmer was unmarried. Sparsely decorated with stout homemade furniture, there was a table and three chairs, two cots in the corner, and a large clock ticking loudly on the mantle. The great open hearth was littered with shavings, as though someone had recently been carving.

Please sit," the farmer invited, his voice surprisingly gentle.

"Nancy! Dan!" Billy cried, as he suddenly came bounding though the open door.

Tom was rattling through a wooden box which appeared to contain small pieces of wood. Scooping up a handful, he brought them over to the table. Billy grinned mischievously and picked up one of the sticks, bringing it to his lips he gently blew on it. To the couple's amazement, the cabin was filled with the sound of geese.

"That's amazing!" said Dan. "It sounds so real!"

Nancy picked out one of the sticks and rolled it over in her hand, examining it carefully.

"It's like a whistle, but longer, and the holes are different."

"Blow it," Billy said eagerly, pointing to her mouth.

Blowing gently, she frowned when no sound came, glancing inquiringly at the Indian. Billy continued to grin as he made a motion with his hands for her to turn it around. Complying, Nancy tried again, startling herself when the stark call of a loon enveloped the room. Tom Irvine, standing by the fireplace, quietly stuffed his pipe with tobacco and smiled thoughtfully as he watched them examine the remaining carvings.

"They're beautifully carved," Dan murmured, "but how do you tell one from another, especially if its dark?"

"Easy," grunted Tom, pausing to light his pipe.

"I know!" interrupted Nancy. "There are some small notches cut into the same end the sound comes out, you can feel them with your fingers."

"Right," Tom nodded, looking at Billy who was nodding enthusiastically.

"Did you make these?" Dan asked Billy.

"Billy carve," he said with a serious expression. "Mr. Tom make them talk."

As they drove back down the long driveway away from the farm, it was hard for Nancy to contain her elation by the sudden turn of events. She sighed loudly and happily patted the parcel of bird callers in her lap.

"So, you're happy now, are you? Now you can always find me no matter where I am!" Dan teased.

"Well, you have to admit, it will be much easier to keep track of each other now."

"And your plan to use them on the water, is ingenious! I think these callers are going to work miracles for us."

As they turned from Craigflower to make the approach to the Pt. Ellice Bridge, they realized it was loaded with pedestrians and had to slow to a crawl. Nancy's eyes shone with mischievous develment as she untied the parcel on her lap. Her fingers searched for the notches as Tom had shown her, slyly choosing a long-stemmed one knowing it would have a loud duck sound.

As Dan eased the car past the crowd, he saw her raise one of the callers to her lips. The effect was loud … and magical. Just as they reached the end of the bridge, Nancy blew several sharp blasts. The people were so surprised they jumped out of the way.

"See," Nancy laughed, as they sped away, "we've just found another use for them!"

When they got closer to town, Nancy made a request. "Let's go down Douglas and see what's happening to the orphanage land, Dan."

"Right, we haven't been that way for awhile, have we?"

Skillfully maneuvering the car though traffic, Dan wrinkled his nose at the smell from the Albion Iron Works chimney that belched black smoke high into the air. At the top of the hill, they swung sharply into Douglas Street their view stretching all the way to the City Hall. They were surprised to see several burned out shells which they assumed had been homes and wondered why they were still standing, making the street look quite untidy.

Dan eased into the curb in front of the huge construction site at the new Hudson's Bay building. It was still not completed and wouldn't be for some time it appeared.

"See little one, it's all gone," he murmured, talking to her as he had so long ago. He reached out and took her hand. Bringing it slowly to his lips, he gently kissed her fingers.

It was as if she hadn't even noticed. "Why are they taking so long, Danny? Isn't the Hudson's Bay Company going to finish it?" He put her hand down and sadly looked at the grand-looking building with its boarded up windows and tatty posters.

"It's supposed to be one of those big, fancy department stores they seem to be building now, but something has slowed them up. I suppose it's got something to do with the economy and the threat of war, Nan. We're fortunate in our jobs but if you read the papers, you'd realize many businesses are beginning to suffer and it will no doubt get worse. I guess the owners changed their mind," said Dan.

"Do you think we'll ever be able to forget that awful place, Dan?"

"Forget it now, love," he ordered, gently. "It's all in the past. Now its just you, me, and Aunt Meg ... and a life of adventure."

"What a mess," she sighed, suddenly feeling quite depressed and wishing she hadn't asked to come here. "Let's go home, Danny."

Meg met them at the door and by her excited manner, they knew she had something to tell them. "Feel like going out to the Gorge Park tonight? They're having a special fireworks show at ten o'clock!"

"That sounds like a great idea," agreed Dan, knowing it would cheer Nancy up. "How did you find out about it?"

"Read it in yesterday's newspaper," Meg replied. "After I packed for our trip to Gordon Head tomorrow, I caught up my reading. We should get there early, so we can look around a bit in the daylight. The flowers will be lovely and the Japanese Gardens are open, too."

Discussing it over supper, they agreed that catching a streetcar would be better than fighting crowds with the car. So, with everyone helping, they cleaned up the dishes and did last minute preparations for the morning. They knew they would be having a late night and would need an early start in the morning if Nancy wanted to see the sunrise.

At eight o'clock, they gathered blanket, coats, and a cushion for Meg, and made their way up to the bookstore on Wharf Street to catch the 'No. 5' tram.

It was a nice evening and they met many not-oft-seen acquaintances as they watched streetcar after streetcar rumble by, full to bursting with happy people. Eventually, one stopped with room for a few more passengers and they were among the lucky ones who managed to squeeze on. Two kindly young men gave their seats up to Meg and Nancy, and Dan stood beside them hanging on for dear life as it jolted along.

"TERMINUS, EVERYBODY OFF," yelled the red-faced conductor, twenty minutes later.

Once free of the jostling crowd, Dan gripped the arms of his companions and led them toward the park. Looking back, they noticed that the empty streetcar was turning on its loop getting ready for its return journey. They had lots of time to stroll in the gardens before dark and Meg was thrilled with all the lovely floral displays.

They soon found themselves caught up in the excitement generated by the crowd, all eagerly waiting for sunset which was still at least an hour away. Deciding to go to the hotel for a drink, they stopped at the playground to watch the young children on the swings and merry-go-round.

"They have such wonderful toys for children these days, don't they?" mused Meg, thinking of her own childhood. The only swing she remembered was in a neighbour's old tree and their usual neighbourhood ball was just an empty can.

Down the path toward the water, they noticed that people had begun to lay out their blankets claiming a space to watch the fireworks. They decided they had better hurry to get their drinks.

Dan noticed a waiter in hotel uniform come out of the back door. He appeared to be carrying a tray on which stood several bottles of beer. He was heading in the direction of the streetcars. *Pre-arranged for the drivers and conductors, no doubt,* he thought. Although he wasn't able to see the man's face, it was the rolling manner with which the waiter walked that alerted him. Watching intently for a few more seconds, Dan could contain himself no longer. Moving away from his companions, he shouted, "WHALE TO STARBOARD, DUMPY, LOAD UP THE CANNON!" Not only Meg and Nancy, but everyone nearby stopped to see what was happening.

"DANNY BOY, WHERE ARE YOU?" came the instantaneous reply. Looking all around, Jack Dumpford finally spotted his waving shipmate. With a loud whoop, he handed his tray to the surprised conductor and tore across the tracks toward them. "Hullo Danny ... ladies, never thought I'd run into you out here!" Come on in through the back door, inside's in bedlam!" Then he disappeared into the crowd intending them to follow.

Eliza Marshall watched Nancy and Dan usher the older woman up the pathway and walked across the porch to meet them. "Follow me, folks," she instructed, smiling pleasantly. "You'll find this a much easier way."

Leading them through the back door, they went along a passage and up two flights of stairs into a bedroom suite with a large balcony window that had been thrown open offering a wonderful view over the park. Eliza indicated eight chairs which were neatly arranged in front of the window and they sat down.

"You'll find you have a superb view of the fireworks from here," Eliza announced, turning to welcome the young people. "And you must be Aunt Meg," she said kindly, shaking the older woman's hand. "I'm so pleased to finally meet you." After getting them settled into their chairs, she moved toward the door. "I'll send up some drinks and if you would like something to eat, just tell the waiter."

"This must be the best seat in the whole park," announced Dan, "yet we're the only people up here."

"Mrs. Marshall must consider you her friends," said Meg.

As the last streaks of a pink sunset disappeared and the blue skies finally darkened, they heard the band begin to play. Sometime later, a waiter brought their drinks and many of the park lights were extinguished. He asked if they wanted something to eat but they gratefully declined. A hush settled over the audience and tired children bundled in blankets and adults of all ages waited expectantly for the fireworks to began.

The sky suddenly erupted with beautiful shooting stars, soon joined by magnificent pinwheels and fiery waterfalls, as many colours and the sound of explosions rent the air. Meg was obviously enjoying herself as her loud oohs and aahs matched those of the audience below. As the last blue star fizzled and dropped to the ground, the park lights came back on, giving the crowd a chance to heave én masse toward the waiting streetcars.

Eliza appeared again, ordering them to stay where they were until the rush had gone. "It's a mad house out there," she exclaimed. "I'm going to get you some tea while you wait for the rush to get away." Before they could object, she was gone again.

In a few minutes, Dumpy arrived carrying a large tray with cups, saucers, glasses and a delectable selection of delicate cakes and pastries. Another waiter had jugs of coffee, tea, and water. Pulling up a chair the ex-seaman joined them pouring himself a glass of water.

"Golly, I miss the sea and the *Belfast* already," he exclaimed. "It don't feel the same working on land." Packing his pipe with tobacco and removing a match from his case, Dumpy gazed longingly at the waters of the inlet. He flicked alive the flame and passed the match over the bowl of his pipe.

"Did you get my message? Are you all set for Seattle on Thursday?" Dan asked.

Taking another puff, the seaman nodded.

"Afterwards, we might have a permanent job for you on *our* boat," Dan added, rather matter-of-factly.

Dumpy's reaction was electric. Jumping from his chair in surprise, he mistakenly grabbed the hot bowl of his pipe. Dropping it into his jacket pocket, he quickly dunked his burned fingers into his cold water. "Tim and Ned are leaving the *Belfast* here?" he asked excitedly, but disappointment quickly clouded his eyes at Dan's negative nod.

"It's for drinking, not sticking your paw in, you fool!" Eliza snapped as she entered the room. "Off you go and earn your keep, there's still a crowd in the restaurant."

Confusion appeared on Jack's face causing him to hesitate ... he had many more questions to ask.

"Are you still here?" asked Eliza, causing Jack to scuttle away. Now, she turned her attention to Meg, who was looking more than slightly uncomfortable. Even Nancy and Dan, who had not seen this side of Eliza before, were a bit embarrassed. Drawing a small bottle of gold-coloured liquid and two small glasses from the pockets on her apron, Eliza turned to Meg. "Would you join me for a little nip of scotch, dear?"she asked softly.

Nodding silently, Meg relaxed a little and made a new mental note. This was another first for her, she'd never known a hotel owner before ... and a woman at that ... and now she was having a drink with one! "Have you known these two long?" Meg asked.

"About a year," Eliza replied, stopping to take a sip and obviously savouring the taste, "but I've also heard an awful lot about them. The hotel owner's face broke into a smile. "Why even Tricky Dicky McBride talks about you. I think I must've heard your life stories! I have nothing but admiration for all of you, guts, drive and ambition, you folks certainly seem to have them all by the stories I've heard!" A strange softness now crept into the businesswomen's eyes. "You're a lucky lady to have those two holding your hand, Aunt Meg!"

Rising abruptly, she moved toward the window, quickly touching the corner of her eye. "Drink up!" she called, lightly. "The crowd's almost gone and it looks like the trams are half empty now."

Eliza's hint was unmistakable. Nancy smiled as she helped Meg from her chair. Going out to stand for a moment at the balcony rail, the Scot took one last look at the panorama of lighted gardens.

"There was an article in the paper recently, about a woman named Mrs. Butchart who is building a beautiful garden out of her husband's limestone quarry," she said. "I wonder if it will be anything like this one day?" Then she turned and allowed Nancy and Dan to lead her away.

Chapter 21

Mist hung like a blanket over the edge of the cliff, and the sea beyond, as Meg cooked Sunday breakfast on Nancy's fancy new stove. Nancy had gotten them all up by six o'clock and they had arrived at Gordon Head less than an hour later being disappointed that the fog was going to spoil their sunrise. However, the freshness of the air here was so different from that at the harbour, Meg was very glad they had come.

Meg shooed Nancy and Dan out the house telling them to go enjoy themselves. She'd call when breakfast was ready. Half an hour later, she looked out at the fog and went to the kitchen cupboard where Nancy had put the whistles. "Och, I think I'll try this thing out," she said aloud.

When the blast of a whistle penetrated the thick foggy air at the base of the cliff-steps, Nancy looked toward the house and laughed. "It's Aunt Meg calling us, Dan; she's using the whistle. Breakfast must be ready!"

The Scot heard them coming up the cliff-steps and smiling, she hurried back to the kitchen. As they ate, the sun began its slow rise in the eastern sky, cutting through the mist with its invisible rays, until first the clifftop and then layer upon layer of islands came clearly into breathtaking view.

"I think we need a canoe to explore the coastline," said Dan, "and a good pair of binoculars."

"Slow down, son," Meg chided. "First, we talk about whistles. We need a code ... something easy we all understand and can remember."

"You're right, Aunt Meg," Nancy agreed, going to the cupboard to retrieve all the whistles. Feeling the grooves and carefully choosing each whistle, she handed one to each of them. Amidst laughter and whistle calls they demonstrated their unique sounds deciding together what each would be used for and how, writing it all down. They decided to keep the bird whistles for emergency situations when they didn't want it to sound like a whistle. This satisfied Meg and they all practiced until the codes were safely ingrained in their heads.

The sound of a car negotiating the drive, saved their ears from further torture and they moved to the front porch to see the Jorgensen's big green car roll to a stop.

Nancy rushed down the steps to meet them. "You're our very first visitors!" she called excitedly, as Jeb stepped out of the driver's seat.

"No, they're not," he said, defiantly. "I was here last week!"

"That's right, Mr. Judd," Meg agreed, "but you don't count, you're almost family!"

It was an innocent remark but Jebediah's eyebrows raised in pleased surprise. He'd been drawn to Nancy and her new family from their very first meeting and to be called 'almost family' pulled at his heartstrings. Jeb had lived his entire life as a loner and had never married. Hunting down lawbreakers was not particularly conducive to staying in one place. The profession he'd followed had almost destroyed his trust in people and yet he had become unusually attached to this mismatched Canadian family.

Terry O'Reilly's voice cut through the old detective's thoughts, loudly suggesting that Nancy and Meg show Beth the house, while Dan showed them the dock. The women gratefully moved into the house and the men started down the stairs with Dan in the lead.

Before Jeb had gone far, he stopped, peering down at the water. "You get any fog here this morning?" Catching Dan's nod, he continued gruffly. "Then we'll need to get a fence put up right smart, we don't want anybody falling over!"

Trotting nimbly down the now familiar stairs, Dan stopped again and looked back up at Jeb. "Just who is it you think might fall, Jeb?" he asked, his eyes twinkling merrily.

"Meg!" Jebediah snapped, blushing slightly through his dark tan. "But it could happen to any of us."

Terry O'Reilly glanced over his shoulder, chuckling at the old man's embarrassment.

"Leave him be, O'Reilly," Gus admonished, quietly, then looking thoughtfully out to sea, he stepped onto the dock. "This dock must be almost invisible from the sea!" Walking to the end of the jetty, he scowled into the water. "Well built," he muttered, "but it's going to be a bitch to load a boat!"

"No, it won't!" Dan laughed, pulling his whistle from his pocket.

The ladies were in one of the bedrooms when Nancy heard the three sharp blasts. Leaping into action, she excused herself and tore down the stairs.

"Where's she going?" Beth asked, startled by the girl's behaviour.

"Watch!" Meg answered, going to the window and pointing toward the cliff.

Nancy went to the top of the stairs and peered over the edge. She saw Dan waving and strained to hear his words.

"SEND A BOX DOWN THE CHUTE!"

Hurrying into the new shed, Nancy quickly found an empty box and loaded it with a rock. Heaving open the trapdoor in the floor, she slid the box onto the chute and let it go.

The whole operation had taken less than four minutes when Dan heard the box thump against the stopper bar inside the cave. Glancing upward, he saw Nancy waving.

"IT'S HERE!" he called.

"How in heaven's name did you do that?" Gus demanded.

Reaching into the bushes, Dan revealed the neatly camouflaged door. He slid back two large bolts and opened it, revealing the entrance to a cave and the end of the chute, holding a box. The curious Americans crowded around, eager to see Dan's contraption.

"Well, bless my soul!" Jebediah laughed. "It's just like a child's slide."

"Smart!" Terry agreed.

"It's more than smart," Gus hissed. "It's hidden. There's nothing to see. I'll bet my last dollar you could load forty cases in forty minutes!"

"Easily," Dan laughed, removing the box and closing the door again. "Now, how do you like our Cunningham pier?"

"It's brilliant!" said Gus, stomping off up the stairs with Terry following close behind.

The old detective shielded his eyes from the glare of the sun and gazed out across the water. "What's that island out there, Danny?"

"San Juan," Dan replied. "If we had good binoculars you'd be able to see the limeworks. The white buildings stick out like a sore thumb.

"Mine are in Gus' car," Jeb offered. "Why don't you run up and get them."

In a few minutes Dan was back. He offered the case to Jeb but was ignored as the old man continued to gaze seaward. Sliding them from their fancy leather case Dan read the label, MADE BY CARL ZEISS, GERMANY and marveled silently at the quality. Raising them to his eyes he made his adjustments and focused on the target.

"Look, Jeb!" he exclaimed, "you can see the lime kiln … and Mount Baker looks so close! You can even see a mist lifting off Baker's foothills. These are great!"

Taking the binoculars from Dan, the American scanned the distant island, easily picking out the white buildings and Dead Man's Bay, before handing the glasses back.

"You don't have a pair, son?" Jeb asked. Dan shook his head. "Well, you do now. You keep 'em, they're yours!"

"No, no!" Dan objected. "They must be worth a small fortune."

"You've no say in the matter!" Jeb retorted, starting up the stairs. But he suddenly stopped, sat down and looked up at Dan with a fiercely somber face. "Listen lad," he said, quietly. "I'm not very good at expressing my feelings, so I'm only going to say this once."

Pausing, the old man's eyes clouded over as he took a deep breath. "Meg called me family up there at the house awhile back. That set me a-thinking, Danny … of how much I want to be part of you three. I'm almost 62-years-old and think it's time I settled down a bit. I know the story of how you three adopted each other. Well damn it, I wish you'd all adopt me!" Jebediah's eyes fastened their pleading expression momentarily on the young whaler and then down at his feet. Only waves lashing at the dock could be heard for ten full seconds when Jeb finally spoke again. "Meg and me would be good company for each other when I come to town and I've no shortage of money!"

Dan's mind was spinning back in time, his own memories crowding his thoughts as his heart heard his friend's own personal pain. He remembered his own motive for his rekindled friendship with Nancy … and the family Meg had helped them create.

Putting the binoculars back into their case, Dan moved to the stairs to stand in front of the older man. Gently resting his hands on the old man's knees, his voice crackling with emotion, he said, "You keep your money, Jeb. We'll just take you ... and I'm sure the women will gladly agree to the terms!"

A rush of air escaped Jebediah's lips knowing his self-inflicted days of loneliness, endless hotel rooms, and mental anguish were over. Their eyes met and the old man found himself basking silently in the warm glow of acceptance. Reaching out his hand, Dan took it firmly and a silent understanding passed between them. Then pulling the older man to his feet, they slowly climbed the stairs together.

Before their heads cleared the top of the cliff, they heard the sound of another car negotiating the drive. The unmistakable sound of Jack Duggan's Irish brogue hailed them from a hundred yards away, as he hung out the window of Harry Maynard's big black Packard. In a few minutes, Harry had gently eased it over the bumps and come to a stop beside the Jorgensen's Dodge Tourer at the side of the house. The back doors suddenly flew open spilling two women into the dusty driveway. Millie and Nellie gathered their skirts and baskets and rushed toward the house where they noisily greeted the three women waiting on the porch.

Dan made the introductions amongst a great deal of laughter and good natured banter and the women moved into the house for another tour. The men walked to the edge of the cliff and stood conversing in low tones pointing first out to sea and then down at the docks.

Suddenly, a window in the kitchen noisily opened and Nancy's voice called, "We're going to need a fire, Danny. Millie's brought enough steaks to feed the army!"

"Better do as we're told," Jeb muttered, grinning broadly at Dan.

Terry O'Reilly lent his expertise and giving everyone instructions they began building a pseudo Hawaiian-style cooking pit. Dan went to the shed for shovels and they dug a large hole, neatly placing leaves and rocks in the bottom in some unexplained and preconceived manner. The young Irish-American turned out to be quite the artist at building fires. The men gathered dry wood, and Terry cut some of it into small kindling.

"How are you going to get the meat cooked on top of this?" asked Jeb, scratching his head. "I've never seen the likes of this contraption before."

"Do you have some fence wire, Dan?" asked Terry.

"Sure I do. I'll get it."

When Dan returned with the wire, Terry rolled it out over the top of the pit. Then he made a second layer, making it stronger to keep the steaks up out of the fire, weighing the sides down with rocks.

"How about showing me the dock, Jack," Harry suggested, moving toward the stairway. "Looks like they've got this well under control without us."

Gus was taking no interest in fire building either. Instead, he watched the men as they ascended to the dock, smiling to himself when he noticed that Jack had omitted to show Harry the cave.

Terry continued his task at the large open fire, rushing around tending the cooking to the delight of the ladies and the amazement of the men. They'd never seen this side of the violent Irishman before.

Obviously selling protection to the Jorgensen empire and trading with fear amongst the waterfront roughs was only one of his many talents. O'Reilly had always been a mystery to Jeb, never talking of his past or his future and disappearing for days at a time. Having known Terry for three years now, Jeb was still searching for answers, quietly grasping at every clue. Several had fallen neatly into place … like the way he pronounced a few words which could only mean New York … and that pointed to the Irish immigrant district with its reputation for violence and death.

Unknown to Jeb, dark-haired Terry O'Reilly was the son of a minister in the immigrant Irish district of New York. His strong-handed father had often tried to beat an education into the boy. But if results are the measure of success, all he created was a tough uncaring youth who took what he wanted from others using the power of his fists. Spending a spell in a state corrections facility as a youth, forced on him by a dour-looking revengeful judge, gave him the reputation and connections to form his own gang. The gentle side of his nature that rarely came to light, was from his mother, a women he adored although she had died while Terry was still a ward of the state. Released several years later to the freedom of the streets and a life of crime, he quickly became a leader and managed by luck and skill to stay one step ahead of the law as he moved his gang from place to place.

A chance meeting with Gus Jorgensen had apparently transformed the tough gangster's thinking. The Swede gave Terry a chance to show him what he was really made of, thus proving to the belligerent young Irishman that some men *are* capable of fair play and keeping their word. Hence, Terry's fierce loyalty to the Jorgensens.

When a wonderful mouth-watering aroma began to envelop the air, they all moved into the house and sat down to enjoy Terry's steaks ... cooked to perfection. Millie and Nellie's salads and Meg's freshly baked fruit pies completed the appetizing meal. Gathering up the dirty plates, the women were unanimous in their praise of Terry's cooking technique, bringing a tinge of red to his cheeks.

Opening the last case of Harry's Crystal Springs beer, the men sat relaxing on the large veranda. "Listen to those giggly women," he laughed. "They sound just like a bunch of schoolgirls!"

"My Beth doesn't laugh like that very often," Gus mused. "She's enjoying the company, just like we all are, and I think it sounds lovely. It's been a nice day with friends."

When their conversation turned to the likelihood of war in Europe, Jebediah intervened. "We have our own war in Seattle with the Anti-Saloon League on the rampage and an Act before the US Congress to make Prohibition national. They already have it in a few states," he grumbled, "and it's spreading ... too fast, for my liking!"

"Idiots," Harry chuckled, "if they do that, I'll just have to ship you some." It was meant to be a joke but it caused a silence to settle over the group.

"You'd do that, Harry?" Gus asked, raising an eyebrow.

Everyone turned to Harry eager for his answer.

"It wouldn't be illegal in Canada," he said finally, thoughtfully sipping his beer. "And that, gentlemen ... ," he said firmly, pointing to the nearby island, "is the U.S. of A!"

A ripple of nervous laughter ran through the group, realizing what he was intimating. Jack Duggan cleared his throat to draw their attention.

"You'll need a fast boat and a damned good sailor," he offered, pointing at Dan with the stem of his pipe.

"Dan's a good sailor," Harry laughed, "but this is an impossible place to load from."

"But, my friend," Gus grinned, "you'd like the business if we made you our buyer ... no cut-price merchandise ... all high quality ... at your going rate!"

Climbing to his feet, Harry recognized that this proposition might have enormous potential ... and no risks for him as far as he could see.

"Delivered where?" he asked, suspiciously.

"Right here!" Gus laughed. "In that shed over there. Is it a deal?"

Jumping to his feet, Harry offered his hand to the American, feeling Gus' firm grip as he shook it vigorously. These were men of honour and this agreement would never be broken unless agreed upon. Jack winked at Dan and called to his wife.

"Come on, Nellie, bring Millie. I think we're off."

Nancy came running out of the house, wagging her finger at the builder as she called from the porch. "But you never told us why you came out here today."

"That's easy, love," Millie whispered, slipping her arms around the redhead's slim waist. "We needed Jack to show us the way, so we decided to bring enough food for a picnic."

"You certainly did that!" exclaimed Nancy, hugging them all. "Thanks for coming, it's been so much fun. We'll have to do it again."

"Are you staying here now?" Beth inquired, as Jack's black beast pulled away and they all waved a final farewell.

"We're still getting organized, but the Joyces will be off in a few days and then we'll move Meg out of the office," explained Nancy, as Harry came to stand beside them. "We've come out because I'm on holidays."

"Are you ready, sweetheart?" Harry addressed his wife. "We need to get Terry down to the dock in Victoria. Thanks Nancy, see you all soon."

The Americans climbed into Gus' car, but Terry, who was waiting at the front to crank her into action, grumbled at Jeb for being so slow. Then Dan made a surprising announcement.

"Hold on a minute! Jeb's staying here. We'll bring him in with us tomorrow!"

Gus waved that he had heard and nodded to Terry to move into action. Soon the Dodge Tourer's engine thundered into life, Terry jumped in the backseat, and it slowly began to move up the track.

"Thanks, son," Jeb grinned sheepishly. "Have you asked them yet?"

Dan shook his head and glanced over at Meg and Nancy who had obviously heard Jeb's comment and were sending them puzzled looks. "Alright, now we're on our own ladies," he began. "I have something to tell you, so let's all sit on the porch."

Chairs were re-arranged, sweaters were donned and they all sat back enjoying the refreshing sea breeze that was now blowing gently over the edge of the cliff.

"Isn't this idyllic, Mr. Judd?" Meg murmured, turning to Jeb. "What a wonderful place to spend the last few years of our lives."

Not surprisingly, Meg had again included Jebediah in her plans for the future, bringing a touch of red to the older man's face. Nancy's eyes met Dan's and it was as if she could read his intentions before he voiced them aloud.

Reaching for his hand, Nancy spoke softly and the others had to strain to hear. "Jeb's been talking to us about retiring. Why doesn't he come and live with us, Danny? We've lots of room and he'd be company for Aunt Meg."

Dan smiled, and turning, winked at the older couple as he stood up and pulled Nancy to her feet.

"I think you have an excellent idea, Nan," said Dan. "Aunt Meg, we think you need some company and have decided, if you will agree, that Jeb should come and live with us." And before anyone could say a word, he pulled Nancy down the steps after him.

"Where are we going, Danny?" she asked, as Dan dragged her toward the cliff.

A wispy smile crossed Meg's face, her heart taking a leap as she shyly glanced at the Pinkerton man. Jebediah's confidence returned and he flashed her a wink in return. This was a new experience for Meg, being paid playful attention by a man of Jebediah's Judd's distinction. She respected the old American detective, thinking of him only as a friend, but there was no mistaking his actions ... the old devil was flirting with her!

On the highside of fifty years of age, the thought of a man in her life had long ago been pushed to one side. "Behave yourself, Mr. Judd," she murmured. "You're flirting with me!"

Chuckling softly, Jebediah watched Dan and Nancy over the porch rail, holding hands as they walked to the edge of the cliff.

"You're right, lass, I am," he whispered, still keeping his eyes on the young couple. "But for once in your life, wouldn't you like to feel like those two? And Meg, if I might call you that, it's high time you called me something other than Mr. Judd!"

"They're mighty special people, those two are," Meg said, her voice barely audible. "They deserve to be happy ... Jeb!"

The shadows began lengthening and the sun slid behind the hills. Meg heard the familiar sounds of Nancy's singing as it drifted up to them on the warm evening air. Reaching for Jeb's arm, they slowly walked to the edge of the cliff. Below, they could just make out Nancy's white dress as she and Dan stood in the darkness of the little cove.

"Where's that singing coming from?" Jeb asked, looking all around.

"Why, it's Nancy, Jeb. Didn't you know she could sing? She's an angel in more ways than you know."

As she sang, the notes were picked up by the breeze and came floating back over the cliff. Meg caught her breath, tears stinging her eyes. Even in the near darkness, Jebediah noticed Meg's mood change and wrapped a comforting arm about her shoulders.

"They're right, Jeb," she muttered, as the singing stopped. "I could use some company. I hope you'll consider staying."

"Meg, with an offer like that, I'd be a foolish man if I refused!"

Taking Jeb's proffered arm, they walked slowly back to the house.

The lights in the house gave a welcoming glow to *Cunningham Manor* as Dan and Nancy came to the top of the cliff-steps. Turning around, Dan's eyes searched the almost black emptiness over the water, waiting for the moon to show its first faint light.

"There's a boat out there," he growled, abruptly. "Find me the binoculars, Nan."

Scooping up the instrument from the porch rail, Nancy could hear the laughter of the old folks, coming from the kitchen.

"I think those two are really enjoying each other," she said, handing him the binoculars. "Fancy yourself as a matchmaker, Mr. Brown?"

His mind on other things, he adjusted the focus and peered intently into the twin eyepiece, moving them slowly over the sea. "There it is!" he whispered, holding the binoculars steady.

"Who is it?"she asked.

"It must be Sam Smith, that hermit Jack told us about," replied Dan. "I can see his little dog bouncing around in the boat."

"I'll bet he sees everything, the nosy old devil," said Nancy.

Hand in hand they walked toward the house. Dan dismissed the sighting of the old loner as meaningless, but strong evidence nevertheless, that he knew the coastline as well as he knew the land even in the dark.

Walking into the kitchen, they smiled at the two older folks warming their knees as they sipped on hot tea in front of the stove. On the table beside them stood two glasses and a bottle of scotch whisky.

"So you two have found something in common," Dan laughed, pointing to the bottle of Highland Glory.

"Just a wee dram for medicinal purposes," Meg admitted, blushing slightly.

Pulling up two more chairs, Dan and Nancy joined them.

"Those binoculars of yours are really good in the dark, Jeb," said Nancy. "Dan spotted a small boat out on the water. Turned out to be Sam Smith, that hermit Jack mentioned he had met out here one day."

Jebediah's eyes narrowed as he listened intently, his lifelong training sending warning signals screaming through his brain. "In the dark?" he asked. "Careful, lad. I think we'd better make a friend of that old man. He could become a nuisance or an ally."

The common sense of Jebediah's words left the group to their own thoughts, momentarily.

Then Nancy looked up at the ceiling and quietly began thinking aloud. "A man and his dog," she murmured. "His weak link is the dog … make a friend of the animal and the man will follow."

"Absolutely right," agreed Jeb. "We'll feed that dog every time we see it!"

Out on the water, old Sam pulled on the oars of the old rowboat borrowed from an unsuspecting farmer in the next bay. He was careful to keep it in a position so he could see the new house on the clifftop. One by one the lights went out as the house fell into darkness. Sam waited patiently for another thirty minutes before dipping his oars and pulling for the cove with the brand new boathouse.

He talked quietly to his dog, Flash, who was lying at his feet. "Rich folk … new dock … and no boat," the old loner grumbled. "Stay close, or they'll shoot ya, boy!" he warned the animal as the row boat gently bumped the dock.

Behind a large boulder at the base of the cliff, Jebediah was crouched watching as darkness consumed the cove, and now moonlight aided his mission. He had found a leftover piece of steak in the icebox and now with binoculars around his neck and revolver tucked into his belt, he set it on the ground near his feet. On top of the rock in a well-wrapped package was another piece of steak and some bones.

Old Sam stepped onto the dock, his Indian instincts alert as he sniffed the air. Flash growled when his nose picked up the scent of the meat and ran over to investigate. Sam followed closely behind until the dog stopped, whimpering. In the moonlight, Sam could see there was something on the ground that was bothering Flash and he nudged it with his battered old boot, glancing furtively around. The hungry mutt picked up the piece of meat forgetting about everything else as he gnawed on it contentedly.

Jebediah's hand reached around the boulder and grabbed the collar of the unsuspecting intruder. Startled, the old man groaned and tried to pull away. Then, he heard the unmistakable click of a revolver's hammer and he stopped moving and began to shake.

"Hungry?" Jeb growled, stepping from the shadows and resting the barrel of his gun on the old man's nose. "Or are you just trying to be a nuisance?" Chuckling, he watched the terrier escape, diving back into the boat still clutching the uneaten meat. "Well?" said Jeb ominously.

Jeb could just see the whites of Sam's eyes as his pupils rolled back in fear. Now in his sixtieth year, Sam was used to roaming the nearby hills and cliffs and was still an extremely agile man despite his years but he didn't often face a problem like this. His mother, a half-breed, had conceived him in a moment of passion with a visiting Nisga, a guide for the Hudson's Bay Company. She had died young and unwanted by his people and viewed with suspicion by the settlers, Sam had spent most all his life alone in the forest. He wasn't worried about dying, he knew it would come eventually, and he had already had enough altercations with the white folk to know that most of them didn't have the guts for killing. But he wasn't so sure about this one, he was different.

Releasing his grip on Sam's collar, Jeb deliberately made a show of uncocking his revolver and sliding it smoothly into his belt. Reaching behind the boulder, he unwrapped the package. It took only a moment and the dog was back sliding submissively on its belly toward the unresistable smell.

Now," said Jeb, placing the cold steak in Sam's hand, "you eat, too."

It took several minutes of gentle coaxing to persuade the hermit to accept the food but when he did it had an amazing effect. He must have been hungry for he tore at the meat voraciously, grunting with pleasure as his strong teeth made quick work of the tasty piece of meat.

"Listen, Sam," said Jebediah, patiently. "Can you understand what I'm saying?"

Nodding his shaggy head, the old man stopped eating and looked at him with wide eyes.

"You know the law of your father says if I give you your life, you belong to me," Jebediah lied.

Sam's eyes grew larger than ever, as fear crept through his body once more, gaping at his captor as spittle dripped onto his shirt.

"The law says," Jebediah continued, "that when you're hungry, we will feed you, but you must protect us in every way or I have the right to kill you again." *How the heck do you kill someone twice,* Jeb thought, laughing inwardly, but he'd tamed this old recluse and now came the training. "We shall be going away for a while. It will be your job to take care of our property.

The man nodded vigorously, wiping his mouth with the back of his grubby hand.

At breakfast, Jeb told them all of his meeting with Sam and his dog.

"That was most brave of you," said Meg. "It could have been dangerous."

"I like your solution, Jeb," said Nancy, thoughtfully. Then changing the subject, she announced, "Don't forget we have to pick up the truck this afternoon, Dan!"

"Gee, there's so much happening, I had forgotten, love!" he teased. "We'll have to get some cash at the bank first."

They were almost ready to leave for Victoria when the telephone on the wall jingled. Meg picked up the receiver.

"Joyce Bros.'s office!"

"NO, AUNT MEG!" called Nancy, from the next room, hurrying to the doorway. "It's *Cunningham Manor!*"

"Sorry, sorry," Meg wriggled under her embarrassment. "It's Cunningham Manor," she said into the receiver.

"I know it is, Meg!" the voice on the telephone laughed. "This is Emerson Turpel from the shipyard. Can I talk to Nancy?"

"We are releasing the *Southern Bell*," Emerson said, when the redhead came on the line. "Can you be in my office on Wednesday morning at ten to sign the papers."

"It's my birthday, Mr. Turpel," Nancy moaned.

"Well then, happy birthday, young lady," he snapped, "but business must go on," and he hung up quickly. Resting the receiver back on it's hook, he looked across the desk at a grinning Gus Jorgensen.

Nancy put the telephone down. "I have to work on Wednesday morning," she announced. "Mr. Turpel rightly reminded me that we have an obligation to Mr. Jorgensen that must be completed."

"Not on your birthday!" Jeb groaned, feigning disappointment.

"Don't you worry, Jeb," Nancy soothed him. "I'm on holiday and I'll still have the afternoon free."

Knowing glances flashed between the others, wondering if their secret could be kept intact for another two days.

Ned was waiting for them as they pulled up in Jeb's car. He seemed a bit jittery and they all understood his eagerness to wind up their affairs so they could be off while the weather was good. Meg had read that the Panama Canal was nearing completion and if all went well, they wouldn't have to sail around the Horn again.

Later that afternoon, Dan and Nancy walked expectantly over to the car showroom. Brian Harper was looking out of his window and saw them coming.

"Look Dan, it's ready!" Nancy exclaimed, as they came through the door and saw the blue Ford.

Brian welcomed them profusely, strutting around the new vehicle again pointing out Willie's work and the effort he had made to satisfy their needs.

"How will you be paying?" he inquired, trying to sound casual and forgetting they had earlier mentioned a cash payment.

"You can have cash," replied Nancy, nonchalantly, watching his eyes carefully. Then lowering her voice, she continued. "Or would you rather have gold, Mr. Harper?"

The instantaneous twitching of his eyebrows sent the suspected message. It was true what she'd overheard in the dining room … this man had a compulsive desire for gold. Even the fingers of his right hand deep inside the pocket of his pants were feverishly fingering some loose change. Nancy flicked her eyes up at Dan before she held out her hand for the account papers, quickly checking the price before making a comment.

"Cash or gold, sir?" she purred.

"Gold," came back the instant reply as beads of sweat appeared on the salesman's brow.

305

"How much gold?" she asked quietly.

Dan grinned as a mechanic arrived to give him some instruction on the new truck, pulling him off to one side so they didn't interfere with Nancy's negotiations. He could still hear the conversation as she manipulated the salesman's greed to her own advantage. Recognizing she might need his help, he sent the man away saying they would finish the conversation later.

"You're not going to let him have old Jack's nuggets are you, sis?" Dan growled in mock annoyance. "They're worth three times as much as the dust."

"I'll give you twice the going price if it's all in nuggets," Brian insisted, taking the bait.

"Oh no, you won't," Dan snapped. "That's seven ounces of nuggets!"

The businessman's eyes darted between them, his excitement rising. Gold fever had struck him again. Brian Harper had dreamed of being a goldminer for years, obsessed by thoughts of striking it rich and becoming enormously wealthy. But life had played a cruel trick on him, making his weak body physically incapable of standing the hardship. A small legacy had allowed him to move west, successfully starting an auto agency in the fast growing western city. Business was booming for Brian, as more cars took to the streets despite the labour unrest and recession, however, it was anyone's guess how long it would last with the threat of war in Europe. Capable and assertive, he faced the world, confident of his future, but when gold came into play, he often became a snivelling fool.

Nancy put her hand into her purse and pulled out a small cotton bag. Handing it to Dan, the crunching sound clearly told Brian the bag held nuggets.

"No ...," Nancy decided, suddenly. "We'll pay in cash."

It was almost the last straw for the businessman whose eyes never wavered from the bag Dan was holding. Walking into his office, Nancy counted out four hundred and twenty dollars in crisp new bills, stacking them neatly on his desk.

"Are there papers to sign, Mr. Harper? What do we do now?"

Sad-faced and dragging his feet, Brian sat down at his desk. "Sign here," he muttered, pointing to the line at the bottom of the paper.

"Now all you need are the number plates. You acquire them from the Registrar at the Provincial Police office on Langley Street. When you return with them, the truck is yours!"

Dan and Nancy chattered excitedly as they hurried into Langley Street, clutching the papers. A dismal office buried beneath the Law Courts at the corner of Bastion Street gave the young couple little feeling of welcome. They stood at the counter before the solemn-faced constable in khaki uniform. They answered many questions which he labouriously penned into his book. The ten dollars registration fee required more writing before the constable handed Dan the number plate and a single sheet of rules.

"My goodness, I'm glad to be outta there," Nancy sighed, as the heavy door slammed behind them.

The tall Langley Street buildings blocked out the sunshine, giving the old street a cold foreboding look as they sauntered back to the showroom. Mr. Harper and the mechanic stood waiting in the yard. The little blue truck was ticking over gently behind him.

"One question, Miss Nancy," Brian asked, having recovered his composure. "Why didn't you give me the gold?"

Nancy's lips twitched slightly as she silently walked around the truck. Dan slipped into the driver's seat.

"It would have been too easy to cheat you, Mr. Harper," she replied, getting into the seat beside Dan. "And we don't do that, sir!"

Brian Harper's expression was of stunned resignation as the vehicle pulled away from the yard. Turning to return to his office, he was pondering Nancy's words when his grandfather's voice came to him. "When want is in, wit is out!" Brian heard the old man's words clearly and a moment of understanding flashed before his eyes. *Could it be that the redhead, a mere slip of a girl, had just saved him from a terrible mistake?*

Dan carefully negotiated the traffic on Wharf Street, turning left at the entrance to the wharf. Jeb and Meg came rushing out to inspect the new truck. The detective explained all the parts to the Scot as she peered into the driver's cab area with its three pedals and a lever.

"My word, that looks confusing," Meg muttered, shaking her head.

"Why don't we all go for a drive, son," Jeb suggested.

Dan got out the crank and after one turn the engine noisily purred into life. Nancy, then Meg, scrambled into the front seat allowing Jebediah to close the door behind them. He climbed into the back, folding his long legs into the small space, as Dan slid back into the driver's seat.

Pulling smoothly away from the curb, they turned left onto Wharf Street and carefully maneuvering through traffic at ten miles an hour, they soon arrived at the railway station and turned up Johnson. They had to slow for horsedrawn traffic but Douglas Street was wider and watching carefully he crossed the maze of tram tracks.

"Keep more to the left, Danny," Nancy advised, giggling. "You're driving down the middle of the road!"

Smiling through the glare of the evening sun, Dan dropped his speed as they reached the entrance to Beacon Hill Park. He took them past the aviary and the Zoo and then out onto Dallas Road, honking his horn at pedestrians who leapt out of his way in alarm. With a devilish twinkle in his eye, Dan smoothly slipped the clutch pedal all the way out, adjusted his lever, and moved it into high gear.

"Not too fast!" Meg cautioned, a hint of fear in her voice, as she gripped tightly to Nancy's arm. She would have liked to have stopped to look at the flowers but Dan was obviously not sightseeing today.

Past the Dallas Hotel, the blue truck raced at more than fifteen miles an hour. A moment of quick action from both hands and feet, brought the truck to a halt at the streetcar tracks as he waited for the James Bay tram to pass. Meg swept the hair from her face and took the opportunity to catch her breath.

They were forced to a crawl, due to the large array of cars and horse drawn cabs entering the city from James Bay. Meg now had plenty of time to sightsee as they slowly went up the causeway past The Empress. Here, too, the streets were congested with traffic and pedestrians taking advantage of the warm evening. Reaching the Post Office at the corner of Wharf, Jeb jumped out of the back when they slowed to make the turn.

"I'll bet I can beat you home using shank's mare!" he laughed, and soon was away ahead, waving as they lost him in the crowd.

Stopping to light his pipe before he went down to the office, Jeb watched as the truck slowly came around the corner and negotiated its way toward him. When it pulled up in front of the office, he was there to open the door. He helped Meg back down onto firm ground.

"Danny," she admonished the driver. "I think you drive that thing much too fast!" Not waiting for an answer, she went into the office and sat down.

After a hastily prepared supper, they sat around the table discussing the list of regulations provided by the registration office. *No motor vehicle,* it said, *shall be driven faster than ten miles an hour within city limits, or fifteen miles an hour on the main highway.* Use of the horn was also detailed, causing Jebediah to burst into laughter.

"Who's going to enforce all these laws ... not a policeman on foot, that's for sure," he said, doubtfully.

A knock on the door brought Nancy to her feet. It was Fred Barrett. Dan introduced Jeb as the fourth member of their family, newly elected, and the men laughed and shook hands.

"You can't do any better than that," Fred chuckled. "Do you still need me to crew on that freighter, Dan?"

Nodding, Dan noticed Jeb's eyes focused on Fred Barrett's cap and the initials sewn on it. The old detective frowned, not relishing the thought of being in close proximity to a Canadian customs officer when returning the *Bell* to Seattle.

Nancy noticed the sudden stiffening in her friend's back but decided this was not a good time to question him. Dan noticed it too and had a feeling what was worrying Jeb. He briefly mentioned that he knew Fred because he had saved his life many years before. Satisfied, the detective relaxed, joining in the conversation until Fred left.

"I should be off, too," Jeb muttered. "Maybe I should go get my things and stay out at Gordon Head."

"Perhaps I should go, too," Meg suggested.

"No, Aunt Meg," Nancy sighed. "We have to help Ned and Tim wind up any loose ends tomorrow. They need to be off by Friday." Disappointment flooded the old lady's eyes until Nancy put her arm around her and whispered softly into her ear. "Don't fret, Aunt Meg, we're all moving out there on the weekend."

Cleaning up the business for the Joyces was a relatively easy task. Tim visited the bank, while Ned sold most of their excess equipment to a steady stream of buyers who answered Meg's ad in the newspaper. After the sales were finished, Dan noticed that sitting off to one side was an old small-bore cannon that had hardly been used since he had worked for them.

"Nobody wanted the toy?" Dan laughed.

"That's for you, son," Ned told him, smiling when he saw the look of surprise on Dan's face. "Best darned scattergun I ever saw and it'll shoot a five pound ball."

"What in heaven's name do I need that for?" Dan frowned in bewilderment.

"Sit down, lad," said Ned, indicating some barrels nearby. "If my guess is right, there's going to be Prohibition over there." His arm pointed in the general direction of Washington State. "And when that happens, you and Gus Jorgensen will be in it up to your necks, and that little toy ...," He nodded his head at the tiny cannon, "will make somebody think twice before messing with you!"

"Who do you think that might be?"

"Crooks, lad, robbers, and maybe even pirates. Them devils will steal the whiskers off a dead man's chin!"

A smile crossed Dan's face as he began to grasp what his old mentor was trying to tell him. "One little demonstration with that thing and you think nobody will want to fool with us?"

"Don't ever misjudge those boys, lad, now ...," Ned continued, "me and Tim are going to treat everybody to supper at the Fish and Chip Shop on Broad tonight." He stood up and headed toward the boardwalk. Shouting over his shoulder, he called, "You tell the girls and we'll meet you there at six."

Out at Gordon Head, Jebediah sat on the top step of the cliff-stairs. With his binoculars, he looked out over the calm waters of Cordova Bay and the Straits of Georgia beyond. He suddenly got a drift of a nasty odour, making the hairs on the back of his neck bristle. Warning bells went off in his head ... he was not alone. Slowly, his hand lowered until he could feel the butt of the pistol tucked into his belt.

Suddenly Sam Smith's sad-eyed terrier peeked around his elbow and whined pathetically.

"Damn," said Jeb under his breath, sighing with relief.

Fondling the dog's head, he glanced over his shoulder to see the old hermit standing at the edge of the timber line, submissively fiddling with the cap in his hand.

"HUNGRY?" Jeb called, receiving an instant nod.

After feeding both Sam and his dog from rations in his own bag, Jeb talked to the old woodsman again about keeping an eye on the property. Listening intently, his head cocked on one side, he nodded his understanding. Suddenly, he spoke in a deep hoarse voice.

"If I see anybody paying this place an interest," he wheezed. "I'll put a rock on the top step, and if they're out on the water I'll put another one on the next step down."

"Good lad," said Jeb. "That's an old Indian trick."

Admiration for this unusual white man had already begun to form in old Sam's mind. Despite their altercation of several nights before, he was beginning to think of him as a friend, now harbouring only the faintest trace of suspicion. After all, the old woodsman had never had a friend before and in all the years he had roamed this area, nobody had ever offered to feed him. Respectfully touching his forelock, Sam shuffled off back to the security of the forest with Flash running happily beside him.

Jeb's mind at ease once again, he returned to a state of peace, completely comfortable with the quiet of *Cunningham Manor*. He settled into a chair on the veranda. Looking out across the strait, he wondered how long it would take before Prohibition changed their lives.

Chapter 22

A lovely bouquet of colourful dahlias and daisies mixed with fragrant lavender, greeted Nancy on the kitchen table Wednesday morning. Going over to sniff the flowers, she was greeted by the mismatched notes of a *Happy Birthday* duet from Dan and Meg as they came up behind her. Breakfast turned into a joyous time as they tried to make the last days in the Joyce office happy ones.

They had no sooner finished breakfast, when Meg stood up. "Out you two, I'll clean up this mess!"

Meg paid no attention to their protests, so Dan took Nancy's hand and led her out onto the dock. They silently watched the early morning activities in the harbour that had already played such a large part in their lives. Holding each other close, they walked along the several jetties greeting friends along the way.

"We've come a long way from that orphanage, little sister," Dan said at last. "You're a woman now. At last …."

Heavily booted footsteps sounded on the boardwalk and the loud voice of Capt. Percy Neville interrupted them.

"We're out here, Captain," Dan called.

"Sorry, old chap," the Captain apologized, seeing Nancy. "The regiment's leaving and I wanted to say goodbye."

"Hold it, soldier boy," laughed Dan. "Say hello to my sister, it's her 18th birthday today."

Percy gaped at the redheaded beauty unfolding herself from Dan's arms. He fidgeted nervously, stumbling over his words. "Y-your sister? I th-thought she was your wife!"

Flashing the Captain a smile that brought an instant blush to his face, Nancy giggled. "Not this year, sir, but I will be one day!" Then leaving both the men staring after her, she scooted off to join Meg.

With heart pounding, Dan watched her disappear through the office door. As if in a daze, he turned back to Percy. "Leaving for where?" he asked.

312

"To the mainland for more training," Percy replied in a clipped voice. "It's not too late to join up and come with us."

Dan shook his head as thoughts of the future skipped through his brain. It had been a strange twist of fate that had thrown he and Percy together that night at the Ship Inn in this distant outpost of the British Empire. As they shook hands, they were not to know that their next meeting would be on the battlefields of Europe under very different circumstances.

Dan watched as Capt. Neville, the consummate soldier, strode purposefully up the boards, disappearing onto Wharf Street.

In the office, Nancy was gathering up the papers she would need for her meeting with Emerson Turpel. Meg watched as she neatly arranged them in order, nodding her head in approval at the girl's systematic approach. She couldn't help but smile when she thought of the hours they'd worked together as she trained Nancy. Her natural aptitude for learning coupled with her quick and active mind had already made her a formidable opponent in matters of business and Meg was exceedingly proud of her.

"Time to be off, love," she murmured, hearing a clock strike the half-hour.

Dan was already at the truck waiting for her. After setting the levers, two quick pulls on the crank had the little truck purring and eager to go.

Emerson Turpel smiled to himself as he looked out the window and saw the Model-T truck easing to a stop in front of his office. He didn't often have the chance to work with a woman but he couldn't imagine this young waitress presenting him with any problems.

Introducing herself to the woman sitting at a desk in the outer room, Nancy was quickly shown into Mr. Turpel's office. Welcoming the girl very formally, he indicated an overlarge chair at the side of an enormous mahogany desk. Nancy moved as if in a dream, totally overwhelmed by this man's office and its sumptuous furnishings. *If this is a shipbuilder's office, I wonder what a millionaire's office looks like*, she thought, thinking of Gus Jorgensen.

A light tap on a side door brought a grim-looking little man with spectacles balanced on the end of his nose and a big sheaf of papers tucked under his arm, into the room. Emerson introduced him as their accountant, Mr. Biddle.

"Right," declared Mr. Turpel. "Let's get down to business."

Together they ran through the account, with Mr. Biddle explaining each charge to Nancy. As they covered the final few items, Nancy's eye noted the total amount. The accountant relaxed and handed her a pen.

"Sign here, miss," he said, indicating a line with his finger.

"No, sir!" Nancy responded, frowning. "There is one charge too many on your list."

"What!" Turpel exclaimed, visibly making the grim-faced accountant dither. "Show me," he snapped, moving forward.

Deftly flicking through the sheets of charges, Nancy pointed to one item marked, *Dockside Equipment $550.* Emerson Turpel scowled at the item then glanced up at the girl.

"Well?" he growled.

Holding the place with one finger, Nancy's free hand shuffled through the papers again until she found what she was looking for. Showing him, she pointed first to its heading and then to the details, *Dockside Equipment $550.* Emerson picked up the papers and glowered as he looked at the two charges. The accountant shuffled backwards a step going red in the face.

"They're duplicates, sir!" Nancy purred.

"Yes, I can see that. Make the adjustment, Biddle!" Emerson ordered, handing the papers back to his nervous employee.

Sitting back in her chair, Nancy watched as the befuddled accountant fled from the room. Emerson smiled across the desk at her, checking his pocket watch when the clock on the wall struck eleven.

"Would you like a job, lass?" he asked, resting his elbows on the desk. "Ned said you were smart, but I say you're downright brilliant. It took a sharp eye to catch that little error. I wondered why Jorgensen trusted you with such a big job, now I understand."

Ten minutes later, they were interrupted by a faint tap on the door and the accountant timidly returned handing the hastily revised papers into the outstretched hand.

"That will be all, Biddle."

It was 11:40 when Emerson leaned back in his chair, satisfied the deal was now satisfactorily complete. On the desk in front of him lay the bank draft from Jorgensen shipping.

"You're taking the *Bell* to Seattle tomorrow?" he asked.

"Yes sir, on the first tide. Two of the crew will be coming aboard later this afternoon."

"I had better inform Ken Macpherson," he murmured, rising from his chair. Holding out his hand, Emerson Turpel shook hers and smiled broadly. "Young lady, it's been a pleasure dealing with you … oh, and happy birthday!"

Leaving the shipyard offices quickly, Nancy found Dan waiting outside. She walked over to the truck feeling very pleased with herself.

Emerson watched through the window as the truck made its way slowly out of the yard. He had known Nancy for quite some time now—as the very pleasant and efficient waitress at the Balmoral, but today he had gained a new respect for her and he found himself wanting to know more about this beautiful girl and how she had become so close to Dan. He had watched Dan Brown grow from a strapping lad into a man, in the employment of his friends the Joyce brothers. He knew they had a special relationship and treated him more like a son than an employee.

It was common knowledge on the waterfront that he had been trained by the brothers and was the finest gunner on the westcoast, and a good seaman, too. Ned Joyce had once mentioned in conversation that Dan was the bravest young man he had ever had the pleasure of working with.

Weaving the Model T along Wharf Street through the congested midday traffic, Dan parked beside the office and offered Nancy a hand out.

"Why are we coming back here?" she asked.

"I'm hungry and Meg said she'd leave us a sandwich to tide us over. I also want to load some equipment to take out to the house."

Together they pulled the handcart, loaded with the miniature cannon, five-pound shot, and a barrel of gunpowder, up the dock and loaded it into the back of the truck.

315

"What is it and what are you going to use it for?" she asked as they finished.

"I'll explain on the way out to Gordon Head. Let's go find that sandwich."

Fifteen minutes later they were heading up Fort Street. Getting out of the city proved to be somewhat frustrating but Dan knew he had to kill some time so he wasn't worried. At Blanshard they turned north and spotting a unit of marching soldiers, he decided to investigate. He caught them up just before the Hudson Bay construction site. A train bound for Sidney sitting at the Blanshard Street V & S Railway Station, was belching black smoke which enveloped the poor soldiers. Dan stepped on the gas pedal and they hurried past.

"Our little truck certainly makes good time," Nancy commented, as they turned off Quadra onto Hillside, not noticing they were barely going the speed limit.

"It's fun to drive too, Nan, you should try it!" Dan teased, enjoying the feel of the little truck as it happily chugged its way up the hill and turned onto Cedar Hill.

She made a face at him and moved closer momentarily putting her head on his shoulder. Taking their time, they meandered along the old Indian trail and Dan relaxed at last noticing that Nancy wasn't even aware that he was going slower than usual.

"The air is so fresh and clean out here. Don't you just love the smells of orchards and freshly cut hay? I want to stay here forever!"

"I can do without that fresh smell of manured fields though!" he objected, holding his nose as they passed another farm where some men were spreading manure on one of the fields.

"Oh, you'll get used to it!" she assured him with a giggle, snuggling closer again as she, too, grasped her nose.

At last turning onto Ash Road, Dan began to feel nervous again. Taking out his pocket watch for the third time, he noted they were still twenty minutes early. He pulled slowly up to the open gate noticing the many rows of narrow tire tracks. He didn't say anything, calling Nancy's attention elsewhere, hoping she wouldn't notice.

Moving along the road to the house, he noticed the several rows of cars half hidden in the trees. Nancy couldn't miss them but he pretended not to notice. He began tooting the horn to announce their arrival and Nancy shot him a puzzled glance turning toward the cars.

"Look!" she exclaimed. "What are all those cars doing here …, Danny?"

Sticking to their pre-arranged plan, Dan quickly pulled the car to a stop on the side of the house and turned off the engine. As it spluttered into silence, Nancy's keen ears caught the faint sound of a piano taking her attention away from Dan.

Slowly alighting from the truck, her eyes curiously followed the sound as Dan steered her toward the front veranda. Suddenly, she stopped, her mouth dropping in astonishment as a crowd of people surged out the doors and onto the porch. The crowd kept getting larger and soon spilled down the stairs toward her. As they did so, their voices rose in unison loudly singing *Happy Birthday*.

As everyone rushed over to greet her, tears of joy and surprise were already dampening the 18-year-old's eyes. So many of her friends were here, both new and some unseen for years, as well as workmates and customers—Waldo and Margaret, Harry Tabour, Mary, Katherine, Billy and Rose, and even Louise, whom she hadn't seen for so long, and all their close friends. Tears now rolled freely down her face.

But there was no time for visiting yet, as the surprise had only begun. Dan, still standing nearby, took her elbow and persuaded her to move toward the house as everyone milled around hugging and greeting her as she went by. In a few minutes, she found herself standing in the doorway of their new living room.

She noticed it immediately, there was no way it could be avoided. "I thought I heard a piano as we drove up," she exclaimed. "Where has this come from? I didn't order a piano!" Then, not being able to resist, she walked slowly toward it and sat down on the little round stool. Running her hand over the highly polished black surface, she turned puzzled eyes on Dan who merely smiled and shrugged his shoulders, as she had done so often before.

At that moment, Harry Maynard stepped forward and cleared his throat. In a very serious manner, he held his glass high in the air and proposed a toast to "our beautiful 18-year-old with the voice and personality of an angel."

"Here, here," they all cried, taking a sip of their drinks in unison.

Harry motioned for silence. "Well, Nancy, I imagine you'd like to know about this piano, wouldn't you?" He saw the helpless expression on her face and continued. "Well, we all got together and chipped in for a birthday present and we had so much money we just had to get you a piano!" Amidst the uproar of laughter, he gave her a sly wink and walked over to hug her.

Nancy could barely think straight let alone find words to speak. She was having great difficulty keeping herself calm. Finally, she stood up and faced the group, resting her hand on the piano for support. "Y - y - you mean, th - this piano is really mine!" she stammered. Seeing Harry's smile, she began shaking her head in disbelief. "No, no, that isn't possible!" she objected. "A piano costs a lot of money!" In total confusion, she sat back down on the stool.

Millie stepped up to join them. Going over to Nancy she put her arm around her shoulders. "Nancy, we don't want you to question our decision. Actually, it was a purely selfish one shared by those of us who can afford the most. We all love to hear you sing and most of all we love you and want you to be happy. We all know how much singing means to you and when we come to visit you and Dan in this magnificent house with its breathtaking view, we would dearly love you to sing for us. For that we, and especially I," she smiled, "needed a piano ... and we could think of no better present to give you for your eighteenth birthday! So let's just enjoy it, shall we?"

By now, not only Nancy was crying but most of the women in the room had gotten out their handkerchiefs. Dan stepped forward, handing her his own handkerchief. Meg pushed through the crowd with a cup of tea and slowly the group dissipated, some helping with food and others going outside.

All afternoon *Cunningham Manor* was filled with the sounds of happy laughter and friends talking. More guests trickled in and they all enjoyed the sumptuous food supplied by Harry Tabour and her friends at the Balmoral. Asked how it had been transported, Waldo admitted he had brought it over in one of his depot hacks.

As the sun began to dip behind the trees the revelers began tiring and soon everyone was sitting outside on the grass at the clifftop or on the veranda. Millie walked over to the piano, that the men had pulled out onto the porch, and began to play some well-known songs.

For the next half hour their voices joined én masse in a wonderful sing-along. Then before Millie could begin another, Jack moved to her side and touched her hand.

"Sing for us, Nancy," he pleaded in his loud, but beautifully gentle, Irish brogue. "Let's see how you like your piano."

A quietness came over the gathering as Nancy rose from her position on the grass and went to join Millie. The pianist handed her a piece of sheet music. Nancy looked at it briefly and smiled, appreciating Millie's excellent choice.

She moved to the railing and looked out at the faces of the waiting crowd. Her mind flashed back to the early days and her lonely childhood, of Dan, Billy, Louise, and the many other special friends who had gone out of their way to help her over the past seven years. A feeling of gratitude consumed her heightening her emotions, but she swallowed hard and turned to give Millie the ready signal.

Millie's experienced hands once again flew over the shiny new ivory keyboard sending the joy of her music aloft. As she began the introduction to the Irish favourite, *Galway Bay*, Nancy looked out over the water and took a deep breath.

Gus and Beth sitting on the grass, eagerly awaited this performance knowing nothing of Nancy's talent until contacted by the Nellie about their gift idea. They had willingly given a substantial sum toward the piano, purchasing it in Seattle and shipping it to Victoria at their own cost. Nancy had become such a special friend, they too felt it warranted an exceptional gift.

Everyone's eyes now fastened on the redhead as the piano became softer and Nancy began to sing. From the very first note, she had their complete attention. Not surprisingly, upon hearing the familiar melody, Jack Duggan also took up the tune and seeing Nancy's approving smile went to stand near her at the stairs. The mature, rich Irish tenor blended perfectly with the youthful, sweet soprano, and their voices rose majestically, soaring across the clifftop.

Jebediah sat bolt upright in his chair next to Meg. Snatching his pipe from his mouth, he stared in disbelief at the girl he thought he knew so well. This was not what he had heard a few nights ago.

"Sit back, Jeb, and relax!" Meg whispered, with a knowing sparkle in her eye. "They've only got started!"

319

Beth leaned against her husband as they sat on their blanket. She, too, was mesmerized by this new discovery. Turning to look up at Gus, she realized he was experiencing the same degree of amazement and his grasp tightened on her shoulders. Looking around the group, she noticed many expressions of surprise and rapture. *We aren't the only surprised guests,* she thought, with a smile.

Millie swung right into *Beautiful Dreamer* and Jack kissed her on the cheek and went to sit down. Then, with hardly a pause for a quick drink of water, Nancy moved smoothly into a catchy number from the deep south, lightening the mood of her audience who clapped in time with the music. She sang several verses of the popular tune complete with funny antics. Laughter greeted the end of the song and when someone shouted, "MORE!" she held up her arms for quiet.

"Friends," she began, in her characteristic quiet manner. "You have made this the best day of my life and I will never forget it. Thank you for being here and sharing my 18th birthday. Thank you for this wonderful piano ... and thank you for being our friends. Millie showed me a new Scottish song recently and I'd like to sing it for a very special lady ... my Aunt Meg. Then I have one last number ... for my Dan," adding quickly, "he sulks if I leave him out you know!"

A ripple of laughter ran through the guests. Millie, unsure of the tempo Nancy wanted, played the introduction and prepared to follow her lead.

The wind always blows your heart back to the highlands, rang through the trees, stunning the listeners with its beautiful lyrics and haunting tune ... a song which most of them had not heard before.

Memories of her homeland tugged at Meg's heart, bringing tears gently coursing down her face. Her fingernails dug into her hand, hurting so much she flinched causing Jeb to look at her to see if she was alright. He now reached out, resting his hand gently on her arm. He had never before heard such singing, this girl truly was the angel Meg had claimed and her singing was pure magic.

When the song concluded, Millie also dabbed at her eyes. She would never get used to this girl's extraordinary talent it seemed. "Right, love," she said softly, handing her a sheet of music. Millie began to play the introduction to *Because,* a song that Nancy had mentioned to her at Christmas. Unbeknownst to the girl, Millie had

320

found the music in one of her friend's collections. Steeling herself against the heart wrenching words and Nancy's anticipated interpretation, she concentrated solely on her playing.

When Nancy began singing there was absolute stillness in the air. Even the wind seemed to have stopped in honour of this magical moment. *"Because you come to me with naught save love,"* she sang looking directly at Dan.

Sniffles were muffled by hankies and every man bowed his head as Nancy sang to the man she adored. Not a leaf moved in the forest. Waves under the dock were silenced and all along the clifftops the notes echoed, as her declaration of love mingled with the slowly fading light.

"My word!" Gus gasped, his arm tightening about his wife's waist. "And we didn't even realize she could sing!"

At that moment, Dan stood up and began to walk slowly toward the veranda. As the last words of the song floated away on the still night air, Nancy melted into his arms.

For a split second the silence was deafening and then the air was rent by thunderous cheers and clapping. It was obvious that these people knew only too well that what they had witnessed here today was something very special.

As the cheering died away, Waldo's voice boomed through the air, bringing them back to reality. "Time to go home, everyone!"

Goodnights were brief, but sincere, as the party quickly broke up and the first of the procession of cars slowly made its way out through the trees.

Meg stood up shakily with Jeb staying close to steady her as they made their way over to Dan and Nancy. Thanking her for the song, she reminded them they had another big day tomorrow.

"You all have a long trip ahead of you tomorrow."

"Not really, Aunt Meg," said Dan, taking Nancy by the hand and leading her inside, "this is just a short one as sea journeys go, but we do need to be up early to get that freighter on its way. We're on a tight schedule now so Ned and Tim can get off on time come Friday."

"So you all go on and get to bed," ordered Meg as she made her way out to the kitchen. "What I don't get cleaned up tonight will wait for tomorrow. I'll have nothing else to do with you away all day. She

321

found several women in the kitchen ahead of her. "Some of the girls already did a pile of dishes, so it's not as bad as it looks," she said, trying not to sound as tired as she felt. "Go on now. You girls go on home, too, it's getting dark." She gave them each a hug and pushed them out of her kitchen. A few minutes later, everything grew quiet as the last cars disappeared up the driveway. She looked about the room, sat down tiredly, and emptied the teapot into her cup.

As the long line of cars picked their way along the narrow county road, Gus turned to his wife, a keen follower of the Arts in Seattle. "It seems like such a waste of a marvelous talent, Beth."

Reaching for his hand in the darkness, she carefully considered her answer before speaking. "Yes, it does, doesn't it, dear. What a wonderful talent to have and she doesn't even know how to read music. A natural voice with no training and I don't think she has any idea ... she just sings straight from her heart. I wonder if I could persuade her to ...," she mused, her voice trailing off.

"Persuade her to do what? I think we know Nancy well enough to realize she wouldn't want to become a professional singer. It would take her away from Dan and Meg."

"No, no, I mean charity work, that sort of thing. She's already done it once, here in Victoria. I heard someone talking about it tonight. I'll have to give it some thought."

"You've got to hand it to those young people, Beth. Against all odds they have succeeded, and I have no doubt they will continue to succeed. You don't see it often. Those two are bound by loyalty and we should be proud to call them friends!"

"You're so right, love. I look forward to watching them over the next few years. Oh, I do hope Dan doesn't have to join the service like our boys. It would be such a worry for Nancy and the others," said Beth, sighing deeply.

Silence, save for the dull engine noise of the car, enveloped them as darkness brought a coolness to the air. Beth moved closer to her husband, resting her hand comfortably on his leg and he held it gently. They turned onto Cook Street and from the top of the hill they could see the welcoming lights of Victoria twinkling in the distance.

Chapter 23

In the half-light of a misty morning, Dan sat trying to read the morning newspaper on a capstan at the Point Hope dock waiting for the Jorgensen's to arrive. On board the *Southern Bell* just behind him, Dumpy and Tim who had settled into the engine room the night before, were now making final preparations to leave. Gus had brought up several extra men to act as crew and coal stokers and he could hear them shouting to each other over the noise of the engine.

Familiarizing himself with the wheelhouse and navigational instruments, Ned glanced out the window as Fred Barrett strode confidently across the deck. He smiled to himself as he often did when he thought of that day so long ago when Fred had rescued Dan. That incident had cemented a strong bond of friendship between he and Dan, one that had remained to this day. Ned had often expressed his gratitude to Fred as Dan had become like a son to him over the years ... that was the one disturbing thing about leaving. The green Dodge turned into the shipyard thankfully disturbing Ned's thoughts.

About time they got here, Dan thought to himself as he folded the newspaper, glancing up at Nancy when she appeared at the railing. She called to Beth who hurried up the gangway to meet her.

"You'd think they were going on a Mediterranean cruise, instead of Seattle. Never can understand women!" said Gus, his eyes twinkling. Then, he visibly cringed as the screaming blast of the shipyard's steam whistle called for the day to begin.

Kenneth Macpherson's harsh Scottish brogue rang through the air as he ordered his men to hoist Gus' car aboard the freighter. Quick action by the dockyard crew and their crane soon had the Dodge Tourer swinging in the air, landing smoothly on the freighter's deck.

"GOT YOUR PILOT?" the Dockmaster yelled to Dan at the rail.

"YUP," came back his reply. "WE'VE GOT NED AT THE WHEEL AND FRED BARRETT ON THE BOW."

A wave from the Dockmaster to his linesmen and the freighter was set loose. Slowly it eased away from the dock, backing into the channel and swinging wide. Once turned, the *Southern Bell* moved forward toward the now wide-open railway bridge at the foot of Johnson Street. Nancy excitedly pointed to the opened bridge. She had always been fascinated by this bridge and finally seeing it from the water side was a special treat.

Ned sent the freighter into a deep sweep of the harbour, then straightened her out. She slid gracefully between Laurel Point and the infamous Otter Rock, a giant rock formation which had always been a hazard to shipping in the harbour. Setting the bow directly on Colville Island, the *Bell* slowly moved toward the mouth of the harbour before turning to face the open sea.

"Take her, lad," said Ned, handing the wheel over to Dan. "She's all yours," he said proudly, sadness unexpectedly gripping him. He turned away watching Dan's reflection in the window as the younger man stood confidently at the helm, his eyes scanning the strait.

Hot cups of rum-laced tea were prepared by the women with the aid of some of the crew more familiar with a ship's galley. Delivered on unsteady legs, the men welcomed the tasty hot drink. In the wheelhouse, those who were not involved with duties, gathered around Dan as he headed on his southeasterly course into U.S. waters.

The jesting and chatter began to revolve around Prohibition and the referendum soon to come before Seattle voters.

"It won't happen," said Ned, doubtfully. "They have it back in Maine and it ain't workin worth a hoot."

"And if it does?" asked Jeb slyly, winking at Gus.

"Hell, I'll run it in for you!" the old whaler growled.

"But you won't be here, Ned," Gus reminded him, gently.

"Well then ... Dan will!" Ned muttered. He was looking out the wheelhouse window at the two women as they held tightly to the rail, wind blowing through their hair and whipping their skirts about their ankles. He didn't notice the quick clash of eyes and the silent message that passed between the two Americans. "Just a touch west, son," he advised Dan, his experienced eye noticing they were slightly off course. "Then south past Point No Point and down the middle of the channel all the way."

It was a perfect day to be on the water, as light clouds kept glare to a minimum. As they moved through the picturesque San Juan Islands and into Puget Sound, sailboats dotted the water, keeping a wide birth from the freighter. Beth, so familiar with this often-viewed landscape, pointed out sights of interest along the way often giving a fascinating commentary.

Nancy noticed several unusual homes built high on the rocks of the islands, their long steep steps leading down to small jetties. Further along, a boat shelter caught her eye amongst the sea-washed rocks and above, a dwelling just visible amongst a grove of tall trees. Outcrops of rock pointed their jagged heads above the water, daring passing ships to come closer. Beautiful colours touched the treetops, as the sun peeked through the clouds kissing a million acres of virgin forest and in the background always the breathtaking beauty of snow tipped mountains.

"It's no wonder we call it God's Country!" Nancy called above the noise of the wind, pointing toward several splendid mansions. She asked Beth if she knew anything about them. Beth explained that this was the old headland at Port Townsend. The homes had been built by rich millionaires who many years before had wrongly anticipated the future growth of the area as a great city and port. Unfortunately, Seattle had become the choice of commerce, leaving the mansions to stand starkly beautiful in their lonely vigil on the headland.

Five hours after leaving Victoria, Fred came into the wheelhouse to refill his cup with the tasty tea mixture. We'll be in Seattle in thirty minutes, that's Bainbridge Island up ahead," he announced, pointing to starboard.

Dock 79 was their destination as Ned took over the helm again, sliding the freighter down the line of ocean-going vessels that dwarfed the smaller freighter. Dan's keen eyes saw the sign long before the others.

"There it is," he called, pointing to the empty space between two other ships, with the numbers "79" boldly displayed. He watched with interest as Ned expertly eased the *Bell* into her temporary home.

It was a masterful docking, loudly applauded by Fred and the others as eager dockworkers fastened her lines to the large capstans. Tim killed the engines with a bone-jarring thud and followed Dumpy up the ladder arriving on deck just in time to see the Jorgensen's car being hoisted into the air by a giant crane. At the same time, another car sped along the wharf stopping with a screech just as the Tourer arrived safely on the dock.

"It's O'Reilly and Peter," Gus announced, shaking his head at Terry's driving habits. "You men go with Terry. We'll take Dan and Nancy. Let's go find something to eat!"

Finnegan's Restaurant and Bar at Fourth and Mercer, a regular haunt of Terry's, was owned by Al O'Malley, a genial, overweight Irishman, well-known to the Jorgensen's group. Thick carpets greeted their feet as they stepped into a world of splendor with crystal chandeliers, murals, and gold-coloured paint adding a touch of elegant grace to the high-class dining room.

"It's fancier than The Empress!" Nancy whispered to Dan, as they were shown to a table.

Service was quick and efficient, the food excellently prepared and presented, though Nancy noticed with interest that the servers were young males and all were Chinese. *I wonder why?* she thought. *There must be some motive.* Being an experienced waitress, she knew the value of good-looking girls with poise, how a wink and a smile could disarm the grouchiest man from complaining. These black-eyed, stone-faced waiters who moved around the floor with the smoothness of a dancer and the litheness of a cat, sent an ominous chill down her spine.

Later, hunger satisfied and the dishes all whisked away, the group was chatting loudly across the tables when Big Al came over to greet them.

"You're Canadians," he began, noting the strangers, but with eyes only for the lovely redhead. "Would you like a tour of my establishment?"

"A tour?" Nancy asked, incredulously. "You mean the kitchen?"

Smiling, Big Al beckoned them to follow. With Nancy and Dan beside him, he led them along a dimly lit passage, tapping three times on the door at the end. A low hum of noise could be heard as the big door swung open. Nancy gasped at the scene before her. Lights and mirrors were everywhere. Well-dressed men bent over several large tables strewn with piles of money.

"What are those little coloured circles they have in stacks?" she whispered.

"Those are gambling chips and each colour denotes its value," Al explained.

A roulette wheel, under a spotlight, spun wildly as several men watched eagerly. Occasionally, there was a rumble of happiness or displeasure from one of the men but usually only the clicking of the wheel or the muffled sound of voices was heard. To one side was a huge bar consisting of a long mirrored wall and counter with high round stools, and everywhere, young Chinese men in white shirts and black trousers served the customers drinks and food.

"Whoa, look at this!" Dumpy exclaimed, pushing forward eagerly.

"Hold it, lad," Ned snapped, reaching out and grasping him by the arm. "This ain't for the likes of you, m'boy!"

"Let me give you one quick lesson," offered Al, now with a serious expression as he moved in behind the only empty table in the room.

The big Irishman scooped up a deck of cards and sat down on the dealer's chair. Inviting his guests to watch carefully, he shuffled the deck with blazing speed and dexterity.

Gambling is for fools, son," he said softly, aiming his comments at the still embarrassed young crewman. "Watch ... four aces," and four aces were dealt face up in front of the crewman. "Now, you put them back into the deck," he said, offering the cards to the young man.

Dumpy smiled wryly. Under the watchful eyes of the group, he replaced the cards spacing them out in the deck before handing the cards back to their host.

Al made a bit of a show flexing his fingers and again shuffling the cards many times, so quickly it took Nancy's breath away. "Son," he said, "here's your four aces!" Four aces flew across the table landing in front of Dumpy who gasped in surprise. "Let me give you some advice, m'boy. If you want to hold onto your money, don't ever gamble. There's always someone like me just waiting to take it from you!"

327

Dumpy seemed speechless but inwardly he had fully understood Big Al's friendly demonstration. He vowed to himself never to play cards with a stranger again. Jeb chuckled, hoping Big Al's demonstration was remembered by these young people.

"Why are you hidden away in the back? And why all the Chinese waiters?" Nancy asked, once they were out in the hallway again.

"They're *my* men!" Terry growled, proudly. "Everyone of them is a skilled fighter. They keep this place trouble free!"

"Right. Interlude over. Let's go!" Gus announced, suddenly. "Thanks Al, put it on my tab. I'll explain the rest to our friends in the car!"

As the green Tourer moved out of Finnegan's carpark and picked up speed, Gus explained. "The reason for the secrecy Nancy, is Prohibition ... due to new laws, no liquor can be made in this state. Before long, Seattle will be totally banning all liquor sales to the public. The consensus is that the Anti-Saloon League are going to win this year's vote. They're going to turn us into another of their blasted dry states!"

Beth rolled her eyes mirroring her husband's frustration.

"Now I understand. That's why you were so interested in our dock at *Cunningham Manor!*" Nancy quipped from the backseat. "This may cost you a bundle, Mr. Jorgensen!"

Dan's arm eased over her shoulder pulling her closer as the car turned onto Perkins Lane. A short distance along, two large iron gates opened giving them their first view of the large and pretentious, Jorgensen waterfront estate. The only indication was a sign declaring, 1 PERKINS LANE on the gate. Peter drove slowly down a wide, circular driveway, giving them a chance to view the magnificent estate with its beautifully manicured lawns. Lining the driveway was a row of little trees pruned into fascinating shapes. Nancy had seen trees like this in Victoria, but never so many in one place.

Colourful flowers in spacious gardens and winding walkways spread about the expansive property. Behind some trees, a tennis court and a horse paddock could be seen. The house was three-storied and built completely of stone and brick. A two-storied, four-car garage stood off to one side. Nancy had never seen such a large house in her life and as the car pulled into the large porte cochére, it towered grandly above them.

"Oh my!" sighed Nancy, staring at the large mansion with its massive wooden doors.

Gus got out and opened the back door offering the awestruck girl his hand as the others tumbled out onto the ornately tiled entranceway.

The door opened and a uniformed older man waited to greet them. Following quick introductions, explaining that this was Joseph, their long-suffering butler, Gus showed the men into his study. Beth, linking arms with Nancy, said they only had time for a quick cook's tour of the house because they had very little time before they had to return to Victoria.

"It's all show," Beth whispered, when they were leaving the austereness of the first floor and climbing the magnificent staircase. Hanging above them was a chandelier even more glorious than the one Nancy had drooled over at Finnegans. "Visual power to intimidate the politicians, my dear!" she laughed, enjoying the girl's reactions. "Now let me show you where we really live."

Beth now seemed in a hurry as she led Nancy along a corridor toward what seemed to be the rear of the house. Opening a door, they entered a large room that was comfortably furnished with a chesterfield, two love seats, various other comfortable-looking chairs and many family pictures in frames of all shapes and sizes.

She invited Nancy in and quietly closed the door behind them telling the girl to sit down and relax before flopping into a large upholstered chair herself. Gazing around the tidy but cluttered room, Nancy noticed the woman's slippers laid out near Beth's chair and men's slippers beside another comfortable looking chair.

She smiled. *This place is obviously lived in.* "You mean you and Gus live up here?" she asked. "It's a perfect hide-a-way!"

"No love, this is home where we can relax and just be ourselves," Beth said seriously. "You've got one, too, you call it *Cunningham Manor* and you'll learn to love it as much as we love this room!"

Going over to one of two large windows, Nancy soon realized why this room was special. From this high vantage point, one could see for miles around … a full 180° angle afforded them a marvelous view of the islands with scores of sailing boats at play in the summer sunshine ... and the sea beyond. Below, her eyes came to rest on a private dock with a small sailboat and a magnificent yacht standing side by side. Over to one side was a significantly smaller, blue speedboat.

A knock sounded at the door and a servant respectfully asked if madam needed anything, which Beth declined waving him away.

"Are these your children?" Nancy asked, looking at a picture of two young boys on a small table nearby.

A sad look overtook Beth's natural, happy exterior. "Yes, two boys," she murmured, a faraway look in her eyes. "They are grown up and both are in the Belgian army. With war in Europe imminent, I can't help but worry about them."

"Do you really think war is coming, Beth? Why will that affect us over here?"

England, love," Beth sighed, clearing her throat. "England stands for freedom we're told, and where she fights, so does Belgium and many other countries ... Canada will be one of those countries. Is Dan going to sign up, Nancy?"

Colour drained from Nancy's face as instant terror struck deep into her heart. The thought of Dan going away sent her mind into a spin. She'd watched the soldiers marching through Victoria and heard the businessmen talking but they'd been so busy that serious thought of the war had escaped her.

"I don't know, Beth, we've never talked about it," she whispered, haltingly.

"I'm so sorry, Nancy. I've upset you, dear!" Moving toward the girl she put her arm around her and led her out of the room changing the subject. "We'd better go see what the men are up to, you will need to be getting back to Victoria soon." Linking arms, the women walked back down the stairway. Hearing their voices, Terry came out of the study and stood waiting for them in the foyer.

"They're all down at the dock," he announced. "I'm to take you there." Leading them out the front door, they walked through the gardens to the back of the house and down a slight incline toward the water.

No matter how she tried, Nancy couldn't get her mind away from the thought of war. When she saw Dan and the others clustered around a sleek, duel-engined blue speedboat, she just knew she had to do everything in her power to protect him. She now realized that war was more inevitable than she had wanted to admit.

Dan was standing in the blue boat and when he saw them, he leapt onto the dock and hurried over. "Look Nancy," he called excitedly. "That powerful-looking little blue monster is ours!"

Taking Nancy by the hand, he led her toward the boat. Before they had gone many steps he realized something was wrong. Feeling her tension and seeing the worry on her face, he stopped, his excitement subsiding. Putting his arm gently around her shoulders, he turned her so he could see her face. Now being unable to hide the tears that welled in her eyes and unable to speak, he looked questioningly at her, concern radiating across his handsome face.

"What is wrong, Nan?" he asked, feeling his throat tighten.

"Please don't leave me, Danny," she whispered, emotionally. "You're all I've got."

"Silly girl," he murmured in her ear, kissing her lightly. "You're mine forever. We have to go. Come on, let me show you the boat."

Jebediah was watching and noticed the sudden change in Dan's mood. He knew something was wrong and his instincts told him that Nancy had said something to cause this, but what? A feeling of foreboding flooded over the old detective.

"Come on, let's get outta here," called Ned. "I want to be home before dark!"

Goodbyes were quickly exchanged and Beth hugged Nancy, telling her they'd see them again soon.

Jeb's keen eye noticed the special look that passed between the women. *They've talked about something that has upset her,* he thought to himself, as Nancy came to sit beside him.

The powerful engines of the little blue boat roared into life, stirring the water at the bow into a thick white foam. One last wave and the speedboat slid smoothly away from the private dock with Dan at the wheel.

Choppy water greeted their entry into the channel and Dan slowed their speed momentarily. At quarter throttle, they rounded the corner with Fred pointing out landmarks. The first was Discovery Park, then Edmonds, as Dan turned up the middle of the channel aiming for Point No Point following the wild coastline of Whidbey Island. Halfway to Port Townsend and Keystone, a pod of killer whales joined them, easily keeping pace with their lazy rolling motion.

"I knew they were there," Ned laughed. "I could smell 'em!"

Everyone joined in laughing, knowing it sounded pretty unlikely but nevertheless most of them knowing it was true. Fred disputed the claim with some straight-faced humour asking Ned if he'd changed his underwear in the past week. As the good-natured argument raged, Dan glanced over his shoulder and called Nancy to join him at the wheel. Sliding out of the seat, he let her sit, standing close behind her and she tucked her long hair into the collar of her coat.

They had been running for almost two hours when the blue boat slipped into the Straits of Juan de Fuca, leaving the American islands in their wake. Dan moved closer and put his arms around her, gently taking her right hand and placing it upon the throttle lever. He nuzzled his head into her shoulder and together they eased more power to the engines. Picking up speed they skimmed the top of the waves until it seemed like they were flying.

"HOLD ON!" he yelled over his shoulder to the others. With both their hands on the wheel, Dan quickly moved the boat left and right, checking the craft's response. Holding Nancy firmly, he threw the boat into a sharp turn ... the blue craft heeled over beautifully. Streaking away, almost at right angles to its previous line, Dan kissed Nancy on the cheek.

"What a boat!" he shouted, into her ear.

Catching his enthusiasm, she tried to put her worries aside. She knew now that before her holiday was over, she and Dan must have a serious talk about their future. Almost shutting down the engines, he swung the tiller hard over and settled the boat down into the water ... then pouring on the power again, he spun it around, whizzing across the water.

"Take us home, Nancy," he ordered, a touch of sadness in his voice as his thoughts strayed to their next task ... saying goodbye to his mentors and friends, the Joyces.

Nancy meanwhile, feeling surprisingly at home behind the controls, swung the bow toward Victoria Harbour, and eased back on the throttle. A heavy vapour scented with lavender assailed their nostrils as they neared the soapworks on Laurel Point's rocky shoreline. In no time, the familiar shape of the *Belfast* came into sight rocking gently at its mooring. Listening to Dan's instructions carefully, the exhilarated redhead expertly docked the blue craft, with hardly a bump.

At the office, Dan paid Dumpy and Fred for their help and watched as they walked away toward the city. Ned and Tim said they were going up to the Lighthouse and left quickly, obviously feeling the pain of separation, soon to be a reality.

After a short discussion, it was agreed that Dan and Nancy would grab something to eat from the office and get the boat around to Gordon Head before dark. Jeb said he would drive his car out to *Cunningham Manor* to check on Meg, returning with them by boat in the morning to see the Joyce's off. Then he and Meg would bring the blue truck back home later in the day.

Suddenly, the distinct sound of bagpipes was heard in the distance, coming closer. Hurrying up to Wharf Street, they were just in time to see the soldiers from the local regiment of the 48th Highlanders, in full dress regalia, come around the corner by the Post Office. They watched in awe as the kilted soldiers marched in perfect formation. The skirl of the pipes blended with the pounding drums and the haunting sounds filled the air, bouncing off nearby buildings. By now quite a crowd had gathered and everyone clapped and cheered as they passed.

"It's a shame Meg's not here to see this," exclaimed Nancy, turning toward Dan. But Dan was not listening. He squared his shoulders and stood up even straighter coming firmly to attention as the music of an ancient land stirred his blood.

Jeb noticed the colour drain from Nancy's face as she looked up at him. *It looks like I've solved my mystery*, he thought. *It's this blasted war. The poor lass is worried sick that Danny will be signing up."*

As the last of the proud regiment turned up Johnson Street toward the E & N Railway Station, the sounds died quickly away and they walked silently back to the office.

Three-quarters of an hour later they were on their way out of the harbour with Nancy again at the wheel. As they passed Shoal Point, Dan gave her instructions on the reef just below the water, adding graphic details of its danger to shipping. At Ogden Point, she slowed as she rounded the corner, looking back and shaking her head in wonder at the growing expanse of the massive undertaking. Seeing it from the water gave one a much different perspective of it's magnitude. All along the coastline, Dan gave her a commentary of landmarks and bays. This certainly was his world and she consoled herself with the realization that he would only leave it under dire circumstances.

"Look, they're almost finished the new building on Gonzales Hill!" he called, breaking into her thoughts as he pointed to the top of the rocky crag and the new construction at the Dominion Astrophysical Observatory. Then, as the craft scooted around the tip of the island, he gave her more instructions. "Give Oak Bay a wide birth and aim for that point of land over there. That's Ten Mile Point. Swing around it and you're almost home, Nan."

Nearly two hours later, Nancy nosed the boat up to the dock below *Cunningham Manor*. She felt a tremendous sense of achievement and when Dan hugged her, she knew he was bursting with pride.

Meg and Jebediah stood on the clifftop taking turns using the binoculars as they watched the sleek blue craft pull up to the jetty below. Nancy looked up and saw them, waving furiously.

Over supper, they discussed the morning boat trip back to Victoria before sunup. Then Meg remembered she had a surprise for them.

"You have a trip to Seattle to make, too. Harvey and Briggs from Wharf Street delivered forty cases of liquor while you were away."

"Forty cases?" asked Nancy, not believing her ears. "Where are they?"

"In the shed," Meg replied, "where they should be, out of sight!"

A quietness settled momentarily over the group, then Jeb cleared his throat and dropped an envelope on the table. "Delivery time and place," he said slowly, "and five, one hundred dollar bills!"

Dan's hand reached for the envelope, a smile playing around his mouth as he emptied it onto the table ... then pushed the money toward Nancy. Her nimble brain did a quick calculation while Dan read the letter.

"Twelve dollars fifty, a case," she said. "Is that a fair price, Jeb?"

"It is for now. Jorgensen can get it delivered overland for the same price," Jeb assured her.

"Then why doesn't he do it?" asked Meg.

"Think about it," said Jeb. "Gus said Seattle will vote dry next year. Their mayor, Hiram Gill, has joined the Anti-Saloon League in an effort to get re-elected. So, Gus is merely getting his line of supply set up ready for the big clampdown."

"Gus wants it delivered by eight tomorrow night to his private dock," Dan informed them, reading from the letter. "We should have no trouble doing that after Ned and Tim leave. It's only a four hour run in the new boat."

Just after sunrise, the blue speedboat slid into the blanket of fog draping the cove. The moon cast its last eerie grey shadows upon the black sea welcoming the sun as it peeked over the horizon.

"Take her east, watching the tide. It can get rough out here," Dan said into her ear. "I'll direct you as we go."

Foghorn blowing, they moved almost silently through the water. Lights blinking on stern and bow, they peered into the dark waters searching for the ever-present deadheads and unexpected boats.

"Due south now, for fifteen minutes. I'll watch the time."

A light over the compass allowed Nancy to follow orders, though visibility through the foggy darkness left the girl wondering just where they were. Streaks of brilliant dawn were beginning to filter through holes in the fogbank causing sparkly patches on the water. It was going to be a perfect day.

"We're past the southern tip, it's getting easier to see now. West, Nancy ... and put more speed on," he called urgently. "Open her up ... come on, let's go!"

Nervously Nancy's hand adjusted the throttle and the craft picked up speed bouncing violently as it cut through the now choppy waves. She quickly looked back to see how Meg was faring, not having heard a word of protest since they helped her down the cliff-stairs. *Of course, I wouldn't hear anything over the engine anyway*, she thought, smugly. However, it appeared Jeb had everything well in control with his arm around her shoulder holding a blanket about her for warmth, Meg actually looked like she was enjoying herself.

Suddenly the fog lifted, allowing them a glimpse of the shoreline below Beacon Hill Park. Feeling more confidence, she opened the throttle, experiencing the exhilaration as the boat screamed at almost full speed across the water, it's nose high in the air. Slipping past Ogden Point, they saw a freighter entering the harbour, and she eased back on the throttle.

"Follow that freighter," Dan called.

They were quickly gaining on it when she felt Dan's hand on her shoulder. "Don't crowd him, love. Give him plenty of room. It's the *Thermopylae* heading for the rice mill on Store Street."

Moving closer to the shore, Nancy swung a tight arc past The Empress and the Harbour Master's wharf before turning in under the *Belfast's* stern. The area was already crowded with well-wishers milling about to send the popular brothers on their way. Several of them willingly assisted by grabbing lines and Fred and Jim offered hands to the older folks, pulling them safely onto the dock.

Silently, the men parted making way for the new arrivals to climb aboard the old whaling ship. Tim and Ned, now alone on the deck of the *Belfast*, offered the woman a hand up and Dan approached his old friends for the last time. Conversation was stilted and uneasy and knowing the men wanted to be off, the women said their last tearful farewells and Dan gripped the men fondly in an emotional embrace. For one brief moment, the brothers looked sadly alone waving from the old ship, and then suddenly, it seemed like every ship in the harbour was blowing their whistles.

It was a joyous, but sad salute to the grand old lady of the sea and its stalwart owners. Tim waved one last time and disappeared below as Ned tooted the *Belfast's* whistle and slowly eased her away from the dock. Picking up speed quickly, the whaler was soon out of sight.

A short while later, Dumpy and Fred sat at the office table talking with Jeb and the others as Meg silently made tea.

Dan and Nancy were outside, being detained by Mr. Hagenbuch, the sign writer, who wanted to discuss a new sign for the wharf.

"What new sign?" Nancy asked. "We haven't discussed that yet."

But the old sign writer was adamant, he'd been commissioned and paid by Ned and was determined to complete his assignment. The pencil in the old man's hand worked like magic and with an artistic flourish he quickly pencilled several designs on the sketch pad and handed it to the young couple.

Studying them for a minute, Nancy pointed to one of them. Dan knew what she was thinking. *"Brown and Wilson Speedy Deliveries By Sea.* Yes, it's perfect," Dan agreed. "How soon can you have it up, Mr. Hagenbuch?"

"I'll be back Wednesday," came the quick reply. Receiving a nod from Dan, the sign writer scurried away, and arm in arm, the new owners walked into their office.

"I'll get your tea," Jebediah announced, rising from his chair.

"Oh no, you won't," Meg growled, pushing the American gently back into his chair. "That's my job and I intend to keep it for a while!" she said, ruffling his hair as she passed behind him.

Serious faces listened intently when the young couple told them of their plans to start a new business, offering a fast service delivering goods and messages to the islands and coastal towns.

Dumpy shrugged his shoulders, his brain not quite comprehending the multitude of opportunities it would bring. He had no aspirations of moving up the social ladder or going into business. Jack was a follower, a good conscientious worker who liked to have someone to look up to. He would always be just a crewman.

In contrast, Fred and Jeb's reactions were of elation. Jeb caught the inference to the delivery of liquor to Seattle and Fred grinned at the American's reaction promising to send customers their way.

"How are you going to manage it, living out at Gordon Head?" Fred asked, doubtfully.

"Easy," Nancy smiled, her eyes turning onto Jack. "Dumpy will work in this office taking orders and delivering them to and from Gordon Head getting help from Meg when needed. Danny runs the boat but Dumpy will be on call just in case. We may have to purchase another boat for local deliveries."

337

Dumpy's face lit up. "You mean I have a regular job again?"

"That's correct, Dumpy," Dan assured him.

"Anything for this side of the Island or The States goes from Victoria," Nancy continued. "Salt Spring, and everything on the other side, goes from Gordon Head."

"Brilliant!" Jeb chortled. "I can help you with the boat."

Dan looked thoughtful for a moment, then a smile spread across his face. He reached across the table and took Nancy's hand. "No, I don't think that's necessary, Jeb. Thanks anyway," he said quietly, seeing Nancy's green eyes sparkle. "I already have a partner!"

Meg handed Dumpy some keys and began to lecture him on office procedure. She was still wagging her finger at the young man as they said their goodbyes and headed for the dock ... knowing Jeb would bring her along later when she was ready.

With Dan at the controls, they headed out of the harbour turning east towards home. With only a ripple on the water and a gentle southerly breeze, they made their way along the rocky coastline. He thought of the new life they had laid out before them ... a remarkable achievement for a pair of orphans, and especially for that lonely little girl he had worried about so long ago.

The thought of looming war suddenly enveloped him and a chill went up his spine. He looked back at Nancy, her hair blowing freely in the wind. Sensing his attention, she turned, and a glittering ray of sunshine caressed her auburn hair transforming it into a brilliant crown.

A feeling of tremendous peace and joy swept through Dan's body. He knew that no matter what fate had in store for them, nothing could change their love for each other.

Watch for the exciting conclusion in

Book Two of the Victoria Chronicles